From
DUST

FREYA BARKER

Cover Design:
RE&D - Margreet Asselbergs
Editing:
RE&D – Dana Hook
Proofreading:
Prima Editing & Proofreading – Daniela Prima

TABLE OF CONTENT

DEDICATION

To my amazing children, Sanne & Stijn.

So proud of these guys growing up to be fantastic individuals, no thanks to that crazy mother of theirs!

I love you guys! Even if you tease me relentlessly about the books I write.

xox

CHAPTER ONE

It's cold.

I think it's April, but I can't be sure. I haven't been interested in staying connected to the world for so long now, I couldn't even tell you the day of the week, let alone the time of day. I generally take my cue from what I feel and see. When the sun starts going down, I know the wharf will be virtually abandoned, and I feel I can finally leave the small shed that has been my home for a while now ... a few months? Maybe it's been a year already, I couldn't tell you with the way time just seems to drift on endlessly.

The seasons are usually pretty easy to distinguish, but we've just had a particularly cold winter and it feels like it is lingering too long. I feel like I've been wearing every last stitch of clothing in my possession for a very long time now. It's been a bitch trying to get them clean at the outdoor tap on the edge of the dock. There've been many times this winter that I've gone rank with the cold temperatures; too cold to peel off even one of the layers of clothing to wash them, or myself for that matter. Who cares anyway?

Tonight I have a particular destination in mind. I heard the big delivery truck rumble past my shack earlier today, heading for my *neighbor*: a pub and grub called The Skipper. That usually means it's Thursday, because on Thursdays, The Skipper serves an all-you-can-eat menu, and that means that tonight, the dumpster in the alley behind the pub will be rich with leftovers.

I usually wait until I'm sure the place is good and locked up, but I haven't eaten more than a few bites of an apple somebody had discarded on the dock the day before yesterday. It only had a few bruises and I washed it carefully at the tap, but those few, richly flavorful bites put a rare smile on my face. It's not often I manage to get my hands on anything *fresh* tasting, let alone a whole apple.

I guess I could panhandle and buy some food like I've seen a few others do, but something holds me back, no matter how hungry I get. Begging would not befit a Donner, or so my parents have hammered into me. Funny, that after all these years, *that* is still as deeply ingrained as guilt is for a good Catholic.

I shake my head before my thoughts start drifting into areas I don't want to visit and pull my flannel shirt tighter around my shoulders to ward off the chill. *Damn, it's cold.*

Keeping to the shadow side of the alley, I tentatively edge my way to the dumpster that promises food for a few days, keeping my eye out for the big motorcycle that is often parked right beside it. Its usual spot is empty, which means the big, burly, and angry looking man isn't here tonight, or he's left already. I watch him sometimes when he drives by. I've come to the conclusion he must work there since he's there quite often. With that dark and dangerous air about him, it's difficult to keep from looking when I hear his motorcycle rumble past my shed. But tonight the coast is clear, and it appears the place is shut down. The only visible light is the weak bulb above the pub's back door, and that is on all the time.

My stomach starts rumbling, already reacting to the food smells wafting from the dumpster. When it comes to food, I'm thankful for the lingering cold weather. There have been too many times in the heat of summer where I've been so overwhelmed with the stench of a garbage can or dumpster, that I wasn't able to stop from puking, but not so tonight. Tonight I can smell frying grease and garlic. The odd hint of herbs and spices filters past my olfactory sense. I'm hungry and my mouth is watering.

Using the dumpster's frame, I climb up and over the side, trying to be as quiet as I can—just in case. When I settle my feet amid the garbage, I scan the immediate area around me. *Jackpot.* A box of now familiar looking paper packages sits within reach. One of the things I've come to appreciate about hopping The Skipper's dumpster is that they wrap the leftover food in the paper lining of the baskets it's served in. Then they gather them all in one of the delivery boxes until it's time to dump them out. As a result, the leftovers are relatively untouched and it somehow makes the food taste better. Weird how once the thought of eating anything someone else had touched—let alone discarded—would have been enough to make me gag, but now, I'm just grateful. Grateful for the prospect of a full belly, and with the chill still in the air, the option to save some for another day before it spoils.

"Please don't."

The soft plea freezes me with a french fry halfway to my mouth. So preoccupied with stuffing my empty stomach, I didn't hear anyone approach. My hand drops the fry and I scramble to the far corner of the dumpster, looking up from under my eyelashes at the woman peeking over the side of the dumpster. I've seen her before; a tall blonde, about my age, with blue streaks through her hair. I've seen her go in the back door of The Skipper before and guessed she was an employee.

Her soft eyes and half-smile fill me with shame. Pity is devastating when it's directed at you, and I've never felt it as strongly as I do now. Wrapping my arms around my waist against the chills running through my body, I turn my eyes away so I can avoid looking at myself through her eyes.

"I'll make you something fresh. Do you want to come in out of the cold?"

My eyes flick to the back door before returning her steady gaze and I shake my head. The thought of being exposed to more pitying eyes would surely undo me. As tempting as it would be to walk through that door behind her and be able to sit down to a plate of food, I'm scared that I won't be able to return to this bleak existence I've resigned myself to afterward.

"I'm the only one here. We've closed up for the night and I was just putting the last of the garbage out." She winces at her own words, probably realizing the implication of her garbage reference. "Please ..."

When she reaches her hand out to me, I can't resist stretching my own to touch it. It's been so very long since I've had any direct human contact that the moment our fingers touch, tears I thought had dried up long ago start rolling down my face. A craving to bask in her warmth some more has me following her gentle pull on my hand and I find myself clambering over the side of the dumpster. Meekly, I follow behind as she leads the way through the back door without a word, only stopping briefly at the threshold. The warmth rolling out of the open door is so inviting, I hesitate, wondering if I step through this door—if I allow myself this comfort—will I ever be able to turn back again. My heart pounds in my chest as I force myself to follow the woman inside the dark hallway, letting the door fall shut behind me.

A steaming plate of breaded fried fish and fries sits before me on the large battered table in the bright, industrial kitchen. I wearily eye the woman as she cleans up the kitchen without a word. The smell of the pot of fresh coffee she put on is causing my mouth to water and I tentatively shove a fry in my mouth. *Oh God, this is good.* The crisp texture and salty flavor burst over my tongue. With the woman temporarily forgotten, I start shoveling the food in my mouth as fast as I can.

A glass of water is set on the table beside my plate and the woman sits down in a chair on the opposite side of the table.

"Don't eat too fast—it'll only give you stomach cramps," she says quietly. "My name is Vivian, but everyone calls me Viv. I've seen you around a few times." Her eyes hold mine as she reaches for my hand again to give it a quick squeeze. "Will you tell me your name?"

Fear of being exposed has me shake my head, but it doesn't seem to matter to Viv because she just continues to talk.

"I started working here when I was only fifteen. We lived next to the Lucas family then—they own the joint—and I jumped at the chance to earn a little extra money washing dishes. With four older brothers, we never really had a lot to spare for frivolous things. At that age, I wanted to be able to buy CDs and clothes, grab the occasional lunch at the diner with my friends, and the money I earned here allowed me to do that." She smiles wistfully. "Never really left after that. Not even after graduating from high school. I just kinda stuck around and became as much a part of The Skipper as Gunnar is."

At the mention of the strange name, I look up, wondering who she is referring to. Noticing my interest, she explains. "Gunnar Lucas is the owner now. He bought his mother out after his dad died five years ago. I had just come out of a long-term relationship which had knocked me on my ass when Gunnar pulled me aside and told me I could keep waitressing as I'd been doing, or I could finally start living up to my potential. He offered me the job as manager and I jumped at the chance. I haven't looked back since."

I'm dumbfounded by the amount of information she parts with, barely noticing the fact that I've finished my plate. Just listening to her talk is like a soothing balm to my shredded soul, but it's the open and honest way she talks about herself that has me open my mouth for the first time in years.

"Sydn ... Syd." My voice sounds hoarse and cracks from lack of use as I catch myself spilling my full name. I can't give up that much of me; not even to this seemingly friendly and empathetic woman.

"Syd." She echoes back to me. "Nice to meet you, Syd. Love the name, it fits you." The smile on her face seems genuine and I tentatively smile back.

"Listen," she continues, "I'm a pretty forward person and I hope I don't offend you in any way, but I just lost an employee today, which is why I'm here so late—I had to do her work and mine. She cleaned the pub before hours, but when she called this morning to say she wouldn't be back, it left me pulling a double today since Gunnar is out of town." She runs her hand through her short head of hair and takes a deep breath. "Anyway, excuse my rambling, but what I wanted to ask you was if you would be interested in the job?"

I'm stunned, and it must show on my face because she immediately grabs for my hand again and scrambles to explain.

"Look, I don't know your history or how you got where you are today, but I'm generally a good judge of character—something honed by years of working in a pub, I guess. You seem like someone who doesn't really belong on the streets. There's an inherent poise about you and I get the feeling you simply fell on some really hard times."

It's hard for me to stop the moisture gathering in my eyes and I direct my gaze down. I'm not sure whether to run or to stay here and bask in the warmth Viv exudes. I swallow hard and look up from the table, braced to find pity staring back at me, but all I see is an encouraging smile.

"Why would you do that?" I manage.

"What? Offer you the job?" She leans back in her chair and seems to consider the question. "Karma." She says firmly. "I believe strongly that sometimes things are just meant to happen a certain way. Don't ask me why, my brothers rib me about my *new age* views all the time, but the reality is that I was given a great opportunity when Gunnar put me on the spot and demanded I live and not just exist. I guess I see something in you that deserves the same. The fact that the day I end up one employee less is the same day I meet you is not a coincidence in my opinion."

A brief silence follows, in which I let her words sink in and find myself actually considering her offer. Is this something I want? Something I need to do? An hour in the presence of Viv has me scrutinizing my situation, and if I'm totally honest with myself, I agree with her. Regardless of my dark and twisted path, I don't belong on the streets, and frankly, just hearing someone's voice directed at me has lifted a little of the dark cloud that always seems to hang over me.

"Okay," I whisper, excited but scared out of my wits. A big smile creeps across her face and she waits a minute, giving me a chance to say more, but I don't know what else to say.

"Great. Can you be here tomorrow morning at ten? I'll make sure to bring you a uniform. Don't worry," she smiles at the eyebrow I raise, "it consists of only a T-shirt and jeans. I'll make sure you have a few extra shirts. We'll do the work together for a while, at least until you are comfortable."

"Are you sure?" I can't help but ask, overwhelmed by the radical turn my life appears to be making in such a short period of time.

"Sure I'm sure. There is a shower in the upstairs apartment you can use whenever you want and food is on the house. You have no idea how much I appreciate you doing this."

I know what she's doing. She's making it easier on me to accept the help, and make no mistake, I realize this is a helping hand. The irony is it actually makes me feel a little better about accepting it, but there is a small problem.

"I don't have a watch," I'm embarrassed to admit.

"Shit. Right. No problem," Viv answers, taking the blue watch she is wearing off her wrist. "Here, use this. I have a shitload of these at home in all colors of the rainbow. Got them in bulk because I tend to lose them so I have a few left at home."

"Thanks." I'm pleased my voice is coming through a little stronger.

When Viv closes the door behind me, the cold air hits me hard, but my full belly, the plastic blue watch around my wrist, and the prospect of what could well be a turning point in my life, has me smile against the stiff breeze coming off the water.

CHAPTER TWO

Syd

At ten o'clock the next morning, I stand huddled in the corner between the dumpster and the wall, my eyes peeled to the back door.

After lying down on my makeshift bed in the shed last night, I started having second thoughts. Most of the clothes I own I'm wearing, and none of them have seen the inside of a washing machine in years. The occasional rinse under the outside tap, would've hardly done the job, and the same goes for me. I can't really remember the last time I've had a proper shower, and I'm wondering if Viv is having second thoughts about her offer. Surely, she must have smelled the slightly sour odor coming off me.

Suddenly, this whole idea seems out of my reach and I start feeling nauseous. Viv had set the alarm on the watch, but I was terrified of it not working. Worrying about that, along with the negative thoughts cycling in my head, had me wide-awake all night. When the alarm actually went off this morning, I was still shivering from the last minute rinse and wash I decided on after hours of tossing and turning.

The back door of The Skipper opens a crack and a now familiar blue and blonde head peeks out.

"Syd? Are you here?" Viv turns her head and when her eyes find me, she cracks a smile. "What are you doing in the cold? Get yourself in here." She must sense my apprehension because she steps outside and faces me fully. "Look, there is no one else here yet, at least not up until eleven, so we have the place to ourselves for a bit. That'll give you time to try on the clothes I brought." Holding out her hand in invitation, she gestures for me to precede her inside.

Part of me wants to ignore her, but a bigger part wants to go inside. I don't think opportunities like this will come along often, if ever, and the thought of perhaps learning to stand on my feet again spurs me on. With a small smile for Viv, I pass her and head through the door. "You're gonna have to come upstairs with me where you'll have some privacy to change."

Gathering up my courage, I swallow hard and turn to look her in the eyes, "I'm not exactly clean."

"I figured you might want a quick shower, which is why I've set some stuff out in the bathroom up there. Come on, time's wasting." She nudges me to the stairway, apparently not at all put off by my admission. *Huh.*

The water is so warm, I want to stay under the stream forever, but Viv is waiting on the other side of the door. The big fluffy towel she left out for me to use is so gentle against my skin, it brings tears to my eyes. When did this happen? When did I become so estranged from a kind word or a soft touch?

An inadvertent glimpse in the mirror shows me an absolute stranger; one that smells faintly like the bottle of shampoo I used to wash my hair. My hair is now so long that it reaches past my waist. I've always been a dark, strawberry blonde, but I can't recall my hair ever being this wavy, even wet. My bluish-gray eyes staring back at me are familiar, but not the dark circles around them, nor the hollowed out face. My almost skeletal body is so unlike my rather plump one, I can't even find one familiar part to it, except perhaps ... low on the stomach, between my prominent hip bones where there is a scar. I know that scar well because it's one that evokes memories I am quick to suppress.

A knock on the door jolts me out of my musings and I quickly wrap the towel around myself.

"You okay in there?"

"Almost done," I assure Viv, making quick work of pulling on the jeans and T-shirt sitting on the hamper. The shirt is big enough to hide the fact that the jeans are falling off my ass. *Jesus.* With a last wistful look at the pile of dirty rags on the ground next to the hamper, I open the door to face what might well be my restoration.

"If you finish washing the glassware, I'll jump into the kitchen to start on prep. Come find me after."

"Okay."

Viv smiles and leaves me behind the bar with my hands in delicious warm water.

After the first time my jeans started slipping off my hips, Viv produced a length of rope that was now holding them up securely. A bit embarrassed about my now scrawny body, I was quickly assured that I'd have some padding and muscle to fill out my frame soon enough. She would see to it.

After walking me through my job duties and showing me where to find the cleaning supplies, she has us start out cleaning the washrooms before taking on the pub. Every morning she wants the glassware washed. The perfunctory rinses they get when the doors are open are not enough to her liking. So, while Viv wipes surfaces and sweeps the floors, I'm relegated to dish duty, and I don't mind one bit. The warmth of the water is slowly making its way into my bones and I feel such utter contentment in that moment, until a sound from behind me has me turning. Two sets of curious eyes are facing me and it's all I can do not to crawl under the bar right now.

"Hey, what happened to Maria?" The tall, pretty-faced man asks. Searching the place as he stands there, I can only assume that he's looking for the missing Maria. Still not comfortable speaking, I just shrug. The gorgeous girl standing beside him tilts her head to the side as she observes me. She's pretty and polished with shiny, dark straight hair that flows down to her shoulders, and a perfectly made up face. I feel like yesterday's garbage in comparison. How apropos. I *am* yesterday's garbage, quite literally.

"Can you talk?" The edge is clear in her voice as she continues to regard me through slitted eyes. "You look damn familiar."

Her last words have me trying to shrink in on myself. The shame of being recognized as someone living off the streets is something rather new and harsh. I'm a little surprised I care, where I was so without care before. Not sure what to say, I'm rescued by Viv, who comes in from the kitchen.

"Great, you guys are here. I can introduce you to Syd. She's here replacing Maria. Syd, this is Matt and Denise. Denise generally works the bar and Matt serves with me, but we sometimes switch it up."

"Nice to meet you, Syd." Matt reaches out and with a quick glance to Viv for reassurance, I place my hand in his, receiving a small squeeze.

"You too," I mumble.

"I'm sure I know you from somewhere," Denise says with her head still tilted to the side and her hands firmly on her hips. Not knowing what to say to that, I simply shrug my shoulders. Once again, Viv seems to know to jump in.

"Wouldn't be surprised. Syd lives pretty close, don't you Syd?"

Picking up on the fact that Viv won't speak about my living conditions, I finally open my mouth. "Not far at all. In fact, I have a view of Holyoke Wharf from my window." From the corner of my eye, I see a little smirk on Viv's face, which encourages me to look at Denise straight on.

"The apartments at the end of the dock? That's where you live? Wow, those are hard to come by. Been there long?"

"Just about a year or so." I don't confirm or deny her assumption, and feel justified that I've not told a lie.

Viv claps her hands. "Come on guys, we're wasting time here. Let's get to work. Syd, you almost done there?"

"Just a few more," I tell her.

"Why don't you let Denise finish up now that she's here and you can give me a hand in the kitchen." Without another word, she turns on her heels and disappears into the hallway. I grab for the towel and dry my hands, feeling eyes on me the entire time. When I look up, Denise is already working at the sink, but Matt is standing by the doorway, eyeing me up and down. Ignoring the invasive looks, I slip past him and hurry to join Viv in the kitchen.

"Never mind Denise. She always behaves like that around other females ... like she needs to establish her rank in the pack."

I can't stop the snort that escapes when I get the implication of Viv's words. Yeah, Denise does seem like a bit of a bitch. Viv has one side of her mouth lifted and shoots me a wink.

"Let's get these vegetables chopped. You okay with a knife?" I nod when she hands over a large chef's knife and gestures to the huge cutting board, the size of half a door, piled high with onions, peppers, and other assorted produce. She spends the next ten minutes showing me how she wants them all sliced and diced before leaving me to go do something by the stove.

"You cook too?" I ask, watching her stirring in the various pots and pans on the large industrial stove.

"I do, but we have a cook coming in at noon for the lunch crowd. I usually serve the lunch crowd and most of the time Gunnar is here to tend bar in the evenings, so Denise and Matt serve the dinner crowd. We also have a few part-time employees who are scheduled on weekends, days off, or when one of us gets sick, which is practically never. I get to cook in the evenings and I do the morning prep. It's what I love to do. What about you? You like cooking?" She throws me a look over her shoulder.

"I used to," I say carefully, not wanting to think back to the times I would prepare entire gourmet meals without blinking an eye. I'm determined to move forward and not look back.

Apparently, getting my reluctance to part with more information, Viv simply says, "Good. We'll just have to make sure you will again."

I'm not holding in the smile that is forming on my face. If I leave the past and focus on the here and now and the path ahead—like is so often suggested—I feel good ... *content*. It feels like a milestone of sorts.

"So what do you think?" I ask, as Viv scrutinizes the piles of chopped and sliced vegetables I've created over the last hour or so on the cutting board.

"I'm happy with what I see, but are you up for this? Working here five hours a day?" Her gaze now lands on my face, trying to gauge my response.

"I think so. I don't want to disappoint you; not after all you've done for me."

A spontaneous laugh bursts from Viv. "I haven't done anything that wasn't at some point done for me. And I have a feeling that I may come out of this with a new friend; something that hasn't come easy for me over the years. You'll do fine." She looks at me with warmth in her eyes.

"I'd really like that. I've not had a friend in so long, though, I might've forgotten how to be one," I tell her with a shrug.

"How to be a friend? There's absolutely nothing wrong with being just who you are."

I feel a lump forming in my throat and work hard to swallow it down. Noticing my struggle for composure, Viv suddenly turns businesslike. "All right then. Your hours will be 11 a.m. to 4 p.m., Tuesday through Saturday. Sundays and Mondays, you'll have off. I'll start you at $8 an hour for the first month and after that, we'll go up to $8.50. Do you have a bank account?"

I slowly shake my head, the implications of working again finally hitting me. I've worked so hard staying off the grid, not wanting to be connected to my past, that I've let everything go. I'm afraid if I open a new account or get registered anywhere, my past will find me one way or another.

"You running, Syd?" Viv asks me with some concern.

"Only from my past," is my simple answer.

"Okay then, I'll try to keep you off the books and pay you cash for now. Every second Friday is payday, but this is something that we may have to contend with at some point."

"Th-thank you," I stammer, relieved that this isn't a deal breaker. Not yet, anyway.

"We'll work it out. Now before you leave every day, I would need you to wipe down the bathrooms again. They won't be as bad as in the mornings, but we try to get a fresh start for the evening crowd."

I nod in response, depositing the mounds of vegetables in the bins Viv has placed on the counter.

"Why don't you go see about them now. It's getting close to two o'clock already."

I wash my hands at the sink and am about to leave the kitchen when her voice halts me. "There's a laundry room upstairs. If you want to wash your clothes while you work, you're more than welcome to. And until you get on your feet, I don't see why you can't come in here at ten in the morning, which is when I'm usually here, and have a quick shower before you start. Only if you want to."

"Thank you," I mutter again, and without turning around, I head over to the closet where the cleaning stuff is stored.

I've just finished the ladies' room and I'm on my knees picking up the paper hand towels that landed under the sink instead of in the garbage in the men's room, when the door behind me opens. Before I have a chance to turn around, a deep, rumbling voice comes from behind me, freezing me on the spot.

"Who the fuck are you?"

The question is launched with such force, it has me scrambling to the far wall on my hands and knees before turning around to face whoever is so pissed.

The man before me is massive. His thick thighs are encased in jeans, and the size of his shoulders would not be out of place on a lumberjack. In fact, he looks like one with his flannel shirt, not unlike the one I have, but oh my God, the face scowling back at me is the most intimidating thing about him. Disheveled salt and pepper hair, a few days of dark growth on his square jaw, and the deep set of dark eyes are enough to have me cower further into the wall at my back. He is much more impressive up close than he is riding his motorcycle at a safe distance.

"Gunnar!" I can hear Viv's voice from behind him. "The fuck are you doing scaring the shit out of Syd?"

So, this is Gunnar.

CHAPTER THREE

Gunnar

I hear Viv yelling at me, but can't take my eyes off that scrawny pile of bones with the biggest eyes and gorgeous copper-colored mane of hair, sitting on my washroom floor.

I need to piss like you wouldn't believe and I'm this close to fucking wetting my pants like a child. Tearing my eyes away from whoever she is, I stalk past her and relieve myself in the first stall, not bothering to close the door. No time. A groan escapes me when I can finally let go. Fuck, that feels good, and I don't give a damn that I'm standing here pissing with an audience behind me. I've been on the road for a long fucking time and haven't been able to hit a washroom since the plane I was taking back to Boston from Phoenix hit a pocket of turbulence halfway through the flight. That nasty-ass stewardess—or flight attendant it is these days—was blocking the damn door and sent me back to my seat. Probably because I didn't care for her obvious come-ons. But who the fuck makes suggestive remarks to a guy who is obviously traveling with two kids? *A skank.* The moment we landed, we got stuck in a flow of people and I don't particularly like leaving the kids unsupervised outside an airport bathroom. I figured I could hold out until we were on the road but decided to just hoof it to the bar, first dropping off my guys at their mom's. Of course she picked that moment to start bitching about dumping the kids on her when we had already agreed on this schedule change

28

weeks ago via e-mail. I've been gone for a week with them, visiting my mom, and told Cindy I'd drop them off around 3 p.m. because I'd need to check on the pub. I trust Viv, but it's a lot to take on my shift as well, and for an entire week at that.

"Jesus, Gunnar. Close the door, will you? You're gonna have Syd here quit on her first day!" Viv yells as she slams the stall door closed. Some mumbling and shuffling of feet follow and I'm glad to hear the washroom door slam shut as well.

Syd? That little thing's name is Syd? What kind of fucking name is that for a girl? My stream downgrades to a trickle. I shake off and tuck my business away, zipping up as I push open the door to get my hands washed. The washroom is empty. Seems Viv has taken her new charge out of here and is probably somewhere, trying to calm the little bird down. Christ, she looked like she was terrified. I feel kind of bad about that but holy shit, my bladder was bursting and I find some weird chick on the floor of the men's room.

I splash some water on my face in an attempt to rinse away some of the travel fatigue etched on my face. I'm getting fucking old at forty-four.

There are voices coming from the kitchen so I stick my head in to find the little bird sitting on a chair and Viv fussing over her. I better get this apology shit over with since I know Viv well enough to know she'll make my life hell if I don't. One reason why she handles all hires and fires is because I apparently don't have *people skills.*. My people skills work well enough when I pour drinks. Plenty of women appreciate my people skills too. At least, I think they do, although it's not in my nature to check up with them after I leave them well-fucked in their beds. Never mind.

Don't bring that shit home ... not ever. My kids are with me every other week and that house is as much theirs as mine. My eyes turn back to take in that fantastic hair falling over the creeped-out chick's back. She has streaks of blonde in different shades, but the overall effect is of burnished copper. Amazing for someone looking so gaunt everywhere else to have such bright bluish pools for eyes and a mass of shiny hair.

Sucking in a deep breath, I move into the kitchen. Viv lifts her head when she sees me approach and throws me a cautionary glance. The little bird, or Syd—whatever her name is—picks up on it and slowly turns around. The moment she looks me straight in the eyes, I have to suck in another deep breath. She must've been a knock out once, but the dark circles around those expressive eyes, the prominent cheekbones, and sharp chin are evidence of a hard life. Damn. What has Viv dragged in now?

"*Ahem.* So ... I guess I should apologize for barking at ya," I tell her, noticing the long waves framing her face. She flicks her eyes down and seems to disappear into herself without saying a word. "I've just been on the road—long trip. I didn't expect to find a woman crawling around in the men's room. Sorry if I scared you."

It's becoming increasingly uncomfortable talking to this little person sitting frozen in front of me, refusing to meet my eyes again. I glance at Viv, who gives me a little smile of encouragement. *Jesus.*

"So, yeah ... Syd, is it? Welcome to The Skipper. I'm Gunnar, but I guess you probably heard Viv call me that already. Anyway," slowly her head comes up as she focuses her eyes on me again, "glad to have you on board." I stick out my hand and she tentatively slips her tiny one in mine. A little squeeze and she pulls right back, but not before I feel the hair on my arms stand up from the charge that comes from touching her.

"Thanks."

Her voice is like rough sandpaper—so unexpected from a petite frame like hers.

"Right. Gonna check on the pub. Meet me in my office in half an hour?" The last I direct at Viv, whose smile has morphed into a smirk. *Smartass.* She can probably tell I can't wait to get out of here. With one last nod at Syd, I turn on my heels and make myself scarce.

Denise is standing behind the bar, chatting up some young guys having a beer. They must be tourists; I've never seen them in here. It doesn't take long for her to spot me.

"Yay! You're back!" The damn girl's almost jumping up and down.

"Yup." I do my best not to engage with her too much. I know she has some kind of fixation on me, but that shit will never happen. *Hell no.* The thought sends shivers down my back. She's technically young enough to be my daughter, but a damn good employee. I can't argue that.

"How are things up here?"

"Just great. No problems at all," she says in a breathy voice, while stepping in too close to me. I'm relieved to see Matt walk up with a simple wave and I use the distraction to reclaim a healthy distance from Denise.

"S'up, boss? Have a good trip?"

"Not bad. Phoenix is nice and hot. Bloody freezing when we got back to Boston, though. Took half the drive to Portland to get the damn truck warmed up. Everything quiet here?"

A look is exchanged between the two of them before Matt answers.

"Pretty quiet. We had the baseball team come in for drinks Wednesday and they were pretty rowdy with their captain away." He nods at me. The boys of The Anchors, my beer-league ball team, make it a habit to come in every week, even outside of the season. Wednesday is our regular game night, but it'll be another month before we actually start playing again. Doesn't stop them from showing up every other Wednesday of the year as well. They're a good group of guys, but damn noisy.

"Yeah?"

"Yeah—but Viv told 'em off good. We had a few families still here eating and the guys weren't minding their language. Viv threatened to ban them for life if they didn't mind their manners. That scared them straight; no one wants to mess with Viv." He grins.

I chuckle. Smart move not to mess with that woman. She may look all soft and girly, but she's got more brass and bigger balls than most men I know. Not to mention a mean left hook. I know, I've been on the receiving end of it.

"Good. Anything else I need to know before I dive into my office?"

Again, they look between each other, but this time it's Denise turning to me.

"Actually ... you know that guy who was in here last month scoping the place out?" I nod while she fiddles with the towel in her hands. "He umm ... he was back, only this time he came right up to the bar and started asking all kinds of questions."

"Like what?"

"About you, mainly. At first he chatted me up about the menu; wanting to know the crowd favorites. But when he started asking about the day-to-day workings and wanted to know details—like the number of employees and the busiest nights and stuff—it made me a little uneasy. It wasn't just idle chit chat, Gunnar. He asked a lot of questions about you, like when you're usually here, how long you've owned the place and who owned it before you. I don't know who he is, but both times he's been in here, he's been eyeing up the place." Denise looks a bit nervous when Matt jumps in.

"Are you planning on selling?" he blurts out, taking me completely by surprise.

"Am I what? Fuck no. Not in a million years. This place has been in my family for donkey's years. We get good business from our regulars and a decent amount of walk-ins from tourists, so why the hell would I want to sell?"

"Phew, good. I like my job. Matt and I just got to talking, and well … we were worried. Viv said it was ridiculous; that you'd never sell, but it's nice to hear it from you."

"Next time he comes in, let me know. Think I'll introduce myself and tell him if he has questions, he can come to me."

I'd like to find out what this guy wants. Over the years, there have been a few individuals interested in buying me out. Heck, I've even had a well-known chain restaurant try and sway me with a wad of cash, but I've given up a lot to keep this pub in the family and I'm not about to change that over a fat wallet. Those only last so long.

I close the door to my office to call Tim. He's on the ball team but works for the City of Portland in the Economic Development Department. He might be able to find out if there are sharks circling.

When my door opens a bit later, Viv catches me stifling a yawn. I'm wiped already and the evening rush, which is always busiest on a Friday night, hasn't even started yet. Traveling and the abrupt temperature change are getting to me. Fuck, I'm getting old.

"Tired?" Viv asks, as she sits down in the chair across from me.

"A bit. Just got off the phone with Tim. Matt and Denise told me about the guy who's been asking questions about the pub. Reminded me a bit of when Red Lobster sent someone over here to try and convince me to sell. Tim's gonna see if he can find out if there've been any applications for business licenses or anything else, to see if someone is interested in setting up shop here. I'm not afraid of competition; hell, most of the time I think it'd be good for a few more places to open up around here and help draw crowds, but I don't like the focus on this particular pub." I run my hand through my already mussed up hair, trying to stifle another massive yawn, unsuccessfully.

"Yeah. It made me a little uncomfortable when I heard too. I'm sure if there's anything to find out, Tim will. Tell me about your trip? How was your mom? Did you have a good time?"

I give Viv one of my rare smiles before answering. She is probably the one person I can trust completely. I've known her forever and I'm glad she stuck it out here because I couldn't ask for a better manager, hands down. Doesn't mean I don't worry about her. She's like my little sister. We were neighbors growing up and since I've been friends with her oldest brother since elementary school, she's been part of my life too. She went through some shit a few years back, but she's come out stronger on the other side. Still, I'd like to see her find a life—maybe some happiness—outside of The Skipper. I have my kids to drag me out of my routine from time to time, but Viv just sticks close to the pub and her family.

"Was good. She's living it up with her daily yoga classes and her bridge club. I don't think the kids came out of the pool for more than meals, so they were happy. As for me, it was good to see her. I'm glad she's made a good life for herself there, but I was pretty happy when it came time to come home. Fuck-all to do but sit around, and that gets me antsy. She did want me to ask you when she can expect your visit."

Viv chuckles, "Incorrigible—that's your mom. Maybe one of these days."

"So tell me about this new employee of ours?"

"Syd? Yesterday morning Maria calls me to say she was quitting. She found another job with a hotel up the coast and she gets full-time hours there. Not happy about her leaving me high and dry with no notice, but what can you do? Can't blame her for trying to find a job that gives her more hours. I just wish she'd given me some notice. Anyway, I happened to bump into Syd—who I've seen around from time to time—and we got to talking. Long story short, she was able to start right away and so far, she's working out great."

As soon as Viv starts talking about the new employee, her eyes turn to the window, as if she doesn't want to look me in the eyes when talking about her. I'm not getting the full story here, but I trust Viv's judgement. Not bothering to try and pry more information out of her, instead I voice my concern over the small woman in the men's room.

"She doesn't look too healthy to me. You sure she's up to the physical labor?"

Freya Barker   FROM DUST

At this, Viv's eyes return to mine. "Positive. She'll work out fine. She's had a bit of a rough go of it, but with some decent meals and a job, she'll be on her feet in no time. She worked hard today and you don't have to worry about her because she's coming in on my shift."

I give her a long, hard look, making sure she gets the message that I know she's holding back on me before responding.

"I'll leave her in your capable hands then."

The small smile sliding over her face confirms that somehow, the wool has just been pulled over my eyes, but I'm too tired to care ... much.

36

CHAPTER FOUR

Syd

"I'd better go," I say to Viv when she pulls me out of the washroom. No way in hell can I stay.

"Nonsense. His bark is worse than his bite. I just never got the chance to warn him."

She pulls me into the kitchen and pushes me down onto a chair.

"Look. He usually doesn't get here until after three o'clock. You won't even have to bump into him. You'll see, it'll be fine."

The next thing I know I hear him clear his throat behind me before he launches into a rather rambled apology. At least that's what I think it is. I have a hard time hearing anything he says because I'm drawn to his eyes; deep green and sincere. As mesmerizing as they are, I pull my eyes away and focus on the ground instead, for fear of losing myself. I don't like the unsettled feeling he gives me, although I have to admit, I'm not really scared of him.

When he calls my name, I slowly lift my head to meet his gaze, which hasn't left me. I can feel it. Noticing the hand he has stretched out, curiosity has me reaching out mine. It disappears in his large calloused one and I respond to the pressure of his hand by giving a little squeeze back, trying very hard to ignore the feeling of hot tingles spreading over my skin.

"You okay?" Viv immediately checks when he's gone from the kitchen.

"I'm fine."

Biggest cop-out response of the century, but effective because she doesn't push. Instead, she suggests I grab a plate of food before I'm done for the day. By the time I leave through the back door of The Skipper—back in my familiar and musty smelling garb—I'm a little sore from the physical activities, but I'm showered and I've got a full stomach. I'm pretty confident I'll be back tomorrow ... I think.

The two days I've been off have been so long and boring, I'm actually glad when Tuesday morning comes around.

Funny how you spend years not talking to anyone, not socializing, and being perfectly content to be that way, then to get it and realize you want that connection.

Viv has been incredible. I don't think I've ever known anyone like her before, not even in my past life. She doesn't seem to care that I have little or nothing to say and is content carrying entire conversations virtually solo. I find myself craving the sound of her voice. It shuts up the ones in my head; the ones that constantly try to remind me of things I'd rather forget.

This past Saturday I'd been back, even though I wasn't sure I would be until the back door shut behind me. Viv was there, ushering me up the stairs so I could change and encouraged me to use the shower if I wanted to. I did. Things like standing in a stream of warm water or eating hot food were at some point in my life taken for granted, but not anymore. I struggle with the feelings of guilt, the sense that I don't deserve to feel *good*, but the lure for some comfort is too great so I push those feelings back.

Saturday was uneventful. When Denise and Matt arrived, they simply called out a "hello," but dove straight into their tasks. Thank God for that. I'd rather be left to my own devices. To be around other people continuously and have to interact is a bit overwhelming. So much so that by the time the end of my shift came, I was looking forward to two days of solitude and silence, only to find myself missing the human contact.

The back door is open and as instructed by Viv, I simply enter and head upstairs to shower and get changed. Blissfully warm and clean in my uniform of jeans and a T-shirt, I walk into the kitchen to find Viv already at work on the kitchen prep.

"Hi," I mutter, still a bit hesitant about using my voice.

"Oh hey, Syd. We've got a busy day ahead of us in the kitchen. Tuesday mornings, we get most of our standard deliveries for the week. The beer truck will get here first and usually our other suppliers come just before the lunch hour. After the washrooms, do you think you can go through the produce and see what needs to be tossed? I'd like to try and clean the shelves a little before the fresh load comes in."

I simply nod. I was in the cold pantry, off the side of the kitchen, on Saturday to grab some more onions for the prep. It's a long narrow space with stainless steel shelving on either side, the smell reminding me of damp earth and fresh cut grass. I didn't mind being in there. I've been surrounded by the smells of the wharf for so long now—fish, stale water, wet wood, and rotting garbage—the earthy scent from the produce is a welcome change.

The morning goes by fast with cleaning and the constant flow of suppliers. Beer kegs, boxes of liquor, crates of fish, meat, and any other staples of food are brought in through the back door. I'm dodging strange men left, right, and center, but can't escape the curious looks. Managing to avoid small talk, I hide mostly in the pantry. I'm cleaning when the door opens and a man carrying a crate of vegetables walks in. The moment he spots me, he squints his eyes with a smirk on his pockmarked face and lets the door fall shut behind him. A little panicked, I look over his shoulder to the door and at the same time, back up until I feel the cold wall against my back.

"Well hello. Haven't seen you before. Why are you hiding in here?"

His voice is surprisingly high-pitched, but with a thick Boston accent. I don't like the look in his dark eyes. He looks ... predatory. My mouth opens and closes a few times, trying to formulate the right words to get me out of here, but nothing comes out. This is not my first rodeo, I've been accosted before, but usually outside where I had room to maneuver. Here I have my back against the wall and my only escape route is behind the man in front of me.

"Cat got your tongue, or can't you talk?" he says, looking me over from top to bottom while licking his already wet lips. The moment he steps forward, I try to duck around him, but he grabs a handful of my shirt and yanks me to a halt. "In a rush?" he whispers, using his body to push me back against the wall, trying to push his hips between mine. I turn my face to the side to avoid the stench coming from his mouth and survival instinct takes over. With both hands, I push at his chest, but even though he isn't that big, I can't seem to move him, and it only makes him chuckle.

"Come on now, sweet thing. Don't play hard to get." He coos as he grabs my hands and holds them tight over my head in one hand while the other starts kneading my breast. At the same time I pull up my knee, the door swings open. There is no way I can stop the momentum and my knee makes solid contact with his crotch. He lets go of my hands instantly as he doubles over.

"You fucking kidding me?" I hear Gunnar's voice from the doorway. Next thing I know, the creep is being yanked back and out of the pantry, but before I can catch a breath, the sound of fists flying registers and I rush into the kitchen where Gunnar is pounding on the guy.

"Stop!" My voice is barely above a whisper, but Gunnar hears it. With his fist poised to strike again, he stops and looks at me, dropping the delivery guy to the floor with blood streaming from his nose. Stepping over him, Gunnar is in front of me with his hands on my shoulders, checking me for injury as he slides his hands down my arms. An involuntary shiver runs through me.

"Did he touch you?"

The small shake of my head has him squinting his eyes.

"Don't lie to me," he says, lifting my wrists where red marks are already forming, gently brushing his thumbs over the red, soon-to-be bruised skin.

"What the fuck is all this ruckus?" Viv comes barreling into the kitchen, taking one look at the guy on the floor and then up at Gunnar. "What did Jack do now?"

"I didn't do anything," the muffled voice comes from the floor. "I was just putting away your supplies when that crazy mute bitch kneed me in the nuts. I didn't do anything!"

The word *crazy* is like a red flag to a bull for me and I yank my hands from Gunnar's careful hold and step over to

41

Jack, who is starting to sit up. I plant one sneakered foot on his crotch and lean down.

"I'm not *crazy,* you dirty sleaze bag!" I spit out, so angry I almost miss the look of surprise on his face. "And as you can tell, I'm not mute either, asshole." I push my foot down just a bit until I see his grimace.

No more surprise on his face, but I see pure anger, and it's directed straight at me.

"Whoa, little Bird." Gunnar's voice sounds close to my ear as he steps up behind me with his arm around my waist and easily lifts me a few steps away. "Want to file assault charges?"

My heart stops in my throat. Hell no. That would require filing a police report and the implication of that is not something I'm willing to consider. I vehemently shake my head no, struggling a bit against the strong band of his arm still wrapped around me. He lets me go, but immediately turns me around to face him. He dips down and looks me straight in the eyes. "You sure?"

"Positive," I whisper.

"You okay?" Viv asks, putting a mug of warm tea in front of me and a hand on my shoulder. All this touching. I forgot the feelings it could evoke from revulsion, to heat, and finally to comfort. I almost wanted to curl into the safety of Gunnar's arms earlier and now I find myself leaning into Viv's touch; almost starving for affection like a neglected dog.

Years of frozen emotions are starting to thaw and the process is almost painful. How long has it been since someone cared? How long since I cared? It's been safer not to—to keep enforced walls up and people out—but this place, these people, are crumbling my walls.

"I'm fine." Again with the *fine.*

"Jack's tried shit before with me first, and then once with Denise, but that was nipped in the bud. I guess catching you alone in the pantry was too much of an opportunity for the bastard to pass up on." She sits down across from me and eyes me with concern. "Gunnar called his boss. Told him he was lucky we weren't filing charges against his employee. He was promised that Jack Barnes would no longer be an issue."

"I can handle him," I say with much more bravado than I feel.

"I'm sure you can. That was the most I've heard you say in one stretch, when you were crushing his measly balls with your foot." She snickers at the memory. "He's hopefully learned his lesson. Still, I'm glad Gunnar was here to help with deliveries. The frying pan I would've used on him would probably have made a mess."

The rest of my shift goes by without a hitch. After I put the last of the cleaning supplies back in the closet, I head for the kitchen where Viv and Matt are sitting at the table, having a late lunch by the look of things.

"Come sit down before you head out, Syd. Grab a bite with us. You haven't had anything yet either." Viv motions to one of the chairs. I feel Matt's eyes on me as I slide into the seat opposite him. We haven't really exchanged any words since I was introduced to him, other than a "*hi*" in passing.

"Want some fish stew?"

On my nod, Viv ladles some of the fragrant stew in a big bowl and my stomach growls audibly.

"That hungry, huh?" Matt chuckles beside me and I can't help but smile and shrug at him.

"So, I heard what happened this morning. That's crazy. Did he hurt you?"

Before I get a chance to answer that, Gunnar walks into the kitchen, his face full of rage.

"That bitch," he spits out before plunking down on the chair beside me. I freeze on the spot at his proximity.

"Who, Cindy? What's she done now?" Viv asks while sliding the steaming bowl in front of me. "Eat," she nudges me.

"She's bailing on her week with the kids. Bitch can't even make it a full week before dumping them again. Emmy has a play at school tonight her mom promised to go to. She was so excited to show her, but now Cindy's saying 'something important' came up and she has to go out of town and won't be able to make it. She's dropping the kids off here after school with all their stuff, leaving me to deal with the fallout, as usual." He rakes his hand through the unruly hair he seems prone to and sighs deeply. "And the fucking babysitter is out of town until the end of the week."

"She's an idiot. Still can't figure how she can't seem to appreciate the amazing kids she has." Viv gives his shoulder a squeeze. "They can keep me company in the kitchen, and if it gets too late, they can crash upstairs. No worries."

"I'll set them up with my iPhone. I've got lots of new games they'll like," Matt contributes, earning a raised eyebrow from Gunnar.

"Thanks, although I have my doubts about the games. But it means tonight I should be at Emmy's play and we'll be short staffed. Also, Dexter has already made it known he doesn't want to go, so he was gonna hang with me here while I work. He'll just have to deal and come along." A deep groan illustrates his frustration.

"I can stay and help."

I swear the words just come flying out without passing through my brain. *Oh my God.* And from the startled looks around me, everyone else is as stunned as I am at my words. Although their reactions are more likely over the fact that I actually spoke, they don't have a clue why my offer is something completely out of character. They don't know me at all.

I tend to avoid kids like the plague. They wouldn't know that, nor will they because that part of me is locked away tight.

"Actually," Viv says with an eyebrow raised, "that could work out quite well. I'll join Matt and Denise up front and you can help Dino in the kitchen and watch Dex."

"Dino?"

Viv laughs at my question. "Dino is our chef. His real name is Francis, but he threatens to hit us when we try to use it. The *Dino* will become obvious when you see him."

"You sure?" Gunnar's gritty voice asks beside me and I turn to meet his eyes.

"Me?" I ask tentatively. When he nods, I simply nod yes back, but shit, I'm really not sure at all.

"He's a good kid, Dexter. He won't give you any trouble and I'll only be gone a couple of hours. Sure you don't have somewhere you gotta be?"

I hold back the giggle that threatens to come out at that question and my eyes flick over to Viv, who seems to have kept the fact I'm homeless to herself.

"Nowhere." I tell him.

CHAPTER FIVE

Syd

Dino is behemoth, and I mean massive.

I just finished my final clean of the washrooms when I venture over to the kitchen and find a large bull of a man coming out of the pantry. My instincts are to turn and run, which is something I would've done out on the streets if I encountered someone as intimidating as him, but when I take a step back out the doorway, I bump into Viv who's come up behind me.

"Ah, you're early. Perfect," she says to him as she slides past me, grabbing hold of my arm to pull me further into the kitchen. "Dino, this is Syd. She's replacing Maria and she's great in the kitchen as well. Gunnar has something he has to go to for a couple of hours tonight and Syd's gonna hang around to help in the kitchen while I take over bartending duties. Syd, meet Dino, our chef."

"Hi," I choke on his name, a little unnerved by the intense stare directed at me from under his heavy brow. A grunt in response is all I get as he turns away and starts laying out the supplies he collected from the pantry. When I quickly glance over at Viv, she winks at me with a smile on her face, handing me an apron.

"Dino will tell you what to do."

My eyebrows shoot up, questioning whether the grunting Neanderthal can even speak, only causing Viv to snicker beside me. A light shove in my back from her propels me to step beside him at the counter and without looking at me, he slides over a cutting board with a knife.

"You do know how to use a knife?" The deep rumble of his voice is even more imposing than Gunnar's, but surprisingly, the tone is soft.

"Yup." Is all I say, picking up the knife and starting on the peppers he's lined up on the counter.

Half an hour later, with a bin of diced peppers done, I feel him standing behind me. "Hmmm, not bad. How are you with onions?"

"Okay."

"Not one for small talk, are you? Nice for a change," he grumbles, referring to Viv's chatty personality I assume. Oddly, it makes me feel more comfortable in his presence.

"Not much to say."

"Hmmm," he says again. "Tackle the onions next."

Just as I'm about to grab the first one on the pile, I hear a kid's voice from the door.

"Hey, Dino!" A young boy walks into the kitchen, backpack slung over his shoulder. "Who are you?" His eyes find me frozen with the kitchen knife in my hand.

"Daniel ..." The name I tried so hard to forget stumbles off my lips before I can think. Memories of a little boy—both happy and painful—assault me and the knife slips out of my hand, bouncing off the board and cutting my leg on the way down to the ground. I can't get myself to tear my eyes from the boy in front of me whose eyes have gone bigger than saucers.

"You're bleeding," he says, looking at me with worry all over his face.

Snapped out of my memories, I glance down at my jeans that now have a red stain quickly spreading.

"Shit, girl!" Dino turns me toward the kitchen table and shoves me down onto a chair. "Thought you could handle a knife?"

"Sorry ... it slipped," I mumble while he tries to have a look at my leg.

"Sit tight while I go get some supplies. Dexter? Keep an eye on her," he says, leaving the kitchen and me alone with the scared looking boy.

Dexter. That's the kid's name, right? Gunnar's son?

"Are you okay?" he asks me timidly and my heart aches at the tears pooling in his eyes.

"Hey, I'm fine ... honest. It's just a little cut. It doesn't even hurt."

"Why did you call me Daniel? My name is Dexter," he says, concern replaced by curiosity as he regards me.

"You just reminded me of a little boy I knew," I find myself saying.

"I'm not really that little. I'm nine." Dexter pulls himself up to his full height and pops his little chest out, making me smile.

"I can tell. You're gonna be as tall as your dad."

"Everyone always says I look like him," he says proudly.

"Sure do." I smile at him, winning a small smile back. I lift my eyes to the door, spotting Dino who is leaning against the post, listening, and a first-aid kit in his big paws.

"Dex, why don't you go up front and hang with Viv? I need to fix Syd up."

At the mention of my name, Dexter looks at me. "Syd?"

"Yup. That's my name. Nice to meet you, Dexter."

With a little man's chin tilt and a wave of his little hand, he's gone, leaving me with Dino's dark eyes focused on me, making me more than a little uncomfortable.

Freya Barker   FROM DUST

"Been married for twelve years so don't take this the wrong way, but I need you to drop your pants."

I'm poised to object, but the sticky flow of blood against my skin tells me to suck it up, so I stand, untie the rope at my waist and let the still zipped up jeans drop before sitting again.

"Christ, woman. You're skin and bones," Dino mutters as he starts wiping the substantial gash in my thigh with alcohol wipes. I grimace at the sting but sit still, taking this pain as my punishment too.

"Seemed chatty enough with little Dex, there. Been around kids a lot?" He asks, not looking up from the care he's giving the cut on my leg, so he doesn't see the look of panic I feel threatening to settle on my face ... I hope. I take a deep breath and with a nonchalant air I don't feel, I respond without revealing too much.

"Not really. Been a while."

"That so? Well, Dex and Emmy are great kids. They're here quite a bit so I guess you'll be seeing a lot more of them." He briefly looks up before going back to the task of doctoring me up. I sit quietly as he pulls the edges of the cut together and closes it with butterfly bandages. I think I've done enough talking for today, but Dino isn't done.

"Just so you know, I'm not half as scary as I look. Not a big talker myself, but a good listener. Remember that."

Gunnar

"Dad?"

My little guy stands in the doorway to my office where his big sister has already taken up residence with her homework.

"Hey, squirt. Where've you been?"

"Kitchen." Just like his father, Dex doesn't like to waste words. Would probably piss me the hell off if he were older, but from the little guy, it's just cute. He's not moving from the doorway though, just shuffling his feet a bit where he stands. Quiet kid normally, so I know I'll have to ask before he says anything.

"What's the matter?"

"I think she's hurt pretty bad—the lady in the kitchen. She was bleeding a lot," he says without really looking at me.

"Hurt? Is it Viv?" I ask, shooting up from my chair. With two strides, I'm in front of him.

"She says her name is Syd. And, Dad? She called me Daniel. I think I scared her and that's why she dropped the knife."

A sick feeling settles in the pit of my stomach thinking about that waif of a girl getting hurt. She's as fragile as a baby bird already. *Damn.*

"Stay here with Emmy, kid. I'll go have a look, okay?" With his head bobbing in agreement, I take off for the kitchen.

I catch Dino's question about kids just outside the doorway and her tentative sounding response. She hasn't strung more than three words together at a time to my knowledge so far, so the news she was chatty with my son surprises me. She doesn't see me, but Dino—who is sitting on his knees in front of her—throws me a quick look over her shoulder before saying something in a low voice I can't quite catch.

"What happened?"

At my voice, Syd twists her head around to find me right behind her. Her jeans are puddled around her ankles and her exposed legs tell me she's even more malnourished than I suspected. I'm almost sickened at the pang of lust that stirs my cock at the sight of the pale expanse of skin and the plain cotton panties she's in. *Fuck me.* It hasn't been *that* long since I've had someone for a skinny little bird like her to rouse me, or has it? Can't fucking remember now. Spotting the cut on her thigh and the butterfly bandages Dino has obviously placed on the cut, goes a long way to snuffing out any sexual thoughts. *Thank God.*

"Sorry," she says, apprehension in her eyes. "The knife slipped. I'll pay for the jeans."

I shake my head, trying to understand. "Jeans?"

"That Viv gave me? They're cut too."

Still at a loss, I look to Dino for answers but he just shrugs and stands up to his full height, towering over her. "You woozy?" he asks, watching Syd closely. When she shakes her head no, he turns to the sink to wash his hands.

Before I have a chance to say or do anything, Syd is pulling her jeans up over those skinny legs, carefully avoiding her injury. The large bloodstain and the rip in her jeans give me a clearer picture, as does the fact that she has to hold them up with a piece of rope. I need a talk with Viv. "You need to go lie down or something?"

She looks at me suspiciously before turning her eyes to the ground. "I'm fine."

"Still. I'd feel better if you took a load off for a bit. Half an hour, tops. Use the apartment upstairs. It has a comfortable couch, and after that, we'll see how you feel. Whether you need to go home or not, we'll manage." With nothing more than the faintest of smiles, she slips past me, into the hallway.

"Sure she doesn't need to see a doctor?" I ask Dino.

"Nah. It's long, but not so deep. Reason she was bleeding like a stuck pig is 'cause the girl has no fat on her body ... at all." He looks at me hard. "I mean nothing. She's skin and bones. Where did you find her?"

"I didn't, Viv did. She told me Syd had run into some hard times, but I'm thinking there's more to the story."

Dino nods in agreement. "Sure seems that way."

With Syd upstairs and Dino once again focused on his stove, I set off to find my manager for a talk. I find her setting up the bar for the evening crowd. "Tell me more about Syd." I dive in without preamble, startling Viv who hadn't heard me walk up.

"Oh, hey! Syd? What do you mean?" She feigns ignorance, but I know her too well. She can't lie for shit.

"You know what I mean. I just sent her upstairs to go lie down. That woman is not well. Where did you meet her?"

"Upstairs?" Her confusion is clear on her face. "Why? Did something happen?"

I tell her what Dexter told me and what I observed in the kitchen. She looks ready to run upstairs and see for herself when I hold up my hand to stop her. "She's fine, or at least she will be after she lies down for a bit. I need to know, Syd. That woman is so malnourished and so damn pale; something is off with her."

"Shit. I know, Gunnar. I kept it to myself 'cause I wanted her to have a chance to find her feet, so you have to promise me not to jump to conclusions."

I answer the plea in her eyes with a shrug of my shoulders. I can promise not to jump to conclusions, but I fucking well reserve the right to form those on my own.

"She's homeless. Well, technically, she lives in the shed down the alley, but she has nothing. I found her collecting food from the dumpster last Thursday night. She was so scared when I caught her, Gunnar. It broke my heart."

"Who's to say she isn't some junkie who's gonna rob us blind the first chance she gets? Seriously, Viv, what the fuck were you thinking?" I'm pissed to have been put in this position, but I can't risk what I—no—what my family has spent the last several decades building. She's got to go.

"You promised," Viv spits out, her mouth an angry line. "I know you, and I know how you think. Hell, I even know *what* you think. She's not like that. I can tell. Gunnar, please don't. Give her a chance. I realize she's a big question mark but you know what? She hadn't spoken or been spoken to in a long fucking time when I found her, and already she is interacting with most of us and she works really hard!"

I have my mouth open to respond but Viv cuts me off with her hand. "You send her away now, you'll set her back further than where she was when I first saw her. Please."

Fucking hell. Those puppy-dog eyes of hers are filling with tears. The times I've seen Viv cry in all the years we've known each other can be counted on one hand. She's just that tough. Not now though. I can't figure what has her so invested in having Syd here, but something does. Turning Viv by her shoulders, I guide her into the hallway in the back where I pull her in for a hug.

"You're a pain in my ass, you know that?" I tell her, resting my cheek on her head.

"I know ..." she snuffles into my chest.

"We'll see how it goes, but one wrong move and she's out of here, okay?" I draw a line in the sand but truth be told, I don't know if I'd have the heart to put her out anyway. Fucking little bird does something to me.

"Ready, girl?"

I've just left Viv in charge of the pub and have to hustle to get my girl to her play in time; Dino's already fed both kids some dinner at the kitchen table. Looks like Syd found her way back downstairs, looking a little better than earlier. She's sitting at the table, apparently much more at ease with Dino and my children than she is with me since she seems to avoid looking me in the eyes.

"Ready, Daddy?" Emmy jumps up and grabs her backpack. I walk over to where Dex is sitting and ruffle his hair.

"You gonna be okay here for a bit, kid?" The enthusiastic nod of his head is answer enough. Without forcing the usual rule of answering with words, I lean down and kiss his head. "Be good for Dino and Syd, okay?"

"Yes, Dad." I catch Syd observing my interactions with the kids closely, but the moment she senses my eyes on her, she flicks her gaze back down to the table. *Huh.* Maybe it's me. The girl is an enigma.

In the truck, I can't help but notice Emmy seems withdrawn and is staring out the window, her long blonde hair covering part of her face. She has her mother's looks but thank God, not her attitude. Emmy is soft hearted and sweet.

"You nervous, kiddo?"

She nods but doesn't turn her head to face me. Worried she might be more nervous than I had anticipated, I grab her hand in mine, squeezing it.

"You'll be brilliant, you know that right? You're my daughter. How could you be any other way?" I tease her, knowing how to coax a smile out of her, but it's not working and when I see her shoulders pull up around her ears, I know she's crying. I pull into the first free parking spot on the side of the road that I see. "Hey. Emmy, look at me."

"Daddy, we're gonna be l-late," she hiccups, finally turning her face so I can see her. Her eyes are wet and big fat tears slowly roll down her cheeks. I reach out and brush them away with my thumb.

"What's going on, honey? I thought you were looking forward to tonight. What happened?"

"I was, but when I got mad at Mom for making other plans, she said because I don't have a leading role, it's a waste of time anyway." Emmy starts sobbing now and I hate it when the kids cry—especially Emmy—who doesn't do it very often. Leaning over, I pull her against my shoulder where she continues to sob. I try to control the urge to curse her mother out loud, but I don't want to add to Emmy's stress. I know she kept this from me because she hates to see us fight, and unfortunately, that has happened more than it should. With a bit more care than I usually would, I try to undo the damage Cindy has caused.

"Listen, *I* have been looking forward to this ever since I found out I was gonna get to take you instead. *I* happen to believe you are very talented, very beautiful, and capable of playing any role you set your sights on. That's why it doesn't matter what role you play, because I *know* you will blow everyone else out of the water."

She lifts her head off my shoulder and gives me a watery smile and a nudge to my side. "Da-ad ..."

Grinning, I give her a quick kiss on her forehead before steering the truck back into traffic.

"Tissues in the glove box, girl. Wipe those tears and let's go knock 'em dead." When I throw her a wink, I'm happy to see the upward tilt to her lips remains as she furiously wipes at her cheeks.

The smile on my girl's face when she bows in front of a loud and appreciative audience later that night is tucked away with the other bright moments I will treasure always, unlike the dark space I reserve for my ex and her destructive nature. *That* space is overflowing and I know I have to take some action soon or she will suck all the happy out of my kids, like she's done with me already, years ago. I'll kill her before I let her kill the light in my kids.

CHAPTER SIX

Syd

"So what other homework do you have?"

I look at Dexter, who is squirming a little in his seat. I can see Dino smile from the corner of my eye as he is prepping the next order, but don't allow my eyes to wander.

"Come on ... I can tell there is something else," I nudge Dex, who rolls his eyes before responding.

"Fine. Math, but I hate it and I don't understand anything my teacher told us today." The firm set of his chin reminds me of his father and that makes me chuckle. Dex is so innocent in comparison with that man. For one thing, Dex doesn't make my stomach churn like his dad does every time he comes within talking distance of me. Also, Dex is kind of cute when he does that stubborn thing, where Gunnar only looks more intimidating.

"You do know that Batman is really good with numbers, right?" I try, earning a weak and tentative smile.

"I bet he never had to do math homework though." The little smartass makes me chuckle. I should've known he'd be too old for games like that.

"The only way to get smart though." I lift one eyebrow in a silent challenge and with slow, deliberate movements, never losing eye contact with me, he pulls his math book from his backpack.

I have to bite my lip to keep from laughing at the way he gives in *under silent protest.*

He's been working on his homework now for about an hour while I help Dino with cooking and plating. I'm surprised they give little kids so much work to take home. My initial shock at seeing Dexter in the doorway has long since gone, and I find myself enjoying the boy's company and occasional questions.

I hate to admit it, but that half hour Gunnar forced me to take did me a world of good. The cut on my leg pulls a little, but other than that, it doesn't hurt too bad at all. The first few minutes on the couch upstairs, I was afraid he'd follow me upstairs, but exhaustion and shock finally pulled me into a dreamless sleep. When Viv came to check on me, I was already up, my body well accustomed to self-regulation. I really don't need an alarm. Ever since ... well, since the last time I overslept, I've been able to wake myself up on cue. It's been five years now; five years of learning to just close my eyes and let go.

With a shake of my head, I turn back to Dex, only to find him staring at me.

"What?" I ask him.

"Dino asked if you were okay helping me with math. If not, he will after he's done."

A quick glance at Dino shows him with one eyebrow raised in question. *Shit.* I must've really wandered off for a minute there.

"I'm good with math. In fact, math was my favorite subject all through school." I stop myself from exposing too much, finding myself way too comfortable here in the kitchen. "Show me what you've got."

For the next half hour, I'm able to show him the basic workings of decimals and fractions. He's actually smiling when he finally closes his book. "You're really smart. Where did you learn all that?" he wants to know.

"In school. Just like you, I had a hard time understanding math at first, but then I changed schools and got this great teacher who really helped me understand. I've loved math and numbers ever since," I tell him, a little uneasy with the close scrutiny he's subjecting me to, but encouraging him to do well outweighs my concern for the second set of ears in the room.

"So how come you work here and not at a bank, or some other place where you can use numbers? You're really good at it."

A heavy, almost painful pressure sits on my chest. I did once, but I'm not going to give him that answer. It's one I'm not ready to explore myself. "I may just do that at some point." I know full well I'm avoiding the actual question. "But I really enjoy working here too," I cautiously add.

The next thing I know, Dexter jumps up from the table and makes for the door. "Dad! You're back!" He launches himself at his father, who looks at me with intense eyes. Crap. How much has he heard?

"We're back, kid. And your sister was out of this world, she was so good!" Emmy stands beside her dad, beaming from ear to ear at the compliment and I can't help but smile.

"Awesome," Dino rumbles from behind me.

"That's great, Emmy," I add softly, and I'm rewarded with the same bright smile. It hits me right in the chest as well, but runs through me like a soft breeze, blowing the dust that has settled on my heart.

"Ice cream to celebrate?" Dino suggests, which is met with an enthusiastic "Yesss" and a fist pump from Dexter and a "Yay!" from Emmy who plops herself down at the table beside me. Gunnar stays in the doorway.

"You guys gonna be okay here while I check out the pub?"

"Yes, Dad."

"Fine, Daddy."

With one last look in my direction, he turns down the hall, lifting the tension from my shoulders immediately.

It's almost ten when Viv pushes me to the door. "Go. You've been here for twelve hours already. Go get some rest."

Reluctantly, I leave the warm and safe haven of the kitchen for my cold blankets on the floor of the shed. Funny how quickly you get used to the comforts of life again. The freezing air outside hits me in the face and I can't stop a full-body shiver running through me. It's a cold night, but it's clear, showing the bright stars against the night sky. Tempted by the view, I turn left toward the water instead of heading straight for my shed.

I sit on the side of the dock, my feet dangling over the water below and try to focus on the view alone. It was something I'd always been good at; compartmentalizing. Focus on one thing and have everything else disappear, but my mind keeps returning to the day behind me. I feel exposed. My emotions seem to be coming alive under the influence of good people and warm food. My heart is defrosting and it hurts like my fingers do when warming up after being outside too long in the cold. The dull ache in my chest is getting sharper by the day and the children's appearance today only made that worse. Or is it better? I don't know. I don't know what'll happen when I can no longer stave off the memories and it all comes flooding back. I'm scared, but not scared enough to turn my back on The Skipper. It represents something I've gone without for a long time: hope. I'm drawn to it like a moth to a flame, but even the knowledge I'll get myself burned isn't enough to keep me away.   I'd grown so used to waking up disappointed I was still alive, I didn't think the day would ever come again where the morning would arrive and I'd be relieved to still be there. Hope brings with it the possibility of loss. I've experienced loss, and I don't think I'll survive it again.

I'll just take things a day at a time—a moment at a time. It's something I've become very adept at—living in the moment.

A sound behind me startles me out of my thoughts and I turn around, but can't see anything. Probably just an animal going through the garbage, I tell myself. God knows I've encountered plenty of them roaming the docks under the shelter of night. With the cold already settling into my bones, I get up to head to my blankets. Once inside my shed, I roll myself in my bedding and drift off to sleep with the knowledge there'll be a warm shower and a meal waiting for me tomorrow.

Gunnar

Been a long fucking day. The kids are safely upstairs asleep and I'm seriously considering spending the night here instead of hauling them out of bed and home. Cindy left a bag of clothes for them when she dropped them off this afternoon so they'll have something clean to wear to school tomorrow. I sent Viv home earlier, who was dead on her feet, and Denise and Matt left not long thereafter. I've been wrestling with numbers the past hour, trying to find a way I can afford to hire on a full-time bartender to ease the load on us. With the kids' mother so increasingly unpredictable, especially after hearing the mindfuck she put over on Emmy, I'm seriously considering applying for full custody. However, if I want to do that, I'll have to find a way to be available to them without it having an impact on the pub. I know any judge will look at my lifestyle and find working night shifts in a drinking establishment while my kids are either looked after by a babysitter or here with me, is not conducive to a healthy, nurturing environment.

When the numbers start to blur in front of my eyes, I decide to take out the trash and head upstairs. Fuck going home tonight; I'll just crash on the couch.

With a box of kitchen garbage and a black trash bag in hand, I push open the back door. The blast of cold air gives me a full body shiver. In the few steps it takes me to reach the dumpster, the distinct smell of smoke hits my nostrils and looking around for the cause, I see an orange glow down the alley. I quickly dump the trash, pull my phone out and dial 9-1-1 while walking toward the flicker of flames.

"Fire on Holyoke Wharf," I tell the operator, "the alley behind The Skipper. Looks like one of the old storage sheds." As soon as the words leave my mouth, I remember Viv saying Syd lives in a shed and I take off running, tucking the phone back in my pocket. The small building is engulfed on the backside with flames licking over the flat roof to the front. "SYD!"

With smoke getting thick around me, I rip off my flannel shirt and tie it around my face. The heat this close is intense. I don't get any response so I call out again, hoping this is not where she beds down at night. *Fuck!* What was I thinking, sending that frail woman back out here.

"Syd! You in there?"

"Please ..." I hear from the other side of the door.

I try to open it, but there's something wedged against the door on the inside. I have to wipe burning embers out of my hair, as the wind blows the flames in all directions.

"Step back! I'm coming in!"

Taking a step back, I haul out with my leg and manage to kick the door open to where I can now get in through a decent opening. Once inside, I'm almost overcome by the thick black smoke, but when I reach out with my hand, I manage to grab onto what feels like an arm and I pull it toward me. Wrestling myself back through the narrow opening, I pull Syd out with me. The fire is now coming around the sides, and we need to get the hell away, so without stopping to check her over, I swing the tiny woman in my arms and run to the back door of the pub. I have to get my kids to safety in case the fire starts moving this way. Once inside, Syd starts coughing and struggling in my arms. "Hold still, woman. I'll put you down in the kitchen."

No sooner have I set her down on the kitchen table, Emmy comes running in. "Daddy, fire!" She stops dead in her tracks when she spots us and I see the fear in her face.

"It's okay, honey, it's not here," I cough out. "Fire trucks are on their way." And just then, I hear the sirens. "Go back upstairs with your brother for now. Make sure he stays where he is, okay?" With a frightened nod, she runs back up the stairs.

Still holding onto her shoulders, I start looking over Syd for injuries while she continues coughing up smoke. It's hard to see anything with the thick layer of soot covering the both of us. "Gotta get you to the ambulance out there."

Immediately, she begins struggling to get out of my hold. "No h-hospital," she manages.

"You've probably suffered smoke inhalation. You've gotta get checked out."

But Syd shakes her head furiously. "No. Please ..." *God dammit.* I don't know what it is about this woman and I'm sure this'll come back to bite me in the ass, but I can't ignore her terrified plea.

I pick her up again and take her upstairs where I leave her in the bathroom with a pile of towels and a frightened Emmy with instructions to stay put while I talk to rescue services outside. A quick check on Dex finds him still sleeping soundly, despite all the activity outside the window.

Outside, I track down the first rescue person I see and explain that I was in the shed checking to see if anyone was in there, but found it empty. When the firefighter tells me to stay put and wait for the police, I explain I have to get back to my kids, but to send whomever over to The Skipper. I'll leave the back door open.

I make my way back upstairs to find Syd with her arms around a crying Emmy and I move in to take my daughter from her arms.

"We're fine, honey. Just dirty from the smoke, that's all. The fire trucks are here and are already putting out the flames, I promise." I meet Syd's eyes over my girl's head and I see defeat in them. Not pain, not fear, but defeat. That is almost worse than dealing with my daughter's tears. What happened to this woman?

When the crying slows down to some snuffles, I urge Emmy back in bed with her brother and walk toward the bathroom to get cleaned up, but a knock from downstairs stops me. Syd's panicked face pokes out of the bathroom. "Go on, get cleaned up. I'll take care of this."

With a nod, she disappears back into the bathroom. I'm glad her coughing seems to have stopped or it would be hard to hide her from the police officer standing at my back door, looking for answers.

I explain about taking out the garbage and noticing the fire down the alley. I also tell him I kicked the door down, staying as close to the truth as I can, but he still regards me suspiciously. "Are you saying you barged into a burning building just to *check* if anyone might be inside? That doesn't seem risky to you?"

"Come on ... you must know that vagrants crash there from time to time? I just reacted, not thinking much at all. When I realized it was empty, I came back here to check on my children right away. Look, can I get cleaned up? I'll be happy to go over it some more tomorrow, but my kids are scared upstairs and I could do with a shower," I point out. With a reluctant nod and a last suspicious glance my way, I show the officer the door and promise to stay available for further questions.

By the time I walk into the apartment, I find Syd wrapped in a throw blanket, curled up, and fast asleep in the chair. Figuring I'd only wake her up if I moved her to the couch, I leave her where she is. A quick shower and a last check on the kids later, I flop down on the couch, close my eyes, and drift off.

"Dad ... wake up."

I squint my eyes against the morning light streaming in through the windows and it takes me a minute to figure out where I am. Dexter is leaning over me with his hair neatly combed, and his breath smelling faintly of toothpaste.

"Hey, buddy," I struggle to sit up and look around the apartment, finding it empty. "Where's your sister?"

"Downstairs in the kitchen with Syd." *Fuck.* Right, the fire.

"Syd told me to come wake you up. I'm gonna go back to eat my breakfast."

My boy takes off running and is almost at the door when the information registers. "Breakfast?" I call after him.

"Yup! Pancakes. Gotta go!"

Less than two minutes later, I walk into the kitchen, dressed in some old track pants and a T-shirt I found in my old dresser upstairs. My kids are at the table chowing down on what looks to be a substantial pile of pancakes and are laughing at something Syd says. She stands with her back leaning against the stove, smiling at them. That smile. Fuck me.

She must've heard something because her eyes lock on mine and before I can say anything, she comes walking straight toward me, nudging me back into the hallway. What the hell?

"Don't say anything about last night to Dex. Emmy tells me he already has bad nightmares sometimes."

I'm stunned. She's never looked me in the eyes for longer than a minute and she sure as hell has never spoken in full sentences that I know of. Part of me wants to be offended that she tells me how to handle my kids, but I can't argue her reasoning, or her apparent genuine concern. I guess she takes my silence the wrong way because her gaze turns to the ground and she starts fidgeting with the edge of the men's flannel she is wearing. "I'm sorry. They woke me up this morning and you were still sleeping. I thought I could get them ready for school, but then I realized you'd need to drive them." She peeks up through her eyelashes and continues, "They've got clean clothes on and brushed their teeth already ... shit ... I guess I should've told them to do that after breakfast, right? I forgot. I'm sor—"

I put my hands on her bony shoulders and dip down to look her in the eyes. "You tell me 'sorry' one more time and you're fired." At that, her eyes shoot up with a spark of fire coming from them. "Whoa, just kidding, Syd. Let me say thank you, okay? Getting them ready, making them pancakes for breakfast? That's more than they ever get at their mom's, so thank you for that. And for letting me sleep a little longer."

She shrugs her shoulders under my hands, making me aware I'm still holding onto her and I pull my hands back. That felt too nice. "Gonna run them to school real quick and pick up some clean clothes at home. You need anything?" I see something flick over her face before she shuts it down and shakes her head no. Like hell. "Gonna be out anyway, so tell me what you need," I insist.

"I don't have a toothbrush. It burned in the fire," she whispers, suddenly shy again.

"I'll pick you up a toothbrush and I'll give Viv a call to see about getting you some clothes. But when I get back, we're gonna talk—you and I."

A quick nod and she turns back into the kitchen, chatting with the kids like it's the most natural thing in the world. Running my hand through my hair, I wonder how it is that yesterday I was ready to kick her out on her ass, not sure if she was trustworthy, and today I let her cater to my kids and offer to pick her up a goddamn toothbrush. Confusing as hell.

CHAPTER SEVEN

Syd

I love cooking. It's been so long since I've been behind a stove but it appears I've forgotten little. When I looked for something hearty to make the kids before school, I spotted the bin of flour in the pantry and it all came back to me—pancakes. I made way too many, but I figured maybe Gunnar would want some when he comes back, Viv too. Covering a baking tray with tinfoil, I place the pancakes on top and slide them into the oven to keep them warm before sitting down with a cup of coffee from the big pot I finally figured out how to work.

I feel like a million bucks. How's that for irony? My only *home* burns down with all my earthly possessions inside and I may well be in trouble with the police for evasion, but for the first time in years, I feel like I have the tools for a new start. That is if Gunnar doesn't toss me out on my ass. Even that possibility doesn't stop the slow-building feeling that I'm at the beginning of something more. The fire seems almost cathartic—cleansing—burning up any remainder of my past and setting me free. Of course I still have a roof over my head to consider, which is a huge worry, but oddly enough I feel little anxiety over that at all. I'll try to get into the Florence House shelter on Preble Street for tonight. It's a bit of a hike, and although it's not a long-term solution, it will be a warm place to lay my head at night for now. That is if they have room to take me in.

"I have a proposition for you." Gunnar stands in the doorway with his hands on his hips. His comment pulls me out of my thoughts and I'm momentarily startled since I hadn't even heard him come in. *Huh.* I'm normally very attuned to my surroundings out of self-preservation and I'm surprised at how easily I've let my guard slip. His words excite me for some reason and I tilt my head, looking at him.

"Proposition?"

"Yes," he confirms, a frown marring his forehead, as if he's unsure himself about what he's thinking. "It would appear we're each in a bit of a pickle and there may be a way to solve both of our issues." He moves into the kitchen and pours himself a coffee before sitting down at the table in front of me. I don't say anything, just wait for him to continue. "But first, you have to explain to me why you were avoiding the hospital and the cops last night. Are you in trouble with the law? 'Cause if you are, I don't know if this is going to work."

I swallow hard, trying to figure out how much, or how little, I can get away with sharing. How much can I trust him with? Although he scared me at first, nothing he's done since has given me any reason to believe he is anything but a caring father and a considerate boss. Besides, the man may well have saved my life last night. I owe him. "I'm not in trouble," I try, but judging from the look on his face, it's not enough.

"Need more than that, Syd,"

Fuck. Okay, I didn't really expect that to fly, so I venture on carefully. "I, uhh ... I don't want to be found."

"You running away from someone?" His entire demeanor changes before my eyes; lips in a straight line and eyebrows scrunched together. "Are you in danger?"

I quickly shake my head. "Not in so many words. I just need to leave my past where it belongs, and that's behind me. It wasn't a good place for me." I carefully gauge his reaction.

"You know you're being evasive, right?"

"Yes, and I'm sorry. It's just that I've been on my own for a long time—years—and I'm not used to sharing anything."

Gunnar glances at his folded hands on the kitchen table, the corner of his mouth tilting up. "That doesn't come as a surprise. You've hardly been forthcoming."

"I'm sorry." His head shoots up and he pins me with an angry glare, making me turn away.

"Enough with the 'sorry' already. Gotta stop apologizing for everything."

"Okay, I'm sor—, I mean, I will. Stop, that is. At least I'll try."

The little smile is encouragement enough for me to give him a little more. "I've done things I'm not proud of. Things I can't ever make right."

"I get that, but there's always a way to make amends or turn things around. Hell, I made the biggest mistake of my life marrying my ex, but if I hadn't, I wouldn't have my kids."

I'd like to tell him that my clouds don't have that silver lining, but I keep it to myself instead. With a deep sigh and a hint of disappointment, he seems to come to terms with the fact that I've shared about all I'm comfortable with.

"All right, here's what I'm thinking. I need someone to help me look after the kids after school; someone who will be here to check on homework, make sure they're fed and all that. They seem to like you and it looked like you handled them just fine. You don't have a roof over your head and need a place to stay. The apartment upstairs has been vacant since I bought the house and I only use it to crash when it's been a particularly busy night and I don't feel like going home, or to give the kids a place to sleep when plans get fucked up like they did yesterday."

A hint of excitement sparks in the pit of my stomach and I know it must show on my face because he smiles and shakes his head. "You think you can keep doing your work and take on the kids after, then it's yours. We'll consider that payment for the childcare." I can feel my face cracking open with the unfamiliar smile that I can't hold back. I'm nodding furiously, making Gunnar chuckle. "There may be times where the kids need to crash there for a few hours though. That gonna be a problem?"

Hell no! Not a problem at all, although I would agree to just about anything right now. Could it be I'm this lucky? I know I don't deserve this, but I'm not stupid. I'm not going to turn this down. Overwhelmed and a bit teary-eyed, I look him straight in the eyes. "Not a problem, and thank you."

"You crying? Christ, please don't cry. I don't need none of that." He looks distinctly uncomfortable and now it's my turn to chuckle. "I'm hungry," he says, quickly changing the subject. "Got any of those pancakes left over?"

"Yup. Still warm in the oven."

"Then load me up, woman. Oh, and make sure to pile up a few for yourself as well. You're too damn skinny—that's gotta change."

That's how Viv finds us a little later; chowing down on breakfast in companionable silence. I load her up with the last few pancakes and while she eats, I let Gunnar fill her in on last night's events and our agreement. After she fusses over me to make sure I'm fine—which I am, save for a few singed hairs, a small burn on my arm, and a sore airway— she hands me a bag of clothes, full of stuff she swears is too small for her. With the bag, the toothbrush, and the toothpaste Gunnar picked up, I run upstairs to clean up and change while Viv offers to take care of the breakfast dishes.

Standing under the hot shower, washing away the lingering smell of smoke, I feel myself coming down a little from the emotional high I was on earlier. Sure, my immediate issues seemed to be resolved with the offer of a roof over my head. Hell, it's more than I've had for a very long time, and the new purpose the work gave me sparks some hope for a future, but the risk of getting too close to these people only looms larger. Already Viv has sharper eyes than I'm comfortable with and Gunnar and his kids are finding ways to slip under my skin. The place where my heart sat frozen in my chest for so long is becoming too warm a place. *Caring.* It's a dangerous emotion; the beginning of something that cannot end well. It's a vulnerable place where if I let my guard down, heartbreak can only follow. There was a time when hope and love were feelings I took for granted, in the form of an innocent little boy whose big eyes showed all the wonder and beauty of the world around him.

"Mommy, why do dogs have four legs and we get only two?"

The dark-haired little boy is sitting at the breakfast island, coloring a crude picture of a speckled puppy in his book.

"Not sure, baby, but I think it's so they can run faster to catch the ball. Besides, we get two arms to make up for it."

"But I want to run faster," he says, a little frown creasing his high forehead.

"Hmmm, but then you wouldn't be able to give your momma such special hugs now, would you?"

Reaching over, she picks up the child in her arms where he clings like a monkey, his spindly arms wound around her neck. Smiling at his strong squeeze on her, she bends her head to blow a raspberry on his exposed little neck, causing him to giggle out his healthy belly laugh.

A door slamming downstairs brings me back to the image in the fogged up mirror in front of me. I suck in a breath of air in an attempt to clear my chest of the heavy weight that rests there. With a corner of the towel, I wipe away at the condensation on the mirror and find a vaguely familiar face; eyes wet with tears. I wipe at them furiously, and swallow down the blackness that threatens to overwhelm me. *Not now.*

In a hurry to escape the destructive thoughts, I get dressed as quickly as I can in a pair of cargo pants and another staff T-shirt from the bag Viv gave me and make my way downstairs.

In the kitchen I find Matt and Denise have arrived. "Morning." Both their heads turn in my direction, and I'm met with a smile from Matt and a rather blank stare from Denise. Wonder what's up with her.

"Hey, Syd," Matt says, "did you see the burned shed in the alley? Damn, we're lucky the flames didn't jump and take the pub with it with that wind last night."

My eyes flick to Viv who gives her head a little shake, assuring me these two have no idea that was my home. I decide to try for a neutral answer. "Very lucky," is all I say.

Easily distracted, Matt turns back to his coffee and the conversation with Viv I obviously interrupted. Not so much Denise. She observes me with her head slightly tilted to the side, as if waiting for me to trip up. I remember her saying she'd thought I looked familiar, and a sudden fear that she might connect me with the burned out shed has me hurrying out of the kitchen to get started on my chores. Bad enough that two—well, make that three since Dino seems to see right through me—people who already know more about me than I'm comfortable with. I certainly don't need Denise and Matt as added risks to my full exposure. It hasn't even been a week since Viv caught me and already my tightly controlled, self-imposed, solitary existence has unraveled.

"The fuck? Again?"

A now familiar voice sounds behind me as I'm on my knees, on the floor of the men's washroom, picking up the discarded hand towels that missed the garbage. *This* time, instead of scurrying away, I giggle as I pull myself up on the sink. A disgruntled Gunnar is right behind me with mild irritation making place for a reluctant grin on his rugged features.

"Fuck, Syd. Do I have to clear my washroom schedule with you before I can take a piss?"

"All yours, boss. I'll move next door," I chuckle as I squeeze past him. But the chuckle quickly dies on my lips when the brush of our bodies sends unexpected tingles down my spine. A quick look up reveals the deep jade color of his eyes, darkened with heat. *Whoa*. Tilting my head down, I try to hide the flush staining my cheeks.

"Thanks."

I hear the word behind me—uttered in a low growl—before I let the door to the men's washroom slam shut behind me. I lean my head back against the door and blow out a big breath. This is getting a little bit dangerous.

Gunnar

Holy shit.

I'm pretty sure she felt that zing too, and I'm happy she seems to choose to ignore it as well, but there was no mistaking the physical response or the bright blush on her cheeks. My mind immediately travels to flushed cheeks for an entirely different reason, like having Syd underneath me after I've made her come a time or two. As soon as the image pops up, I stamp it down. Not going there. I can't have that, even at the bottom of my wish list, let alone on top. Probably just the lack of action lately. Maybe it's time to find a willing body to help me exercise these thoughts right out of my head. She's too young, or at least I think she is. She's so damn tiny. Emmy is at least as tall. I wonder how she was ever able to survive on the streets. Of course she's plenty smart from what I can tell, and although shy and quiet, she doesn't allow anyone to mess with her, judging from the treatment she handed that sleazeball, Jack Barnes. Which reminds me, I should probably put a bug in the cop's ear about him. I have a suspicion that he may have been hanging around, looking to get back at me, or maybe even Syd. He could've been waiting for her to get off and followed her, but I just find it hard to believe someone would intentionally try to harm someone in such a horrific way, no matter what may have happened. If it's arson, I'd be more inclined to think it was something else driving it; that they weren't aware of anyone inside when they torched the shed.

As if on cue, the phone rings on my desk.

"The Skipper."

"Gunnar Lucas please?"

"Speaking."

"This is Sergeant Winslow of the Portland Police Department. We met last night?"

I vaguely recognize his voice. "Yes, I remember. What can I do for you?"

"I just received a call from the fire inspector. The preliminary investigation shows arson is likely the cause of the fire. Mr. Lucas, were you aware that shed is listed as your property?"

What? I never knew that. Never even bothered to look twice. I always assumed it was part of the small charter company that's housed in the building across the alley in the back.

"Well, no. I had no idea. This place has been in my family, going back many years. When I bought my folks out, I never had reason to check the deed. We used the same lawyer."

"I see. Well, I assume you'll be putting in an insurance claim now?"

Wait a fucking minute. I can see where this is going and I'm not liking it one bit.

"Is there something you're implying here, Sergeant Winslow? As I said, I had no idea the shed was part of the property, and frankly, I have no idea whether it even falls under the current insurance policy." I work hard to keep my temper under control, knowing it wouldn't do me any good to let it loose.

A deep sigh sounds through the phone. "I'm not sure I was implying anything, Mr. Lucas. I'm simply following up on some information that came our way this morning."

The hair bristles at the back of my neck. "What kind of information?" I bite off.

"Can't really go in to that with you, Sir. This is an active investigation at this point, but let me just say that we will make sure to take a closer look at the source of the information."

A list of possibilities runs through my mind, not the least of which is Jack, but I'm reluctant to talk about him because it involves revealing Syd. So who else would be on my relatively short list of enemies? Cindy, probably, or at least she will be when she finds out I'm going for full custody, effectively cutting off her money train. A picture of the guy who's come in a few times asking questions pops into my head, but other than being nosy, he hasn't made me feel that uncomfortable so there's nothing to indicate he should be considered an *enemy*.

"Please do, because I'm not sure who'd benefit from passing on false information to you guys."

"Leave it with me, Mr. Lucas. I'll be in touch."

With that, he hangs up, leaving me stewing behind my desk. Days like these, I wish for a normal nine-to-five job. Seems like the devil always shits on the same heap.

CHAPTER EIGHT

Gunnar

"Dad? Can I go over to Tasha's house after school?"

"What about homework?"

"That's what I'm gonna be doing—we have a project due tomorrow."

I stick my head around the bathroom door to look at Emmy leaning against the wall in the hallway with a cheeky little smile on her face.

"Tomorrow? And you wait 'til now to start on it?" To say we've had an easy time of it since the kids were dumped off by their mom a few weeks ago would be an exaggeration. Cindy dropped them off, saying she was going out of town and she still hasn't returned. She called last night and upset Emmy when the girl tried to get her mom to say when she'd be back. When I took the phone from Emmy to get some answers, she hung up on me after yelling, "It's none of your business!" Still a bitch. If I had any doubts before about hitting her with a full custody claim, last night took care of those.

I've been in touch with my lawyer and the application is being drawn up. Not only that, I've been passing on all the little bits of information the kids have dropped about Cindy's behavior. More than once, Emmy's apparently had to clean up after her drunk-ass and that shit's *not* okay with me. The kids've been keeping a lot of stuff that goes down at their mom's house from me. I get it—she's still their mom—

but hearing that she spends most of her time while the kids are with her, drunk out of her mind, makes me see red.

If not for Syd, who's been taking care of them after school, I might've lost it a few times. Dealing with the custody issue, the aftermath of the fire, as well as the looming prospect of a restaurant chain moving in on the other side of the wharf—something Tim discovered for me—I barely have the energy or patience to deal with anything else. That woman seems to have the magic touch with my kids, listening to their after-school chatter and making sure they keep up with their schoolwork. She even feeds them before Mrs. Danzel—their longtime babysitter who stays with them five nights a week—comes and picks them up.

That's another thing to put on my list: solve my staffing issue so I can have some more time with my kids. *Christ.*

"Dad?" My daughter's voice penetrates my thoughts. "Did you hear anything I said?"

"Sorry, girl. Just have a lot going on. What was that?"

"I said I *did* work on it with Syd. Me and Tasha each had to do part of it on our own and then finish it together. It was assigned for us to work on as a team, so can I go?" I have to hide the smile that threatens to break through. Emmy's hint of attitude is an almost welcome sign after how withdrawn she's been since her mom took off.

"Yeah, you can go, but I want you home before dark, okay? I'll let Mrs. Danzel know to expect you later."

She smiles big before throwing her arms around my neck for a hug. "Thanks, Daddy!"

I kiss her hair, set her back on her feet, and watch her skip off down the hall.

"Emmy?" I call after her.

"Yeah?"

"Lose the attitude, okay?"

I don't get to The Skipper until after the noon hour. I had to drop off the kids at school and meet with my lawyer to update him on what's going on. Walking into the kitchen, I find Viv at the counter and Syd standing by the stove, both giggling about something. The sound of Syd's laugh has my cock twitching in my jeans. *Fuck no.* In an attempt to disregard my physical reaction to her, I snap at her.

"Syd. My office when you can." I turn on my heels and walk out, followed by Viv's instant reply.

"Hello to you too, asshole!" Don't know what the hell I called her into my office for, or why I had to behave like an asshole—Viv called that—but I know I needed to stop the sound of Syd laughing. It scares the crap out of me, the way my body reacts around that girl. It spells trouble, something I can't have right now, not when I depend on her to look after my kids. It's a fucking minefield.

I pop into the pub to find the regular lunch crowd and a few new faces well taken care of by Matt and Denise and wander into my office. A few seconds later, there's a knock at the door.

"It's open!" In walks Syd with her beautiful mass of hair hanging to cover her face, which is aimed at the floor. I can't help but notice the improvement in her appearance. She was stunning right from the get-go, but so painfully emaciated it was difficult to guess at her age. Syd looks like the mature woman she is, now that she's filling out and getting some curves. I'm guessing mid-thirties? She no longer has those clear eyes sunken deep into her face, and her cheeks are fuller and flushed most of the time she's in a room with me.

"You wanted to see me?" she asks, not even looking up at me. *Fuck.* I've been a dick. Not only have I avoided her like the plague these last few weeks, not ready to deal with my confusing fascination with her, but I just ordered her around like a dog.

"Please," I try not to growl at her, "have a seat." She takes the chair in front of my desk, perching herself on the very edge. The tension coming off her is palpable. "How are you doing?"

I see a quick glimpse of her eyes before she turns them back down. "I'm fine." That's been her standard answer to anyone asking her and it's starting to tick me off, so I get up and walk around the desk to stand in front of her.

"Hey, can you look at me?" When she still doesn't lift her eyes, I reach out and stroke the long strands of hair behind her ear before tilting her face up with a finger under her chin. The impact of her skin under my fingers and her big, shiny eyes on mine is immediate, and I can't resist running the back of my hand over her downy cheek. The fire in her eyes has me drop my hand instantly. "I need to know how things are working out for you, Syd. I've no complaints about your work, and the others all seem to like you fine. Even the kids are well-looked after because of you, but how are you coming along?"

I can see her swallowing hard before she opens her mouth to answer. "I'm doing okay. I enjoy working here, especially in the kitchen with Viv and Dino." A small smile hits her lips. "Emmy and Dex are great kids. They really are, and I love spending time with them."

"And upstairs? Got everything you need?" She stubbornly refused to accept my offer two weeks ago to get her set up with some new stuff. She said she managed on her own long enough and actually seemed pissed off about it. The look she gives me now tells me I'd better not broach that subject again. She's a feisty little bird when she wants to be.

"I have more than I'd learned to be satisfied with for a long time. I have a bed, a warm shower every day, and it's more than enough. In fact, it's more than I deserve ..." Her last words are so faint I almost miss them. The meaning behind them seems clear. She feels a great amount of guilt over something. I haven't missed the occasional flashes of blatant pain in her eyes, nor have I missed the wistful glances she sends in the kids' direction. That, coupled with her initial reaction when she first met Dex, has me thinking she's left something very precious behind.

For a moment she seems so forlorn, I react instinctively and pull her up from her seat and into my arms where she stiffens at the contact. "Hush. It's just a hug," I whisper into her hair. Damn, she smells good, and with the angles softening on her body, she feels fucking fantastic in my arms. I feel her relax a little and tentatively her arms slip around my waist and her cheek presses against my chest. "When you need to unburden some of what you've been carrying around, I'm right here." Without thinking, I press a kiss on her head.

When she leans back and looks up at me, those expressive eyes shimmering with tears, it's all I can do not to claim her mouth. Especially when the tip of her little pink tongue appears between her lips and licks them slowly before speaking. "Thank you for that," she whispers. The door opens and Syd instantly jumps back when Denise steps in.

"How many times, Denise? Fucking knock before you barge in on me!" It's not the first fucking time she's pulled this, and ironically, it's only when I'm alone or have a woman in here with me, be it Viv or the rep from one of our liquor suppliers, who happens to be female. I'm not an idiot, I know she's interested—she's made it apparent on more than one occasion—but I'm not touching that with a ten-foot pole. I see Syd shrinking under Denise's intense scrutiny and want to pull her back into my arms, but something tells me that would only make matters worse.

"Sorry," Denise says in an unimpressive show of remorse. "Just wanted you to know that the keg is almost empty."

"Need a new one now?" I pin her with a glare when I catch her throwing a dirty look in Syd's direction.

"Well no, but it'd probably be good before the dinner crowd." She opens her eyes wide when she looks back at me.

"Fine." I lift my hand in a dismissive wave, hoping she'll catch the hint. She does, but not after sending one last dirty look at Syd. *Bloody hell.*

Syd

Denise has never been my favorite, but after that uncomfortable scene in Gunnar's office, it's clear she hates my guts. God knows what I ever did to her, but I better stay out of her way. Part of me is glad she interrupted because I was slowly forgetting myself, wrapped up in those strong arms of Gunnar's, almost ready to climb that man like a monkey. Her barging in like that saved me from making a complete ass of myself.

First chance I have, I beeline it out of that office and back into the kitchen where Viv is still stirring my soup.

When I came down this morning, she asked if I'd be interested in putting a special together for that night's all-you-can-eat menu. Having missed being in the kitchen, cooking, I was all over that. With her approval and a pantry and freezer full of the necessary ingredients, I had the stock simmering on the stove before I even started cleaning. We'd just finished chopping the veggies and pulling the meat off the chicken when Gunnar showed up. Now all that is left to do is let it all simmer while I turn my attention to the pesto bread I've planned to go with it.

"So, what did Gunnar want?" Viv asks, with her hands wrist deep kneading the first batch of dough I just handed to her.

"Not sure. Just checking in to see how I'm doing, I guess." I shrug, trying to avoid eye contact with her. I don't feel like explaining what happened. I'm not quite ready to fully explore that myself, but her sharp eyes pick up on something.

Looking at me with a gleam in her eyes, she nudges my arm. "You like him." Ignoring her, I focus on adding ingredients to the next batch of dough, but I can feel a blush heating my cheeks as Viv chuckles.

It's not until after the kids have been picked up by their babysitter and I'm ready to head upstairs that Viv pushes a little. "You know, he's a good man underneath that angry façade he puts up, right?"

Standing at the bottom of the stairs where she catches me, I drop my head, overwhelmed by a wave of sadness. "Not gonna happen, Viv. It can't happen for that exact reason. I don't deserve someone like that."

Before she has a chance to say anything else, I run up the stairs, shutting the door to the apartment firmly behind me. I slide down to the floor with my back against the door and shove my hands in my hair. *This.* This is exactly why I've avoided people for so long. The danger of getting too close is just too big. I wanted to start living again and embraced the opportunity, but at what cost? Already there's a risk people could get hurt—the kids could get hurt. If anyone finds out what I've done, they'll turn on me, just like everyone else has.

"God dammit! Look at you—you're pathetic!"

Jacob is hovering over me. I'm curled into a ball on the floor of the bathroom where I had taken my bottle of Vodka first thing this morning, right after he left for work. Work. I haven't been back, nor have I wanted to. I haven't cared, just like I don't care now. I don't care about Jacob, or lying on a bathroom floor that hasn't seen a mop in … how long has it been? It hurts to even think about anything that happened before *even something as mundane as mopping the bathroom floor. It's better to just take another swig so I can stop thinking altogether.*

The bottle hits against my teeth as Jacob knocks it out from between my lips, only to crash against the wall of the tub and break, spilling its contents.

"Were you drunk? Huh? Even then, were you drinking? Is that what happened?" Jacob yells, his voice bouncing off the tiled walls of the bathroom. Desperate to escape his voice and stop it from echoing inside my head, I crawl on hands and knees to where my bottle—my solace—is slowly emptying onto the floor. I don't feel the shards cutting into my hands and knees. All I see is that beautiful liquid seeping into the bathmat.

Next thing I remember is waking up in a stark, white room with no color on the walls, or on the bed I'm shackled to. My arms are bound to railings at the side of the bed, gauze under the leather shackles on my wrists.

I don't know how long I've been sitting on the floor just inside the door before a knock startles me into action. Jumping up off the floor, I run my hands over my face, wiping at the tears on my cheeks.

"Syd! You in there?" Matt's voice comes through the door.

"One minute!"

"Denise just went home sick and we're pretty swamped. Could use a hand for an hour or so."

"Be right there!"

A cold splash of water on my face and a quick glance in the bathroom mirror, I figure I'm good to go, barring any close scrutiny.

Downstairs, the sounds of a busy pub filter through the hallway and I make my way into the kitchen, only to be stopped in the doorway by Dino.

"Up front, honey," he says, shoving a tray full of bowls filled with Mexican bean soup and bread in my hands. I'm a bit confused. I've never worked in the actual pub before and I'm not sure I want to. It's too much exposure.

"But—"

"Go. Gunnar wants you out there and the food is getting cold."

Hands shaking, I make my way down the hall, careful not to spill anything. The noise just gets louder the closer I get. I walk through the door on the side of the bar to find Viv manning the tap and a big grin on her face.

"Crazy in here tonight, Syd! Welcome to the nuthouse!" She has to yell to make herself heard above the din of the place. "Those are for The Anchors' boys."

At my blank look, she points at a large round table by the window where Gunnar is standing, chatting with a rather large group of men. "The Anchors. Gunnar's baseball team."

Right, but I thought they gathered on Wednesday nights. I remember Gunnar telling me about that. I walk over to the table, avoiding eye contact with anyone. When Gunnar spots me, he steps to the side, clearing a space on the table for me to put the tray down.

"Here," he says, sliding the bowls of soup and bread in front of some of his friends while I stand mute beside him, feeling curious eyes all over me.

"Guys, quit fucking staring and eat your soup before it gets cold. This is Syd, and she works here, so don't bug her," he growls at his team.

"Wasn't looking to bug her, Guns, just familiarizing myself with the hot mama I'll be thinking of when I whack off tonight." A younger guy, maybe late twenties, with a backwards cap on his head, and a big smile on his face pipes up to the hilarity of the men, but with one glaring exception—Gunnar.

I'm ready to turn tail and bail, but Gunnar puts his hand on my shoulder, firmly holding me in place and with the other, swipes the ball cap off the guy's head with a smack.

"Hey!"

"Didn't I just fucking say not to bug her? A bit of respect, you fucking lowlife!"

I shrink away, expecting fists to start flying at any moment, but instead, the whole table starts laughing and ribbing the young guy. He seems to be taking it all in stride with a cocky smirk on his face.

"This your new woman, Guns?" a tall, lanky looking man with teasing eyes asks. I can hear Gunnar growling beside me. Ignoring the question, he grabs me by the arm and pulls me through the bar and out into the hallway where he swings me around to face him. Letting me go, he drops his head and runs his hands through his salt and pepper hair, which now stands out in every direction.

"Sorry, Syd. This night is fucked up. Denise left sick just as the boys arrived and we were already close to full capacity. Normally they're here on Wednesdays, but some of them went to a league meeting last night so they showed up tonight instead. I haven't been able to go since the kids are with me full time, but they're all good guys, really. They just get a bit rambunctious at times." He lifts his eyes to check for my reaction and I give him a smile to show I can deal, lifting a bit of the worry that dulls his eyes. "I need you to run the orders from the kitchen. Matt and I will run the tables and take the orders. We'll make sure Dino gets them, so all you need to do is deliver the food to the tables. You won't have to be in there all the time."

My heart warms a little at the opportunity to help, and also to the consideration he shows me. "I'll be fine." At the look of mild irritation on his face, probably at the use of my standard line, I smile and assure him again. "I will. I'm good, Gunnar. Go back inside. I'll take care of the food."

A barely there smile lifts the corners of his mouth. "I owe you."

"Hardly," is my response and I quickly turn toward the kitchen, feeling his eyes on my back with every step.

Hanging in the kitchen with Dino isn't a hardship. For all his scary looks and imposing size, the man is a pussycat and makes me feel completely at ease. He tells me about his family and chats with me about cooking in between runs, or when I'm not rinsing the glassware behind the bar.

"That soup of yours is a big hit tonight," he says as he scrapes the last of it out of the massive pot and into a bowl. "Tried some earlier and I can see why. If you have more recipes like that—good, hearty, one-pot meals, I'm thinking we should do a *Syd Special* every Thursday night." He looks at me with an eyebrow raised.

Feeling oddly pleased, I nod eagerly, excited about the prospect of cooking more. Dino chuckles and shakes his head. "Still not much for words," he mumbles. I just shrug my shoulders as he hands me the tray to take inside. "This is for the boss man."

The dinner crowd has slowed down tremendously and other than a few stragglers—including the table of ball players—the place is almost quiet in comparison. I can actually hear the oldies' rock playing in the background now. I head over to the team's table and hand over the basket of fries to Tim, the tall, slim guy who was teasing Gunnar before and introduced himself to me my second time at the table. I place the soup in front of Gunnar who had pulled up a seat and slide the two heaping baskets of wings in the center, along with a stack of plates and napkins for those interested. I'm about to head back to the kitchen when Gunnar grabs my wrist in passing. "Good soup, little Bird."

A pleased smile steals over my face. "Thanks."

"Why don't you call it a night? Long day for you. We'll talk tomorrow."

His face is as relaxed as I've seen it in the last couple of weeks and I can't seem to resist putting my free hand over his, still holding my wrist. The moment I voluntarily touch him, his eyes turn dark and a little muscle twitches in his jaw. I feel his thumb stroking along the veins on my wrist where my heartbeat pounds. I can't move. I know I'm staring and I'm getting lost in the tender touch my body has lived without for so long, but I'm unable to pull away. I'm grateful for the interruption when one of the guys calls his name, drawing his attention away from me. I pull back my hand and make myself scarce. Viv looks at me with a sparkle in her eyes as I approach the bar, but before she can say anything, I wish her a quick good night and head upstairs.

CHAPTER NINE

Gunnar

"Viv! Can you come in here?"

Exasperated, I lean back in my chair, hands behind my head. All morning I've been trying to get the feel of her heartbeat under my thumb out of my mind. I affect her. That much was obvious from the rapid pulse and the dilation of her pupils when I looked into her eyes. Fuck, mine were probably doing the same. Can't deny that little bird has a huge effect on me too. On top of that, I was just in the stockroom and the bottle count is off. We've got a pretty simple system where every time a bottle of liquor leaves the stockroom, or a new keg is tapped, we mark it down in a register. In addition, Viv keeps check of the empties that go out as well. It's something we started doing a few years ago when we discovered one of the summer temps using my stockroom to supply his drunken nighttime beach parties. Two things I don't have any understanding for are thieves and drunks. Ironic, since I own a bar and deal with drunks quite often, but dealing with an ex who would as a matter of course start drinking at the stroke of noon has given me a foul taste in my mouth. Escaping into a bottle is a sign of weakness if you ask me.

I usually check every Friday, but missed last week because of a doctor's visit with Dex. Just a regular check-up to monitor his asthma and get a new prescription for his inhaler, something the doc assures me he will probably grow out of. Anyway, in the hustle of getting him from school to the doc's office, and back to school with his brand new *puffer,* I'd run out of time to check the stockroom before getting next week's order in.

This morning's count shows I'm short two bottles of scotch and three of vodka. Now it happens we miss marking up one occasionally when it's busy, but five bottles in a week, or maybe two, is a lot.

When Viv still hasn't shown after five minutes, I get up to find her, register in hand.

"There you are. Did you hear me calling?" I walk into the kitchen to find her working on prep at the counter, her back to me and her head bobbing. "Yo, Viv!" I yell when she still doesn't acknowledge me, making her jump. She swings around, grabbing her chest with one hand while pulling the earbuds from her ears with the other. Loud music seeps into the kitchen ... *Queen,* if I'm not mistaken.

"Jesus! You scared me," she huffs.

"Well no shit, woman. Not surprised with that shit turned up so high. I'm surprised you can still hear anything at all." I gesture to the iPhone sticking out of her pocket.

"*Queen* is *not* shit," she argues, "it's only the best rock music of all time."

Can't argue that, so I barge right in. "We've got a problem. Count's off on the bottles. Can you have a look and see if anything tweaks?"

She turns off the music on her phone, walks over and grabs the book from my hand. Leafing through, she mumbles to herself. "This doesn't make sense. I checked the empties last week against the book and they matched up. Let me go count them now."

I've poured myself a coffee by the time she's back with an incredulous look on her face. "Okay, this is just weird. There are five more empties than have been signed out."

"Let me guess," I offer. "Two scotch and three vodka? We've got a problem here, Viv. Not many people working here, it shouldn't be too hard to figure this shit out."

"Everybody knows the system though. If they wanted to take a bottle, wouldn't they have marked it?" she asks, worry reflected in her eyes.

"They could've, although it'd likely have thrown up a red flag if we saw one person sign off on a lot more than usual. I mean, that's the reason we've got this system, right? To have some accountability?" I drop my head in my hands and scratch my scalp. My thoughts are going in a direction that doesn't sit well with me and when I look up at Viv, I can tell she knows what I'm thinking.

"Don't," she pleads.

"You know it and I know it, Viv. *Fuck*. I don't wanna think it, but we have to consider all possibilities. How did those empties stay here, but the bottles weren't signed out? Only one person isn't familiar with the register and we know dick-all about her background."

Viv just shakes her head, worrying her nails with her teeth until she blurts out, "Not buying it, Gunnar. I don't care what happened before she came here, but that girl had a hard time accepting any help to begin with. Sure doesn't make sense she would suddenly start stealing."

Relief at her words relaxes my shoulders, which have been tight from the moment Syd's name popped in my head. Still, it brings home how little I know about her. Not even a full name and I have her looking after my kids? I get she's not ready to talk about the shit that was her life, but eventually she'll have to open up … right? I mean, it's not like she's fucking Cher, who manages to go through life with only one name. Regardless, I don't think Syd's responsible. It never felt right, but Viv confirming it makes me more convinced. "Okay, Syd's out. How then? One of the suppliers? Did we get shortchanged on our order somehow?" I'm genuinely puzzled.

"Let's keep an eye out. Check the stock daily for a while and no more leaving the door unlocked. The others will have to come see one of us for the keys."

Her suggestion is sound. Still, I hate that it's necessary. I get up, plant a kiss on Viv's head, and go lock the stockroom door.

Being a Friday, the lunch crowd is a decent size. Everybody's busy so I jump behind the bar and let Denise help on the tables.

"Draft Bud, an orange juice, and a dry white, big guy." Denise leans on the bar, propping her chest on the edge. *Big Guy*? She's verged on being inappropriate with me all afternoon and it was irritating to start with, but now she's really pushing it.

"Gunnar's the name. I'll answer to Boss, but you're pushing it now, Denise. Knock it off 'cause I'm not interested. Never was, and it's not likely to happen now." I know I can be a dick, but shit. How often do you need to hear *no* before you get it? I don't slow down filling the order, but don't miss the sharp intake of breath and the angry pinch to her face.

"Mind grabbing me a bottle of Pinot Grigio from the back?"

With a loud smack, she drops her tray on the bar before turning on her heels. Matt walks up, his eyebrows raised as he watches her disappear into the back.

"The hell is up with her? Caught her earlier giving Syd a hard time. Something about the glasses not being 'properly cleaned', but it was bullshit. They looked fine to me. It's also not the first time she's done it either. She's being a bitch. Must be that time of the month or something." For a normally laid-back guy, that came out pretty forceful. Can't recall Matt ever making noise about something and I wonder how come he feels so protective of Syd. Not sure I like that. She's my concern.

Whoa. Where the hell did that come from?

"Boss?" Fucking Denise calls from the back. Why can't she come here and ask whatever it is she needs to know?

Irritated, I throw my towel on the bar and slip under the flap on the side. "Keep an eye on the bar." I direct at Matt who rolls his eyes.

Denise is leaning against the wall beside the stockroom, one hip cocked out with her hand resting on it, looking very provocative, but only pissing me off more. "What?" I bark out, having had enough of these games. If she doesn't knock it off and fast, her ass is going to be on the street.

"Can't get in. Somebody locked it," she pouts.

"I did. This why you called me out here? Could'a just come and got the keys." Angry, I fish the keys out of my pocket and unlock the door.

"Why?" She grabs ahold of my arm. "We've always had it open, so why lock it now?"

Something about the way she asks seems off and I decide to test her. "Numbers were off, so I decided only Viv and I check the stock."

Her eyes go big before they get a calculating gleam in them and she leans toward me, whispering, "I didn't want to say anything 'cause I really like her, but the other day I saw the new girl put some bottles with the empties. You think maybe …" She lets the sentence trail off and never takes her eyes off me. It's clear she's waiting for my reaction.

I'm not an idiot. I can smell the set-up a mile away. She was clearly not happy finding Syd in my office when she barged in yesterday, and she's been all over me like a wet rag ever since. Even Matt says she's been dogging Syd. Reigning in my anger, I figure I'll give her a little slack so she can hang herself; feed into her con. "You think it's Syd?" At her eager nod, I push a little. "Could be. Don't know much about her."

"Exactly," she hisses, "you don't and you know most homeless people are alcoholics." The glee in her face is unmistakable. She's fucking eating her own crap.

"And how would you know she was homeless?" I ask, leaning down and getting in her face. "We never discussed that with you or Matt because it's none of your business, which begs the question: how would you know that?"

Taking a step back from me, her face blanches, but she tilts her chin in defiance. "Heard you discuss it with Viv. You must've left the door open."

Fuck that, she eavesdropped. I decide I've had enough of this game. "That's it, Denise. Heard enough of your bullshit and now you're done. Pack your stuff and get out." The shock on her face this time is genuine.

"You can't do that!"

I straighten up and look down at her. "Watch me," is all I say. With a small amount of satisfaction, I watch her stomp toward the bar, so I follow her, watching her collect her things. I plan to escort her out the back door but she aims for the front door instead, intent on making a scene, it appears. She stops with the door handle in her hand and tries for a final word.   "You'll regret this!"

I just wave my hand to get her gone, convinced she's only spouting empty threats.

Big fucking mistake.

Syd

"Take a break."

Viv gives me a pointed look after she sees me yawning for the umpteenth time. Yesterday was a long-ass day and I slept for shit. By the time I hit my pillow last night, I'd been dead to the world, but nightmares soon woke me up; sweating, and in a tangle of sheets. Seems my subconscious doesn't care much for the little taste of happy I snag every day. Whether it be from the kids, who've become my purpose every day, or yesterday's exchange with Gunnar, the darkness that lives inside forces its way out at night to make sure I don't forget. Knowing this, seeing as it's happened almost every night since moving into the apartment, I didn't bother to try and go back to sleep. Instead, I tried to distract myself by watching old black and white movies on the tiny TV in the living room.

With the daybreak, I grabbed a travel mug filled with coffee and a blanket, and went out to sit on the dock to watch the fishing trawlers head out for the day. It's cool, but the worst chill of April seems to have passed, and wrapped in my blanket with my hands around a warm mug of coffee, I'm quite comfortable. My mind drifts to the people at The Skipper; people who took a chance on me, even knowing I was holding back. Even without knowing something basic like a last name, they judged me at face value, which wasn't much to begin with, but to them, apparently it was enough. It's such a new experience for me, having always been judged and mostly found wanting. I'm lucky, I know that, but it doesn't stop the guilt from steadily gnawing away at my resolve to pull myself up. Vivid green eyes are at the forefront of my mind—eyes that change in color and intensity, depending on mood and circumstance. Eyes framed by incongruently long lashes in a lined, hard, but strong face. Dark and brooding with always a hint of gray-flecked scruff, and strong white teeth between those full lips that seem to counter the gruff appearance. I've seen his features soften, every time he looks at his children, and often with Viv. He cares deep. And for a moment yesterday, it looked like his face softened for me, as if he perhaps cares a little for me too.

By the time the chill starts to settle into my bones, the dock is alive with activity and I'm no longer comfortable being out here. It's almost time for my day to start anyway.

Over the past few weeks, I'd gotten into the habit of cleaning the bar first before Viv even got there, wanting to relieve some of the pressure on her. Seems she's constantly doing for me and I need to feel I'm giving some back. Objecting at first, she finally appears to have accepted that whether she approves of it or not, I'm going do what I do.

But now, here I am swaying on my feet from lack of sleep and a full day and night of work yesterday, which is exactly why I don't argue with her, but calmly take off my apron, walk over and surprise her by wrapping her in a hug. I don't have much to give except something I haven't done in a long time. Surprised, she initially stiffens before I can feel her body relaxing and her arms surround me too.

"Thank you," I whisper with my face buried in her neck. A light touch strokes over my hair before she sets me back a little and looks me in the eyes.

"Didn't need the thank you, but I appreciate it all the same," she smiles. "Now go get an hour of rest before the kids come back from school."

With only a nod, because speaking right now would be impossible around the big lump that's lodged firmly in my throat, I turn on my heels and walk out the door. When I reach the bottom of the stairs, I hear voices at the other end of the hallway, and what I can hear chills me to the core.

It takes me two minutes to pack my meager belongings in the old backpack I carried around for over a year. I'll take nothing that wasn't mine when I came here.

This is my punishment—my mistake for letting my guard down even a little and allowing myself to feel. But in the end, I'm once again being judged and found wanting.

Worse.

This time I haven't done anything wrong, but they wouldn't see it that way. It's ironic how I never revealed that part of my past that could condemn me, yet it didn't matter. I will always be condemned anyway. Never before has the temptation to relapse been bigger. There is definite irony there somewhere.

I manage to sneak out the back without anyone seeing and slip down the familiar alleyway. I know where I'm going; don't even have to think about it too hard because not so long ago, I was thinking of doing exactly this, that is until the promise of a different, and better future came along. And I, in my moment of self-delusion, thought I could have it.

It takes me an hour and a half to find it … Preble Street. I ring the bell at an ornate, large older building that says "Florence House" on the sign in the small front yard. It's the one place in Portland where I hope to find temporary shelter, at least until I can find another shed, garage, or abandoned building to keep me out of the elements.

I ignore the pain ripping at my chest and instead remind myself that this is Karma … *My* Karma … my burden.

A very tall, gray-haired black woman opens the door and takes me in with her eyes from top to bottom.

"Abusive husband?" is all she says and I shake my head no, not quite sure how I should explain how I got here, but knowing I'd probably have to give them something. Sticking her head out the door and looking up and down the street, she finally pushes it open and motions me in.

I'm led to a small office at the back of the long, narrow hallway and sit down as indicated.

"I'm Pam, what's your name?" the woman asks me in a much gentler voice.

I hesitate, wondering if I should give a false name and continue hiding, or whether I should just be me and deal with any consequences as they come. Having had the warm knowledge that there are people—good people—out there who care, I decide I've hidden enough. I'm tired of living under the guise of night, tired of being anonymous, and tired of being alone. After having had a taste of social contact, of gentle hands, and the bittersweet feeling of hope, I simply can't go back.

"Sydney Donner."

My own name sounds loud and strange in my ears and I look at the woman who has patiently waited me out to see how she'd react. I go for broke. "I'm an alcoholic, and I've been dry for a year, at least I think it's been a year."

"Nice to meet you, Sydney. Now tell me as little or as much as you want about why you are here."

By the time she shows me to a tiny, but private room up on the third floor, I've told her everything. Well, almost everything. The moment my exhausted head hits the pillow, I'm asleep.

CHAPTER TEN

Gunnar

"Hey Dad, where's Syd?"

I look up from my endless struggle with the books and now the added task of finding a replacement for Denise, to find my girl leaning in the doorway.

"Hey, girl. She's not in the kitchen?" I get up and walk over to give her a quick hug and kiss before walking ahead of her down the hall.

Dino is doing dinner prep and Dex sits at the table. "Hey, buddy. How was school?" I ask him while ruffling his hair, which is getting a bit too long. He just shrugs his shoulders, not really answering me. I make a note to take some time and talk to my boy. "Viv gone too?"

"Went upstairs to check on Syd. Says she sent her upstairs maybe an hour or so ago to take a load off," Dino says turning around. "Not really like her to miss the kids coming in. She must've forgotten to set an alarm."

A small niggle of unease crawls over me, but before I can make sense of it, I hear footsteps rushing down the hall and Viv bursts into the kitchen. She opens her mouth to speak but on seeing the kids, tries to smooth out the panic on her face.

"Gunnar, can you come check on something with me?" The silent plea in her eyes in unmistakable.

"Sure. Kids, just hang with Dino. I'll be right back."

I follow Viv to the stairs, where she turns and whispers, "She's gone."

I stop in my tracks and shake my head. "What do you mean she's gone?"

"Come up. I'll show ya."

At first sight, nothing is wrong. Everything seems to be where it should be except for Syd, who's not here, but then I walk into the bedroom and see the bed neatly made and clothes carefully folded and stacked at the foot of the bed. On top is the toothbrush I'd gotten her.

"That's everything I gave her," Viv says softly from behind me. "Every single piece of clothing, including the torn jeans from when she cut herself. All she took was that ratty backpack and the few clothes she owns."

A sick feeling settles in my stomach when I walk back into the living room and see a stack of bills sitting on the kitchen counter beside the coffeemaker. I walk over to see if she's maybe left a note, but there's nothing—just a small pile of cash. Viv grabs the money and starts counting. I don't know why, but I already know what she's going to say when she looks up at me with tears in her eyes. "Everything is here, not a dollar missing. She left every last penny she earned these past few weeks. Why would she do that?"

I grind my jaw, trying to keep a lock on the sudden rush of fury I feel. Something Viv said earlier nags at me. "Did you notice anything?"

Viv shakes her head. "Other than that she looked exhausted, she was fine."

"How long ago did you say it was she came up?"

"Maybe a little over an hour? Why?"

"Because I wonder if she overheard Denise and me talking. Unless she heard it out to the end, it would've sounded pretty damning. *Fuck!*" With one swipe of my arm, the coffeemaker goes flying off the counter and crashes onto the tiles on the floor. My instinct is to run out and try to find her on foot, but I have no idea where she would've gone. Her shed is gone and I doubt she would stick around the wharf, thinking I accused her of stealing booze. What a clusterfuck. The pub short not one, but two staff members, my kids downstairs in the care of Dino, and the little bird who started worming her way under my skin out on the streets with nothing but the clothes on her back and no money.

I pull out my phone and call Tim.

"Kitchen's closed. I'll take over the bar, you go home to your kids." Viv slides in behind the bar with me and tries to shove me out.

Mrs. Danzel was able to pick up the kids earlier and promised to feed them. Dex had bought the story that Syd had to leave suddenly on a family emergency, but Emmy was looking at me, unconvinced. Even when they walk out the door to Mrs. Danzel's car, she stops and turns. "Daddy? You promise she'll come back?" The tears shimmering in her eyes has me grab her by the neck and pulling her to my chest.

"I'll try to make sure she does, girl." *Fuck*. There isn't much else for me to say and it's tearing me up. After seeing them off, I head in where I catch Dino suggesting to Viv to check the local shelters.

"You think she went to a shelter?" I ask him.

He shrugs his shoulders. "Might've. It's still cold during the night and she doesn't have that roof over her head anymore. If I found myself on the street suddenly, I'd probably head to a shelter while trying to sort myself out."

Half an hour later, Tim, along with a couple of our teammates, Paul and Frankie, come in. Tim's brother is a cop, which is why I called him. There wouldn't be anything they could do, but I'm hoping Tim will be able to convince his brother to keep an eye out for her when patrolling. Frankie would occasionally help out in the pub during the busier summer months, and was willing to jump in. I guess he brought Paul since at some point in time years ago, he was on the streets for a while, here in Portland.

Viv takes Tim up front where the patrons are starting to fill the tables and the rest of us sit at the kitchen table where Dino can listen in.

"So, what if she doesn't wanna be found?" Tim offers.

"Look. The woman is haunted already by something in her past she's unable to open up about with any of us. I don't want to add to her load, but I can't have her believe I think for one minute that she took the booze." I put my hands behind my neck and try to stretch out the tension. "If she decides she still wants to be gone after she finds out we never suspected her, then ..." I hesitate and Tim looks at me with his eyebrows raised. "Then I guess I'll just have to let her go."

"What exactly does she mean to you, boss?" Dino asks from behind me, so I turn around to face him.

"What are you talking about?" I challenge him, but he just looks at me as he always does, cool as a cucumber.

"Just saying, but unless she means something, might be best to just leave her be?"

He pisses me off and still I find myself answering.

"Something ... Nothing ... I don't know. I just can't stand the idea of her out there based on a misunderstanding, thinking we didn't trust her. Fuck, that *I* didn't trust her."

She had charmed all the guys last night. After the shaky first introduction, she'd hung in like a trooper, gifting those she brought food for with one of her rare little smiles. Tim didn't hesitate for one second in offering to drum up some help after contacting his brother.

"Mike said he'd ask around after shift tonight to see if anyone's seen her. In the meantime, Paul and I are gonna do some driving around."

That was five hours ago. It's dark outside now and the dinner rush is mostly over, except for one last table and the regular Friday night bar crowd. We no longer need everyone on the floor, which is why I'm actually considering Viv's offer.

Just as I'm about to tell her so, the door opens and Tim and Paul come through. Tim waves and indicates they'll take the round table by the window and sticks up two fingers for beers. Viv sees him too and is already filling a pitcher with draft.

"Go," she says, pushing the pitcher and some glasses in my hand, "but come tell me quick, okay?" Viv's been as worried and preoccupied as I have, but we have a pub and grub to manage on a busy Friday night. Still, the guilt of not being out there, looking, is killing me. The thought of that little bird out there by herself ...

"You may wanna sit down," Tim starts.

"Was planning to," I snap and brace for the bad news that seems inevitable. "What've you got?"

"Well, we did a drive and in some cases, a walk around most of the wharves. Stopped at some spots Paul pegged as 'regular' hangouts, but came up empty. No sign, no word, and not a glimpse. Some of the guys on the street knew who she was from the physical description we gave them, but said they hadn't seen her in a long time." Tim stops for a breath and Paul jumps in.

"We stopped at the homeless shelters last, figuring she may have headed to one of those, but she's not at any of them, either. Last place we were at though, one of the volunteers told us about a women's only shelter on Preble Street, but she said we wouldn't be able to get in. Security is tight for the protection of the residents since a lot of them are escaping violence at home. She wasn't sure if they'd take on homeless women, but might be worth the try."

"I'll go." Viv comes up from behind me and slides some nachos and dip on the table in front of the guys. "You're talking about Florence House, right?" she asks Paul, who nods. "I know someone who works there. If she's there, I can find out ... maybe talk to her? But it won't be tonight 'cause they've got a ten o'clock curfew. Place goes on lockdown and won't open until tomorrow." She walks off without looking at any of us as we stare after her. They're probably wondering how she's so familiar with the place. I've got a good idea, although she'd never told me things had gone that far.

"Well, thanks guys—for tonight. Appreciate it. Drinks on the house, yeah?" Both lift their glasses in salute. "I'll check in with you tomorrow, Tim." At his nod, I make my way over to the bar where Viv is rinsing glasses.

"Why didn't you come to me?" is the first thing out of my mouth. It comes out sounding angry and causes her to whip around with an irritated look on her face.

"Seriously? He went nuts for a while there, Gunnar. I wasn't gonna crawl back to my family so they could see how low I'd sunk. Besides, if I'd have shown up at any of your places, it would've just put a target on your backs."

I'm still angry when she walks up and slides her arms around my waist and I can't help but hug her back. "It was good in a way, you know? Hitting rock bottom like that? At least the climbing out under my own steam was. It's what needed to happen then. You or my brothers would've swept in and rescued me and then my self-confidence would never have recovered."

I hate it, but she's absolutely right. Any one of her brothers or I would've known at the time, no doubt we'd have stepped in and taken over. We'd have also likely ended up in jail, because the miserable fuck would've been beaten to a pulp. "Where is he now?" I mumble in her hair and I feel her shoulders shaking under my arms.

"What?" I lean back and see the teasing sparkle in her eyes as she laughs out loud. "Wanna go beat him up now? After all these years? He's long gone, Gunnar, and such an insignificant part of my life in hindsight, he's not even worth mentioning." She smiles at me and I can't help but smile back. She's a pretty kick-ass woman, my Vivian, and would've made a perfect girlfriend or wife if I could see her as anything other than a sister. Never happen.

Pushing against my chest, she wiggles out of my grip. "Move, freak. I have drinks to pour."

"Sure?" I can't help asking.

"Positive, now go home to the kids. Tomorrow we see if we can find your girl," she says, a mischievous gleam in her eyes.

"My girl, huh?"

"Sure are behaving like it," she returns. I just shake my head and take off for home ... to my kids.

Syd

A soft knock on the door wakes me to a room full of bright sunshine. Disoriented, I look at my blue watch, the one I'd forgotten to take off when I left. It shows almost eleven in the morning, when I lift my eyes and take in my surroundings. *Holy crap.* It takes me a minute to recognize I'm at the Florence House. I remember being exhausted and spilling my guts to Pam yesterday afternoon and her showing me my room. That was almost sixteen hours ago. Sixteen fucking hours of sleep. I don't think I've ever managed to do that, not even as a teenager. There were no dreams though, at least none I can remember.

Another knock sounds, this one a bit louder. Looking down, I see I'm still dressed as I was yesterday, so I call out. "Come in!" Fully expecting Pam to walk in, I'm shocked to see Viv standing in the doorway.

"There you are," she smiles with suspiciously shiny eyes.

"Viv? What—"

A few big steps and she plops down right beside me on the bed, pulling me into a hug.

I'm at a loss. I'm confused as hell to see her here. A glance over her shoulder shows Pam softly pulling the door shut after throwing me a little wink. *What the hell?*

"You took off." Viv pushes me back a little and looks at me sternly. "You didn't stay, didn't ask, you just took off. We've been so worried about you."

I shake my head to clear it because this is not making any sense to me. "You don't understand, Gunnar—"

"Stop. Gunnar has been out of his mind. He's had his buddies roaming the streets for you last night. Worried sick, he is."

Convinced I'm going crazy—or she is—I jump out of bed on the other side and start pacing. "I heard him. He thinks I took things from him. Bottles. I heard them talking about it." I know I'm rambling a bit, but I can't stop.

"Syd, look at me," Viv urges, leaning forward on the bed. "He didn't ... he doesn't. No one did. Not someone who has a hard time accepting even the smallest of kind gestures. We knew that person couldn't have turned around and taken from the stockroom. What you heard was Gunnar playing along with Denise to get to the bottom of what she was up to. It was her."

I shake my head again, trying to take it in. "But why? Why would she do that?"

"Jealousy would be my guess. For the two years she'd been working at The Skipper, she tried to get into Gunnar's pants. She tried some stuff with me early on until she figured Gunnar and I are more like siblings than lovers. Didn't mean dick to Gunnar either way, he's done with manipulating bitches and can smell them a mile away. She never had a chance, but when you came along and Gunnar had you looking after his kids right off the bat—something he'd never trusted her enough to do, by the way—I think she saw you as a threat, so she tried to pin something on you. I guess she figured because we don't know much about your background, we'd fall for it." She stands up and comes around the bed to grab me by my shoulders. Dipping her head down, she looks me straight in the eyes. "It never would've worked, Syd. You may keep your secrets close to your chest, but you're not that person. I know it, and Gunnar knows it."

"No. No, no , no," I shake my head violently, pulling out of her grip. "You don't know, Viv. You have no idea the things I've done." I can't listen to her saying these things to me. I'm not a good person. I've done nothing to deserve this. "I'm an alcoholic." I stand up as straight, as much as the churning of my stomach allows, waiting for her reaction to my words.

Without flinching, she folds her arms and tilts her head. "How long since you've had your last?"

My mouth falls open. She should be disgusted with me; angry or disappointed at least, but instead she immediately concludes I no longer drink. "A year I think ..." I mutter, still staring at her as if I see water burning.

"And it hasn't been hard for you? Working around it all the time?"

Taken aback by the question, I take a minute to consider. Had I been tempted? Not that I could recall. In fact, the thought of drinking alcohol now kind of makes me sick, so I shake my head no. "Really, I haven't. I ... I don't even really like it. It just kept me numb." When I see new questions in Viv's eyes, I add, "For a very long time, I needed not to feel. I wanted to forget."

"And now?" she pushes in a gentle voice.

"Now? Now I just look forward, trying to forget what's behind."

"Good. Then let's skip this joint and take you home." She grabs my pack by the side of the bed, takes my hand and pulls me to the door.

Pam stands waiting on the other side and hugs first Viv, telling her it's good to see her again. *Again*? Next she pulls me in for a hug also. "I'd like you to come back and visit. We can talk some more?"

I'm surprised by the invitation, but ever more so by Viv's contribution. "Pam is good. She's been my counselor for over five years now," she smiles encouragingly.

"Oh." That's all I can think of to say. Luckily, it makes her chuckle.

"Remember that bad relationship I got out of?" When I nod, she continues. "I ended up here for a few months, trying to get out. Pam was instrumental in building me back up to where I could face the outside world. She still keeps me sane, except now we call it *maintenance*." She laughs and Pam joins in.

"Okay," I say to Pam, "I think I'd like that."

"Good." Pam smiles at me before Viv pulls me out the door. "Let's go, we've got a lunch crowd needing to be fed."

That makes me giggle, and it feels good.

It really does feel like coming home when I walk in the back door. The smell already so familiar.

"Why don't you run upstairs and freshen up. Your clothes are where you left them on the bed, so come down when you can."

"Okay."

With a spring in my step that was definitely not there yesterday, I make my way up to *my* apartment.

First thing I grab is the toothbrush still perched on top of the pile of clothes and I rush in the bathroom to brush my teeth.

I'm barely done wiping my mouth on the towel when heavy footsteps come pounding up the stairs. A bit apprehensive, I walk into the living room, just as the door slams open and Gunnar comes in. Without even stopping, he reaches me in three steps, never looking away from my eyes. When he grabs my shoulders and gives me a little shake, I figure I should probably be scared, but I'm not. I can feel the anger radiating off him but all I can see in his eyes is worry and something else I can't explain.

"Fucking took ten years off my life, Syd," he growls, sounding out of breath. "Don't ever do that shit again." With a swift yank on my arms, I find myself enveloped, my face against his chest and his arms wrapped around me tightly. His face is pressing into my hair and I swear he's inhaling my scent. "Can't figure how you'd believe I'd think you responsible for something like that. Jesus," he mumbles in my hair. I suspect he says it more to himself than to me, but I slip my arms around his waist and give him a squeeze.

"I'm an alc—" I don't get a chance to finish before he lifts me up off the floor, sits me on the counter and grabs my face in his hands. The green of his eyes is so dark, I can barely see where the pupil ends. For a moment, he just stares at me before his eyes slide down to my mouth. I know what's coming and even though I don't deserve it, I can't help but lean in, craving the moment his mouth takes mine. He stops just before our lips meet.

"Fuck it." Is what I hear before I become deaf to everything but the blood rushing in my veins as his lips slide over mine, his slick tongue demanding entry. Oh God, the sensation. My mouth opens on a groan and his tongue boldly claims the space, stroking my far more hesitant one with alternating strong strokes and teasing licks. With his mouth plastered to mine, he pulls me to the edge of the counter. Wedging himself between my legs, I instinctively wrap them around the backs of his thighs. My restless hands roam over his broad back and up his shoulders, and I whimper when he pulls his mouth away, leaving his forehead resting against mine and panting hard.

"We've got customers," he whispers.

"I'm so—" His lips cut me off with another hard kiss.

"We'll talk later, little Bird. We've got people to feed."

CHAPTER ELEVEN

syd

"You okay?"

Viv is standing at the counter, smiling a little secret smile as she watches me walk in. "Fine." I manage, trying to ignore the blush that is making its way up from my chest. I can feel it gain ground.

"Okay, we'll leave it at that for now," she says, turning her attention to the oil in the fryer, but not losing her smile. Without saying anything else, I grab my favorite chef's knife and start chopping the vegetables she's already washed and let my mind wander.

Even in my best years, I haven't experienced anything as exhilarating as when I saw the intensity in Gunnar's eyes focused on me. A bit surreal that just as I squelched the persistent ember of attraction when I overheard him yesterday, he manages to whip it into a fired frenzy at the first touch. The promise we would talk later, only partially succeeded in cooling the flames. I don't understand how it is I'm affecting him. Nothing he sees or knows about me is remotely appealing. Perhaps it's because of the kids.

I know I'm falling in love with Dex and Emmy and it scares me to death because I can tell they're falling for me too. Kids are easy to read. These two carry scars already, which makes trusting for them even harder, yet they started opening up to me. I both love and hate it, as afraid for them as I am for myself. They've already been abandoned once and I—I've been ground down by my loss; only a collection of particles that threaten to be blown apart and scattered by a strong wind. I've only just begun to gather myself from dust. Another blow would surely decimate me.

I promised myself not to let fear paralyze me, and the fact Viv and Gunnar were looking for me should be enough to feel cared for, and I do. I'm just not sure that I would ever survive if the full extent of my past came out. For now, I'll give them as much as I think they can handle, or better yet, as much as I'm able to handle. But the children? I don't know how to hold back with them.

"You're back!" Small arms wrap around me from behind and I can't help the smile that settles on my lips when I turn around and look down into Dex's bright, open face.

"I'm back," I say simply, but when I look up, I see Emmy standing hesitantly in the doorway.

"How's your family?" she asks. Confused, I turn to Viv who is sending signals with her eyes, but I'm not really computing.

"Yeah," Dex pipes up. "I thought you were gone for good." He buries his face in my belly and my hand strokes his head. I get it and I feel like shit. I have a choice. I can perpetuate whatever lie they've told them to explain my sudden absence, or I can tell them the truth because I can already see that Emmy is too smart to fall for lies. I can't do that to her, regardless.

"Come sit for a minute." I indicate for Emmy to come sit at the table too, but she just stands behind a chair, waiting. "I made a mistake yesterday. I was upset over something I didn't really understand, and instead of asking for an explanation, I got scared and ran."

I turn to Dex when he tugs on my shirt. "Why were you scared?"

Jeez. How to explain that? "I was afraid to get hurt. You know how the people you care about most can also hurt you the worst?" Dex nods and looking up at Emmy, I see her swallow hard. Yeah. These kids know all about that and it rips me up to think I almost hurt them to save myself some pain. "Well, that's what I was scared of."

Dex snuggles into my side and Emmy pulls out the chair and sits down on the other side of the table.

"Did that happen to you before?" Emmy wants to know and this time, it's my turn to swallow.

"Yes, it did," I say simply. It seems to be enough for Emmy who nods thoughtfully, but not for Dex.

"Who hurt you?"

I lean down and kiss his forehead. "It happened a very long time ago and they can't hurt me now, and that's all that's important. Now, who wants some cookies and milk?"

The enthusiastic *yes* from both instantly lifts the atmosphere in the kitchen and when I look up to find Gunnar in the doorway looking at me, it goes straight to electric.

Gunnar

"Dad, look! Syd's back." Dexter spots me, jumps up and runs through the kitchen to jump into my arms. I look at my boy before lifting my eyes back to her. Without breaking eye contact, I set him back on his feet.

"Can see that, kiddo."

Oh, I see her all right, and now I not only can't get her big liquid blue eyes out of my head, but her smell, her taste, and the feel of her in my arms as well. By the way she's biting her lip and her eyes turn a dark blue, she remembers it too.

Viv tried to stop me from rushing upstairs when I came in with the kids earlier, but the moment Viv mentioned Syd was up there, I had to go see for myself. I lost the battle to keep my distance. Yes, not knowing anything about her except her first name—or at least what she calls herself—bothers me, but now I'm determined to get to the bottom of it. This intense attraction that only seems to flare hotter after kissing her, is not something I've experienced before.

"Uh, you guys have any homework? I missed yesterday so I don't know what you got done." Syd asks, and I notice I'm still staring at her, but I'm not the only one noticing. Viv's turned her back to the stove and has her arms crossed, flicking her eyes back and forth between the two of us. Even Emmy has an eyebrow raised as she looks in my direction. Right.

"Homework, guys?" I prompt them and both kids start pulling books out of their bags. "You get it done, maybe Syd will let you hang upstairs and watch some TV, but better not mess with her stuff." With a last glance at Syd's pink face, I turn back to my office.

I don't quite get there because Matt is standing in the doorway to the pub, waving me over. When I reach him, he points over his shoulder into the bar.

"Check out the booth on the far wall."

Fuck me. Sitting there with a menu in his face is the guy who's been around a few times asking questions. It's the same guy I described to that Sergeant Winslow. Either the guy has gonads the size of basketballs, or he had nothing to do with the fire.

I did say I'd walk up and introduce myself, so I step around Matt and without taking my eyes off the guy, and walk up to the booth. "Hi. Gunnar Lucas, and you are?" He lifts his eyes off the menu and lingers on my outstretched hand for a moment before they hit my face. Reaching out, he grips my hand firmly before letting go.

"You greet all your patrons this way?" Is the first thing out of his mouth, and already I hate his cocky attitude.

"No," I say sliding into the booth across from him, "only those who come around asking questions of my staff instead of manning up and asking me." The eyes looking back at me turn dark with what I presume to be anger. It would appear the clean cut, slick looking suit has a temper. Good. People with tempers generally let things slip, so I decide to push a little more. "Any particular reason you seem to have such a hard-on for my establishment? Or is it simply my pretty face that keeps bringing you back?"

The tick in his jaw shows me he's losing the battle holding onto his cool. Time to bring it home. "You know, you're welcome to ask me anything, that is unless you want me to contact Graham Bull at your corporate office directly?"

The lift of his eyebrows is evidence that me having this knowledge is a surprise to him. I do my homework, *asshole,* but more than that, it's all I need to confirm this idiot in front of me is hired by Soul Filets, the chain that apparently has their sights set on opening a restaurant right here, on Holyoke Wharf. Graham Bull was once a well-known chef who sold his soul—how appropriate—to the devil when he started branching his successful restaurant in Charlotte, and its clones have been climbing up the Eastern seaboard. It would appear Portland Maine is next, and on my wharf. I'm not afraid of competition. Hell, when you think about it, other than having fish on the menu, we deal with totally different clientele so no, having another restaurant on the wharf isn't really a threat to my livelihood, although it might take a dent. What has me concerned is the ruthless and underhanded ways in which Graham Bull and his corporate cronies have actively tried to undermine and boycott any food serving establishment within a mile radius of their proposed new locations. His reputation in the food industry is not a good one.

Setting the fire in the shed seems extreme, even for their standards, so I don't know what to think, but what I do know is that you can't turn your back on these guys, not for a second. The location of The Skipper on the wharf is unique in that the water is visible from both sides of the pub as it's actually *on* the wharf and not at the base of it, as most other establishments are, and it would seem the proposed new Soul Filets would be as well. They may very well want more than just to disable me.

All this is playing in my mind as the suit and I are locked in a stare down, which he eventually breaks.

"Fine. I'm on a fact gathering mission for Mr. Bull, simply collecting data, testing out the competition."

I push up on the table so I'm leaning over him. "There is no competition. He's welcome to open up his restaurant as long as he leaves my pub alone. There's plenty of fish for both of us, but if I find out you or your boss had any hand in that convenient fire on my property the other day, I will come after you." At the mention of the fire, he lifts a single eyebrow. "Now that that business is out of the way, what can I get you?"

It's a packed Saturday night. After the kids come say goodbye when Mrs. Danzel picks them up, the place is hopping and I don't have a moment to even think. Luckily, Frankie comes back to lend a hand, so with me behind the bar and Viv and Syd helping Dino to process the orders, we do all right, but I know Frankie's a temporary solution and somehow I have to get this staffing issue sorted. If I want to make a good case for sole custody of my children, I'll have to start spending more time with them instead of leaving them in the hands of babysitters. So rather than one more full timer, I'd really need two.

The moment the kitchen closes at ten, things start slowing down. The pub's still full, but now it's mostly drinkers, not eaters, and I can leave Matt behind the bar. Walking into the kitchen, I find Dino's already gone and Syd and Viv cleaning up. With tomorrow being Sunday, these two are supposed to be off, but with the changes lately, our regular schedules are screwed up.

"Guys, give me a hand here." Both of them turn around when they hear my voice. I sit down at the large table and indicate for them to do the same. "We're gonna need some serious help. With Cindy in the wind, I have the kids. Make no mistake, I wouldn't want it any other way, but it complicates the schedule and I really need to have some time to spend with them."

Viv pipes up immediately. "Take tomorrow. I'll be here and call Frankie again." I shake my head.

"Viv, you've been double-shifting it already—both opening *and* closing half the time—and I'm not gonna have you work six or seven days of that. Something's gotta give. Frankie's all set for tomorrow, he's gonna be here at noon as long as we need him. I'm gonna work up a schedule for next week and call in some more summer temps to fill the holes, but we're gonna need more full-time. Mrs. Danzel's set to mind the kids at home leaving me free to come in."

"No."

I'm surprised at the forceful tone coming from Syd who's shaking her head.

"I have nowhere else to be and I like being here. I'll come in." She suddenly looks a little shy and starts rambling. "That is if you trust me. Dino will be here, and Matt too. I can do the morning prep and Dino comes in earlier on Sundays anyway, right? I can shuttle the food orders and do cleanup, and with Matt and Frankie up front, we should be okay?"

It's more of a question than a statement and the insecure pink blush on her cheeks is pretty cute.

"Trust is not an issue, Syd, but you need rest too," I gently remind her. Surprisingly, she reaches over and grabs my hand and I see Viv's eyes widen.

"The kids ... they need you to spend some time with them. Please?"

I'll be damned. Now the little bird is going to bat for my kids. My eyes move to Viv who looks back, smirks with one eyebrow raised and shrugs her shoulders. "Don't look at me. I'm with her," she says, cocking her head in Syd's direction, who promptly releases the hand she was still holding.

"You sure?" I have to dip down my head to catch her eyes. She's kept them downcast since dropping my hand. At my question, they bug open and she smiles big.

"Yes, I'm sure."

Since Syd will be working tomorrow, I send her upstairs to get some rest, leaving Viv to finish cleaning while I retreat to my office to try and bring some order to my chaos.

Syd

I lean my forehead against the tile, letting the hot water run down my neck and back, indulging in the luxury. My thoughts are on Gunnar. Small things, like the feel of the coarse hairs on the back of his hand or the sound of his deep rumble when he talks. The way his normally dark face can transform into something beautiful with just the lift of his mouth, and the touch of his lips on mine that seem to have sparked an almost constant state of arousal since. I didn't need to feel his long erection pressed to my center when he stepped between my legs to bring my body to life, his taste alone did that.

But the memory of that hard length between my legs has me sliding my hand over my body. Reacquainting myself with shallow dips and rises and finding harder edges than I'm used to. The tingling in my lower belly and between my legs is vaguely familiar and with the image of the broad, callused hand I was holding earlier in my mind's eye, I trail my fingers through the curls at the apex of my thighs in search of relief. The instant my fingertip encounters my swollen clit—prominent from between my lips—my languid pace becomes frantic. Panting with my mouth wide open, my cheek plastered against the shower wall, I need one hand to keep me standing while the other pumps two fingers into my cunt.

Not hard enough. Not nearly hard enough.

I slide down the wall and lay back at the bottom of the tub with my legs spread up and wide, my second hand now adding much needed pressure and friction on my clit. With my eyes rolled back in my head and involuntary sounds escaping my mouth, I finally tip over the crest and shatter apart on a loud yell.

Fuck! I immediately scramble from the tub and turn off the water, wrapping myself in a towel. Would somebody have heard me?

I stand without moving with my ear to the bathroom door for minutes before realizing that given the volume of the music downstairs, there's no way someone would've heard.

Tired, clean, and sated, I crawl into bed where I promptly fall asleep.

CHAPTER TWELVE

syd

The sun is beautiful and bold, rising up on the horizon. The sky has an orange hue and gives off the impression of warmth, even though the morning temperatures are far from it. It's going to be a gorgeous day.

There are no people milling around on the dock when I sit down in my favorite spot, dressed for the chill and a cup of coffee warming my hands. Other than the regular morning exodus of fishing trawlers, there isn't a lot of human activity. Just the way I like it.

This right here is what attracted me to Holyoke Wharf to begin with. One morning, probably a year or so ago, after waking up with a street-grade, *high gravity* hangover, I found myself lying at the end of this dock. A sunrise, much the same as this morning's, was slowly warming my chilled and shivering body. I just didn't know whether I wanted to be warmed. The cold in my bones matched the frost on my heart and I crawled to the edge, peeking over the side. The kind of pain I was enduring needed to end, and the cold water below seemed to offer the solution. I was ready. About to heave myself over the edge, I noticed a fishing boat heading out, a flock of seagulls swirling around the trawler and in its wake. I remember thinking how beautiful a sight it made against the backdrop of the rising sun and the thought stopped me. If I could still find beauty in this pit of despair, maybe I wasn't ready to leave life after all. That was the last time I drank. It was also when the wharf became my sanctuary.

The memories come flooding back, each one further back in time, and rather than stomp them down, I allow them to flow over me, bringing with them the emotions I've worked so hard to suppress. Safe in the sun and at my favorite spot, I cry. For the first time since ending up on the street with nothing but the clothes on my back, I cry for what I'd allowed my life to become.

It's cleansing.

I can feel my will to move away from the past strengthening with each tear, and when the sounds of activity around me filter into my awareness, I get up and walk back; back to where my future begins.

"Mornin'."

Dino's deep bass sounds from behind me and I turn to face him.

"Morning." I smile back at him.

"Early start, I see?" He indicates the counter lined with bins of chopped vegetables.

I'm almost done with prep and it isn't even ten thirty yet. I shrug my shoulders at him and he just shakes his head.

"Want to do the special today?" he asks, wrapping the chef's apron around his hips. "Figure you probably have some ideas—might as well put whatever fire you got going on this morning to good use."

I do. I have a fire in me today. I can feel it. I also have ideas and immediately blurt out, "King Edward skillet!"

Dino turns around with a blank look. "King what?" I quickly explain the basic recipe and hearing the combination of grated potatoes, onions, peppers, and bacon, seasoned with cayenne and cumin, then topped off with cheese, Dino is on board.

"Don't have skillets big enough, though."

"Sheet pan will do too, as long as we grease it good," I suggest.

The warm fragrant smell of the skillet in the oven is already filling the kitchen when Matt comes in sniffing the air.

"Mmmm, smells fucking great in here. Watcha cooking?"

I promise him a piece to taste when it's done and he heads down to the pub to get it ready for opening. Frankie comes in ten minutes later, much the same, and another piece of skillet is promised. With Dino setting up for the standard menu fare, I'm off to get my bucket and mop to tackle the washrooms.

The day is busy, but we manage well between the four of us. I'm told Sundays are often *lunch-heavy* in terms of patrons, Sunday dinners often being a family affair. I remember those.

"But my parents will be here soon. Can't it wait until Monday?"

I've been in the kitchen most of the day, preparing a full out gourmet dinner with Daniel sitting in his high chair because Jacob thought it would be a good idea to have a family dinner, only to announce at eleven o'clock this morning he's got work to do at the office. I don't even want my parents here, to be honest. It'll just be another reason for my mom to point out my shortcomings and my dad will have an opinion about the way I parent Daniel, which is too soft according to him. Boys need to be taught to be tough, and in his opinion, I baby him too much. How can you baby a fourteen-month-old baby too much?

"I can't believe you made me organize this, and now you're gonna bail on me? Nice, Jacob ... real nice." I slam the phone down on the counter, the sound startling Daniel who starts to cry. Just as I have him lifted out of his chair to comfort him, the doorbell rings to announce my parents' arrival.

After the first fifteen minutes, I'm ready to scream and slip into the kitchen under the guise of checking on dinner. Taking the phone into the pantry for privacy, I dial Jacob's number to beg him to come home and rescue me. My parents still think he walks on water and his presence will at least distract them from me. I'm almost ready to hang up after five rings, convinced he's ignoring me, when it's answered. Not by Jacob—no—by a breathy sounding female.

"Hello?" she purrs, followed by a high-pitched giggle and the rumble of a man's voice in the background.

"Hi, yes—can I speak to Jacob please?" My voice sounds almost as shaky as my hands are, holding the phone to my ear.

"He's busy right now, can I—mmmmm—can I take a message?"

I hang up the phone, my stomach churning.

The voice I heard whispering in the background was Jacob's. It was unmistakable.

"Open up for me."

I know this, because he said those same words to me, just last night.

Gunnar's called in twice today to make sure things were under control. The first time he spoke to Matt, and the second time is a little after nine and he asks to speak to me.

"Everything okay?"

"It's fine."

The growl in my ear makes it clear Gunnar does not like my answer. "Syd ..."

"It's good, Gunnar. It got a bit busy over lunch but dinner's been easy, and we only have a few drinkers tonight. Dino's left already and Matt's gonna lock up at eleven, as usual."

"Call me when you're upstairs," he orders.

"I'm fine," I repeat.

"Syd. Call me."

Although I bristle at the tone, I also hear concern in it. Concern for me, and that affects me more than I'm ready to admit. "Okay," I concede, and without saying anything else, he hangs up.

I've been able to sort the kitchen out and do a last run through of the bathrooms when Matt pokes his head in the ladies' room.

"We're all shut down for the night. Are you about ready?"

"Just a few more minutes, but why don't you head on out? I'll just finish this and I'll be done."

"Okay, if you're sure. I'll take the trash on my way out," he says, ready to go.

"Just take the kitchen box. I'll do the bag; I have some more to add when I'm done here. Just leave it in the hall for now." A lift of his chin and he's gone.

It doesn't take me long to finish cleaning the washroom and put away the cleaning supplies. I empty the trashcans into the garbage bag and put them back in the washroom with clean liners before tying up the bag and carrying it out the back door, leaving it cracked open a bit.

A chilly wind comes off the water, rustling some loose trash around the alley. I heave the trash bag over the side of the bin just as I hear the phone ringing inside. Knowing that it's probably Gunnar getting impatient or something, I turn and make for the back door. I barely have my hand on the handle to push it open when suddenly my head is yanked back by my hair. My hands fly automatically to my head to try and keep my scalp from being ripped off. All I hear is a ragged breathing behind me as I fall backwards, the only thing preventing me from smacking my head on the stones is the hold on my hair. I try to look behind me, but only catch glimpses of a large man as I'm being dragged away from the door.

"Help me ..." I try screaming, but panic has my throat constricted and barely a sound comes out.

"Shut the fuck up, crazy bitch! You got away once, and cost me my fucking job. Not gonna let you get away with that." Bending down, he pulls me up by an arm, not letting go of my hair with his other hand. Tears are running down my face, but despite my blurred sight, I recognize his face right before he pulls me against him, one arm now wrapped around my chest. Jack. The guy who'd almost forced himself on me. The guy I'd nailed in the balls. I took him once, I figure I can do it again so with all my might, I start kicking back at his knees. When I land one, I hear his yelp loud in my ear, right before he flings me around and I go flying and slam into the side of the dumpster, the breath knocked from my lungs. Gasping for air, I lie in a crumpled heap in the alley with Jack three feet away, grabbing his knee.

"Fucking crazy cunt! Gonna pay for that!" The spittle is flying from his mouth and his lips are drawn back from his teeth. He looks like a feral dog. He's completely beyond reason.

I scramble to my feet as he reaches for me and push off to run, but he gets a hold of my shirt. Once again, he holds me pressed with my back against him and arm banded around my ribs, but this time his other hand is around my throat, cutting off my airway. I struggle to draw air, feeling all strength leave me and I realize I'm fighting a losing battle when black spots appear in my vision.

Next thing I know, I'm tossed onto a concrete floor. It reeks like rotten fish in here and the ground underneath me is slimy with scales. It has to be one of the buildings on the other side of the wharf, where the fish are brought ashore and prepped for shipping. The only light in here comes from the street lighting outside. The slam of a door has me turn my head and I watch Jack come toward me with a predatory gleam. Trying to scramble back, I get barely any purchase on the slippery floor and get no further than the wall behind me before he's on me. With his legs on either side of me, he straddles my abdomen and grabs my throat again with one hand while the other starts pulling at the button on my jeans.

"Had to shut the door. We're gonna need ourselves some privacy." I recognize the foul stench coming from his mouth as he leans down in my face.

Oh, fuck no. Hell no.

I haven't survived this long, living on the streets to be raped by this piece of shit, who's apparently pissed out of his brains if the thick alcohol fumes coming from his breath are any indication. My attempts at stopping his hand from yanking on my jeans, are stopped with a closed-fist blow to my face, whipping my head to the side. While momentarily stunned, he's able to strip my jeans down my hips.

"You stop fighting me, I'll may make it good for ya. Should'a let me at you the first time." I have to turn my head quickly to the side as vomit explodes from my mouth. Jack rears back and pulls his hand from my throat. "You fuckin' puked on me, you crazy-ass bitch! But if you think that's gonna stop me, you've got another thing comin'."

Standing up, he pulls me up with him and slams me facedown on one of the stainless steel cutting tables. The impact sends a shard of pain slicing through my face. He stretches my arms above me and holds them there in one hand while shoving down my panties with the other. I struggle against his hold and try to lift my head to look for something—anything—I can use to my advantage. A large hook with a wooden handle at the end sits just out of reach and I try to move my whole body in that direction, but he has me pinned tight.

"Stop fucking moving!" he yells in my ear, pushing my head down on the table again with his now free hand.

Over his erratic breathing behind me, I can hear whimpering and realize it's coming from my mouth. I'm almost paralyzed with fear and if there's one thing I've learned living on the streets, you *never* stop moving; stop moving, then you've lost already. With that reminder, a new surge of anger floods through me. I twist and wiggle, trying to free my legs and move away from his leg that's wedged between mine. But his boot is holding my jeans down and effectively trapping my feet. The sound of his zipper makes me dry heave as I hear his mumbling behind me.

"Sweet little ass is all mine. Can't wait to fuck that little ass. Bet it's nice and tight. Ah, yeah, baby. What hole should I stick it in first?" In his eagerness to get his jeans down, he lets go of my hands. Immediately my right hand starts searching for the only thing I have within my reach. With one hand now keeping me down by the neck, his other hand slips between my legs and he shoves a finger inside me.

"Gotta lube you up. Want you tight, not dry, baby."

With tears running down my face and gagging against the burn of violation, my fingers finally encounter something and I don't hesitate to wrap my hand around it.

"NO!" I scream as a burst of adrenaline allows me to push up and turn my torso, whipping my right arm around with the hook now clenched in my fist. I find purchase and relieved, I feel him back away. When I turn around, I see him hold the side of his head, the wooden handle sticking out through his fingers and blood seeping out between. He stumbles backward until collapsing on the floor.

I killed him.

Blind panic has me pull my feet clear from my jeans, run to the door and fling it open. I'm not thinking; I'm moving away from the horror behind me.

"SYD! Where are you, Syd?"

The familiar voice is up ahead and knowing I'll find safety there, I take off running until I bump into a solid chest and find myself lifted off my feet.

"Jesus Christ! Little Bird ..."

It's the last I hear before darkness takes me again.

Gunnar

"Daddy, do we have to go to bed?" Emmy tries in her sweetest voice, in hopes I can be swayed and Dex puts on his most angelic face. Little manipulators.

"School tomorrow, guys, and I've already let you stay up this late. Come on. Let's get you upstairs and get your teeth brushed."

The disappointment doesn't seem to be too great because both of them turn to go, but not before pointing two prominent bottom lips my way.

"Born actors, those two," Tim says behind me, coming in through the sliding door after sneaking a smoke on the back deck.

"Sure are. Guaranteed they'll be asleep before their heads hit the pillow."

After tucking my kids in—something they still seem to want me doing—I grab a few brews from the fridge and join Tim in front of the tube.

He'd come over earlier to help me extend my deck, something I've been wanting to do since I got this place. The yard's a good size and the deck the previous owners had built was too narrow; it would only fit a couple of chairs at most. This summer I want to be able to eat outside with the kids, and eat at a table. Besides, it'd been a pain having to go down the steps and around the side of the deck to where the BBQ sits, every time I want to grill, which is a lot. The bigger deck easily allows for the cooking station to be set up just to the side of the sliding doors from the kitchen, which will make grilling in the winter a less daunting task.

We ordered some Chinese and managed to finish off the railing around nine, with the outdoor lights on because it was pretty dark already.

I hand Tim the bottle and drop my exhausted body into the recliner.

"How are they doing?" I indicate the screen where the Red Wings are trying to fight off first round elimination by the Bruins.

"Tonight's the night," Tim says, an avid Bruins fan, just as Lucic is sent to the box … again.

"Fucking guy doesn't stay out of the penalty box. I don't know if they will. Boston's power play's gotta be the worst in the league," I observe.

"Have some faith, brother."

"Whatever," I grumble, my mind already wandering to the pub where they should be closing shortly. Early night on Sundays. Monday is the only day the pub's closed, so closing earlier on Sunday nights allows everyone to get a decent night's sleep before their day off.

We watch Detroit tie it up in the third with only two minutes left in the game and when the whistle blows, Boston hasn't been able to respond, despite the fact they had the goalie pulled the entire two minutes. Overtime.

While the commercials are up, I quickly dial the pub because Syd hasn't called yet like she promised. It's coming up on eleven thirty. Place should've been locked up by now. The phone, which has an extension upstairs, just rings and rings before going to voicemail. Thinking she might be having a shower, I give her a few minutes before calling again, all the while trying to talk my cock down as I'm imagining her with water sluicing off her naked body.

I call repeatedly with no answer. Suddenly, I'm restless and get up. "Gonna head over and check on the pub real quick." I tell Tim, grabbing my jacket off the back of the kitchen chair.

"Something wrong?"

"Nobody's answering. Syd was gonna call after they locked up."

"You've got a hard-on for that little waif, don't ya?" he says with a big smirk on his face.

"Fuck off. I've gotta go. You good here for a couple?" It'll only take me about five minutes to get to the pub at this time of night, and at my speed anyway.

"Yeah, I'm good. Set to watch overtime anyway." With his hand up, he waves me off.

I grab the truck, which is sitting in the drive. The bike's parked in the garage where I prefer to keep it overnight. Bike would've been easier since I can park it behind the pub without blocking anything, but tonight I just leave the truck in the alley by the dumpster. Not like there'll be any deliveries late on a Sunday night.

First thing I notice when I get there sends a chill down my spine. The outside light is still on and the back door is open a crack. Inside there is no sign of Syd, nor up in the apartment either. I pull out my phone while walking back outside and contemplate calling the cops. Problem is, she could be out by the water as I've seen her do from time to time, and I'd have the cops over here crawling around. She might take off. She already made it clear she wanted nothing to do with emergency responders last time. Standing on the back door step, I can just see the water's edge this side of the dock, but there is no one there. She could be on the other side. As I turn my head, my eyes catch something on the ground by the front wheel of the truck. A shoe. Looks to be one of Syd's runners. *Fuck.*

I don't hesitate then and put in a quick call before running into the alley, yelling her name. Just as I pass the burned out shed, I can hear a scream and my heart about pounds out of my chest.

"SYD!!" My voice bounces off the buildings. "Syd! Where are you?"

Running toward me is a half-naked woman, her signature copper-colored hair identifying her immediately, which is good because her face is covered in blood. I have to lock my knees to avoid buckling as she runs straight into my arms.

CHAPTER THIRTEEN

Gunnar

"Mr. Lucas, please sit down."

"I'll stand, thank you."

Not gonna let some punk-ass cop dictate whether I sit or stand. Waste of my goddamn time anyway. I need to get back to Syd's room.

"Just a couple more questions, sir."

"Well hurry it up. Don't see what the big mystery is anyway. Seems pretty obvious what happened, doesn't it?"

"How well do you know the victim?"

"Jesus, this is useless." I grab my hair, pulling hard, knowing the only way to get back to Syd is to get through his damn questions. "Fine, I'll explain again. She works for me. My manager found her down on her luck and since one of our employees up and left just hours before, she offered the job to Syd."

"Actually, sir, I was talking about the other victim."

I whip around at his words. "Fuck you!" Stalking over, I lean in to within an inch of the stupid prick's face. "Only *one* victim in all this. Only one! And she's lying in a bed down the hall, fucking violated, face bashed in and in shock, and that's where I should be. I'm fucking done!" At that I turn around, ready to stomp out of there when I see Sergeant Winslow standing in the doorway, looking almost apologetic.

"Go ahead, Mr. Lucas. Harper here is done. I'll follow up with you at a more convenient time." A scathing look in the direction of the younger cop makes it clear he's not happy.

Though his proper manners grate on my nerves, seems Winslow is not quite the pussy I took him to be. Without wasting another word, I beeline it down the hall to where Syd's being looked after.

The moment she collapsed into my arms in the alley earlier, I heard the sirens coming down from the other side. Two police cars and an ambulance right behind. I ignored the calls from the officers and walked right up to the back of the ambulance where the EMTs were pulling out the stretcher, Syd still in my arms. I didn't want to let go of her, but laid her on the stretcher anyway when the EMT promised to look after her. The cops were right behind me and I quickly told them what I knew, which wasn't much. They didn't stop me though, when I climbed into the back of the ambulance, but was told a car would follow it to the hospital.

I still don't know much about what happened. The only additional information I picked up is that they found the guy who attacked her in one of the fish shacks down the alley.

An hour and a half he kept me in that fucking room with his asinine questions and with blood boiling in my veins. I stop to take a few breaths outside her door. A nurse is cleaning blood from her face and turns to me when I step in.

"How's she doing?"

The nurse throws me an apologetic look before returning to her task. "I'm not sure I can give out that information, sir. Family only," she says kindly.

I sit down beside her bed and grab her hand. "I *am* her family for now," I say weakly, suddenly feeling every last minute of the last couple of hours. The nurse regards me with a slight tilt of her head before jutting a clipboard with forms at me.

"Then maybe you should fill this out as best you can and make sure you mark that under *immediate relatives.*

With a wink, she walks toward the door where she stops and turns around. "Be back in a few minutes to pick that up."

Unclipping the pen from the top, I start scanning the form, immediately reminded of how little I really know of this woman. Last name? *Fuck.* I've kissed her, observed her closely—too closely—for almost a month, and although I know the tilt of her head, can wax poetic about the color of her hair and will never get the flavor of her out of my mind, I know nothing. Skipping over the last name, I can fill out address, but I'm stopped again when it comes to insurance. *Crap.* I'm thinking I'm safe in assuming she doesn't have any, and there's no way I can slip her in under mine. Next of kin. I hesitate here. With only one option open to me, I quickly fill it out, ignoring the small pang of guilt at my deceit. On a roll now, I return to 'last name' and scribble the first thing that comes to mind before putting the clipboard down and scooting my chair closer to the bed. Picking Syd's hand up, I kiss her palm and tuck it under my cheek when I put my head down.

The rustling of paper pulls me out of my catnap. "So, Mr. Lucas, is it?" The same nurse is back and flipping through the papers on the clipboard. "And Ms. Bird is your fiancée?"

She looks at me with a smile teasing at the corners of her mouth. I just shrug my shoulders. "Fine, I'll let Dr. Sanders know. He should be coming around soon."

"Thanks."

Just as she walks out the door, Syd's fingers start moving in my hand and when I turn back to her, her eyes are quietly observing me.

"Who's Ms. Bird?"

Syd

I've been lying here with my eyes closed, just enjoying the sensation of a warm cheek and bristly stubble against the palm of my hand. It distracts from the aches and pains everywhere on my body.

I know who it is. Funny that—I don't even need to rely on sight or hearing to have that confirmed. His smell is the first thing that registers; a hint of sea and nutmeg, mixed in with the scent of clean man.

I'm about to make it known I'm awake when I hear footsteps approaching and decide to play mum a bit longer. I don't feel like answering the inevitable questions yet.

"Who's Ms. Bird?" is the first thing I ask Gunnar when I hear the nurse leave. His beautiful green eyes turn to me and he sports a little smile.

"It's all I could think of on the spot," he says, his eyes scanning my face before looking down at our hands. He hasn't let go yet. "I realized how little I really know of you when they had me fill out the papers. I may have embellished a bit."

"The last name or the part about the fiancée?"

He looks up from under his heavy eyebrows. "They wouldn't tell me anything and you were out. Didn't have a choice." He leans in closer. "I think the ruse will only hold up so long though. The cops are here too. Have a feeling they may not be easily turned away with a false last name."

I turn away for a moment, trying to gauge the impact this all will have. I may be done with anonymity, at least for those who want to dig.

"Sorry, Syd. Had no choice, really. The EMTs were already there when I found you—or rather, you found me."

I look at him and the regret is obvious in his words, and also mirrored on his face. All at once, another face pops up in my mind, one twisted in anger, and my body starts to shake at the memory.

"It was him ... Jack ... f-from the pantry?" My teeth are starting to chatter as the flood of memories start to wash over me.

"Shhh ..." Gunnar sits on the edge of the bed and pulls me into his arms. A hiss escapes me as a sharp pain stabs my side. "Fuck. Sorry."

He's gentler now, but the soft sounds he makes with his lips pressed to the side of my head do little to stop the tumble of thoughts in my head. The phantom smell of rotting fish permeates my senses and I can still feel the brutal, foreign hands touching me. Sounds and images assault me and just like that, I'm back over the cutting table, being held down by the weight of his body. I fight and scramble, a keening sound coming from my very core. Something is holding me down and panic wants to pull me under. I struggle until a different smell starts filtering through, familiar and comforting, along with a deep rumbling voice in my ear, hushing me.

"Shhh, I've got you, little Bird. No one can touch you. Hush ..."

I open my eyes to see a bright hospital room; not a dark and dirty fish shack. My racing heart slows as, what I recognize to be Gunnar's arms, surround me, rocking me gently back and forth. A sob works its way out, quickly followed by another—and another until I'm crying and sobbing loudly. I turn my face into his neck, inhaling the scent of sea and nutmeg.

"Is he dead?" I manage to whisper through my tears.

"No. Unfortunately," he bites out. "He's in the hospital."

"Here?" I pull back, feeling the panic build again.

Gunnar's warm eyes hold steel when he tells me, "He will never lay a hand on you again. He's under guard and barely hanging on."

Slightly reassured, I try to shift from the odd position on the floor we somehow ended up in, but my body protests. Gunnar sees the wince I'm not able to hold back and immediately gets up, with me in his arms. It's only when he puts me back in the bed that I fully take in his face. It's covered in scratches that weren't there before. I clap my hands over my mouth.

"Did I do that?" I whisper, horrified.

He runs his hand down his face and looks at the blood on his palm before turning his eyes to me. "Hey," he says softly, reaching out to cup my cheek. "It's nothing. I'm just glad that whatever happened to you hasn't killed your will for survival."

I flinch at his words. They strike close ... too close, and he doesn't miss it, but before he can say anything, the door opens to an older gentleman in a white coat. I presume he's the doctor, which he confirms when he introduces himself.

"Ms. Bird, glad to see you awake. I'm Dr. Sanders, and this is?" He indicates Gunnar.

"I'm—" he starts.

"He's—" I say at the same time, but before he has a chance to finish his sentence, I quickly add the rest of mine. "—my fiancé."

I can see from the surprised look on Gunnar's face he wasn't expecting that, but the truth is, I don't want to be left alone with anyone, at least anyone other than him. His surprise makes way for a small smile as he grabs my hand with one of his, and sticks the other out to shake the doctor's.

"Gunnar Lucas."

"Right, you're the gentleman who found her," he says, pointing at Gunnar's bloodied shirt—something I hadn't even noticed yet.

"More like she found me, but yes, I came in with Syd."

"Interesting name, Syd. Is that short for Sydney?" Dr. Sanders looks at me questioningly. A quick glance at Gunnar's face shows me a similar expression.

Resigned to the fact I'll likely no longer be able to hide my identity, I concede. "Yes, it's Sydney."

"Do you mind if I call you Sydney or would you prefer Syd?" he asks gently.

"Either is fine."

"Right. Well, Sydney, you've sustained some injuries that will heal with some simple rest. You have some nasty abrasions on your face, but only the cut right at your hairline needed stitches. It was done very carefully to minimize scarring and what little there may be will likely be hidden by your hair."

My hand automatically goes to my face to explore. The doctor smiles at me encouragingly.

"Also, your ribs are tender but I don't think they're broken. Regardless, the treatment would be the same, rest. The stitches should come out in a week, which is about when I'd want to see you anyway to see how you are healing otherwise." At this point, he leans forward and asks me softly, "This next part may be uncomfortable for you to hear and I think it's perhaps a good idea for your fiancé to wait outside. I can get a nurse if that makes you more comfortable."

The moment Gunnar stands and starts pulling his hand back, I hang on tightly, sending a wordless plea with my eyes. The little reassuring nod is for me when he sits back down, before he turns to the doctor.

"Sorry, Doc. Syd wants me to stay and I promised I wouldn't leave her."

Dr. Sanders is obviously waiting for me to say something. "I'm ready, but he stays."

"Very well. I'm not sure how much of what happened you remember, but—"

"Every. Single. Second." I interrupt him.

"Right. We found evidence of sexual assault, Sydney. We couldn't find evidence of actual intercourse, but you were bleeding when you were brought in. Not a lot, but enough for us to investigate. We found some tearing of your perineum; the skin between your—"

I raise my free hand to stop him from going on. The other hand is wrapped in Gunnar's, squeezing hard, but he doesn't seem to notice. He's clenching his jaw so hard I'm worried he'll break a tooth.

"His fingers," I whisper. "Three I think."

"*Jesus* ..." This from Gunnar, who doesn't let go of my hand, but grabs his neck with the other one, tilting his head back and raising his eyes to the ceiling.

"It's still rape, Sydney," Dr. Sanders says. "Even if there was no penile penetration. The police are outside wanting to talk to you. I can hold them off a little longer, but eventually they will have to question you."

I nod, terrified of what is coming; afraid everything is going to catch up with me and I'll drown for real this time.

"Let's get this over with so I can take you home," Gunnar mumbles beside me.

"Since you have no concussion and don't appear to have any internal injuries, technically you can be looked after as well at home as in the hospital. You did go into mild shock, and normally we would admit you. However, I get the feeling you'd probably feel safer at home, but I strongly suggest you not be alone for the next forty-eight hours as a precaution. I would also like you to see a counselor to help you work through the assault." The doctor puts a careful, but consoling hand on my shoulder and I discover I'm crying.

I don't know if I want to talk to a counselor. I don't know if I want to see the cops. I don't know. I feel so out of control, and I don't even know what to say next. Gunnar steps in and turns to Dr. Sanders. "I'll make sure someone is with her at all times. Give us ten minutes and we'll talk to the cops." He squeezes my hand. "Okay, Syd?"

I answer with a simple nod and the doctor seems to take that as his cue. Promising to get me appointments for a follow-up with him and a counselor, he walks out, closing the door behind him, leaving Gunnar and I alone.

Gunnar's thumb is softly stroking the skin of my hand as he sits on the edge of my bed, quietly. I have my eyes averted, feeling ashamed, guilty, and fearful of being even more exposed than I already am.

"Syd?" His voice rumbles beside me. "What do you need?"

What do I need? I need to be where I was twenty-four hours ago. The urge to escape from the events of tonight, and what is yet to come is equal. Part of me wants to retreat again, wants to get a bottle and disappear into it, but that's a line I can't cross. Another part wants to come clean—tell all—and just purge the guilt, the shame, and the fear. I take in a shaky breath and decide to open up, just a little.

"I don't know what I need. I've long ago stopped thinking in those terms. What I should *do* is face forward. Deal with this and then leave it behind me, but I've been a coward for so long, hiding in the shadows. I just don't know where to start." I finally lift my eyes and only find compassion in Gunnar's face, who quietly listens. "I can't believe I fought him off. For someone who's spent years destroying her life, I'm surprised at how strong the will to live—to fight—is in a situation like that. I'm not used to wanting to see another day for five years now." His slight nod encourages me to go on, but when I try to pull back my hand from his, he holds on tight, not allowing me to create distance. "You've been good to me, Gunnar, but I'm afraid to tell you. I'm so afraid that when you find out, you'll turn me out, and I wouldn't blame you. You, the kids, Viv—you've helped me believe in a future I didn't think I had or even wanted."

"Not gonna turn you out, little Bird," he says, shaking his head, but I'm not so sure.

I breathe in deeply through my nose and rip the band-aid off. Looking down at my hands, I push the words out. "Five years ago, I lost my son. The pain was more than I can handle, and I started drinking to numb myself. I was too drunk to even attend his funeral." I swallow hard to dislodge the persistent lump of guilt stuck in my throat. "My family fell apart with me at the center, hell-bent on destroying myself and everything around me. My family was ... unpleasant; before, during and after. One particularly hopeless day, I ended up on the psychiatric ward at Mass General and was held for seventy-two hours. When they were up, I checked myself out and walked away from the hospital, my family, and my life, such as it was." I take a deep, shuddering breath and risk a glance at Gunnar's face. His eyes are on me but I can't read him. All I can see is the twitching of the muscles in his jaw. Only a small squeeze of my hand is indication he wants me to continue. "My job was gone, and I didn't leave a whole lot of goodwill behind. I ended up in Portland where I coasted on fumes for a while, but eventually drinking myself numb cost me a job and a roof over my head. One morning I woke up on the wharf with no idea how I got there and ready to end my misery. Something stopped me. That's when I found the shed, got dry, and kept to myself. Time ceased to exist as one day just turned into another."

I feel his hand come up to my face and brush away the tears from my cheek. The compassion in his face is back, and I haven't even told him everything yet, but there is one thing he deserves to know.

"I haven't had a drink since that day at the edge of the water and I had the isolation and the cold at night to keep me numb, until Viv."

I lift my chin, looking him straight in the eye. "I lied to you by omission because I knew if you found out, you'd never have allowed me to work at The Skipper, let alone keep an eye on your kids. And I wanted that chance so badly. I needed that push to get me unstuck. Viv's touch was the first human contact I felt in a very long time, but it wasn't until I felt yours that I instinctively knew I was safe."

Gunnar's face is impassive and this time when I pull back my hand, it slips easily from his. He immediately gets up and paces the room until he stops at the foot end of the bed, looking down at me.

"What's your name?" His voice sounds as raw as I feel.

"Sydney Donner. I'm thirty-nine years old and have a degree in accounting. My parents are James and Marilyn Donner, and I have one older sister, Sofia. My husband's name is Jacob Webster, although I guess he probably isn't my husband anymore since he served me with divorce papers when I was in the hospital. I left them behind in my room, but I did sign them. For reasons of my own, I don't want them to know where I am. I want to build again, and not on the ruins of my past. That's where my family belongs."

Gunnar seems shocked at my vehemence. "Christ, Syd—you only get one family."

I can't help but snicker at that. "Right. They have never been kind to me and finding out what I've become is definitely not going to change that. They're part of the baggage I want to leave behind."

He sits down beside me and I'm instantly warmed when he grabs my hand off the blanket. "That's a fuckload to process, and I have a feeling I have just been given the surface, but thank you. I figure that was scary and painful for you." He leans in and his lips press gently to my forehead.

"I want to move forward, Gunnar, but the truth is I'm an alcoholic. And given what I just told you, I think I should go back to Florence House until I can figure something out."

"Like hell you will!" Gunnar jumps up and I inadvertently shift away from him. The move doesn't go unnoticed and he immediately sits back down and grabs my hand again. "Look, truth is I care about you. Fuck. The kids ... they care about you. Viv, Dino, and even Matt. You're making a difference to all of us. I can't imagine the agony of losing a child, and frankly just the thought of it makes me sick to my stomach, so what do I know? I do think neither of us has a clear head right now and, honey, you've just survived another major trauma. So, I propose for now we focus on you getting better. Promised that doctor I'd look after you and that's what I'm gonna do. Now let's talk to the police so we can get out of here."

CHAPTER FOURTEEN

Gunnar

What a fucking bitch of a night.

I'd been afraid she might've been sexually assaulted when she came running at me half-naked and bloodied, but I had to fight not to stalk that bastard's ass in the hospital and make sure he ended up dead. Reining that anger in was taxing enough in itself, but then she started coming clean and my emotions were all over the place—still are. It didn't help that Sergeant Winslow took his sweet time having Syd rehash every detail of what happened three fucking times. The woman was wrung out by the time the nurse came in with her discharge papers and told him it was enough, that Syd needed rest. She never gave him any more personal information than her name and where she lives, and when he asked how long she'd worked for me and had lived there, she became evasive. She told him "for a while," that she'd left Boston and had "bounced around" a little before starting at The Skipper. Winslow looked dubiously at both her and me, but didn't push the issue, at least not yet.

My eyes wander to the clock on the wall; five in the morning. After Syd fell asleep in the truck and I carried her to my bed, I woke up Tim, who'd fallen asleep on my couch. I told him a condensed version of what had happened before he headed home, ensuring me he'd call in the morning. I didn't share anything about Syd's history. Not quite ready to address that myself, but now in the early hours of the morning, lying on the couch in my living room, I can't stop the thoughts crowding my head. The way she looked running toward me, the complex mix of relief, horror, and rage. It worries me that she'd so completely lost her way in the past that she used the bottle as a solution. A definite button for me, since that had been—and apparently still is, according to the children—Cindy's solution of choice: a bottle and oblivion. Only difference is, I get it in Syd's case. I do, but it's also obvious to me that no matter how much she wants to move forward, she has a history that you can't just bury and forget. That shit always comes back up and causes more destruction. She has a lot to work through, and how willing is she? Fucking hell. It'd be so much easier if I didn't care, if I could just back away. I've got kids to think of, an understaffed pub, and sharks in the water. Not to mention a custody issue that won't be easily resolved.

Thank God the pub is closed today. Lack of sleep and emotional overload would kill me.

Resigned to the fact I won't likely get any sleep tonight, I head to the kitchen to put on a pot of coffee when a sound from upstairs gets my attention. It sounds like wailing. Taking the stairs two steps at a time, I find Dex at the top of the stairs rubbing sleep from his eyes.

"S'okay, son." I tell him in passing as I rush into my bedroom where the pitiful sounds are coming from. Syd is thrashing around in my bed, keening the name Daniel, over and over again. Afraid she'll hurt herself, I lie down on the bed and wrap my arms around her as gently as I can, but firm enough so she can't flail around.

"Shhhh, Syd. It's a dream."

My senseless mumbling seems to calm her some. A sharp intake of breath from the other side of the bed comes from Dex, who must've come into the room with me. He's staring at Syd's face, his eyes big as saucers. "Daddy? What happened to Syd? Did someone beat up on her?"

I wonder if I should be concerned that that's the first thing my son comes up with. "Actually, bud ... yes, someone did. Syd was hurt pretty badly and we're gonna look after her for a bit."

He bobs his little white face and I can see he has questions, but for now he keeps them to himself. "Why don't you head back to your room and get some more sleep?" I prompt him, but to my surprise, he climbs into bed on the other side and snuggles against Syd.

"Gonna help you take care of Syd," his little voice whispers. "This way we'll keep her safe."

"Sounds good, kid," my voice comes out hoarse with emotion.

I must've dozed off because next thing I know, Dexter's shaking me.

"Dad, wake up. We've gotta go to school."

Shit. Right—school. I carefully disentangle myself from Syd, who seems to have wrapped around me during the night. Still fast asleep, I'd like her to stay that way a little longer so I raise my finger to my lips, indicating to Dex to be quiet while nudging him out of the bedroom. A quick stop in the bathroom for me before I walk into the kitchen. Emmy seems to have taken charge, generously slathering jam on a stack of sandwiches. Their lunch pails are sitting on the counter with a juice box and a banana besides each.

"I told her about Syd, Dad," Dex says as he slides back into his chair at the kitchen table, in front of a half-eaten bowl of cereal. He doesn't hesitate shoving an overflowing spoonful into his mouth, preventing further conversation.

"Morning, Emmy," I walk over and give my girl a hug and a kiss on her hair. "So yeah, about that—" I proceed to give the kids the bare basics, simply saying that Syd was attacked when she was putting out the garbage. I don't want to scare the kids, but I'm not in the habit of lying to them. Besides, Dex already saw her face, so there's no hiding that.

"I just went to check on her when nobody was answering the phone at the pub, and Tim stayed here with you guys. Luckily Syd had been able to get away when I found her, but she had to go to the hospital."

"Will she be all right?" Emmy's eyes are worried and I'm afraid she's guessing a lot of what I don't say. She's thirteen, and very perceptive.

"She will be, honey. But she'll be staying here until she feels better, okay?"

Emmy nods, a frown creasing her forehead as she finishes their lunches. Such a little adult. It hurts my heart and I don't think I can put all that blame with her mother. I haven't exactly been *present,* either. That's going to change though.

When Dex runs upstairs to brush his teeth, Emmy asks if she can see Syd. Thinking Emmy's imagination might be scarier than reality, especially after hearing her brother's description of Syd's visible injuries, I agree. "Sure. I'll go with you and quickly dress while you get ready for school. I'll drive you."

I follow Emmy up the stairs and when she opens my door, she stops dead in her tracks. Syd's sitting up in bed, sheet pulled up to her chest for cover, but the extent of damage to her face is even more glaring in the light of day. I put my arm around Emmy and take her over to the bed. "Hey. How are you this morning?"

Syd seems to ignore me, her eyes focused on Emmy. "I'm okay," she says, mainly to my daughter. "Emmy? It's just bruises and cuts, honey. I promise you, it looks much worse than it really is." She reaches out and grabs Emmy's hand, pulling her close. With her other hand, she wipes at Emmy's face. "None of that, pretty girl. A few days from now you won't even be able to tell."

A sob escapes Emmy's lips and before I have a chance to hold her back, she flings herself into Syd's arms. I go to pull her off, but despite the wince on her face, Syd shakes her head with a sharp *no,* and folds her arms around my girl's shaking shoulders. Giving them a moment, I use that time to slip into the bathroom with some jeans and a T-shirt so I can get dressed. By the time I get back, Emmy is sitting up on the edge of the bed, a bit more composed.

"Okay, girl. Go get cleaned up quick before I drive you to school. I'll be down in a minute." With a careful peck on Syd's cheek, she's off and I take Emmy's spot on the side of the bed, stroking the back of my hand over the same spot Emmy just kissed.

"Thank you," Syd says with a little crack in her voice.

"Don't wanna hear it. I want you to promise me you'll be here when I get back from dropping off the kids."

When she doesn't respond, I take her face in my hands and carefully tilt her head up so she has to look at me. "Promise me," I repeat softly and watch her eyes go warm as she leans into my hands cupping her jaw.

"I don't wanna run, so I promise." She turns her face and plants a kiss in the palm of my hand.

Wow. Talk about instant reaction. The moment her soft lips touch my skin, my cock jumps to attention. Good thing the kids are waiting downstairs, otherwise this situation could get out of hand fast. But the moment I register the bruising and cuts on her face, I'm reminded of what she'd just gone through the night before. My lust curbed, I manage an almost platonic kiss on her forehead ... *Almost.*

"I'll be twenty minutes or so. Is there anything you want? Anything you want me to pick up for you?"

Syd shakes her head no. "I'm fine, thanks," she says as she settles back in bed.

The kids are already on the porch outside, waiting for me when I get downstairs. In the truck, Emmy turns to me. "Is Syd staying with us?"

"For now she is. The doctor said she needs someone to look after her and she lives alone, so—" I try to respond before Dex interrupts me.

"Awesome!" His enthusiasm puts a smile on my face, even though I feel the need to remind him she's here to get better. Emmy beats me to it.

"Not so awesome for Syd," she states. "She's really hurt."

The enthusiasm is quickly replaced with a worried look on his face. "She'll get better though, right, Dad?"

"Yeah, kid. She will, but it may be a while, you know. Better hold off on inviting her on the trampoline out back."

Last year I got the kids a trampoline at the start of summer and everyone who shows up at the house gets dragged onto that thing. Dex loves it. Emmy did at first, but it's apparently no longer *cool*, or so she says, but I still catch her sneaking out there from time to time. "Okay," Dex says easily.

"Dad?"

"Yeah, Emmy?"

"Why did that man hurt her?"

Christ. Yet another dilemma. How much can I tell them? I don't want to lie, but I also don't want to have them run scared. Cautious? Yes, but not scared, so again I go for as little as I can get away with.

"He's not a very nice man. He tried to touch Syd before and she made it clear she didn't want that. Then he got mean and I guess he had decided to take what he wanted anyway." I check the kids to gauge their reactions. Dex just nods, apparently satisfied with that explanation, but when I look at Emmy, she looks a little white around the nose.

"Did he ... was she ..." she stammers and I grab onto her hand, shaking my head no.

"No, baby. He never had a chance against Syd." I smile, trying to reassure her.

"But she's not much bigger than me."

"I know, but she was much smarter than him. If you keep your wits about you, you don't always need to be big, just smart." I give her hand a little squeeze and leave her to mull on that. God, I hope I handled that okay.

The rest of the drive is uneventful with Dex chattering about his baseball season that starts next month and Emmy staring out the window.

After I drop the kids off, I stop at the Open Window bakery for fresh bagels and coffee. The pot I made earlier that morning is probably like tar by now.

Syd

I'm so sore … and dirty.

The moment Gunnar leaves with the kids, the silence becomes oppressive and although I try to close my eyes, the images of last night's attack start crowding my brain to the point where I need to get out of bed. A door in the hallway reveals a linen closet stocked with towels, and I grab two with shaking hands. I need to get myself clean. Maybe it'll help.

The generous warm spray of water feels good running over my battered body. I grab a bottle of shower gel off the little shelf in the corner and start lathering myself. It smells like Gunnar; a light, spicy fragrance that wakes up my olfactory sense, but when I tilt back my head to rinse my hair, a hint of fish enters my nose and suddenly that's all I can smell—fish … rotting fish. Gagging against the bile rising in my throat, I squeeze more of the gel in my hand and try to rub it in my hair, but the move causes a sharp stabbing pain in my side and I'm only partially successful at rubbing it in my hair. If anything, it seems to make the smell even worse. I grab for another bottle to try, dropping it at my feet in the tub when I try to wash the smell out of my hair. It won't work—I can't get rid of it. A low, whimpering reaches my ears and changes into sobs before I realize it's coming from me. Sliding down into the tub, I pull up my knees protectively and give in.

The smell of his rancid breath, my fear, his hate-filled eyes, and his slimy grin. His hands groping me, along with the sounds of his grunting, and his zipper sliding down. I remember my feeling of utter helplessness when he stabbed my dry core with his fingers, ripping into me. Had I done *anything* to lead him on—to cause him to want to just take something from me—that made him think that was okay?

Did I do this? I'm drowning in images and slowly losing my mind.

"Jesus!" I can hear Gunnar. His voice is like a lifeline I want to grab a hold of. Something—anything—to pull me out of this swirling riptide. But when I feel hands trying to lift me out of the tub, I fight. I need to be clean. I can still smell *him* on me, so I bat at him with my hands, needing him to let me get this stench off me.

"Okay, honey. It's okay. You can sit right there." The low rumble of his voice is soothing and I want to curl up in it.

Safe.

I can feel his hand stroking my hair as he mumbles to himself, and I slowly relax.

"I can smell him." My voice is weak and cracked, like an old music player, but Gunnar hears me.

"Let me wash him off you," he says softly, and I finally open my eyes and find his vivid green ones inches from mine. When he releases his arms from me, I feel the loss instantly and can't stop the pathetic whimper that escapes. "Just grabbing a facecloth from the shelf, honey. Not going anywhere."

True to his word, he's back in an instant, setting a washcloth on the side of the tub before grabbing a bottle of shampoo and thoroughly washing my hair first. When he's done rinsing, he runs the washcloth, liberally doused in shower gel, lightly over my body.

"Did he touch you here?" he asks, carefully pressing the cloth to my neck. I nod and he gently washes my neck and shoulders before sliding the cloth lower, his intense look never wavering from my face.

"How about here? He touch you here?" his hand covered by the thin cloth gently cups my breast, and again I nod. He takes great care in washing my chest and asks permission with his eyes when his hand slides down over my belly.

With his gentle ministrations, the smell of rotting fish leaves me, and I'm infused in a scent I've come to associate with Gunnar.

"Honey, I need you to do this part yourself," Gunnar whispers. His movements still on my lower belly; he takes my hand and puts it on top of the washcloth, sliding both between my legs—his hand guiding the way. When he tries to pull his hand away, I grab his wrist with my other hand.

"Help me."

Together we erase the last of *his* touch.

"Want cream cheese on your bagel?"

Gunnar stands on the other side of the kitchen table holding up a container, waiting for my answer. I'm surprised to find myself hungry, so I nod yes and watch him slather a goodly amount on one of the bagels he pulls out of a paper bag. He amazes me.

After my cleansing session in the shower where his gentle attention pulled me out of the pit of insanity I was threatening to slide into, he set out some threadbare sweats and a much too large T-shirt for me to get dressed in. I should be scared of a man's touch, or at least apprehensive, but Gunnar's touch has been nothing but a comfort. I should also probably have been self-conscious of being totally exposed and naked, both literally and figuratively, in front of him, but there was no shame—no insecurity. Perhaps it's the fact that my body is almost unrecognizable, even to me; bruises covering my too thin frame. A far cry still from the persistent padding I'd always had. Funny how something I always hated is now something I miss.

When he left me to get dressed, I almost begged him not to leave me again before catching myself. Can't let myself become too dependent on his presence. He was being supremely kind, but I can't allow myself to read too much into it, especially now. The fact that his body quite obviously reacted to me, as evident from the large bulge in his own sweats, could simply have been a standard physical response..

I quickly got dressed and joined him in the kitchen where the freshly brewed coffee was hot and the green eyes that scan me as I sit down at the table are smoldering. *Huh. Maybe?*

"This is good," I mumble around a mouthful of bagel.

Gunnar smiles. "Only from the best baker in Portland. I was hoping it might stir up an appetite. Thought that eating something might make you feel a little better." He shrugs his shoulders a little.

"It did. Thank you for this, and for earlier. I don't know what to say."

"Don't. I care about you, Syd." He reaches across the table and grabs my hand. "I—" He abruptly stops and releases my hand to run his hand through his unruly hair. "I called Viv. Don't be angry," he says, holding up his hands when I open my mouth to object. "You were dreaming last night, and it was bad. You were calling out your son's name."

I flinch at the mention of Daniel. Sitting back from the table, he reaches for my hand again before continuing. "Syd, I think you'd do well seeing someone. Not so much because of what the doctor said, but for you. You deserve more—much more—than you allow yourself."

The words slice my heart. If only he knew the full truth of what I really deserve. I certainly don't deserve to be cared for in this way.

Before I have a chance to set him straight, there's a sharp knock at the door and leaving me sitting at the table, Gunnar goes to answer. The sound of muffled voices drifts through the open door, and I recognize Viv's, alongside Gunnar's. Next thing I know, she walks into the kitchen, her eyes shiny with unshed tears. Wordless, she walks right up and wraps me up in a tight hug. Behind her, Gunnar stands and observes with a small, almost apologetic smile.

"I'm okay, Viv." I try to reassure her, swallowing down my own emotions.

"I know," she sniffs, "you're a rock." Releasing me from her embrace, she grabs the plastic bag she dropped at her feet when she hugged me. "Brought some clothes. They'll probably be too big, but as soon as you feel up to it, you and I are going shopping."

Before I can take the bag from her hand, the doorbell rings. My eyes shoot to Gunnar, who has one eyebrow pulled up. Viv is still chattering but I can't seem to focus on anything but the sounds of muted talking at the front door. Footsteps approach down the hall and the sight of Sergeant Winslow coming around the corner has me suck in an audible breath. I'm not sure I'm ready for this again. The solemn look on his face should've been a warning, but still, the words from his mouth chill my blood instantly.

"Ms. Donner, I'm afraid I have some news that might upset you." His face is serious and a cold shiver runs down my spine. Gunnar walks up behind me and wraps his arms around my waist, and not a moment too soon. My knees threaten to give out when Winslow delivers his news.

"Early this morning, Jack Barnes succumbed to his injuries. He never regained consciousness."

I killed a man.

CHAPTER FIFTEEN

Syd

Can't remember much of the past day. I've been trapped inside my mind for most of it. Oh, I was aware of the small sound Viv made when Winslow made his announcement, and also of the strength Gunnar lent me by helping me keep my body upright upon hearing the news, but I had little or no response to either. Too overwhelmed with the events of the past twenty-four hours, I simply checked out.

I know Gunnar brought me upstairs to his bedroom to lay me down, and even stayed beside me for a while with his arms securely around me, but I was too busy fending off the pull of the dark gravity that once again had me in its hold. I don't know who dealt with Winslow or how he was dealt with, but between Viv and Gunnar, I'm sure they had him handled.

I killed a man.

This feeling is horrifyingly familiar, and yet not nearly as excruciating as I remember. But he's dead just the same, and by my hand.

I stare at the far wall, listening for sounds in the house, but all appears to be quiet. From the light outside, it would seem it's late afternoon and I would've expected the kids to have come home from school. The kids. *Jesus.* Gunnar won't ever let me be around them again. *A killer.*

My heart hurts. I thought I'd managed to freeze my emotions again—I'd done it before—but even the thought of Emmy and Dex puts a crack in the coldness I wrapped myself in. Tears roll down my face and I don't seem to have the power to stop them. A sob escapes me, and immediately the door opens.

"Syd?" Gunnar pokes his head inside his bedroom and although I vaguely remember him checking on me every once in a while, I hadn't dared face him. This time though, I turn my head to look at him. Expecting him to be repelled by who I am, I'm surprised to find his eyes warm and full of concern, not accusatory or horrified—both reactions I have plenty of experience with, but kind and caring. *No.* The warmth radiating from him breaks the dam.

In two steps he's on the bed with me and rolls me onto his chest where I cry out everything I'm feeling, hoping maybe he can help me make some sense of it. Strong hands hold me together; one cupping my head and pressing it into his chest, the other banded around my back, tethering me to him. The pain in my ribs is sharp but clean, and I welcome it. It seems to ground me in the here and now instead of back five years ago when my life disintegrated into dust.

I don't know how long I cry, but eventually the tears seem to dry up and my breathing slowly returns to normal, save the occasional hiccup. I lick my lips that are chapped from all the crying, I guess.

"Wh-where are the kids?" are the first words I've spoken since this morning.

"At Mrs. Danzel's. Viv dropped them off."

"You stayed?" I raise my head and look at him questioningly. His eyes are still warm but his jaw is clenched.

"Of course I stayed," he almost growls. "You had a massive shock and you disappeared for a while. Had me worried."

My hand mindlessly strokes his chest and I can feel the friction of his chest hair under his shirt. When my fingers inadvertently brush over his nipple, he hisses and I quickly go to pull my hand back, but he places his hand on mine to keep it in place.

"Even when I shouldn't—when I *know* it's wrong to think of all the things I'd like to do to you—the slightest touch of your hands, a whiff of your scent, can almost make me lose control." His voice is gruff and low, but his eyes are bright and alive. I can feel the heat radiating off him. His words have that flicker of hope I had almost extinguished again, flare to life. He still wants me. *Me*. Despite what I had told him already last night and the news this morning, it didn't appear to make any difference for him.

I have to fight to stave off a new wave of tears and instead, reach for his lips. Soft and tentative on his part, but I won't have it. I want that flame of hope to stay alive, hope that despite the negative spin cycle my thoughts want to swirl in, I am redeemable, so my lips and tongue take. I don't think I've ever kissed this hungrily before. It's as if I want to absorb some of him. My tongue licks along his and although I can feel the struggle he wages to stay in control, his mouth responds to mine with equal hunger, making my body hum.

Too soon he disentangles himself on a groan. "Honey, we need to talk." Right. That's never good news. Not in my experience anyway, but when I move to roll away from him and get up, he holds me back with a hand on my hip. Sitting with my back to him on the side of the bed, I can feel the mattress dipping as he leans toward me, and very softly kisses the small of my back.

"I'll have you soon, little Bird. Very soon. That is, if you'll have me."

Gunnar

It about fucking kills me to pull away from those soft lips, but there is no way in hell I'm able to hold on to my control with her mouth plastered to mine. Her body is battered from the attack and the emotional impact of it is all invisible.

When she suddenly turns away, I know she needs my reassurance. Her body stiffens under my hand when I tell her my intentions and I'm suddenly unsure, knowing she'll likely be unhappy with me after I tell her what I've done.

"Okay," she whispers under her breath.

Taking that for what it is, I slide my legs down to sit beside her. "I asked Viv to contact Pam at the Florence House." I keep my eyes on her to check her reaction. Her lips are thin and when she turns her eyes on me, I can see anger.

"Why?" she asks in a clipped voice.

"Because the doctor's right. Between what you were subjected to last night and the shock of this morning, anyone would be traumatized. Add to that what you've already lived through—and I have a feeling I still don't know the full story—you'll need some help processing. Viv said Pam had been amazing with her. So be mad at me all you want, I don't give a rat's ass, not when it comes to your well-being."

She doesn't say anything but sits still beside me with her head down, eyes focused on some spot on the ground.

Wanting to bridge the distance, I reach for her hand and am relieved when she curls her fingers around mine.

"There are things I can't … I won't talk about. Not with you, and not with Pam." Her voice is soft but her determination evident.

"Then don't. Talk about things you *do* want to talk about. See where it leads."

"Okay. I'll see her." She gives my hand a squeeze before getting up to go to the washroom and I look at her small retreating frame and have to clench my fists to contain the rage that comes surging back. A useless emotion at this point since the man is dead, but still.

Not wanting to allow time for Syd to change her mind, first thing I do is call Viv to see if she can get Pam to come here. I'm all for molding the iron while it's hot. Viv says she was waiting for my call and she'd already spoken to Pam. She doesn't think coming here will be an issue.

Now I need to sort the kids out and get some dinner going.

When Viv announces herself over an hour later with a knock on the door, we are just finishing up dinner. The kids agreed to stay at Mrs. Danzel's for the night, albeit under protest. I'm picking them up early tomorrow morning so they can get ready for school at home. Didn't think it would be a good idea to have them around when Pam is coming to talk.

Syd seems to shrink in on herself when I get up to get the door.

"Hey," Viv says as she walks through the door. A tall black woman with a stern expression, but warm eyes right behind her. "This is Pam. Pam, meet Gunnar."

I grab the hand she points in my direction and I'm surprised at the strong grip. Pam's eyes are assessing and I feel like a fucking bug under the microscope.

"You got somewhere to be?" Pam asks me in a rich, deep voice.

"Nope. Not planning on going anywhere," I answer a tad curt.

"Well, I suggest you find somewhere 'cause having you hovering over her isn't gonna make this any easier."

Wait a minute ... am I being dismissed?

"You kicking me out of my own house?" I look between Viv and Pam. Viv's mouth is twitching and Pam is just staring me down. "Can't fucking believe this ..." I mumble as I walk back into the kitchen where Syd still sits at the table and crouch down in front of her.

"Pam's kicking me out of my own goddamn house, but I'll stay. All you have to do is say the word, even though she scares me a little."

The sound of Syd's soft chuckle makes me feel a little better about leaving her. She's obviously not quite as intimidated by Pam.

"Okay, if you're sure. I'll head over and do some work at The Skipper, so just call me when you need me, or whatever."

"I'll be fine," Syd says, putting her hand on my face. I lean in and give her a quick kiss on the lips before grabbing my keys and a jacket, ignoring Viv's pointed looks when I walk out the door. How about that, three women in my house and I'm standing outside. Fucking hell.

I've spent the last hour going over the pub's finances. Business has been decent, despite the lingering cold. Usually at this time of year, we already have the small patio open, but the weather has been too cool. In previous years, I haven't added summer staff until we set up the tables and chairs outside, but given that we are still short a full-timer, and the fact that I want to be able to take more time for the kids now that they're with me, I'm checking to see if we have anyone on file who'd fit in. Summer staff mostly consists of students, but I do have one or two who might be interested in doing a full-time rotation. I pull their numbers and in the next ten minutes have two interviews scheduled for tomorrow morning. The thought of leaving Syd alone tomorrow to tend to business here sticks in my craw, but I have shit to take care of and can't put more on Viv than I already do. I'm fucking tired. The e-mail from my lawyer stating they haven't been able to locate Cindy to serve her with papers just adds to the worries. I hate the bitch, but she's the kids' mom and for their sake, I hope she's okay.

Just as I shut down the computer and prepare to head upstairs to grab Syd some stuff from the apartment, the phone on my desk rings.

"The Skipper."

"Guns—Viv told me you were there," Tim says. "There's some stuff I heard at work today and thought you might want to know." As project coordinator for the City of Portland, he's privy to information on new, planned developments.

"What have you got?" I ask him.

"Demolition permit was issued on Friday for the old warehouse at the other end of the wharf. One guess who's behind it?"

"Graham Bull of Soul Filets would be my guess."

Tim chuckles. "You would be correct. The application for the permit came with proposed plans for a complete gut of the building. Nothing but the walls will be standing when they're done. Looks like you'll have a new neighbor by spring next year."

"At least they're not throwing some shiny new building on the wharf. I'd have hated that. I don't mind a little competition; I think it'll be good for business in the long run. Just not happy with the way Graham Bull sent a lackey to gather information. I'd have gladly talked to him if he'd had the decency to contact me directly. No need for this covert shit."

"He been in again?" Tim wants to know.

"Not since I had a little sit down with him last time. Got the feeling he was being a little overeager in his pursuits 'cause the moment I brought up calling the big boss, he paled a little. Anyway, I'm glad their intentions are public record now. Much easier knowing what I'm dealing with." I can't hide the yawn that escapes me and Tim is quick to react.

"I just wanted to give you the heads up. I can hear you're tired, but before I go, how's Syd doing?"

"She's tough. That cop, Winslow? He came this morning to inform her that the guy had died overnight. It almost did her in. Totally spaced out on hearing that bit of news, but she's almost too casual about it now. That worries me. Viv called in this counselor she had met at the shelter we found her at. They're at the house now, trying to get Syd to talk some."

"Must've killed you to leave her." I can hear the smile in Tim's voice and call him on it.

"Fuck off. Went against my nature, to be honest, but I've gotta be careful with her. She was violated, Tim. Fucking guy had her bent over a table and was ready to stick his dick where his fingers had already done damage. If it hadn't been for Syd bleeding in my arms, I would've gone back in there and fucking castrated the motherfucker." It feels good letting some of my pent-up anger out; a little bit of pressure off.

"Son of a bitch," Tim hisses. "That poor girl. Give her my best and I'll let you get home. Need anything in the coming days?"

"Nah, if you have a chance, pop in for a drink." I suggest.

"Will do, and Guns? You sound pretty gone for her."

My instinct is to call bullshit, but I'd be lying, so I answer honestly. "Seems that way."

It's nearly eleven at night when I pull into my driveway. I grab the bag of clothes and toiletries I grabbed from Syd's apartment and head inside where I find Pam already gone and Viv sitting on the couch by herself.

"Hey," she says as I walk in.

"Hey yourself. Where is everyone?"

"Pam just left. She'll be back tomorrow and I just finished tucking Syd in your bed." Viv's eyes fill with tears. "God, Gunnar. That woman has been through hell and back, and not just once. It's a miracle she's still standing."

I knew that. At some level, I knew she'd seen hell and then some, but I seem to have pushed that down. And for good reason. With Viv's words, a wave of nausea hits me and I just manage to get to the can before dinner makes a reappearance. Viv comes in behind me, hands me a wet kitchen towel and rubs her hand over my back.

"Sorry 'bout that," I mumble.

"No worries. Had to leave the room a few times myself. She's so fucking contained, I can't stand it. Said a few times that she really doesn't deserve any better, which pisses me off as much as it worries me. I offered to leave her and Pam to it, but Syd just kept hold of my hand, willing me to stay on the couch beside her. She carries some heavy load that I don't think we've seen the full extent of yet."

I look at the tears rolling down Viv's face and pull her in for a hug. "She's got a good friend in you, honey."

"Yeah, well, I wish I could do more," she mumbles against my shirt.

"Me too, honey. Me fucking too."

Viv decides to stay the night in Emmy's room, not wanting to be alone, and I try to go to sleep in Dex's bed, but I'm restless. It isn't until I slide into my own bed behind Syd, my arms tucking her to me, that I finally find some rest. The little bird in my arms doesn't even wake up.

syd

When I wake up, instant panic seizes me when I feel arms banded around my body. I struggle to get free until I hear Gunnar's voice by my neck.

"Easy does it. It's me, and you're safe. Gonna let you go now." Slowly he relaxes his arms from around me, but I don't move. I take a minute to catch my breath before gingerly turning my body to face him. Stiffness has set in overnight, but I feel clearheaded now. His eyes are heavy lidded with sleep still, but completely focused on mine.

Rolling over on his back, he slips one arm behind his head and with the other, rolls me on top of him. My hands find the soft bristle of hair on his chest and I push off to take him in. Thick salt and pepper hair that is never quite in place is now sticking out in every direction. The perpetual scruff on his jaw, framing his strong, full lips. Heavy eyebrows that accentuate his deep set, observant green eyes and a mostly straight, rather prominent nose that seems to have seen a bit of abuse, judging from the bump about halfway down. Not a beautiful face, but a striking one.

He doesn't say anything, but a little smile curves his lips as I slide my eyes down the strong column of his neck to the graying chest hair that starts at the base. I follow the trail my hand makes over his pecs, skimming his nipple, until it rests on his toned abdomen. There is no way I can ignore the thick head of his erection trying to escape the confines of his boxer briefs, but oddly it doesn't scare me. No. I'm surprised to find myself turned on, and although Gunnar hasn't moved during my exploration, his breathing is a bit more erratic and he appears as affected as I am. Tentatively, I slide my hand down to where my fingers are lightly stroking the head of his cock. A light twitch and his sharp intake of breath are evidence he's well aware of my touch.

It's powerful, this ability to freely explore a man's body without feeling any threat. To feel it responding to your touch—reacting to *you*. A stronger and much bigger man allowing you control over his body. How very different it is ... and arousing.

When my fingers slide under his waistband and wrap around the soft steel of his cock, he groans softly as I carefully pull him free. My thumb slides over the broad head, rubbing the moisture leaking from the slit. Gunnar takes a deep breath in and releases his other arm from around me, slipping it behind his head as well. His eyes are shiny slits and his jaw is clenched as he looks down at me, giving himself over completely. With one hand working down his sweats over his hips and the other slowly pumping his shaft, I lean in for a taste. I was never big on blowjobs, but I want him in my mouth—at my mercy. My tongue traces around the ridge and along the slit and my lips close around the tip, sucking lightly and eliciting another groan from Gunnar's lips. It encourages me to take as much of his cock in my mouth as I can with one hand firmly at its base and the other seeking out his balls to roll in my hand. The musky taste of him on my tongue and the girth of him stretching my lips has me moan deep in my throat.

"Keep that up and I'm gonna come in your mouth," he grunts out in a strangled voice.

So I moan again before sucking hard as I let him slide back out of my mouth, causing him to hiss. Looking up at him, I see his mouth has fallen open and his eyes are on fire, and I realize I want to make him come, to make him fall apart at my will. With renewed vigor, I work my mouth and my hands in tandem, hearing the effect I have on him in his erratic breathing.

I can feel when he is almost there; the tightening of his balls in my hand and the rigid feel of his cock in my mouth. When I take him as deep as I can, I swallow on the tip while at the same time tugging on his balls. My eyes never leave his as he jerks in my mouth on a loud grunt and pulses streams of his seed down my throat. Mouth now wide open and eyes barely visible, he twitches and shudders under my hands. I swallow everything he gives me before letting him slide out from between my lips, laying my head on his hip to face him.

When his breathing finally slows down a little, he lifts one hand from behind his head and reaches down to brush the hair off my forehead. The first time he actively touches me and it strikes me how well he reads me. I needed this to take back control.

"Thank you," I whisper, causing his eyes to widen slightly.

"I should be thanking you. Amazing. It killed me not to touch you, but I wanted you to feel free to take what you needed. Guess I never figured how much I needed that myself."

I crawl up to lie by his side and he turns his head to face me, tracing his hand from my shoulder down to my hip.

"I'd love nothing more than to bury my face between your legs right now and not come up for air for days, but I'm taking your lead. You'll tell me when you're ready?" He almost seems tentative asking.

"You trusted enough to let me take control and it was exactly what I needed—what I wanted. I loved doing that to you and it turned me on. I'm still turned on, but I want to carry that feeling with me for a while—let it settle in and build. Being aroused is a victory for me. It's been many years since I've felt anything close to this. It makes me feel alive."

Leaning in, I brush my lips against his in a sweet kiss before drawing back and looking him in the eye.

"You're a beautiful man, Gunnar Lucas. And you don't look half-bad, either."

His deep chuckle follows me as I get up to go to the bathroom, warming me from the inside out.

CHAPTER SIXTEEN

Syd

"What have you got planned for your special?"

It's almost one o'clock on Thursday as Dino walks into the kitchen, straight over to the large pot I have sitting on the stove. "Smells fucking phenomenal."

"Shrimp and pork jambalaya," I tell him, smiling when he grabs a spoon and dives in for a taste.

I've missed cooking. It's been a couple of weeks and I'm glad to be back in the saddle so to speak. Last week Gunnar took me back to see the doctor who removed the stitches and declared me healthy, other than my ribs which might be sore for a bit yet, according to him. Gunnar hadn't been pleased when I announced I wanted to be back in the apartment, but I was adamant. Oh, the temptation to stay with him and the kids was huge, but my daily sessions with Pam made it clear that I still had some work to do on me. And I couldn't focus on me if I was constantly focused on him and the children. Waking up in his bed every morning with his arms wrapped tightly around me is something I missed, but the constant state of arousal I walked around with was starting to get to me. It was something I discussed with Pam and she suggested a bit of distance. Nothing more than a few kisses had happened between us since that morning, but it was getting harder to ignore his prominent morning wood waking up. Pam said that if I still felt I had to hold out, I probably wasn't ready. She said I should trust myself to know when.

The entire time, Gunnar had been true to his word, never pushing for anything and simply waiting for me to make a move. When that move was to go back to my apartment, I could tell he was disappointed, but he helped me pack up and dropped me off all the same. He cares for me. I can tell in everything he does. But I don't want to run the risk of making myself at home in his life when I still haven't found the courage to confront all of my demons. Pam's been prodding around the edges of what is holding me back and seems to know I haven't come clean completely. I know it's a matter of time before all will come out. I just don't know what I will be left with after it does, and I don't want to hurt anyone else.

The guilt I carry as a cloak seems less heavy now than ever before. I'm sure the sessions with Pam have helped. She pointed out that if anyone I cared for had been threatened, I wouldn't have thought twice about defending them, regardless of the outcome, yet when it comes to having defended myself, I can only focus on my perceived responsibility in the outcome. I'm starting to listen and even believe my actions may have been justified.

I've been back above The Skipper for a week now and back at work since then, even though Gunnar forced modified duties on me. Actually, he didn't have to push hard when he asked if I would consider doing the books for him. I frankly jumped at the chance. It's been good. I've been able to create some space in the budget, enough to pay the new cleaning crew who now come in before opening and whip through the place in an hour. Viv or I still pitch in during the day when necessary, but only with a quick wipe down.

Gunnar also managed to get one of last year's summer part-timers to come in full-time. Leanne just finished college but isn't sure yet what to do with her degree. A sweet and bubbly girl, she seems to fit in quite well. With Matt behind the bar permanently and Leanne serving, the rest of us can jump in and out as needed.

Emmy and Dex still come in after school each day, but now instead of hanging in the kitchen the whole time, I take them upstairs to my apartment to do their homework there. A little less distraction for them. We eat jointly in the kitchen and Gunnar tries to join as much as he can. He's been able to take them home at around seven most nights, leaving him the entire evening with them. He seems to be less stressed, so it's working for now. Come summer, when they're off, will be another thing, but that won't be for another month or so.

"This stuff is great. Did you use cumin?" Dino's voice draws me back to the present and the large man spooning a bowlful of jambalaya.

"Yes, actually; cumin, and a hint of cardamom along with the cayenne and brown sugar."

"Mmmm." He mumbles as he sits down at the kitchen table, digging into his bowl.

"Food!" Matt walks into the kitchen behind me, grabbing a bowl on his way to the stove. Gunnar isn't far behind him, and before you know it, the kitchen table has everyone but Viv sitting around it, putting a good dent in my Thursday Special. With a smile on my face, I head down the hall to the bar to see if Viv needs some help now that she's been left to run The Skipper by herself.

"Where the hell did everyone go?" she asks when she sees me.

"Having a taste test in the kitchen." I giggle at the look of disbelief on her face.

"Typical fucking men. Stomach first, responsibilities after," she says, shaking her head. "They better be leaving some for me."

I'm getting a kick out of the positive feedback on my cooking. That and the now familiar sense of belonging makes me almost happy, but I never lose the niggling feeling that someday, when they learn all there is to know about me, I'll be rejected the same way my own family rejected me.

Stopping at the few occupied tables, I clear off plates and take drink orders, the smile still lingering on my face. That is, until Sergeant Winslow walks in, heading straight for me.

"Ms. Donner, could I have a word?"

I turn to the patrons at the table, a family with a little baby who look a little uncomfortable. "Please excuse me for a minute while I help this gentleman?"

With a "Sure" and a "Go ahead," I lead the cop to Gunnar's office, letting him step in before I close the door and turn to face him.

"How dare you walk in here like that, putting a scarlet letter on my chest in front of the customers." I'm incensed at the blatant show of disrespect. Not so much for myself, but for what it could do for The Skipper if rumors started flying. We've had enough speculation fly around the wharf since the attack; last thing we need is law enforcement enhancing those.

"Well now, it would appear our *victim* has grown some claws," Winslow almost sneers.

He's making a mistake if he thinks he can intimidate me. Oh, he might've, even as little as three weeks ago, but what he doesn't realize is that I didn't come out of the attack a victim, I came out a survivor. Something that has only been enforced in the past few weeks and I'll be damned if I let him undermine that.

"Survivor, not victim," I set him straight. "Now what can I help you with that was urgent enough to haul me away from customers?" I make no effort to conceal the sarcasm. He doesn't seem to take the bait.

"You have a knack for surviving, don't you, Ms. Donner? First, you appear out of nowhere, even though you and I both know you were here all along, living in the shed. The one that *happened* to burn down? I recognize burns when I see them, and the ones on your hands seem fairly fresh. Then you are supposedly attacked by a man you say tried to rape you. A man who happens to end up dead by your hands."

I should've recognized the evil gleam in his eyes, but still I'm shocked when he continues.

"Not the first time you've had blood on your hands, is it, Ms. Donner?" Looking very pleased with himself at the pain I feel pulling at my face, he tilts his head to the side. "Did you really think I wouldn't look a little deeper? Since you appeared on the scene, I have an unexplained fire and a dead man. All a tad too coincidental for my liking. My superiors may have decided yours was a clear-cut case of self-defense and are telling me to back down, but I'm warning you; I have my eye on you."

And then I snap.

"You sanctimonious, self-righteous, son of a bitch! Look all you want, you asshole! Feel big now, do you? All big and threatening to a woman half the size of your fat ass and still bearing the injuries of an attack? Yeah, you're a hero all right, Sergeant Winslow. A real fucking protector of the innocent." I know I'm yelling, but I can't seem to stop myself. Yanking open the door, I hold my arm out. "If that's all, then get the fuck out!"

All he has done is smirk at me, but when I open the door and point at it, his face straightens. From behind me I hear, "Better do as she fucking says," in the deceptively calm rumble of Gunnar's voice. He must've walked up when he heard the shouting and steps up to my back, slipping his arm around my waist to anchor my shaking body. "And if I see you here again, I'll get your ass suspended so fast you won't know what hit you."

Winslow's eyebrows shoot up. "Are you threatening an officer of the law, Mr. Lucas?"

Stepping around my body, pushing me behind him, Gunnar gets up in the officer's face. "You've got that right. And I dare you to try me. Don't underestimate me, Winslow. You have no idea of the kind of connections I have."

Appearing a bit shaken now, Winslow throws me a last glare as he walks out of the office without saying another word.

Gunnar

What the fuck? When Viv came running into the kitchen, telling me to get my ass in the office, I had no idea I'd find Syd yelling at the cop. She was doing a decent job at dressing him down by the sounds of it. It was a bit of a turn on to hear her stand up for herself, but it didn't stop the anger from coursing through my body and I had to hold myself back from storming in there and laying the bastard out. Should've guessed he'd be sniffing around again. For some damn reason, he's decided to be a pain in my ass since the fire, but coming after Syd like this? My patience has finally run out.

"You okay, Bird?" I ask her, watching her try to compose herself.

"Fucking asshat."

I can't hold back the chuckle, the language incongruent with the pretty little mouth on the small woman in front of me. She stands with her legs slightly spread, shoulders pulled up to her ears and her fists clenched by her side. If the furious glare at Winslow's retreating back is anything to go by, the man just made a serious enemy. When I reach out for her, she whips around to face me and I can see her eyes go from burning with anger, to burning with something else altogether.

Without further thought, I pull her against me and slam my mouth on hers in an adrenaline-filled kiss. At some point, she must've unclenched her fists because I can feel her small hands sliding under my shirt and up my back, sending shivers over my skin. So fucking good. My own hand slides down to cup her ass while the other tangles in her long hair, pulling her head back. I slide my mouth along her jaw and down her neck to the pulse point where I latch on, breathing and tasting her. She exhales on a groan and pulls herself closer into my body, rubbing her tits against my chest and her groin into my raging hard-on.

Fuck, she turns me on. So deceivingly fragile, but with a core of steel.

I clutch my hand on her ass, which has filled out nicely over the last few weeks. I like the curves on her. With my mouth taking claim of hers again, my other hand finds the swell of her tit, her puckered nipple rolling in the palm of my hand, and this time it's me who groans.

Tongues tangling and hands groping, neither of us hear anything but the other's breathing until we are interrupted by a sharp clearing of the throat.

"Oops. Sorry I barged in."

I swing my head around just in time to see Leanne backing out of the office. Keeping my arm securely around Syd, I turn to face her.

"What's up?" I ask Leanne. who's blushing a bright red.

"Erm ... I just wanted to ask if I could leave a little early tonight, but it can wait." And before I can respond, she's gone.

I look down at Syd, but her face is obscured by her hair. Her shoulders are shaking and concerned she might be upset, I brush the curls off her face only to find her laughing silently.

"What's so funny?" I smile at her when her eyes meet mine.

"You. Me. Dancing tentatively around each other for weeks and shared anger is what finally breaks through the standoff and ignites the spark."

With eyes that look sparkling blue and a wide smile on her lush lips, I swear I've not seen her this beautiful. Her hand comes to rest on my chest and I clasp it between us as I swing her flush against me, bending my head down to hers.

"Make no mistake. That spark was lit a long time ago, but I'd like nothing better than to let it burn free."

Her pupils darken and her tongue slips out to lick her plump bottom lip, drawing my eyes to her mouth. I have to taste her again.

"We have customers," she mumbles against my lips and I reluctantly pull away.

"I want to come see you after closing tonight." My voice sounds hoarse with the effort of holding back. I'd love to slam the door shut, lock it, and use my hands and mouth to learn her body before sliding my cock into her. The thought alone is making me even harder. I adjust myself to relieve the strain against my fly, which makes Syd giggle and hide her face in my chest. I love that sound and I'd love to hear more of it, but first I need to know what Winslow wanted. Almost forgot about that bastard.

"What did he want—Winslow?"

I see hesitation and maybe even guilt as she turns her head away, but I cup her face and turn it back to me.

"Talk to me." I urge, watching resignation settle on her features.

"It's nothing, he ... he suggested I must have some responsibility for the fire and the attack. He claims it's too much of a coincidence." My jaw clenches and she hurries to continue.

"He knows I was in the shed that night, Gunnar. He noticed the burns and made a calculated guess."

I grab hold of her hands, which still bear the faint scars of the burns she sustained.

"I'll put a call in. I wasn't kidding when I told him I have connections. The Chief of Police was a good friend of my father's."

Syd shakes her head. "He mentioned he was told by the brass to back down already. I think he just wants to stir up trouble. He'd done some digging into my past and made sure I knew it." Her voice softens with those last words and I have to strain to hear them.

"Still gonna call, especially now that I know he had no grounds to be here."

She burrows her head against my chest and whispers, "I'm scared."

"Why?" I ask her gently, already suspecting the answer.

"Because what he found out could ruin everything."

"This is about what you've been holding back, isn't it?" When she nods, I stroke her hair. "Syd, there is nothing he could tell me that would change what's going on here, but whatever it is, I'd much rather hear it from you." I kiss the top of her head and can barely hear her soft response.

"I know."

Syd

"You're sleeping on your feet. Get out of here, we can manage." Viv waves a tea towel in my direction as she tries to shoo me out of the kitchen.

It's been a long-ass busy day. Thursdays generally are, with the all-you-can-eat menu. Even with all hands on deck, we've all been running around with barely any time for breaks. I had the kids up in my apartment until Mrs. Danzel came to pick them up, and she's keeping them overnight; something Gunnar arranged on Thursdays because it's the busiest night of the week. She also drops them off at school on Friday mornings.

Haven't had a chance to think much either—not about Winslow's visit earlier or the inevitable *talk* I'm going to have to have with Gunnar. I know I have to. It seems unavoidable the truth will come out now and I'd rather not be surprised by his reaction, but face it straight on. From the moment Viv pulled me from the dumpster out back, part of me has known that this day would come. I'd just hoped I would have some time before it all came to a head. And it might have been possible, if not for the assault. Rape—I should start calling it like it is, or was, rather. Pam has been hammering into me to stop hiding behind pretty words, to stop avoiding things just because they may be uncomfortable. She's been great; calling me out on every evasive answer and not letting me get away with a single thing. She forces me to talk out my feelings of guilt at having taken a life, but at the same time manages to persuade me to see it was a sequence of events I didn't set in motion. It helped finding out it was likely not Jack's first sexual assault. He'd been charged three years ago, but the woman he assaulted had dropped the charges and moved away. Despite the relative ease with which I'm able to discuss everything that happened in the past six weeks, she knows there is something I've been holding back. And even though we've talked about loss, about losing a child, in particular, I haven't opened up all the way yet. After my initial adamant refusal to discuss anything pre-dating my time at The Skipper, she has been able to chip away at my past, revealing bits and pieces by asking innocuous questions. She knows I was in an unhappy marriage. She also knows I have a sister and parents I never speak to. The only thing she doesn't know is what is at the root of my estrangement; what started my downhill path. Or maybe she does—maybe she's guessed. Either way, it seems she won't be the first one to hear it from my mouth. It would appear that dubious honor will be Gunnar's, and it makes me nervous.

Even though it's only eight o'clock and there are still diners, the crowd has thinned some, which is why I decide to follow Viv's suggestion. I'm sure Gunnar will show up as promised after closing and I welcome some time to try and sort my thoughts before he comes.

Upstairs I take a quick shower after checking the entire apartment first. It's something I do now since being back here. The hot spray goes a long way to washing the tension from my shoulders but makes me even sleepier. I dry myself off, towel dry my hair and with the towel wrapped around me, lie back on the bed, just for a minute.

I wake up at some point during the night to the feel of Gunnar's solid body pinning me to the bed in what has become a familiar way. One arm serving as my pillow and his other one wrapped tight around my waist, his leg hiked up over mine. My body is tilted toward the mattress and it's difficult to move without waking him. He obviously found me asleep when he came in and decided to crawl into bed with me.

With my bladder about to explode, I wiggle myself out from under his body and leave the towel that has come loose during the night. Darting into the bathroom, I quickly pee before flushing and washing my hands. Tiptoeing over to the dresser to grab something to wear, the deep rumble of Gunnar's voice startles me. "Come back to bed." Painfully aware that I am stark naked and backlit by the bathroom light, I grab the first thing I can find.

"Just let me put this on," I mumble, trying to find the right end to the shirt so I can pull it over my head.

"Don't," he says simply. "Been waiting to feel your skin against mine. Just let me feel you."

His eyes are luminous orbs in the dark room and the lust in them is unmistakable. I should probably feel apprehensive, but I'm surprised to find myself growing more confident under his study. When I start moving toward the bed, Gunnar flips back the covers, revealing his broad chest, dusted in dark hair with a few silver strands. My eyes follow the trail that runs down to the waistband of the boxer briefs I'm relieved to find him wearing. His gaze burns a tingle on my skin as it traces down my body. I barely get a chance to slide into bed when his arms reach out for me and pull me on top of his body. I can feel the press of his prominent erection against my stomach and it doesn't feel like a threat—more of a promise of what he could do to me. I can't help but rub myself against him restlessly.

"Mmmm," his voice rumbles in his chest. "Don't know if I can just hold you, Bird."

CHAPTER SEVENTEEN

Syd

"Maybe I don't want you to …"

I push myself up and look him straight in the eyes. "Maybe I want you to do to my body what your eyes are promising." With a hand that is slightly shaking, I find the elastic waistband on his boxer briefs and start tugging it down. A lift of his hips off the bed, and they slip down far enough for his erection to spring free.

His large hands slide down to clutch tightly at my ass and I feel my own arousal slipping from between my legs. Sliding one hand down to grab my leg, he pulls it over his hips so I'm straddling him, rubbing my wetness over his cock. The friction of his hard length slipping and sliding between my pussy lips makes me throw my head back and ride.

"Look at me, Bird. Gotta see your eyes," he rumbles; his breathing a little labored. "You run this show, babe, but give me your eyes. I need you here with me."

His hands slightly cup my ass where I sit on his crotch and lift me up. Looking him in the eyes, I can see he is struggling to hold back and I know why he is giving me the reins. I can tell he will be a forceful and demanding lover once he lets go and he is allowing me to move at my pace. I can't wait to tap into that barely contained passion burning in his eyes. But for now, I slide a hand between our bodies and with my gaze firmly fixed on his, I slip my hand around his slick, hard cock and align myself so the crown is poised at my entrance. Leaning forward a little, I touch my mouth to his in a sweet kiss.

"There is no fear with you, only feelings so deep, I'm overwhelmed." With that, I slide myself carefully onto his shaft. The stretch of my tissues from lack of use burns a little but the feeling of fullness steals my breath. My eyes don't waver from Gunnar's face as his mouth slacks open and a deep rumbling groan escapes. His fingers clutch at my ass cheeks and I know I'll have his finger marks to carry with me for days. I don't care. I want him to mark me. I love feeling the barely restrained strength and passion—seeing the effect I have on him by the fire in his eyes and the clench of his jaw. It's powerful to be able to drive someone to the brink of losing all control. And I know he hangs on desperately for me, trying with everything he has to let me reclaim my body.

Slowly, I lift myself and slide back down again, carefully at first and slightly uncoordinated. Gunnar's hands settle on my hips and gently control my rise and fall on his cock, his eyes following its slide in and out of my body.

"Beautiful," he mutters between pants. "Need to have your taste on my lips." His head lifts up further and with one hand behind my back, guiding me toward him, he latches his wide-open mouth onto my breast, his brow lined with intensity. He sucks on me so hard and deep, I can't hold back a deep moan as I feel that pull of his mouth travel all the way down to the walls of my pussy.

"Gunnar ... please."

"What do you need, Syd. Tell me." The words are mumbled around my nipple, urging me.

"Please ... please take over. Take me. Fuck me ..." The plea has not left my lips before he has me lifted off and rolled under his big body. I feel no threat. I am in this moment with him and need to show him by letting him take charge. I want him to.

Lifting one of my legs in the crook of his elbow, he spreads me open and in one strong move, slides balls deep inside me.

Gunnar

The clench of her jaw and the hiss of air from her mouth has me freeze up the moment my balls hit her ass.

"Syd? You okay?" I have to ask, fighting the urge to ram myself into the tight grasp of her pussy over and over again.

"Don't stop. Please don't stop." Her bright eyes plead with me, but the brimming tears bring me to a halt.

"I'm hurting you."

"No. Feeling your hunger is beautiful and unfamiliar, so please, let me have it all." Her hand has come up to stroke along my jaw as she lifts her lips to mine. "Give me everything," she whispers against my mouth.

Eyes locked and lips molded together, I let go. With deep strokes, I piston my hips into the cradle of hers and give her what she asks for, and that's everything. There is nothing in my head and heart but this moment; Syd's giving and my claiming. More than the primal fusing of bodies, it's an opening of the heart. Something I feel deeply when she allows me to see everything in her eyes. I see heat, love, a hint of vulnerability, and beyond all that, a deep trust that I know I'm privileged to receive. I can't turn away and lower my forehead to hers as her hands grab my ass and her sharp little nails pull me deeper inside of her.

It doesn't take much, the tension between us having built to a burning need. I feel the tell-tale tingle down my spine a moment before my balls tighten in warning.

"Come with me," I grunt out as my thumb finds that tight little button right above where my cock slides into her. One firm roll over her clit and I can feel the onset of her orgasm spasm against my shaft. With her mouth slack and her eyes rolling back, she gives herself over. Unable to hold back, my movements become erratic as I pump my own release into her body, groaning out her name.

"Ohmigod ..." Syd breathes out, wrapping her arms and legs around me. I can't do anything but grunt my confirming thoughts with my face buried into her neck, the mane of hair tickling my face. When I catch my breath, I try to roll off her, afraid it'll be too much, but she holds firm. "Don't go. Your weight on me feels secure—safe."

I'm still unable to form a coherent word and simply lie sprawled on top of Syd, my dick going soft inside her and my release slipping out, but I still can't bring myself to move. I realize we haven't taken any precautions, too wrapped up in the moment and I'm surprised I'm not worried. You'd think I'd be smarter than that, but I know I'm clean as of last check—and Syd's been thoroughly checked out in the hospital. There is no way I'll ever regret what just happened. The thought of her in the hospital makes me aware that I'm resting my much heavier body on her healing one and I quickly roll over, shifting so I have her on top of me. She tucks her head under my chin and settles there snugly.

It's not long before I hear her breathing deepen as she falls asleep, just as the cries of the gulls outside mark the onset of morning.

The smell of coffee hits my nostrils and wakes me up to Syd sitting on the edge of the bed, a coffee mug in her hand.

"Morning," I croak out, running a hand through my bed head and taking in all that is her. There is something tentative about her this morning, somehow even more vulnerable than what I saw in her eyes when I was deeply settled inside her.

"Hey," she responds softly and my hand slides under the cover to adjust my cock. The response to her is instinctive and immediate, but I sense this is not the time to give in to my baser needs. I pull myself up in the bed and settle back against the headboard, accepting the coffee she hands me.

"What time is it?"

"Nine thirty. We slept in a little," she says with a small smile.

"Mmmm's good," I mumble, sipping the strong dark brew. Looking at her over the rim of my mug, I can tell she's gearing up to talk and I don't want to push, so I stay silent.

"I'm scared," she says softly, "but I need to tell you something before someone else does." She sits ramrod straight and when I try to reach for her, she shifts out of my way.

"Hey," I try. "Don't move away. Look at me. Let me touch you." She shakes her head and keeps her eyes fixed on the floor.

Freya Barker   FROM DUST

"Please don't touch me right now. You may not want to once I'm done and I don't want to look at you and see your reaction. It's easier this way."

I have to admit, she is freaking me out a little, but I do as she asks and keep my distance. The ringing of my phone on the nightstand interrupts this odd standoff, but I choose to ignore it. This is more important right now.

Funny, there simply isn't anything I can imagine her telling me that would make a difference in how I view her. Not even the fact she used alcohol to self-medicate was enough to turn me away, despite my negative associations with alcohol abuse. I've got fuck-all, but from her body language—the way she's making herself as small as possible with her head down and shoulders turned in—I can tell it's huge for her.

She's wringing her hands in her lap and swallowing hard, but before she gets a chance to say anything, my phone goes off again and she nods toward it.

"Better take that, could be the kids."

Right. Fuck.

I quickly scan the display and see it's Dex's school. I can't ignore this. Something might have happened.

"Lucas."

"Mr. Lucas, this is Wendy McMaster, a student counselor at Reiche Elementary? I have Dexter here in my office and his mother in with the principal. I'm afraid she wanted to take her son with her and had signed him out, but he's not wanting to go, insisting we call you?"

I feel the anger amping up my blood pressure. Something must've shown, because I feel Syd's hand on my shoulder and when I look at her, I see concern in her eyes.

"Glad you did. His mother disappeared weeks ago and I've filed for sole custody. She obviously, finally received the

200

paperwork. I'd like to ask you to keep him in your office until I can get there? I'll be ten minutes."

I stand up, letting Syd's hand slide off my shoulder and go in search of my jeans.

"Mr. Lucas, perhaps you should come through the gym? I'm sorry if I'm being presumptuous, but your wife—"

"Ex-wife," I correct her a bit curt.

"Right, my apologies. Dexter's mother is not quiet. It was quite a scene earlier. I was just thinking you might want to avoid her?"

"Ms. McMaster, was it? I'm not afraid of a confrontation. Simply keep Dex with you until I get there. I'm on my way." I hit end on the phone and toss it on the bed, close the buttons on my jeans, and grab for my shirt.

"Is it bad?" Syd stands by the bed, wringing her hands. I forgot for a minute how invested she has become in my kids. Hit with a stab of guilt, I walk up to her, hold her upper arms, and bend down to face her.

"Cindy showed up out of the blue at Dex's school, wanting to pull him out. He did the right thing and had them call me, but she's still making a ruckus, apparently."

I feel Syd's shoulders square up under my hands and the look on her face spells thunder.

"Gotta go, babe. And fuck if I'm not pissed that even at a distance she can fuck up my life. I wanted you to talk to me. Please don't back out now—I'll be back soon." I give her a hard kiss before she can say anything and head for the stairs. Halfway down, I can hear her footsteps behind me and when I turn around, she's standing at the top of the steps looking down.

"I won't be long," I tell her.

"I'm coming."

"Syd, I don't think—"

"I'm coming. While you deal with that unbelievable piece of work, I'll be making sure Dex is all right." She stands with her arms crossed and one hip jutted out; her mouth a straight line, making it clear she won't budge. Fuck me.

"You're coming. On the back of my bike." I tell her resuming my trek down the stairs, but not before I see her eyes go big and I turn quickly to hide the smile on my face.

Syd

"Hey, honey. You okay?"

I walk into the student counselor's office to see Dex sitting on a couch, sniffling. The moment my butt hits the seat beside him, he throws himself into my arms. It breaks my heart.

After a thrilling, but short ride on Gunnar's bike to his house where we picked up the truck, he drove us to the school. He guides me through the gym entrance to avoid Cindy, who is apparently still in the front office, demanding to take Dex with her. Knocking on the Student Services door, he quickly identifies himself and introduces me to Wendy McMaster, who guides me into her office while Gunnar heads off to deal with his ex.

"I'm sorry," Dex sobs, "I don't wanna go with her anymore. She just showed up and wanted me to go with her. I like it at Dad's—I wanna stay there." He blows his nose with the fistful of tissues I tuck in his hand, my arm still around his shoulders.

"Don't you be sorry about this, Dex. You did the right thing and I'm sure your dad's gonna tell you the same thing as soon as he has a chance."

For a while, we just sit there, my arm around him and his whole body leaning into me, his head on my shoulder. Ms. McMaster has disappeared into the outer office, leaving us alone.

"Why is she like that, Syd? My mom?" The small voice startles me out of my thoughts.

"I don't know, buddy. Sometimes people don't see what is right in front of them until it's missing, and when they try to turn back the clock, they find that it's impossible. You can't go back, but you can go forward, it's just hard sometimes to know how. I think that maybe your mom is having a hard time moving forward. I'm sure she doesn't mean to confuse and hurt you guys, or if she's even aware she's doing it, but don't give up on her. Everyone should be given a chance to do better. We all at least deserve to try."

Dex snuggles in a little closer and I look over his shoulder to find Gunnar standing in the doorway, a wealth of emotions shining in his eyes, but with a small smile playing on his lips.

"Ready, kid?"

Dex, who just now notices his dad, jumps up and runs straight to his dad, who lifts him up. With his arms around Gunnar's neck, I hear him whisper, "Sorry," and Gunnar squeezes his eyes shut.

"You've got nothing to be sorry for. This has nothing to do with you, kiddo. Sometimes adults are not so good at dealing with their problems and they draw kids into them. You did the right thing, telling them to call me. Proud of you, kid." He plants a kiss on Dex's hair.

"That's what Syd said you'd say."

Gunnar's eyes find mine. "Syd's exactly right."

The words from his mouth are more than a response to Dex. I can see it in his eyes. Talking to Dex, he is *speaking* to me.

"Having fun?" Gunnar's deep rumble comes from behind me as I struggle to get bait on my line.

We had picked up Emmy from school right after getting Dex. Gunnar had said he fully expected Cindy to go to her high school after and we hurried over before she'd have a chance to create a scene there as well. Gunnar hadn't discussed what happened during his confrontation with his ex, but his focus was on his kids.

After getting Emmy dismissed for the day for a *family emergency,* he piled us in the truck and drove to Casco Bay, only stopping to pick up some cheap fishing poles and food for a picnic.

I worried about the pub, but he said he'd call Leanne in early and would give Viv and Dino a heads up. After giving those two assurances we would be back before the evening rush, he grabbed my hand in the truck and didn't let go again.

We've had our lunch and I'm trying my hand at fishing while the kids are playing around the lighthouse. Fishing is apparently a skill I'm not blessed with, because every time I feel a nibble, I find my bait eaten, but no fish on the line. Gunnar chuckles each time I reel in to find nothing on my hook, while he pulls in fish after fish, only to release them immediately.

"Yes," I answer, "despite the fact that we've established I can't catch fish if my life depended on it, I'm having a good time. You?" I turn to find him watching me with a smile on his face, something I've seen him do a lot of today. Looks good on him.

"After the rocky start, I'm having the best day I've had in a long time," he says earnestly. "We needed a family day."

The look he throws me is almost a challenge to question his wording, but I don't. I feel it. A sense of belonging with this man and his kids. No words have been spoken, but I know his feelings for me must run deep. It has been evident in his every action, and I know I've fallen hard, for all three of them.

Suddenly, I realize how much I have to lose and my breath sticks in my throat.

"Hey ... what's wrong? You're white as a ghost." Gunnar is beside me in an instant and tilts my face to his. "You sick?"

All I can do is shake my head *no* as I try to stave off the panic that's come over me. "Not sick. This day was wonderful. I was just thinking how much I suddenly have to lose. I had no such worries for the longest time and now ..." I let the sentence trail off and lift my eyes to his face.

"Syd," he says softly, sweeping a strand of hair from my face. "We're not going anywhere."

"I know, but—"

"No. You have a place here with us. With me, Bird." His eyes are warm and loving as he leans in closer, and I can feel in my bones what is coming. "I lo—"

I quickly slam my mouth on his, drinking in the words I'm really dying to hear, but can't. Not yet.

When he pulls back moments later, there's an amused glint in his eyes.

"Did you just cut me off?"

I drop the fishing rod and turn to climb on his lap, sliding my arms around his neck and leaning my forehead against his. "Only because when you say what you were going to say, I want there to be no secrets between us. I need you to know all of me first. You may not want to say them anymore once you do."

"That's fucking crap, Syd," he says, obviously angry. "Nothing could change it."

"All the same, I need you to know." I kiss the frown between his eyebrows and feel him soften again.

"We'll find the time to talk. Tonight."

When I nod my agreement, his mouth slides over mine and his tongue finds entry in a passionate kiss full of promise.

"Eeewww!" Dex is standing on a rock in the water, looking in our direction. Gunnar chuckles when I try to hide my face.

"Won't be saying eeewww for much longer, kiddo. Just you wait."

"Dad! Don't say stuff like that," Emmy pipes up, walking toward us from the direction of the lighthouse. "Disturbing enough to see my father kissing, but it would be *sooo* much worse if it was my little brother." There's a twinkle in her eye as she teases Dex.

Gunnar throws his head back and laughs at the interplay that develops between the kids. I look at the strong column of his neck, the forceful jaw, and the way his face is transformed into something beautiful when he laughs and I realize he's happy.

And right here, in this moment, with laughter filling the air and the mild breeze on my face—I find I'm happy too.

CHAPTER EIGHTEEN

Gunnar

"A Sea Dog old brown, two pale ale drafts, and a diet coke." Matt puts his tray on the bar as he settles in to wait for his order.

The moment we got back to The Skipper from dropping the kids off at Mrs. Danzel's, the busy Friday evening swallowed us up. Syd relieved Viv in the kitchen and I took over bartending duties for the evening.

We haven't had a chance to talk yet. Not with the kids around. I know she wants to know what happened with Cindy earlier, and I'm eager to get whatever is pulling at Syd out in the open, but it'll have to wait. Nothing much to tell on my part anyway; Cindy went off like a banshee when she spotted me at the school, claiming I was keeping her kids from her and she'd be calling the police. All the while, the strong smell of alcohol surrounded her. By the look on the principal's face, I wasn't the only one who'd noticed. Between us, we managed to get her outside where I told her, in no uncertain terms, that her behavior was going to go on record, and that if she wanted to maintain her position in the children's lives, she would fucking need to clean up her act. With a handful of witnesses hearing the exchange in the school parking lot, Cindy made the smart decision and drove off. Not trusting my ex, I went to pick up Dex and Syd so we could go and get Emmy as well. Time to show these kids they have at least one parent.

Walking in on my son snuggling up with Syd froze me on the spot. Fuck if I didn't have to swallow hard against the lump that suddenly got stuck in my throat. Her small body, not very much bigger than my boy's, yet protectively curved around him, shielding him from the world and giving him her love. What she said to try and comfort him cut me deep. The evidence of her own struggles were clear in every word.

"You okay, boss?" Matt asks as I slide his drink order on the tray.

"Yeah, why?"

"Because trouble is coming through the door," he says solemnly. When I look over his shoulder, I know exactly what he means. Trying to create a larger than life image with his massive girth and pretentious handlebar mustache, Graham Bull looks more like an oversized Hercule Poirot than the fast food chain image of Colonel Sanders he's so obviously attempting to emulate, and he's not alone. The familiar face of his inquisitive lackey walks in, right behind him.

Well this should be interesting.

"What can I get you gentlemen?" I dive right in as they sit down at the bar.

"This isn't a social visit." The bite to the Soul Filets' owner's voice is unchecked. The man is out for something, but I'm determined not to let him rattle me. "Do you know who I am?"

I almost chuckle at the pompous ass, but manage to swallow it down. "Sure I do. Your face is plastered all over the Eastern seaboard. Kinda hard to miss, Graham." The casual use of his first name pisses him off, I can tell. Guess he's used to folks bowing down to him, but he'll be hard-pressed to find me doing the same. "I've also had the pleasure of meeting your ... associate? Although he never quite managed to give me his name." I make no attempt at masking my sarcasm. "Since this is a pub, let me pour you gentlemen a drink. Perhaps then you can tell me what it is that brings you here."

"Courvoisier," the pretentious ass says with an eyebrow up, fully expecting me to tell him I can't provide that. Seeing his face drop when I bend down to the shelf that holds our select stock and come up with the familiar cognac bottle, pleases me to no end.

"One cognac coming up. And one for you, sir?" I turn my attention to the other man after placing the bowl shaped snifter on the bar, who shakes his head.

"Anything you have on draft."

"Sea Dog pale ale good for you?" He responds with a nod. Graham hasn't taken his eyes off me the entire time.

"I want to buy your bar."

I don't stop or look up from pulling the draft, not wanting to give Mr. Bull the satisfaction of a reaction. Leisurely scraping the cap of foam back to the rim of the beer glass, I place it on the bar before raising my eyes.

"You do? Well, I'm sorry to have to tell you this, but I'm not for sale, and neither is my *pub*." I place my hands wide on the bar and lean in. "This place has been in my family for decades and I have no intention of changing that."

I observe a slight tremor to the hand of the *suit* lifting his draft to his mouth. Interesting. I understand better when Graham shoots the man a sharp glance before turning back to me. "I was given the impression you might be willing to negotiate."

"Well, you've obviously received faulty information 'cause I have absolutely zero interest in even considering it, for *any* amount of money."

A thick silence falls after my words as he quietly sips his cognac. Regarding me boldly, his sidekick slightly squirms on the stool beside him.

"Mr. Lucas. It has come to my attention that you have been at the core of some trouble recently. A fire, I believe? And a rather nasty incident with one of your employees?"

If I was suspecting it before, I am now almost certain that Bull has Sergeant Winslow in his back pocket and I feel anger pushing up. But it's the dismissive referral to Syd that finally gets to me. With all that I am, I keep from hurtling myself over the bar and wiping the smug grin off the bastard's face.

"You may have been able to buy the dubious support of some of our local law enforcement, Graham, but I warn you; I have my own connections and I can guarantee *they* won't be so easy to buy off. In fact, I think it's about time I demand a proper investigation into that fire. I have a feeling our Sergeant Winslow may not have been as thorough as he could've been."

The slight twitch in Graham's jaw is a welcome sight, but even more gratifying is the blatant wince on the face of his companion. These fucking people keep making the mistake of thinking they're dealing with a small-time idiot. What they don't realize is that decades of great community standing and maintaining good relationships with patrons pays off in helpful connections when you need them. Portland may be the largest city in Maine, but it has a tight community.

"I'd hoped we could come to some agreement today, Lucas, but I see I'm wasting my time." The pompous ass pushes himself back from the bar and stands up.

"If your idea of an *agreement* is for me to cave and sell to you, then you are absolutely wasting your time. There is room enough on the wharf, Bull, if you could only see past your own massive ego. You may find that it could be mutually beneficial to have a little competition to crank up sales." With that I turn away and take an order at the other end of the bar, leaving the two to find their own way out.

Syd

I find Gunnar in his office, head down on his arms on the desk. I slip behind him and slide my hands from his shoulders to his neck, feeling the tensions of the day knotted there. With firm, long strokes, I start working his muscles loose.

"Ahhh, that feels good," he mumbles, his head still down on his arms.

We haven't talked all night, but I heard the reports from Matt when he'd come into the kitchen. There is enough weight on this man's shoulders for now with concern about his children and his business, no need for me to add to it. What I have to say won't go away, so it can wait.

"Why don't you go home? I'll finish the deposit and get Matt to go with me to drop it in the night slot. You go home to the kids."

Gunnar swivels around, grabs my hips, pulling me between his legs and leans his head against my midriff. I run my fingers through his longish hair and he moans, pressing his face into my belly. "I have a better idea," he offers. "We do the deposit together, let Matt lock up and you come home with me."

"You need rest, Gunnar."

"I want you to come home with me," he repeats.

"The kids—" I try, but he quickly interrupts.

"We slept in the same bed for over a week with them in the house, Syd." I hear a smile in his voice.

"Yes, but we weren't 'doing' anything then," I try again, only to be met with a pair of mischievous eyes.

"Are you saying you won't be able to keep your hands off me?"

The man is impossible.

"Fuck, babe. You feel so fucking good," he mumbles in my neck as he slides into me from behind.

I have my hands braced on the tiled wall, one foot hiked up on the side of the tub and Gunnar holding my hips as he pumps inside me. The warm spray from the shower runs off my back. Barely able to contain the sounds that want to escape me, I turn my head and bite into my arm. *So good.*

"You ready for me?" he grunts, sliding one hand between my legs while his body curves around me from behind, pulling my back against his chest. My head falls back against his shoulder as he works my clit with his fingers, his cock filling me up, and I can't hold back when a blinding orgasm overtakes me.

"Ahh ... Gunnar!"

His arms are clasped around my body to keep me upright while he pushes inside me twice more before groaning out his release, holding himself deeply planted inside.

I ended up giving into Gunnar and came home with him, fully intending to simply curl up in bed with him, nothing more, but as soon as Mrs. Danzel left and we walked into his bedroom, he had me up against the wall, his leg inserted between mine, putting the most delicious pressure to my pussy. I almost came from riding his thigh alone. My attempts to deter him were fruitless and within seconds, he had me in his bathroom, stripping me down. My token resistance was quickly washed down the drain the first time he made me come in his mouth, on his knees in the tub.

Now clean, dried, and dressed in one of Gunnar's shirts because I refused to stay naked with the kids in the house, I curl up in the strong arms around me.

"Glad you came," his deep voice vibrates through his chest where my face is planted. "I needed you right here." He squeezes his arms around me.

Tears flood my eyes as I let those words settle inside me. To be wanted like this—needed even—fills my heart. The realization I have a place in his life, in his arms, has me voice feelings I was keeping to myself. "I love you." So softly, yet I know he heard me when the next second I'm on my back, Gunnar hovering over me with his hands on my face.

"I want to look you in the eye when you say that. Tell me." His eyes, dark and swirling with emotion, bore into mine as he whispers, "Please ..."

"I don't kn—"

"Please ..." he pleads again.

I ignore the niggle of guilt. I know I should tell him everything first, but this moment right here, I don't want to let it pass.

"I love you, Gunnar."

Dropping his forehead to mine and with our lips almost touching, he starts to say something, but I lift my mouth to his and swallow the words. The kiss is sweet and languid before turning hot once again. And it isn't until after we both come again, our bodies still connected and heartbeats racing, that he calls me out.

"You can stop the words from my mouth, but you can't stop the feeling in my heart."

"You're back."

Dex climbs onto the bed with a big smile on his face.

"Hey, buddy," I say, wiping the sleep from my eyes, noticing Gunnar gone. "Where's your dad?"

"Gone with Emmy to get donuts for breakfast."

"Yeah? Sounds good," I tell him as he worms his small body under my arm and cuddles up beside me.

"I like the jelly-filled ones, the ones with the powdered sugar on top? Those are the best, but I also like the ones with the pudding? What are those called? They have chocolate on top."

He turns his face to me expecting an answer, and I have to swallow down the emotions. His early morning chatter, the warm little body curled up against me in the easy acceptance of my presence—it makes me feel blessed.

"Boston Cream; my favorite," I smile at him.

"Mine too."

Dex shoots up at his father's words from the doorway and exclaims, "Yesss! Donuts are here," before scrambling off the bed and through the door.

Gunnar's eyes are holding mine as he stalks toward the bed the moment Dex's butt is out the door. I'm caught in his gaze until his mouth almost touches mine. Slipping my hand over my mouth, I turn my head away.

"Morning breath ..." I mumble in way of explanation, but he grabs my hand and drags it away, and just as I open my mouth in protest, he covers it with his and slides his tongue inside, claiming me thoroughly. By the time we come up for air, my hands are tangled in his hair and my breasts are plastered against his chest.

"Christ, you taste sweet," he mutters with his nose buried in my hair. "Have I told you I love your hair? First thing I noticed about you. Even then I wanted nothing more than to tangle my hands in it and kiss you silly."

A giggle escapes me.

"Really? On the floor of the men's room with you hopping from leg to leg with a full bladder? All I remember is how dark and angry, and breathtakingly handsome you were."

"Breathtakingly handsome, huh?" his cocky grin makes me smile.

"Figures you'd get stuck on that instead of the 'dark and angry' part of my description," I say teasingly.

"Hey, I can't control where my mind gets caught up. You've been there ever since that first encounter, firmly lodged, no matter how hard I tried to ignore it."

Loud voices filtering up from downstairs break the moment.

"Dad! Dex stole a donut from me!" Emmy's voice carries up the stairs, her brother's angry one in the background.

Gunnar rolls his eyes and stands up from the bed. "As much as I love seeing you in my bed, I'm thinking you should get some clothes on and come down for breakfast before these two make quick work of the donuts, that is if they don't kill each other first."

A quick peck on my lips and he's out the door and down the stairs, his deep voice negotiating a truce between the siblings as he goes.

Once freshened up and dressed, I head downstairs to find peace returned, as well as a plate with a single Boston Cream donut beside a steaming cup of coffee on the counter.

"Sorry," comes from Emmy who is sitting at the far end of the island. "I didn't know Boston Cream was your favorite."

I turn to look at Dex, who's sitting on the couch in the living room, watching a cartoon on TV. His eyes flick to mine and he shrugs his shoulders. "Had to grab it or she would've eaten it."

The explanation of a nine-year-old is melting my heart. I walk over to where he sits and kiss his head. "Thanks, buddy, but don't fight with your sister."

"Kay," he says without taking his eyes off his TV program.

"And you ..." I tell Emmy as I reach her and slide my arm around her. "You have nothing to apologize for. In fact, if you still want, we can share the donut. Tastes much better shared than eaten alone anyway."

The small smile on her face, and the barely there return hug tells me I just waded through a minefield and managed to avoid a massive explosion. Grabbing a knife from the block on the counter, I deftly slice the donut in half, sliding the plate with one half to Emmy and taking a bite off the other.

Gunnar walks up behind me and slides his arm around my waist, his hand spreading over my stomach.

"You amaze me," he whispers in my ear, sending shivers down my back.

Gunnar

"Are you gonna marry my dad?"

Emmy shocks me with the forward question. She's not usually this direct, and by the looks of it, she's completely taken Syd by surprise too. Her mouth opens but nothing comes out, so she immediately snaps it shut, turning her eyes on me, pleading for help.

"Emmy," I draw my daughter's attention. "Don't put Syd on the spot. We haven't gotten that far yet."

"But she makes you happy. I just want you to be happy like this all the time." From the mouths of babes …

I reach out and stroke my daughter's long blonde hair away from her face. "You and your brother make me happy and I couldn't ever do without you. Syd is my cherry-on-top; the chocolate sprinkles on my ice cream. Life is great with you guys, but better with Syd there too."

"Making me hungry again, Dad!" Dex yells from the living room, making me chuckle.

Emmy has slipped off her stool and has her arms wrapped around my waist and her face planted in my shirt. When I look up, I catch a soft look and suspiciously shimmering eyes. Syd is looking at us with a yearning that's almost tangible.

"Hey, you," I prompt her, "come over here." I hold my arm out to snag her to my side, planting a kiss on her head. Fuck me. Having my two girls pressed against me is enough to choke me up, but the doorbell is an instant cure.

Dex is dashing for the door and before I know it, has it open to reveal an unhappy looking Cindy.

"Mom!"

Emmy slips from my hold and goes to greet her mother, whose hateful eyes have not wavered from the woman in my arms, ignoring her children right in front of her. I can feel Syd trying to slip away, but I won't let her move, only tucking her in closer to my side. Both kids are now looking from their mother to me, worry starting to move over their faces.

"Cindy. What can I do for you?" I keep my anger at her intrusion contained and manage to speak evenly.

A red flush, I recognize as the onset of an alcohol-induced tantrum, colors her face as she tosses her hair back. "What you can do, is give me my kids," she slurs, her hands on her hips in a challenge.

Emmy and Dex are both taking a few steps back from where she's standing. "Mom, you're drunk," Emmy points out but she's ignored by her mother.

"You have that piece of trash around my kids? A fucking wharf rat who probably sold her body for booze or drugs. And a murderer to boot!" Her voice turns shrill as she screams, while Dex stands there with his hands over his ears and Emmy has big tears rolling over her face as she watches her mother lose it completely. I let go of Syd and in a few large steps, I'm in Cindy's face, itching to put my hands around her neck.

"Shut the fuck up, woman!" I bellow, causing her to blanch a little.

I can hear Syd's soft voice coaxing the children away behind me, and as soon as I hear their footsteps going up the stairs and out of earshot, I lean in close to Cindy's face, wincing at the wafts of alcohol coming off her.

"What the fuck is wrong with you? First you go drunk to their school, causing a ruckus after they don't hear from you for fucking *weeks*! Upsetting Dex and making an ass of yourself. Now you come here? Drunk off your ass, wanting to take them with you? Are you fucking insane? You didn't even look at them when they ran to you. Get the fuck out of here. You'll have nothing to do with the kids until you get your ass clean and your priorities straight!" I stop for a breath, and to calm myself before continuing, "And don't you ever ... *Ever* talk about Syd that way again! What you said is slander, Cindy, punishable by law. And let me tell you, I will not hesitate to take action if you open your mouth again."

I take a step back, trying to rein in my anger when I notice the glint in her eyes. The bitch is up to something. I know it before she opens her mouth to speak.

"It isn't slander if it's the truth," she tries, but I cut her off.

"Defending yourself against an attacker is just that, self-defense, you ignorant, vindictive bitch!"

Surprised, she raises her eyebrows.

"Self-defense? What are you talking about? I'm talking about the kid she killed—her own kid!"

CHAPTER NINETEEN

Gunnar

It's the shock of those harsh words. I hear her sharp intake of breath behind me and I'm frozen to the spot when she slips by me and out the door, taking off running. It's the only explanation I have for not stopping Syd or immediately going after her.

It takes all of my restraint not to wipe the smug grin off Cindy's face.

"Get out, now. Or by God I won't be able to stop myself from putting my hands on you."

With her lips in a tight, straight line on her face, she turns to walk out the door, but at the bottom of the steps, she turns back. "Just so you know, I'll be calling CPS. You're not keeping my kids from me."

The lunacy of that statement hits me just as she starts up the car and weaves out of the driveway.

I immediately grab my phone to call Syd when I realize she doesn't have a cell phone. *Fuck!* I quickly dial Viv instead and in as few words as possible, explain what happened and to keep an eye out for Syd. Without waiting for an answer, I hit end and run up the stairs, two at a time, to get to my kids. I find both of them in Dex's room, huddled on the bed together. Dex is sniffling in Emmy's arms while she's holding it together, just barely. The moment they see me, they launch themselves at me. Under the weight of my two

221

children and the final piece of the puzzle that is Syd, I sink down on the bed.

"Is it true? What mom said about Syd? She's a murderer?" Dex's voice suddenly sounds much smaller than his nine years.

"Of course not," Emmy pipes up before I can answer. "Mom is just drunk and mean and I never, ever want to see her again!" Pulling her head toward me, I press a kiss to her forehead.

"Was she lying, Dad?" Dex insists.

Jesus. I don't have to wait for Syd's explanation, I *know* Cindy was spouting off some bullshit. Syd would never hurt someone willingly unless she had no choice, but her reaction to Cindy's words were evidence that there is truth to some of what she said.

"I think your mom wasn't thinking when she talked about Syd, kiddo. I know something bad happened to Syd a long time ago and she lost her child, which is really awful. She tried to tell me what happened but things kept coming up." As the words leave my mouth, I realize how true they are. She was ready to tell me yesterday. She kept hinting that once she did, it would change the way I feel about her. That's why she didn't want me to tell her I love her. I fucking love her.

Lifting the kids off me, I reach for my phone and dial Mrs. Danzel, asking her if she would be able to come over right away. Indicating she'd be here in fifteen minutes, I turn to the kids who are both looking at me expectantly.

"You're going after her, aren't you Dad?" This from Emmy, who never doubted Syd, not even for a minute. I draw resolve from her young, hopeful face.

"Sure am, girl. Gonna find her and bring her back."

"What about Mom?" Dex wants to know. I kneel on the floor in front of the bed so I can look him straight in the eyes.

"Your mom is not in a good place right now, and she's dragging everyone down with her. She needs help getting better. I'll do what I can to see that she gets it, but in the meantime, you two need to avoid her and call me immediately if she shows up anywhere you are, okay?"

The two solemn faces nodding at me nearly do me in. I hate Cindy's guts for what she's put them through, but she's their mother, and I'll move heaven and earth for my kids. Another reason why I need to find Syd and talk this out, because she puts smiles on their faces. Fuck, who am I kidding; she puts a smile on mine too.

I'm positive she ran, thinking I'd turn on her, but whatever it is she thinks she's done, we'll work through. I just need a chance to tell her that—let her know there is no running away from me ... from us.

Giving the kids a quick hug and kiss, I head downstairs so I can open the door for the babysitter when she gets here. I quickly call Viv to see if she's heard or seen anything, but there's no answer. Next I try the pub, hoping she may have gone home. No luck there either. Damn.

When Mrs. Danzel finally knocks, I'm ready to go, my jacket and boots on. In a few words, I explain to her that we just had some drama with Cindy and under no circumstances is she to talk to the kids or come inside. With a quick goodbye yelled up the stairs, I head out, aiming for my truck when my phone rings. I answer as I slide into the driver's seat.

"Gunnar, it's Viv. I know where she is. Meet me on Preble Street, at the Florence House."

"Ten minutes," I tell her, already pulling out of the driveway. Relief courses through me. For a minute there, I'd been worried Cindy might've done something crazy. She left not that long after Syd, but knowing she made her way to Pam takes a load off my shoulders. Needing to get to her as fast as I can, I race through the streets of Portland.

Viv is already standing on the sidewalk and when I pull up in the first available parking spot a little down the road, she's jogging toward me.

"What exactly happened? When I called earlier to ask Pam if she'd seen Syd, all she said was that she was with her and a mess." Viv sounded out of breath and pissed.

"Cindy came to the door this morning, drunk. She saw Syd in the kitchen and went off on her, basically calling her a whore and murderer. Said Syd killed her kid."

Viv slaps her hand over her mouth and her eyes fill with tears as she looks up at me with big eyes.

"No shit?"

"Syd heard her and I didn't move fast enough when she took off running. The kids were upstairs and upset. They'd had a front row seat. *Christ!* That bitch has done so much damage."

Suddenly I find Viv up in my face, a fist clenched in the front of my shirt, hissing, "Don't talk about her like that."

I pull her hand away and set her back a step before leaning in so I can look her in the eyes. "Fuck, Viv. You fucking know me better than that. Cindy, you dumbass. I was talking about Cindy."

Blinking her eyes a few times, and with a slightly embarrassed smile on her lips, she mouths *sorry*.

"I just ... I mean Syd would never ..."

Having wasted enough time on the sidewalk, I grab Viv's elbow and steer her up the path to the front door of the house. Before we have a chance to knock, the door opens. Pam stands there with her hands on her hips, looking at me accusingly. *What the fuck?*

"I should kick your ass for having been married to such a mean-spirited piece of trash. And you—" She turns her glare on Viv next. "—what were you thinking, bringing him here? In case you haven't noticed, this is a shelter—a sanctuary—and you two storming up the path are scaring the shit out of my residents."

Duly scolded, we wait until she's done glaring. "You're lucky I'm gonna let you in to talk to her, but say anything to upset her and I'll—"

I hold up my hands to stop her. "Not here to upset her, but Pam, you don't fucking let me see her, I'm gonna seriously lose my shit."

Without another word, she turns and walks into the house with Viv and I closely on her heels.

Syd

"Hey, little Bird," Gunnar smiles softly from behind Pam as they walk through the door of her office.

The relief that floods me at seeing warmth in his eyes instead of the expected derision brings tears to my eyes, *again.*

The moment I heard the condemning words from Cindy's mouth, I knew I'd missed my opportunity. I should've confessed long ago, but couldn't bring myself to. And when my first real effort at coming clean was thwarted yesterday by Cindy's appearance at Dex's school, I simply didn't have the guts to try again. Not after spending the day with Gunnar and the kids, making me fall in love with all of them even more. Then there were the problems piling up left, right, and center on Gunnar's shoulders already. Rather than telling him what he deserves to know, I told him I love him instead.

So I ran.

I ran with tears running down my face and a crater in my chest the size of the Grand Canyon where my heart used to be. But instead of hiding, something I'd been very adept at, I ran toward help. The cab I managed to flag down got me to Preble Street in short order. Pam only took a second to take me in when she opened the door to my knock before I found myself wrapped in her strong arms. I stood embarrassed in the doorway while Pam paid the cab, since I didn't have anything with me, before guiding me into her office. She didn't speak at all while I rambled, not holding back anything. Didn't even blink when I was telling her about this morning's confrontation and the truth behind it. But the moment I was done purging, she pounced.

"My guess is he'll be here soon," she says cryptically, and at my confused look, she adds, "Gunnar."

I shake my head and I'm about to tell her he wouldn't want to see me when she suddenly gets up and walks out of the office, only to walk back in just now with Gunnar and Viv in tow.

Gunnar kneels in front of my chair and wipes at my cheeks with the back of his hand.

"Could I have a minute with Syd alone?" he says, never taking his eyes off me.

"We'll be in the kitchen." I hear Pam say, but my eyes never waver from his either.

With the soft click of the door latching, Gunnar is on his feet, lifting me out of the chair before sitting back down with me on his lap.

"Not my first choice of locations for me to tell you I love you, but extenuating circumstances and all ..."

I'm sure the look of shock on my face must be what causes him not to finish that thought. *Love me?* "What?" I whisper and he responds by taking my face in his hands.

"You heard me. I love you, Sydney Donner. Or Syd, or whatever you choose to call yourself."

"But how? You heard her—"

"I don't listen to her. I'd rather listen to you. Tell me." I hesitate, not wanting the hope that's flared up in my chest to die a quick death should he turn me away after all. But Gunnar won't have it. "Tell me." With his voice almost a growl and his hands sliding down my neck and over my shoulders to hold me steady by my arms, I take a deep breath.

"Chrissy? Can you get Daniel ready for preschool? I think he's playing in his room. I'm running late for a meeting, but I'll pick him up this afternoon. See ya!"

Christina Valejo, my Filipino nanny, sticks her head around the kitchen door and waves me off. "Go. I've got it."

My head is quickly going over the checklist of things I'll need with me for this meeting. I just finished one of my largest clients' year-end last night and can't afford to forget anything. They're in the process of a merger and need every penny to be accounted for so they can hand a complete financial account over to their lawyers. This meeting is important; if I don't have all my ducks in a row, I'll stand to lose the account and that would put a huge dent in my business. As an independent

CPA, I have only a handful of clients whose contracts have an impact on my own bottom line, and ME Shipping is leading that pack.

Of course it didn't help any that I was only told of this meeting on Friday afternoon. And after a stressful weekend, trying to juggle my four-year-old Daniel, my once again absent husband, and the sudden truckload of work, it's not a surprise that it took me until 2:00 a.m. this morning to finish. I'm cursing Jacob for disappearing on another one of his unexpected business trips this weekend. Our marriage is what it is—which is not good—and I've been able to ignore much of what I know is going on behind my back, but lately he's been a bit too loose in the discretion department.

The first time I found out about his infidelity, I was ready to walk out. I'd always been of a mind that cheating is an absolute deal-breaker, but Jacob's feeble excuses, his tears and pleas not to break apart our family swayed me to stay. The next time I caught him I was just building my business and was so stressed about making it work, I was scared to concede any kind of failure. It didn't help that my parents had always adored Jacob and they had been less than impressed that after a year at home with Daniel, I wasn't going to be a stay-at-home mom and wife. A working mother for a daughter would be a blight on their perfect little world. I knew they would take Jacob's side in any conflict, using my business as the culprit for a failed marriage. Right then and there, I decided I would stick it out, at least until Daniel was a little older and more self-sufficient. My concession was to hire Chrissy, who came highly recommended, and who'd been a salvation for me. I settled into one of the spare bedrooms and Jacob's flings—of which I'm sure he had many—were shoved to the background. He knew better than to wave them in my face.

As of late though, he's been less and less discreet with his extra-marital affairs, and doesn't even try to shield them from me.

With my hands full of folders, my laptop bag, and angry thoughts of my husband fucking his side-squeeze of the moment swirling through my head, I click the button on my remote and the locks of my Mercedes pop open in response. Hurriedly, I toss what's in my hands on the passenger seat and jam the key into the ignition.

A glance at the clock tells me I'll be at least fifteen minutes late and I jam the transmission in gear. My foot is on the gas and I'm already backing out before I even turn to look. I feel a thud and hear a scrape. I slam on my brakes and a quick glance in the side mirror shows a familiar tricycle rolling toward the raised curb on the side of the driveway, where it bangs to a full stop.

Then there is only silence.

I can't.

With the agonizing memories washing over me, I can't bring myself to continue. My screams when I find Daniel's little body crumpled half underneath the car—lifeless—are still ringing in my ears. Flashes of an ambulance ride and snippets of hysterical phone calls jumble through my mind until I see myself sitting in the small waiting room off the ER, a quickly summoned social worker by my side keeping me company and holding my hand.

The safety of Gunnar's arms now wrapped tightly around me, lends me a little courage.

"Jacob walked in," my voice is hoarse from crying and I can't bring myself to look into Gunnar's eyes. "He walked right up to me and slapped me in my face so hard, I still saw stars a day later." Gunnar's arms tighten almost painfully around my body, but I'm grateful for their hold. "All I can remember is the anger and the chaos. The doctor coming in to tell us Daniel didn't make it and security being called to hold Jacob back from coming at me again. I think I would've welcomed whatever Jacob wanted to dole out then. Anything was better than the hell I was in. They sedated me and kept me overnight. The next day, Jacob was back with my parents." The memory of my rumpled and distraught ex beside the perfectly attired and appropriately solemn vision of my parents pulls up a snort.

"That's enough," Gunnar's gruff voice penetrates my memories as he palms the back of my head and presses my face in his neck, his head resting on mine. "*Jesus*," I hear him mumble in my hair.

"They took me home, barely talking to me, their accusing glances enough for me to hide in Daniel's room, surrounding myself with his things, his smell. Chrissy, my nanny, tried to coax me to eat, day after day, and finally I gave in on the condition she bring me a bottle of scotch. I'd always hated the stuff and felt it was fitting I'd try to numb myself with something that tasted ugly and bitter."

I'm silent for a moment, taking in the strength of Gunnar's presence surrounding me, and allow myself to remember the first time I managed to drink myself into oblivion. It was the first of many.

"I missed his funeral. I was so wasted—not even my mother and her continued reminders that I'd already taken their grandson and she wasn't about to let me take their good name as well—could get me sober enough."

The angry growl rumbling from Gunnar's chest against my ear makes me smile a little.

"Sofia—my sister—tried to reason with me. Even months later, she was still trying until I finally told her I didn't want to see her again. I was bitter, angry, and jealous of the happy family she had with Brad and the girls. I haven't seen her or my nieces since ..." My voice trails off with thoughts of my older sister. The one person who'd always stood up for me whenever my parents tried to wrestle me into what they thought was appropriate conduct for a '*Donner*. I wrecked that as well.

Exhausted and tired of talking, I finally lift my eyes to find Gunnar's beautiful green ones looking down at me, deceptively shiny.

A sniffle from behind us has me turn my head to find Pam and Viv leaning in the doorway, Pam's face calm in comparison to Viv's, which is blotchy with tears.

"Sorry, honey," Pam says. "We heard you screaming and came to check. We should've walked away as soon as we saw Gunnar was taking care of you, but—"

"I screamed?" I interrupt her.

"When you were remembering. For a bit there, I lost you. Had to hold you down," Gunnar explains. My memories had hit me hard and reliving them was agony.

"I guess I did lose it because I can't remember that. Anyway," I turn back to Viv, "I'm glad you heard. Relieved in a way." I look around me at all the warm and sympathetic eyes on me. "Surprised too, that you're all still here."

"What did you expect?" Pam asks. "For us to turn our backs and judge you? For what? Girl, if I had your mother in front of me now, I'd mess up her expensive coif. Turn that shit into dreadlocks."

I can't stop the giggle escaping at the visual of my perfectly groomed mother with her hair sticking out in tight twists, and then I burst into tears.

"I'm taking her home," Gunnar announces, and before I can even move, he has me up in his arms and walks me right out the door, down the sidewalk, and to his truck. The moment he has me seated and slides into the driver's seat, he turns to me, cupping my cheek with his hand. "Also not the best place, but it bears repeating. I love you."

My heart full in my chest and my mouth unable to formulate my thoughts, I turn to look out the front window while he starts up the truck and drives us home.

CHAPTER TWENTY

Gunnar

She gutted me in there.

I check her profile as she stares out the windshield when I pull into my driveway. The strain is visible in the tight lines on her face and I wish I could do something—anything—to wipe them away.

Pam had whispered to call her when I walked past her with an exhausted Syd in my arms, and I will. Now that the proverbial can of worms is opened, there is no way to shut it back down. Her memories are going to continue haunting her and it fucking kills me.

I shut off the engine and twist my torso so I can fully face her. Putting my hand on her neck, she tears herself away from whatever it is she sees through the window. I'm sure it isn't the garage door in need of paint. Slowly she scans her surroundings before turning to face me.

"You brought me here?"

"Said I'd take you home, Bird."

"But the kids—" With panic sneaking into her eyes, I have to stop her.

"Are fine. Once I got Cindy to leave, I spent some time talking to them." I try to reassure her.

"Did they hear?"

I could lie to put her mind at ease, but the reality is I don't know if the kids wouldn't blurt something out and make things even more painful, so I opt for the truth.

"They did, *but* they were upset for you. They know their mother was using ugly words to provoke me, and they get that it said more about her than about you."

Carefully I peel away the hands she had slapped over her eyes.

"What are you gonna tell them?" she wants to know in a shaky voice.

"*We.* What are *we* gonna tell them—the truth. I will do the talking but I think both of us should be there." I squeeze her hands in mine as she takes a deep breath.

"I still can't believe you're still here. That *I'm* here. I thought you wouldn't want me around your kids anymore— around you. It's not what I expected to have happen once you knew it all."

Still holding the back of her neck, I pull her toward me as I lean in. Our noses are almost touching and I can feel her shallow breathing against my skin. "It was an accident. A horrible, tragic, unfair, and random accident. I can't even imagine the devastation you've endured and still do. But, Syd? Your ex and your parents should be the ones feeling guilty. No one could have predicted what would happen and therefore prevented it, but they had the power ... fuck, they had the responsibility to help you through your grief. Instead they turned on you. The whole fucking lot of them, loading you up with more guilt on top of the immeasurable amount you were already loading on yourself."

Her head is bowed and tears are dripping down from her face. I tilt her chin up with my hand, forcing her to look at me.

"That is not going to happen here, little Bird. I don't care how long it takes, but I will remind you every time you struggle, what an amazing person you are, how much you are needed, and how deeply you are loved." Leaning in, I kiss her lips and swallow the words she whispers.

"Thank you."

The kids were just inside the door, being held back by Mrs. Danzel. Looking sweet and grandmotherly, the small grey-haired woman had a spine of steel and managed my kids with an ease I'm envious of. If not for her, I'm sure Emmy and Dex would have come storming out of the house the minute we pulled up in the driveway.

By the time I walk in the door, my arm firmly around Syd, Dex is almost jumping up and down. "You found her!" And without hesitation, he barrels into Syd, wrapping his arms around her midsection. Her own arms automatically hold him close, his head buried against her chest. He flips it back to look up at her. "My mom's a meanie. Even Emmy says so. Right, Emmy?"

My eyes inadvertently slide to my daughter who hasn't moved from her spot, her arms wrapped around herself, and her focus on Syd. Syd sees it too, and with more resolve than I've seen on anyone before, she gently unwraps Dex's arms from around her, moves from under my protective one, and takes a step to stand in front of my girl.

"Emmy?" her soft voice gentle and probing.

"I'm sorry—" my daughter starts, but is immediately stopped by Syd, who places her hand on Emmy's cheek.

"Nothing to be sorry for, sweetie. I think we should all have a talk," she says resolutely.

Once again, I'm blown away. The moment she's faced with my kids, Syd pulls herself out of the emotional quicksand of her past to focus on them. Straightening her back and lifting her chin, she takes charge, grabbing Emmy's hand and pulling her into the living room, Dex trailing behind them.

"I'll be heading home. I'll leave you to it." Mrs. Danzel puts her hand on my shoulder and gives it a little squeeze as she passes. "That girl has a hole in her heart I'm afraid no one can mend, but the three of you can pour the rest of her heart so full, she'll barely know it's there." With a little smile, she's out the door before I have a chance to say anything.

After a gut-wrenching conversation with the kids that had everyone in tears, again, I snuck away on the back deck to give Viv a quick call at the pub.

"Hey, boss, how are things going?"

"If I never see a tear again it wouldn't be soon enough. But things are all right, considering."

"What about the kids?"

"They're on eggshells around Syd, almost scared to talk to her. After she went to lie down they asked me a million questions." I run my hand through my hair. "Christ, Viv. I never thought parenting would be this hard. Syd was a trooper and sat with her hands clenched in her lap while I filled in the story during the parts where she was about to lose it. I never imagined—"

"It's unimaginable, that's why. I knew there was something so deeply tragic about her. From the first time I laid eyes on her, she just didn't seem the type. Too clean and well-groomed, despite the fact she'd been living off the street for over a year by then. And when she started talking more, I could tell she was educated. Clear minded too. Knowing her full story, it all makes sense now. I hurt for her, Gunnar." Viv stifles a sob.

"I do too. Fuck me, I do too." I need a minute to collect myself before moving on to practical matters. "Did you get a hold of Dino?"

"Yeah, he's already here, and so are Matt and Leanne. I think we'll be ok, Gunnar. We should be able to manage without you today. It gets crazy tonight, I can always call Frankie or one of my brothers to jump in. Those guys won't have anything useful to do on a Saturday night anyway," she chuckles. "Would serve them right to be called into action— and not the kind of action they're usually after on party night. The women of Portland and surrounding areas will thank me to get those idiots off the street for one night."

Relieved to know Viv seemed to have everything in hand, I'm suddenly anxious to go back inside.

"Gonna check in with you after the lunch rush, yeah?"

"Sounds good, boss. Take good care of her."

"Not a hardship, Viv," I tell her with a smile creeping onto my face.

"Not telling me anything I wasn't already aware of, my friend." I can hear her snicker as she disconnects.

Before I have a chance to head inside, Emmy pulls open the sliding door. "Dad! Syd's having a dream or something. I can hear her screaming." Taking a second to ruffle my girl's hair and tell her not to worry, I rush up the stairs when I hear the loud keening and find Dex is standing outside my bedroom door, worry all over his face.

"Hey, kiddo. Go play, okay? I'll make sure she's all right." Giving him a playful punch on his arm, I go into the bedroom, closing the door behind me.

Syd's on the bed, tangling herself in the quilt I put over her earlier. She hadn't felt like getting undressed and under the covers, so she's still wearing her clothes from this morning. Kicking off my boots, I climb onto the bed and gather her up in my arms, trying to prevent from getting hit with an elbow or flying fist by holding her firmly while trying to calm her with my voice. It doesn't take long for her to settle and open her eyes. Even with her face drawn and tearstained, her large, luminous blue eyes are gorgeous.

"What happened?" Her sleepy voice puts a smile on my face. So fucking cute.

"You were crying out in your sleep. You were dreaming," I mumble, loosening my tight hold on her body. Her hands come up to settle on my chest.

"Was I loud?"

Ignoring the question, I ask one of my own. "Can you remember what you dreamt about?"

Syd fidgets in my arms and turns her eyes away. "Vaguely ..."

"Babe, look at me." I wait until she lifts her eyes before I continue. "Tell me. Don't hold back, Bird. You should know by now I'm not gonna run. Talk to me." I stroke her back, trying to rub the tension out of her body.

"It was Jacob. I dreamt he was trying to shove me into a grave. He forced me toward the edge and when I looked over, my boy was at the bottom; bloodied, and his body bent in unnatural ways." She takes in a deep, shuddering breath, hanging onto her composure by the faintest of threads.

"Jesus, Syd."

"When we were in the hospital waiting room, when the doctor told us Daniel was gone, Jacob grabbed my arm and pulled me into the room, shoving the doctor out of his way." A tear starts rolling and she takes another shaky breath. "He looked so little, Gunnar. So broken. I couldn't bear it so I turned my head, but Jacob wouldn't have it. He moved behind me and with his hands holding my head, he forced me to look at my little boy." She can't hold back the sob that rips out of her chest. "He said, 'Look what you've done,' over and over again until security pulled him away from me."

Too choked up from rage at her ex and hurt for her pain, I kiss her forehead and tuck her under my chin where she snuggles in.

A soft knock on the door breaks the silence and then my son's tentative voice calls out. "Dad? Is she okay?"

"Come in, Dex," I call out, and Syd tries to pull from my arms. Not going to let her. I keep one arm firmly around her as I pull us up to a sitting position.

"Hey, guys. I'm sorry if I scared you. Was I loud?" Syd immediately has her attention focused on the kids. Emmy follows right behind her brother.

"You were screaming so hard, I thought someone was in there with you!" Dex exclaims, climbing onto the bed. "Was it bad? Your nightmare?"

Syd reaches out to ruffle his hair. "It was pretty bad, but waking up to you guys is the best cure."

Dex flops onto Syd's chest and she holds tight to him. Then Emmy shuffles over to the bed and I reach out my other arm to pull her against my other side.

Don't think I can remember ever having felt so fucking torn up inside as I am today. I feel raw and battered from the swirling emotions and I tell myself that is the only reason a lone tear slips, slowly rolling down my face.

Syd

"I'm coming with you. The kids can eat there and hang out at my place."

I'm standing in front of Gunnar, my hands on my hips, emphasizing how deadly serious I am. If he thinks that after the countless times he's proven himself by standing by me—pulling me back from drowning in darkness—I'd let him face his problems on his own, he's got another thing coming.

After a few minutes of quiet snuggling, the kids had gotten restless and trailed out of the bedroom, undoubtedly in search of more exciting ways to spend their time. For me—I could've spent a lifetime in that bed, surrounded by the complete acceptance and warmth it provided, but the shrill ring of Gunnar's phone put an end to that fantasy. The call from Viv that trouble had just walked into the pub in the form of Sergeant Winslow, accompanied by a health inspector, effectively burst our bubble.

With a brief recap of the short conversation, Gunnar announced he had to go see to *business*, alone, while pulling on his boots. That's when I jumped off the bed and got in his face.

His look of surprise at my challenge is nothing short of amusing and I struggle to keep a straight face. "Think it's better if you stay here with the kids. I don't know what I'm gonna be walking into."

"Exactly," I point out. "All the more reason for me to be there."

His lips are drawn in a tight line and I know he's not going to give in, leaving me no choice but to bring my argument home. "You've done nothing but show me these last days that you're only weak when you stand alone. You made me believe it. Well, you're not alone either, so we're coming. Haven't had to face a problem alone since I met you, and I'm not about to let you deny me doing the same for you. Now get yourself ready, and I'll get the kids." Turning on my heels, I leave him sitting on the edge of the bed, a slightly startled expression on his face.

I'm out front with the kids, waiting for Gunnar to lock up the house when I feel him come up behind me on the step. "Don't know why I'm caving. All I know is that new bossy attitude is a real fucking turn on," he rumbles softly in my ear before patting my ass and moving past me to the truck where the kids are already waiting. The smile that spreads over my face feels alien, but so fucking good.

The limited parking space on the wharf is almost full and it's only five thirty. Must be a good crowd tonight and with the tight staffing, not a great time for trouble, even if it comes in the form of a cop.

Gunnar purposely marches us through the alley to the back door, instead of going in the front. Once inside, he leaves me in charge of the kids and heads into the pub. Dino spots us in the doorway and leaves his stove to come give me a hug.

"Hey, girl. How are you holding up?" If his words weren't already a clear indication, the empathetic look on his face confirms it. Viv told him. I bristle at the invasion of my privacy, but Dino catches my stiffening.

"Don't you dare get mad. She's looking out for you. Like it or not, you are part of our fucked-up family, and when that prick Winslow came in here and started spouting off some nonsense about death following you around, she jumped right down his throat. Fierce, that one is. I just happened to be within hearing distance."

Instantly embarrassed that I'd jumped to conclusions, I blush and give him an apologetic smile. "You're right. Thank you."

Turning his attention to the kids who've seated themselves at the table, Dex distracted with his electronic game, but Emmy closely observing us, he walks over and leans on the table between them. "It just so happens I made old-fashioned mac and cheese tonight. You hungry?"

"With ham?" Dex wants to know, a big smile on his face.

"Is there any other way?" Dino answers, earning a "Yay," from Dexter and a smile from Emmy.

In no time at all, the kids are eagerly digging into their bowls of food. Leaving the mouth-watering smells of home-cooked foods behind and knowing the kids are good with Dino, I slip out of the kitchen and into the hallway where the sound of raised voices coming from Gunnar's office gets louder and louder. It doesn't take any effort to pick up on the owners of the voices, or the subject matter, which is *me*.

What the fuck?

Not sure how I became the subject of conversation under the circumstances, but determined to put a halt to it, I

242

barge inside without knocking. I zoom in on Winslow who is sitting behind Gunnar's desk. Ignoring the man standing behind him, the inspector I presume, and even Gunnar who is leaning over the desk, looking ready to pounce, I don't hesitate tearing into him.

"What is your problem with us, Sergeant Winslow? I'd love to know how you explain barging in here on a Saturday night when the restaurant is packed with a health inspector, whom I think would likely rather be at home with his family?" A quick glance at the inspector's face, a burly man in his fifties, tells me he is very uncomfortable and not happy about being in the middle of this. Too bad.

"Bird ..." Gunnar tries to get my attention, but I'm not done yet.

I focus back on Winslow. "How is it I hear you bring up *my* name as some kind of justification for *your* presence here?"

With a nasty smirk on his face, Winslow shoves a piece of paper at me. "That's easy, Ms. Donner. You're here, just like you have been every time we've had trouble on the wharf. The notice you're holding is a copy of a complaint from a patron who claims the food consumed here made her violently ill. A second such complaint just came in earlier today and leaves us no choice but to close down immediately until Mr. Walker here has had a chance to inspect the premises."

I want to scratch the smug look from his face with my nails. "It's bullshit and you know it. I'd like to know who launched these complaints." I wave the paper in his face, but he seems unfazed.

"Can't do that, Ms. Donner. That information is confidential and the complaints are anonymous, although the first one mentions you by name."

That gets my attention. "Me? What about me?"

"Apparently you were responsible for the Thursday Special? Jambalaya, I believe it was?"

I now turn my confused look at Gunnar, whose expression I can't decipher. "Yes, I was, but all the ingredients were fresh that morning. I don't get it. We had no complaints," I respond defensively.

"Actually, that's the interesting part. The complainant indicates having reason to believe she was targeted by you specifically, Ms. Donner, which is the reason I am here. Having a certain ... familiarity with some other cases where your name has come up, alongside this establishment, was sufficient reason for me to suggest looking into it."

To say I'm dumbfounded is an understatement. The anger that spurned me to burst in here is seeping out of me, replaced by a sickening sense of doom. I'm cursed; just when I think I finally may have a foothold to a better future. My life is fucking unfair.

"Winslow, you and I both know that the complaint against Syd is bullshit. Have you even looked at the claimant?" Gunnar jumps in, stepping up beside me and sliding his arm around my waist. Leaning in close, he whispers in my ear, "Should've made you stay at home."

So that turned around on me. Ready to throw myself down for Gunnar for a change, here I am, being held up by him instead ... *again*. I slump against him dejectedly, wondering who the hell would be responsible.

"Well, isn't it interesting you'd bring that up, Mr. Lucas. I spoke to her today in fact. You'd be interested to know it was actually a former employee of yours. She had some concerns around the fact that Ms. Donner is preparing food without a Food Protection Manager license. Something that should concern you, Mr. Lucas."

"I have a license, our chef has a license, and my manager has a license. We don't all need one, and if you did your homework, Winslow, you'd find that in the small print of the Maine Food Code. Only if we are unable to demonstrate appropriate knowledge of the food code would we be in violation," Gunnar fires back.

"Actually," Mr. Walker finally makes himself heard, "I—"

He doesn't get very far, with Winslow cutting him off mid-sentence. "No one asked you," he bites off in Walker's direction. Turning back to Gunnar, his face is almost gleeful. "Then it wouldn't be so hard to tell me which one of you was with Ms. Donner on Thursday, when she was preparing the special?"

In the momentary silence that follows, Winslow gets his answer. We don't even have to say anything because I'm sure the looks Gunnar and I throw each other are testimony enough. *Fuck.* Last thing I want is to bring more trouble on the pub and Gunnar's shoulders.

"*Actually,*" the health inspector tries once again with a sharp look in Winslow's direction, "as long as one of the licensees has appropriately and adequately instructed and educated Ms. Donner, it would be entirely within the Maine Food Code and perfectly acceptable from the perspective of the Health Inspection Program."

The anger radiating off Sergeant Winslow is palpable, and with a purely hateful glance at poor Mr. Walker, he forcefully shoves the desk chair back as he gets up and walks to the door. With a glance over his shoulder, he takes in Gunnar and me.

"Regardless, I'm shutting you down, Mr. Lucas. Right this minute. That piece of paper you're holding gives me every right." With that, he disappears through the door, Gunnar following behind.

I'm left with the health inspector who looks at me apologetically and I feel sorry that he's been dragged into this. "I'm really sorry you were dragged into this, Mr. Walker."

"Please," he says, his hand raised. "I feel bad for you. I've never heard a bad word about The Skipper, and it's never had any issues on previous inspections, so when the Sergeant called and said it was imperative to the health and safety of the pubic to shut this place down, based on some additional information he had received today, I had no choice. I promise to be quick and fair when I do my inspection."

With those words, he too leaves the office.

CHAPTER TWENTY-ONE

Syd

Much later, with all the patrons hustled out of the restaurant with refunds and credit vouchers in hand, and the kids already sleeping in the bedroom upstairs, Winslow and the health inspector leave. In one last aggressive move on his part, he refuses to accept Mr. Walker's verbal report and forces closure to run the remainder of the weekend, until he has a written report on his desk on Monday.

Reality is, this will likely hurt the business. The rule that *where there is smoke, there is fire* upholds, where people will be thinking there was good reason for Health Inspection to close us down for two days. But I'm already thinking about ways to minimize the damage. I might just be able to get some help from Mr. Walker and in the meantime, I want to take care of these dejected faces around the kitchen table. Gunnar hadn't been able to send a single person of his staff home. Even Leanne, who'd just started, showed her solidarity by staying.

Slipping out of the kitchen to the bar, I grab a stack of shot glasses and the bottle in the shape of a sunflower of good tequila under the bar. When I walk back into the kitchen with my hands full, I see almost every eye cautiously on me. A sudden fit of the giggles bursts out when I realize everyone, but possibly Leanne, thinks I've gone off the deep end until I produce a bottle of expensive Perrier from my pants pocket and set it on the table next to the glasses. "That green bottle is for me, guys," I chuckle, cracking the seal on the pretty bottle and fill the shot glasses to the brim for everyone else before picking up my green bottle of Perrier and holding it up.

The tension slips from Gunnar's face as a smile settles in. With flourish, he reaches over and grabs a glass, holding it up as well. Everyone else follows suit.

"To a fucked-up day and an amazing group of people," Gunnar salutes, tossing the shot back before slamming the glass on the table. Everyone else does the same, except for Matt, who sits and regards the glass in his hand.

"Always wanted to know what a two hundred and fifty dollar bottle would taste like," he says before he too tosses the drink back, leaving me with my mouth wide open.

"Say what? Two hundred and fifty?" My hand slaps over my mouth. I turn to Gunnar who seems to take it all in stride. "I'm so, so sorry. I had no idea!" I squeal, but Gunnar simply grabs me by the waist and pulls me down on his lap while the rest of them laugh out loud. "It was the perfect choice, babe. We deserved it."

Gunnar

"Finally got yours," Dino says as he gets ready to leave and stands beside me in the back entrance.

With the sound of only the wind, water, and the echo of Dino's words in my ear, my mind floats to the seriously fucked-up day behind me, looking for the heavy feelings that I'd expect to find, but there's nothing. Oh, there's anger and frustration there, but the weight it carries pales in comparison to the lightness the woman who is upstairs, tending to my children, brings.

"Would seem so."

I can still hear him chuckle as he makes his way down the alley to the parking lot, him being the last one to leave. I turn back inside and climb the stairs to fetch my family and take them home.

"Gunnar ... please ..." Syd begs as I tease her clit with my tongue.

It took me all of five minutes to convince Syd to come home with me. Took another five to get the kids back in bed once we got here. Since then, I've spent twenty minutes with her slick body in the shower, but my patience is gone. I need to feel her. I need to end this day, buried so deep inside her there won't be room for anything but her in my heart and my mind.

Finally getting her out of the shower and into bed, I got to work. I lift my head from between her legs, where I've been teasing her and watch her hooded eyes spring open as I slide two fingers firmly inside her pussy. Bending back down, I put my mouth over her clit and suck hard while my fingers curve up inside her, detonating her orgasm. The walls of her pussy squeeze my fingers and her release coats my hand and my chin as she buries her moans in the pillow she's clasping over her face.

"No hiding," I say, climbing up her body and pulling the pillow away. "I need to see you."

"The kids—"

"They're fast asleep. Not even a bomb going off would wake them after the day we've had."

With one hand on the mattress beside her, the other strokes her body from hip bone to shoulder. She's filled out even more since she started working at The Skipper, and I take my time looking at how her body has filled out. Everything is the perfect size, and I test every curve and valley of her skin. Her breasts, now a generous handful and so soft, I can't resist leaning down and sucking a hard nipple into my mouth, causing her to hiss out her breath.

"Fill me ..." she manages to say, and looking in her eyes, I see her need reflected there.

"Do you trust me behind you?" Looking at me with those big eyes, she simply nods her head. Sliding an arm under her, I pull her further up the bed and help her turn over. "Put your hands here." I help her get on her knees, her hands grabbing onto the top of the headboard. She's beautiful. Her copper-colored hair is rippling down her back and over her shoulders and her full, round ass is sticking up in the air. After rummaging through my nightstand drawer for a condom, I make sure not to take any chances this time. I let my hand slide down the curve of her spine and squeeze the soft flesh of her cheeks before inserting one knee between hers. Spreading her legs wide, I slip behind her, my cock lined up with her entrance. Holding onto her hips, I surge inside her on a groan.

"Jesus, little Bird—there's nothing better."

Feels so fucking good just to be inside her, her wet heat pulsing around my cock. I watch our connection as I ease out of her, before pushing back home. With each stroke, it's more and more difficult not to pound out my need inside her.

"Harder …" Her voice is soft, but firm. "I need to feel you."

I raise my eyes to look at her and see her head turned to the side, her eyes focused away. Following her gaze, I see our reflection in the full-length mirror against the closet. *Holy fuck.*

"Like to watch, huh?" I growl behind her and our eyes find each other in the mirror. "Fuck, baby, me too. You're so fucking beautiful."

Leaning forward, I curve my arm around her, spreading my hand on her lower belly to tilt her ass up a little more. With the new angle, I can hit her sweet spot every time I pump into her. Seeing her eyes glaze over in the mirror and feeling the pulsing of her heat around me tells me she's close. So fucking responsive.

I let go of my control, thrusting my hips to hit her sweet spot every time, her soft moans spurning me on. Sliding my other hand from her hip and up between her breasts, I pull her up, pressing her back against my chest. Her head falls back to rest on my shoulder as my hand curves around her neck, feeling the fluttering of her pulse beneath my fingers. Close. So fucking close.

My hand slips between her legs, finding her clit and pinching it between my fingers. My balls pull up in preparation and as she clenches around me in orgasm, my name on her lips, I furiously pump my release into her— eyes still fused on our reflection in the mirror.

I ease her down to the mattress, and quickly discard the condom before slipping into bed and curving myself around her from behind. In seconds I hear her breathing deepen and I just manage to whisper, "Love you, Bird," in her hair before I drift off.

I wake up with sunshine drifting in the room through the blinds. I'm in bed alone and lay still for a moment to listen for sounds coming from the bathroom, but hear nothing. A tingle of worry has me up and out of bed in a flash. Did she take off? I grab my sweats and pull them on before making my way downstairs. Hearing the voices of the kids and Syd in the kitchen has me leaning against the banister in relief. Thank God.

Realizing I could've prevented a lot of the shit that went down the last few days, had I been more proactive, is sobering. I push off the wall, knowing I don't want to leave anything else to fate.

When I walk into the kitchen, Syd's in one of my shirts, hanging down on her like a dress, barefoot and flipping pancakes on the stove. The kids are on stools at the counter, eyeing every move she makes. I ruffle the kids' hair in passing and step up behind her, slipping my hands on her stomach.

"Hey, Dad. Syd's making pancakes," Dex points out unnecessarily, making me chuckle as I lean my chin on her shoulder.

"I can tell, kiddo. Looks good." I lower my voice and whisper so that only Syd can hear, "*You* look good. In my shirt, in my kitchen, cooking for my family. I like you here a fuck of a lot, Bird."

Putting down the spatula, she turns in my arms and snakes her arms around my neck, leaning back to look me in the eyes. The emotion I catch in hers gives me a jolt, but the words she utters steal the breath from my lungs.

"Feels like home. This, them ... you. It's almost too much," she whispers back. "A few months ago this would've been a dream I'd hurry to squash before I could catch up to the impossibility of it, and now? Now suddenly it's become my reality and I'm afraid to believe it."

I gasp in a breath with the release of tightness in my chest and slam my mouth on hers, drinking in all that she's come to mean to me. "Eeewww!" Dex blurts out, causing Emmy to giggle beside him. Syd's mouth forms a smile under mine as I pull back.

She turns back to the stove and with a small squeeze to her hip, I turn around and cross my arms on my chest as I look at the faces of my children. To my surprise, it's Emmy who carries the wide smile, but Dex's face is clouded with concern.

"Talk to me, kiddo. Something's bugging you, I can tell."

He flicks his eyes down to the counter after throwing a surreptitious glance at Syd's back. Picking up on the hint of tension creeping into the room, Syd turns around and takes in Dex's lowered head.

"First load of pancakes, coming up," she says as she turns back to the stove to pull the pan off the fire and grab the plate already stacked high, sliding it onto the counter. "By the time you guys are done with these, I'll be back. Just going upstairs to clean up."

With a smile and the tiniest of nods in my direction, she walks out of the kitchen and up the stairs.

The message is clear; she's giving Dex space to talk, and I love her more for it.

"Dex?" I prompt him the moment Syd leaves the kitchen. His eyes slide up to mine with a world of heartbreak showing in them, making me realize I didn't have the first clue what lived inside my son's mind.

"What about mom?" he whispers, as the first tear rolls down his face.

"Oh, buddy," I mumble, pulling his little body in my arms and holding him tight, wondering how to explain to a nine-year-old that his fantasy is an impossible one. "Your mom and I were over a long time ago. We were so happy when you two came into our lives, but we weren't good for each other."

"But I heard her say she'd get you back. I thought maybe—"

"That wasn't gonna happen, kiddo. With or without Syd, that was never going to happen again." I don't tell him that I suspect his mother's words had nothing to with wanting to reunite.

"Do you like Syd?" Emmy speaks up beside him, drawing her brother's eyes to her.

"U-huh," he confirms, "a lot. She's nice."

"I do too. She's not mean and drunk all the time, and I like having her around." Emmy leans into him to whisper, "And Dad does too. She makes him smile. I like it when Dad smiles, don't you?"

Dex just nods at her, tears all dried up now.

Out of the mouths of babes.

Syd

Even though it stung a little, I knew I had to give the kids some time to talk to their father. I hadn't yet earned the right to claim space in their house or their lives. Gunnar is impatient, and I can sense his need to claim me completely, which was so tempting. After times in the past months, I was sure I was going to lose him before I even had him, I leapt at the chance to embed myself permanently into his reality, but when I noticed Dex's confusion, I realized it was too soon.

I'm getting dressed, collecting my things from around the bedroom and bathroom when Gunnar walks in, stopping dead in his tracks.

"Going somewhere?" he growls, a hint of anger behind his words. I walk up to him and reach up to kiss his tight mouth, leaving my hands to rest on his chest.

"I meant what I said down there, but I think we're moving too fast. The kids aren't ready for us together yet."

"I call bullshit," he bites off. "I want you here. The kids like you here. I think you're using them as an excuse."

"But Dex—" I start before he cuts me off.

"Dex overheard his mom say she'd 'get me back.' He mistook that to mean she still wanted me, creating a fantasy he's nurtured ever since. Not realizing her words likely had a totally different and much less friendly intent. It has nothing to do with you and he realizes that, as sad as it is, nothing will ever happen with his mom and me because I have exactly what makes me happy." I hang onto every word from his lips, and when he dips down and brings his eyes level with mine, my heart skips at the intensity in them. "*You*," he says and takes a minute to let that sink in before continuing. "They're downstairs right now, talking about what we can do *as a family* today. They know you make me happy. Emmy said she likes the way you make me smile more, and even Dex agreed. It makes them happy. Don't walk away for their sakes, because all they want is to have the kind of *sweet* you've brought into our lives. If you leave, at least be honest with yourself and admit it's for your sake that you're walking."

With that, he suddenly turns and walks out, pulling the bedroom door shut behind him. I just stand there, going over all he's said and wondering if there isn't a grain of truth in his words.

Am I trying to use the kids as an excuse to create some distance? Or is it possible I feel the urge to run because perhaps I still feel undeserving? I get the sense that if I go back to my apartment, I might be walking away from a lot more than just his house, and the thought of losing him—losing them—is paralyzing.

He's right. It's about me and my fears more so than about the kids. I'm a coward. I'm the one who is afraid to go in all the way and am using everything in my power to justify it.

The three of them have their backs to me as they sit at the counter and seem to be making their way through my pancakes as I stand in the doorway and watch them. It's right there in front of me, waiting for me to grab hold of— the promise of a new life. All I have to do is push through the fear of possible loss; of painful rejection. I can't live the rest of my life letting the scars my past burned on my soul, rule every decision for my future.

When I slide my arms around Gunnar's torso from behind and lay my cheek on the broad expanse of his back, I feel him suck in a breath and stiffen beneath me before he lets it go in a big rush of air. His hand comes up and covers my two folded on his stomach, pulling them up over his heart.

"I'm here," I say softly, to which I get a slight squeeze on my hands in response.

"I'm still hungry," Dex breaks the charged energy in the kitchen, which has me smiling and Gunnar chuckling under my hands.

"Right," I say, forcefully dragging myself away from Gunnar and heading back to the stove where more batter is waiting, and a smile firmly plastered on my face.

After the second round of pancakes are devoured, I turn to the kids. "So what do you guys have planned for the day?"

CHAPTER TWENTY-TWO

Syd

"Thanks. Yes, I'll be sure to let Mom know."

Gunnar is just ending his call when I come downstairs from my shower in one of his shirts.

We'd been late this morning after a long and busy day yesterday. The kids couldn't agree on the same activity, so we ended up at the Portland Flea-for-All Market around the corner from Florence House, where Emmy had wanted to go. We grabbed some lunch there before heading off to Hadlock Field to watch the Sea Dogs play. Obviously, that was Dexter's choice and I'd never been, so that was a lot of fun as well.

The kids both fell asleep on the way home and Gunnar ended up carrying each of them upstairs to bed. I was in bed and sleeping hard and dreamless by the time he must've come in.

I chuckle, thinking of Gunnar's frustration this morning, trying to get them out of bed. His hair standing up all over the place from tugging on it when it took the threat of a bucket of water to get the kids up and ready for school.

"What's funny?" he wants to know as he stalks toward me.

"Nothing." I try to hide my smile when he slips his arms around me and pulls me into his chest.

"You laughing at me?"

This time I can't hold back a giggle and it brings a smile to Gunnar's face as he bends down to me. He takes my mouth in a voracious kiss, stealing the breath right out of me. When a groan escapes me under his onslaught, he grabs my ass and lifts me up on the counter he's backed me into.

"God, Bird. What you do to me," he mumbles before sliding his hand in my hair, pulling my head back, and latching his mouth onto my neck. My hands clutch at his ass, pulling his hips closer between my legs; the large bulge behind his zipper rubbing against my aching center.

Just like that, he has me all wound up and so turned on, I can feel myself getting slick for him. Fumbling hands undo the button at the top of his jeans and with frantic need, I yank down the zipper and push his pants and boxers down in one move; freeing his substantial erection.

"Wait," he mumbles against the breast he manages to free when he yanks down my shirt. In one quick move, he has my shirt up and off and I find myself sitting on the kitchen counter in just my panties. "Let's get rid of these. Lift your ass." He drags them down my legs, dropping them on top of my discarded shirt before dropping to his knees and pulling me right to the edge. With his thumbs, he spreads me wide open before he covers my pussy with an open mouth and I drop my head back on a groan.

"Gunnar ..."

The feeling of his open mouth sliding over me, exploring every nook and crevice with his tongue, his teeth scraping over my clit—I can't help but grab onto his hair and push his face into me while I buck under him. Not a thought in my mind, just sheer bliss forcing my mouth open in a silent scream as I explode into tiny fragments.

Before I can recover, Gunnar is on his feet, guiding his cock to my pussy before slamming home, his balls slapping my ass. This is fast and furious, and I'm still riding the crest of my first orgasm when the second one hits and blinds me.

"Fuck me ... Sydney!" Gunnar yells as he erupts inside of me, his body shaking with his release before he covers my body with his and lies on me, panting.

Gunnar

"So who were you talking to earlier?"

I look at Syd who's sitting on the bed, drying her hair. After our baptism of the kitchen counter, I carried her upstairs, back into the shower, and was surprised to find myself hard and ready again. This time not quite as frantic, but slow and deep, I took her against the shower wall.

Not quite accustomed anymore to such a workout, I'm actually a little tender and can't help but wince when I carefully adjust myself in my jeans. The little smirk on Syd's face as she looks at me has my cock twitch in an attempt to revive itself. But I figure age wins out on this one, because the momentary enthusiasm dies down the moment Syd's question brings my telephone conversation back.

"Chief of Police. Been beating myself up 'cause I didn't call immediately the first time Winslow got up in my face. I knew the bastard had a hidden agenda and there's no doubt in my mind now, he somehow got on Graham Bull's payroll. Could've avoided this fiasco if I'd gone with my initial instinct."

"Graham Bull? That's the owner of the new place, Soul Filets, right? Why do you think he's behind it?"

I lean back against the dresser and watch Syd brush out her glorious hair while considering my answer. "Someone who would send a guy to sneak around and gather information is not someone who is willing to play a fair game. I already had an uneasy feeling about the fire and that's when Winslow came on the scene. Winslow who, I might point out, has done dick-all to investigate. The aggressive way Winslow was questioning you in the hospital, then again in my office, only confirmed what I already suspected. He's more than an overzealous cop and the only reason I can come up with that makes sense is that someone is making it worth his while to try and shut The Skipper down."

I run my hand over my stubble while watching Syd eyeing me from under the curtain of her hair, waiting for me to continue. "First I thought Graham's lackey might have set the fire, but after seeing his reaction both times when discussing it, I'm almost convinced he has no first-hand knowledge. No, I'm more inclined to suspect the sergeant himself."

"Winslow? Are you serious? Did you mention that to the Chief?" Syd's eyes are big with shock.

"I did, but very carefully. He seemed to take my suspicions seriously. Didn't even attempt to shake my resolve." I lightly shake my head when I realize the truth of what I'm saying. He hadn't seemed surprised at all, nor had he asked a ton of questions. *Fucking hell.* It was almost like I wasn't telling him anything new.

It's noon by the time we get out of the house. A short phone call from my lawyer to let me know he'd heard from Cindy's lawyer was the first delay—finally—and they were contesting the application for sole custody. Not a surprise. I knew she wasn't going to let things go so easily. She's more interested in winning than in doing what's best for the kids. She must've realized there is no way she'll ever find her way back into my life or my bed. No fucking way.

Then there was my weekly call with my mom. I'd talked to her about Syd in our earlier conversations, but the moment she got wind Syd was here, she insisted on talking to her herself. Syd was beet red when she got on the phone, throwing me dirty looks for putting her in that position. I just grinned. She's so damn cute when she gets riled up. Knowing my mom, I had no compunction over putting Syd on the spot. Mom would love her. She never took to Cindy, but Syd is so far from my high-maintenance ex that she might as well be a different species.

As I thought, it didn't take Mom more than a few minutes to have Syd smiling and relaxed, although after she says her goodbyes, she punches me square in the shoulder.

"What's that for?" I ask, masking my face in innocence, but Syd isn't having it.

"For putting me on the spot like that! She might've hated me."

No longer able to hold back my laugh, she's about to stomp off when I grab her arm and pull her against me, my arms around her waist preventing her escape.

"Was she mean to you? Awkward?"

Syd shakes her head no. "But she could've been," she sputters.

"Babe—you honestly think that I'd let my mom have a go at you if I wasn't absolutely sure she'd love you? I've told her about you and how I feel about you. I don't think you could do any wrong."

I notice Syd's body has stiffened in my arms. "You told her everything?" she whispers.

"Only the things that are important. If you want to fill in details for her at some point, that's up to you, but they'd be just that—details. They are nowhere near as important as you think they are."

Syd drops her forehead against my chest and grabs handfuls of my shirt in her fists.

"She knows you are amazing with the kids and they adore you, she knows you've had loss in your life, and that you stayed here for a week to recuperate after a vicious attack. But more importantly, she knows you've struggled through hard times and came through standing strong, and most importantly, that I love you. And my mother? That last bit is all she's concerned about."

Rubbing her face in my shirt, I can tell she's crying. When she looks up, a big wet spot right in the center of my chest confirms it, as do the big, watery blue eyes regarding me. "Thank you," she mouths at me. I just kiss her pink, full lips.

"Right. Now that we've got that settled, I'd better get a dry shirt on before we head over to the pub to meet with the health inspector."

Because only emergency vehicles are allowed on the wharf, except for deliveries, we have to walk from the parking lot toward the back entrance, where we find an unmarked car and a police vehicle. I look up, expecting Sergeant Winslow to be the one accompanying the health inspector, but I'm surprised to find a younger officer on the step.

"Afternoon," Mr. Walker smiles, appearing much more comfortable now that Winslow is missing.

"Walker." I stick out my hand to shake his before turning to the cop. Might as well test the waters with this one right away. Without any hesitation, the man grabs my hand for a strong shake.

"I'm Officer Bragdon—Mike Bragdon. The Chief sent me to have a word after your business with Mr. Walker here is concluded."

Surprised there are already wheels put into motion by Chief Duffy, I merely nod before turning to unlock the door. The moment I push it open, I hear a whirring sound behind us. I look over my shoulder to see a man with a camera pointed at us, snapping pictures, not at all deterred by the presence of a police officer. "What the fuck?"

Officer Bragdon turns around and spots the cameraman and immediately walks over. I'm following closely behind while Syd and Walker stay on the step by the open back door. Unfazed, the guy locks eyes with me.

"Hi. Geoff Bailey, Portland Herald. Mr. Lucas?" he asks me, waving his press card at the officer. I don't answer, but simply stare back, which he takes as acknowledgement before continuing. "Right. It's come to my attention your establishment, known as The Skipper, was closed down Saturday night in the middle of the evening rush by the Health Department. Can you expand on that?"

Barely restrained anger has me keep my mouth shut, but the reporter is not deterred.

"I understand one of your employees may have been attempting to poison a patron? Is there any truth to that claim? Can we expect an investigation?" he pushes on. It's taking everything I have to keep my hands fisted by my sides. Officer Bragdon pipes up.

"There is no such investigation and the claim was deemed false. Don't know where you have received your information, but I can tell you if one word is printed making false allegations, I will encourage Mr. Lucas to file charges for defamation. And just so you know, he will have not only a police officer standing for him, but also the health inspector."

The man seems to take that into consideration, finally nods and starts to turn away. Two steps out, he turns back and fires another question at me.

"Is it true that this same employee murdered a man only a few weeks ago and continues to be a suspect in a recent fire?" The reporter is wise in continuing to back away as he rattles off his question because by the time the final syllable falls from his mouth, I'm already in motion with my fists poised.

"Gunnar!" I hear Syd yell behind me just before Bragdon grabs my arms from behind, stopping my motion.

"Don't do it," he hisses behind me, "it's words ... only words." And to the other man he barks, "You're treading on very thin ice here, Mr. Bailey. I'd suggest you move along right now or I'll be forced to slap a charge of public mischief or some such thing on you."

A superior smirk on his face, the reporter points his finger at me before turning around and walking into the alley.

Syd

"Milk or sugar?" I ask the police officer, I think Bragdon is his name.

He smiles and nods. "Both, please."

I can't quite get my head around what just happened here. I'm still in shock, but the officer pulled Gunnar into the kitchen and shoved him down onto a chair, Mr. Walker and I following behind. I made a beeline for the coffee maker, needing to have something to do with my hands.

The words from the reporter swim around in my head and as I put cups of coffee in front of everyone, I try to catch Gunnar's eye, but he avoids looking at me. I can't really blame him. All I've done since I've been here is create problems. It's too much. The words he gave me this morning felt as if he was cementing my place in his life, but now I feel oddly disconnected. I'm not really surprised. The distance I feel from him is understandable when every incident involving me is damaging his livelihood. I have to get out of here.

"I uhh ... I've got something to do upstairs," I mumble as I walk out the door, nobody stopping me.

Tears are burning my eyes, but I'm willing them not to fall. Not yet. Not until I'm alone and well away from the pieces of my heart. I have to do this.

People always believe that where there is smoke there is fire, and Gunnar stands to lose everything if I stay here. His ex would unearth everything about me in an attempt to keep him from getting full custody. She already managed to dig up my history but as soon as she finds out about the attack, which was kept out of the press, she will take it and run, straight to the judge. The pub, Viv, Dino, and everyone else working here could lose their jobs. Gunnar could lose something that has been in his family for generations. There would always be part of him associating that with me. I can't do that to him.

And the kids. My God, the kids. I can't even go there right now. I'll pack up and head to Pam's; stay there until I can figure out something.

I'm mindlessly packing the few clothes I've accumulated and stuff them in my old backpack. Whatever doesn't fit I stick into some plastic grocery bags from under the kitchen counter. My breath halts when I hear footsteps coming up the stairs and I freeze when they stop right behind me in the bedroom.

"Ah good. You're packing," I hear behind me and the tears I've been fighting back start rolling down my face unchecked.

"I just need to grab my stuff from the bathroom and I'll be out of your hair."

He doesn't answer and I grab another bag to pack my toiletries. I'm emptying out the drawers of the vanity and with an odd detachment, wonder how I could've collected so much crap in such a short time.

"Wait." I hear him say from the doorway. "Did you say out of my hair? What the fuck, Syd? I thought you were packing up your stuff to bring home with us?"

I lift my head and look in the mirror to find his eyes in the reflection. They're dark with confusion, hurt, and anger, and I turn to face him.

"I'm so sorry. I can't stay here. My God, Gunnar, it's never-ending; the misfortune I seem to pile on your doorstep. Can't you see? You're angry already. You couldn't even look me in the eyes downstairs. What would happen if —"

"Stop!" He cuts me off, stepping right up to me. "I will not allow you to run. You belong with us and you fucking know it! Syd … Bird …" he softens his tone and reaches out to wipe at the tears on my face. "You have to stop taking responsibility for all the negative that happens around you. It's. Not. Yours. None of it is." He finishes gently, wrapping his arms around me and holding on tight.

"But you were so angry," I try.

"I *was* angry. Jesus, Syd. The guy was threatening to bring down my future. I was furious. I *am* furious, but not at you. Never at you." He kisses my hair and I make one last attempt.

"Don't you see? I am a threat. Even just my presence here is a threat to the pub and everyone's future here."

With his hands on either side of my face, he lifts it up to his.

"No, little Bird. You're the one who doesn't see." He plants a small kiss on my lips and leaves them there when he says, "*You are my future.*"

CHAPTER TWENTY-THREE

Syd

It's June.

The vacationers are starting to crowd Portland and The Skipper's business has been increasing. We had a slight slump after being forced to close down last weekend, but most of the regulars never missed a beat and with new faces roaming the wharf, business is getting even better.

Gunnar has called in his seasonal workers for Thursdays and weekend nights when the place is bustling. With the weather consistently nice, we're working to open the patio up this weekend.

Funny, how quickly I've started thinking of he and I as a *we*, a unit. I feel at home in his world—now my world too— and look forward to every day. Guilt still plagues me, especially when I find myself smiling a lot, but my sessions with Pam help me put things into perspective. She's been a godsend, and so has Viv, who's been a better friend than I have ever known.

Last week when Gunnar stopped me from running was the last time I've wanted to. After he took me home with all my belongings, I settled in as quietly as I could, not wanting to disrupt the household with my presence. But in the last few days, Gunnar's been urging me to put my stamp on things, even calling in Viv to get her to convince me to put my mark on his place. We're supposed to go shopping for *household stuff* on Monday when the pub is closed. Emmy wanted to come, but she has school so I promised her we'd take her to The Maine Mall some other time when we can focus on her favorite stores. I haven't been in a mall for so long, I find I'm actually looking forward to it.

"What's going through that head of yours?" Gunnar's voice is gruff with sleep. I turn over and smile into his heavy lidded eyes. Even with sleep creases marring his face, the scruff of his beard unkempt and his hair unruly, he still takes my breath away. Where he would intimidate me before, I now recognize the loving protectiveness that brings out his sometimes prickly personality. He would do anything and everything for those he loves. I'm one of those lucky ones.

"Just thinking. Trying to wrap my head around how lucky I am. From living on the street one day to waking up to you every morning only a few months later. Seems surreal at times." I run my hand over the coarse hair on his jaw, shivering at the sensation on my palm. I had the friction of his scruff on the inside of my thighs last night, when he had his tongue and lips working me until I came so hard, I swear I saw stars.

A slight smile pulls at his lips. "I know what you're thinking ..." he teases, turning his head and pressing a kiss to my hand before lifting me to cover his body. My legs settle on either side of his hips and his hardening cock is hitting me just right. Just as I reach my mouth to his for a kiss, the door slams open.

"Syd? Can you do pancakes today?" Dex jumps onto the bed in my vacated spot and I gingerly slide off Gunnar's body on the other side.

"Today? Why don't we save that for the weekend, kid?" Gunnar interjects before I have a chance to respond.

Dexter's face falls with disappointment, but only for a moment.

"But today is Friday! The beginning of the weekend, so I think we should have pancakes to celebrate." The smirk on his face is priceless and I can't help but laugh at the little smartass. His hopeful eyes are focused on me as I slide out of bed, thanking the Lord I had pulled Gunnar's shirt back on right before I fell asleep.

"All right, sweetie, but you better have your sister up and your butt downstairs in fifteen minutes. And no skipping the toothbrush today."

With a fist pump and a victorious "Yesss," causing Gunnar to chuckle, Dex is up and out of the room in a flash.

"Come here," Gunnar tempts me from the bed. "I wasn't done with you."

"You heard the man-child. I'm wanted in the kitchen," I say as I make a move to the bathroom, but Gunnar manages to snag the back of my shirt as I try to sneak by and pulls me back. With his hand gripping the back of my neck, he pulls me down for a knee-buckling kiss.

"There, now you can go." With a satisfied smirk and a slap on my butt, I'm released.

"Dad! Syd! You guys are in the newspaper!" Emmy comes barreling in from her morning task of grabbing the paper from the driveway.

What?

Gunnar snatches the paper from Emmy's hands and pushing the breakfast dishes out of the way, spreads it open on the counter.

"Fucking piece of shit!" he spits out, looking at a picture of the pub's back entrance, perfectly framed with Gunnar looking over his shoulder at the camera, me right behind him, and on the step below, the health inspector and Officer Bragdon. Impossible to miss is the patrol car at the bottom left side of the image. The title accompanying the image is 'Local Restaurant Forced To Close Their Doors?' with a subheading stating: 'The Skipper is in trouble ...' There is nothing more on the front page other than a brief paragraph with a sequence of events, highlighting an as yet, unexplained fire on the property, a violent attack resulting in the death of a hardworking Portland native, and the shutdown by the Health Department, pending an investigation. Only a reference to page twelve for the full article and our names as identified from the photo.

"This is fucking inflammatory as hell. I'm gonna nail that little bastard's hide to the wall." Gunnar is whipping the pages until he finds the *full article*, a small two column description, basically stating the death was in self-defense, the Health Department reported no issues, and the only thing still unresolved was the fire in a shed on the property.

I put my hand on Gunnar's arm and lean in to whisper in his ear. "Kids." One look at their faces when their father yelled was enough to know he's scaring them. They've had enough irrational behavior from one parent, and seeing their father lose his cool must have them worried. Gunnar's eyes follow the direction of my gaze.

"Fuck," I hear him say under his breath before getting up and walking over to where they're standing, backpacks in hand by the door.

"I'm sorry, guys," he tells the two. "I'm not upset with you. Someone's been trying to make things difficult for the pub and that article in the newspaper is just the last of it." He snags each of them by the back of the neck and pulls them to his chest, bending over them protectively.

Gunnar

"Are we gonna be okay?" Emmy wants to know.

"Always, my girl. Just a bump in the road and nothing your old dad can't handle," I tell her.

We've just dropped off Dex at school, who seems to have forgotten the entire incident already, but Emmy's been brooding. She's standing with her hand on the truck door, leaning in, her eyes filled with worry.

"Honey," I try to reassure her, "there is no problem so big it can't be fixed. Let me do the worrying for both of us, okay?"

At her timid nod, I lean over the center console, beckoning her closer. "Now give me my kiss and get yourself smart in there, girl." I point to the front doors of the school, making her smile before she leans in to give me my kiss. "Love you, Emmy."

"Love you more, Dad," she says in that way that makes my heart swell a little more each time.

"Impossible," I yell after her, blowing her a kiss as she goes.

This little reality check with my daughter has cooled me down. I'm pissed, for sure, but Emmy just reminded me I have all that I need at home—no need to bring home trouble to spoil the goodness I have there. The pub will survive. It's seen the worst storms, economic downfalls, and an assortment of other challenges over the decades, and has still remained standing. It will now too, I'll fucking see to it.

A phone call to my lawyer the moment I get home confirms what I suspect; Geoff Bailey hasn't said anything that could be labeled as defamation. No chance to get him or the Herald to retract their story. His suggestion is to allow him to interview Syd and myself for a follow-up story, but there is no way in hell I'd put Syd through that. Not a chance. Not up for discussion, and I tell her that right off the bat. I'll just ride it out.

"What if he keeps up with the innuendo? If he does another story like this one?" Syd asks beside me. We're on our way to the storage unit where I keep most of the patio furniture during the winter. My parents used to have it upstairs in the apartment, which was used for storage for just about anything before I cleaned it out and moved in after leaving Cindy. Since then it's been kept at the Cumberland Self Storage; not too far from the pub.

"As long as he stays on the side of the truth, there isn't much we can do and I doubt our regular patrons will stop coming because of the negative publicity he's trying to create." I chuckle, turning into the storage facility. "Who knows, maybe it's true what they say; that any publicity is good publicity."

I don't really believe that and from the frown on Syd's face, neither does she.

It doesn't take us long to load everything into the rental truck Dino drives up in shortly after we get there and in convoy style, we take off for the pub where Viv and Matt are already waiting. I want to get this stuff cleaned and set up before the dinner rush. Shouldn't be a problem with all hands on deck to wash the furniture down and set it up.

Luckily, it's mostly just dust covering the tables and chairs. The umbrellas we shake out in the alley before hosing them down. A few buckets of soap work on the rest of the furniture and before you know it, we have it all drying in the afternoon sun.

Dino and Viv are handling the food service and Matt is manning the bar for the lunch crowd while Syd and I are setting up the server's station outside. It's where we store menus, salt and pepper shakers, sugar, and other sweeteners and assorted condiments. "We should try and include some of your Thursday night specials in the regular menu," I suggest to her as I'm skimming over the pages of a menu. "Thinking that jambalaya would do well."

"Seriously?" She pauses with filling the saltshakers and shifts her attention to me. "But wouldn't Dino mind?"

"Doubtful. He's the one who suggested it in the first place. Said something about that recipe having the ability to come a fast favorite." I love the smile that stretches across her face when I tell her this.

"Okay," she says, shrugging her shoulders and pretending to be unaffected, but that big smile is still there, telling how she really feels.

"Deal. After the weekend, let's figure out what numbers we'd be looking at daily and adjust our order."

I chuckle when she starts clapping her hands like a child. So fucking cute. Unable to resist, I pull her into my arms and kiss that smiling face. Nothing matters when I have my tongue in her mouth; the world just falls away.

"Oh, how cozy." Until the one person you're trying to forget walks up.

When I lift my head, I see Cindy is not alone. At some point along the line, she's made a new friend.

"Hello, Cindy ... Denise. What can I do for you?" I try to keep my cool even though it's suddenly clear to me where Cindy got some of the misinformation she spouted last week. Ironic that these two found each other, or is it?

Syd is squirming in my hold, trying to get away, but I hold her in place, tucked against my side when I face the two.

"I see you kissed and made up? I've got to say, you're making this very easy on me, Gunnar." Cindy looks at me with a little smile playing on her lips before it turns into a sneer when she turns her eyes on Syd. "Your little plaything here apparently has been a very busy girl. Denise was kind enough to come to me a few weeks ago with her concerns for my children, but this morning's newspaper sheds an even clearer light on things," she says, waving this morning's Herald in my face. "I'm thinking this might be information a judge would find enlightening, don't you think?"

I'm letting her ramble, even laugh at the unimpressive threat, but I'm still trying desperately not to let go of Syd and use my hands to strangle my ex-wife. Ignoring her and her nonsense, I turn to Denise.

"What do you stand to gain from this? Anything? Gotta say, I'm a bit surprised you'd tie your wagon to this one," I tilt my head in Cindy's direction, "or are you just pissed I never was tempted once to take you up on the blatantly obvious invitations to fuck you?" Syd shifts beside me and I stroke her arm soothingly. The sharp hiss my words elicit from Denise is satisfying. "Never would've fucking happened. Syd or no Syd, there is absolutely nothing you have to offer that I am even remotely interested in, but to mix yourself into this mess, to play with the welfare of my children? You're fucking worse than she is," I point at Cindy. "She's a drunk, has been for years. She's got nothing but her own needs in mind. Any motherly impulses she may have had have been drowned in alcohol. She's already lost all her dignity, and I see that you're quickly losing yours. And for fucking what?"

Denise flinches at the impact of what I say and turns her eyes away, shuffling her feet restlessly. Cindy, on the other hand, is spitting mad.

"I'll have you know I have my diggin ... dig ... whatever!" She can't even get the fucking words out of her mouth, she's that sauced already. Before I have a chance to point that out, Cindy swings on Syd. "It's all because of you." She stabs a finger at her and I'm this close to losing it on her when Syd puts a calming hand on my chest and steps forward, coming face to face with the irate woman.

"You lost him way before I ever got here. I had no part in that, Cindy. You did that on your own, but if you think you're hurting now, imagine losing your children for good. I lost a child. There is absolutely no other pain in the world that compares. You need to think long and hard before you ruin any chance you have for a relationship with them— before your children turn their backs on you. I can promise you that's not something you recover from. The hole it leaves in your heart is permanent." Her words seem to have taken the fire from Cindy's eyes, leaving her wringing her hands nervously. It's like she's confused by Syd's friendly tone. With a gentle smile, Syd adds, "The kids love you, they just don't like you very much right now. You can change that. *Only* you can change that. I love them and want to be part of their lives. But, Cindy? You're their mother. You'll always be their mother, even if you're not behaving like it now."

Fuck, this woman owns me. For as much as I thought I was getting through to these two vindictive bitches, Syd just very quietly and calmly holds a mirror up in front of their faces. Oh, as much as she was talking to Cindy, Denise is clearly affected too. She grabs Cindy by the arm, turns her around and walks away, throwing one last wistful glance over her shoulder.

I pull Syd's body back against me and bury my nose in her hair, breathing her in along with the fresh air, blowing in off the ocean.

"What did that bitch want?" Viv is standing with her hands on her hips by the door when we head inside.

I smile at her vehemence. She's always been fierce in her protection of me and the kids, but apparently Syd's opened up an entire new level of momma bear.

"Nothing Syd couldn't handle single-handedly," I say, stroking my hand along Syd's spine. "I went for Denise, but Syd here brought the truth to Cindy; at least I hope so."

"As awful as she's been—and I'm not making any excuses for her—I think the woman is scared and clawing at anything coming her way." She shrugs her shoulders before continuing. "I just held up a picture of what the future might look like if she continues this way. Don't know if it does any good. I hope so for the sake of the kids, but only time will tell, but in the meantime, I won't hold my breath."

"I take it they saw the newspaper and came to rub it in?" Viv offers.

"Something like that. I've gotta say, having those two teaming up threw me for a minute," I admit.

"I bet ya it was Denise seeking Cindy out, trying to get back at you for tossing her ass to the curb. Vindictive cow was always panting after you, trying to get your attention. Well she got it, but not the way she'd hoped for." Viv chuckles as Syd slips away from me, disappearing into the hallway behind the bar.

"You know she's the best thing, aside from the kids, that's happened to you, right?" she says, watching Syd's retreat.

"Believe me, I know."

Been a busy day. After the earlier confrontation outside, the afternoon and evening swallowed us up. A surprise visit from a few guys from my team to *christen* the patio livened up the place, and the mild evening had the crowd lingering out there longer than normal.

I love the sound of laughter bouncing over the water, and there was a lot of laughing going on tonight.

Syd stayed in the kitchen after one of the patrons asked her if he should be worried that she's the one serving him food. Syd stood frozen, gaping at the man. Viv, who'd been at the next booth with a customer, immediately intervened, telling the guy in no uncertain terms that if he couldn't keep his poor taste in jokes to himself, he could take a hike. Muttering apologies to Syd, the guy quietly finished his meal and left, leaving a massive tip, just for her.

Of course they didn't tell me until after he'd left, knowing full well I'd have ripped him a new one.

After spending a bit of time with my teammates on the patio after the dinner rush died down, I head inside to look for Syd. I haven't seen her for the last hour or so.

"Where's Syd?" I ask Viv who's loading the dishwasher in the kitchen. Dino left after closing the kitchen at ten so there was no one else there.

"Fell asleep with her head on the kitchen table a while ago. Told her to go lay down upstairs until you were ready to go." I walk over and sling my arm around Viv's shoulders, giving her a kiss to the side of her head.

"Thanks for picking up the slack and looking after my girl."

Viv snickers as she pushes me off her. "You kidding me? I'll do anything for the woman that keeps your ass happy. Makes my days a hell of a lot easier."

Smartass.

But with a lighter feeling in my chest than this day warrants, I head upstairs. By the looks of things, Syd never made it to the bed, laying curled up on the couch, fast asleep.

"Hey, baby, time to go home." I slip my hands under her knees and around her waist, hoisting her still too light frame in my arms and carry her downstairs.

"He looks so young," Syd says, looking down at Dexter who's sprawled out in his bed. Asleep most of the way home, she insists on walking in under her own steam. Showing Mrs. Danzel out, I lock up and head upstairs after her, finding her in Dex's bedroom.

"Hard to believe he's nine years old; ten next week," I agree with her, sliding a hand up her spine and around her neck.

"I see him when I dream."

"What do you mean?"

"Each time I dream of Daniel, he looks more and more like Dexter," she whispers,

I guide her gently out of the room, closing the door behind us. Once in our bedroom I push her back to sit on the bed, kneeling before her. When she lifts her eyes I see pain so deep, I can feel it. "I'm losing him, Gunnar. The only photo I had of him is long gone and when I try to picture his face, more often than not, Dexter's is the one who fills my vision. I'm scared ..."

She looks so fucking broken. I'm afraid to touch her until she throws herself into my arms.

Sitting on the floor with Syd in my arms, breaking a little with every sob from her body, I vow to find a way so she will never forget her boy.

CHAPTER TWENTY-FOUR

Syd

"Are you baking me a cake?"

Dexter's excitement over his upcoming birthday party is infectious and he has me smiling as he hops from one leg to another in front of me.

"Do you need to pee?" I ask him, my eyebrows raised.

"Nuhuh. So are you?"

"Maybe ..." I tease him, ruffling his hair. I never noticed how tall he really is. Takes after his father who must be at least six foot three or four. My five foot two frame certainly won't be able to stand up to the genes Dex carries for long. For now though, I can still ruffle his hair to my amusement and his irritation.

"Syd, I need cake. The guys are coming and they're gonna want cake too."

"Are you whining?" Gunnar's deep voice comes from the doorway. "Because you know we don't listen to whiners here, right kid?"

The guilty little shrug he gives his father makes me want to chuckle, but I hold it in. Attitude is rampant with Emmy stumbling into puberty and Dex flexing his male dominant muscles.

"Go to the bathroom and pee, Dex. You're about to blow a leak."

It's all it takes to break the hint of tension in the kitchen and sends Dex snickering at his father's choice of words off to the bathroom, but not before bumping fists with him first.

"Nice language," I taunt Gunnar when Dex is out of hearing range.

He steps into me and slides his arms around my waist, sliding his hands down to cup my ass.

"Man talk. You wouldn't understand," he says with a sparkle in his eyes, making me shake my head as he lowers his mouth to my neck, sucking on the tender skin.

"Kids might come in," I point out rather breathlessly. "You have your mouth on my neck, your hands on my ass. I—" My words are cut short when Gunnar's mouth slides over mine, tugging at my lower lip with his teeth and creating instant havoc on my clean panties. His tongue parts my lips and claims my mouth thoroughly before leaving me breathless and panting.

"I like having my hands on your ass. Like the way it's starting to fill my hands more each day," he growls in my neck where he's returned to his explorations. His hands slide from my ass up the small of my back where one holds me pressed against him, his arousal prominent against my belly, and the other slips around the front and up to lift the weight of my breast. "These too. So fucking gorgeous. I could feast on you all day." Flicking his thumb over my nipple has me release a shuddering breath.

There's nothing I'd like to do more in this moment than climb him like a monkey, but a voice calling from the front door puts a quick end to that fantasy.

"Dad! We gotta go!"

"*Fuck*. Gotta get the kids to school. You ready?" he asks, leaning his forehead against mine. Still rather incoherent, I simply nod.

After dropping the kids off at their respective schools, we hit a Denny's not too far from Viv's place. I've not been to her apartment yet and rather than having her drive all the way to Gunnar's house to pick me up, he suggested taking me for breakfast and then dropping me off for our shopping spree. Gunnar offered to get the ingredients for the double chocolate cake I'm planning to make tomorrow morning and he's picking up the rest of the party stuff as well. My job is to find the game Dex has been after. Apparently, Best Buy has it in stock so I'll pick it up before tackling Macy's, Sears, and the Pottery Barn.

"Two eggs, bacon, sausage, home fries, and rye toast, please." Gunnar places his order after I've already placed mine for waffles and fruit. "Oh, and can you bring us some more coffee?" he asks of the tired looking waitress who says nothing but snaps her chewing gum in response.

"Good thing they serve my kind of comfort food, 'cause that waitress isn't making me feel warm and fuzzy right now," he quips, making me laugh. Immediately he slides his hand across the table and grabs mine. "How are you doing, Bird?"

He doesn't have to explain, I know he's talking about my breakdown before the weekend. Saturday came and went in a flurry of activity, with only a few questions about the newspaper article from loyal patrons. By Sunday we noticed a nominal decline in business but that could have had something to do with the open mic night at b.good's, a local eatery that runs these evenings once a week during the summer.

All in all, I've been busy enough not to wallow in my momentary depression, but the fear remains.

"Not too bad. I don't want to, but I can't help thinking about him," I look at him, hoping for understanding.

"Nor would I want you to," Gunnar smiles reassuringly. "Would you consider contacting your family to see if they would send you a picture?"

The moment he utters *family* has me immediately shaking my head no.

"I don't want them to destroy what I've found. Don't want their accusations in my face."

Squeezing my hand, he draws my attention. "I'd never let that happen. You know that, right?" He waits for my confirming nod before he goes on. "Maybe your sister? Just think about it."

Just then the waitress is back with our orders, saving me from a response, but all through breakfast, I'm thinking about my sister and how much I miss her. I'm not sure she'd even recognize who I am now, or what she'd do if she did.

Gunnar tries to lift my spirits with questions about my pending shopping trip and pushes a credit card my way.

"I'm not taking that," I tell him firmly. "Bad enough you won't let me contribute to the household, but I'm not letting you pay for my shopping. I've hardly had opportunity to spend the money I earn by working for you. It just doesn't seem right to me."

After a few futile attempts at making me change my mind, Gunnar tucks his card in his wallet and pulls me out of the booth, wrapping his arm around my shoulders.

"Just wanna make it clear that it's only because I know you value your independence, I'll let you get away with this," he mumbles in my ear. I can't help it, I laugh. Typical guy to concede defeat only to make it into some magnanimous gesture. His face shows irritation, but his eyes sparkle with amusement.

"How many sheets do I need for one bed?" Viv has been dragging me from store to store with a Starbucks clutched in her hand. I swear she could've done without the added caffeine; the woman is tireless.

"Only one more. You need sexy sheets too. The other sets are great for daily use but you need a set that screams *hot night ahead*." She dons a wicked smile and I can't help but chuckle.

"Have you met Gunnar?" I ask her. "Not like old ratty sheets would stop the man if he has a mind to get frisky. He's happy with the kitchen counter."

"Okay, TMI." She looks at me horrified. "I've eaten at that counter. Regularly have my coffee there. Besides, the man is like another brother, I can't even ... Ewww!"

Laughing, I elbow her in the arm. "You started it."

"Touché. I'm done discussing your sex life. Let's find some throw pillows." She slips her arm in mine and pulls me toward the Pottery Barn where we spend another hour looking at accessories and knick-knacks. Never an ardent shopper, Viv's enthusiasm has me enjoying myself thoroughly. Before I realize it, it's already four in the afternoon.

"We've gotta go," I blurt out, getting a glimpse of the large clock on the wall at Victoria's Secret where Viv dragged me for some sexy undies. Her words, not mine. I've always been quite happy with my comfortable cotton panties. Mostly because I never felt sexy enough to wear anything else, but I have to admit, with the blatant interest Gunnar examines my body, I can't wait to see the effect sexy underwear will have on him.

Viv follows my eyes to the clock, quickly grabs the three sets I'd taken into the dressing room with me and makes a beeline for the register.

"Wait! Where are you going?" I try to stop her, but only have one leg in my jeans. By the time I'm dressed, she's standing by the exit with a triumphant smile on her face, and a fat Victoria's Secret bag in her hand.

"Don't even ..." she stops me with a raised hand when I open my mouth to protest. "You *will* let me do this. Just think of it as a belated birthday present for Gunnar. I'm sure he'll be grateful." She raises one eyebrow, daring me to counter. The best thing I can come up with is to stick my tongue out at her, realizing arguing is futile. She throws her head back and laughs, tugging my arm through hers and pulling me from the store.

Half an hour later, we pull into the driveway at Gunnar's. Or maybe I should start calling it our house? After all, the volume of bags Viv pulls out of the trunk certainly looks like I'm settling in. I'm suddenly embarrassed. Is it too much? Did I go overboard? But before I have a chance to worry myself to tears, two strong arms slide around me from behind and Gunnar whispers in my ear. "Have fun?"

I nod my head and can't stop the smile from splitting my face almost in half. He chuckles, turning me around in his arms and laying a hot and heavy kiss on me right in the driveway.

"Enough!" Viv's voice breaks us apart. "I've had to suffer through Victoria's Secret with her, knowing your greedy eyes would be appreciative," she points at Gunnar, "but I could do without the mouth sex in front of the house." With a wink at me, she saunters through the door, loaded down with shopping bags.

"Victoria's Secret?" Gunnar growls.

I roll my eyes at him. "Really? You're that easy?"

"Only when it comes to you, Bird. Only when it comes to you."

To my surprise, Gunnar insists on cooking that night and invites Viv to stick around. After a tasty meal of grilled kebabs with chicken and vegetables—a seasonal debut for the big BBQ out on the deck—we're sitting out back with sweaters on against the evening chill, sipping a cup of decaf.

"Did you manage to find Dex's birthday present?" Gunnar asks after checking to make sure Dex is inside and out of earshot.

"I did and I got him some other stuff too."

"You didn't have to do that, babe," Gunnar squeezes my hand.

"I had to hold her back from getting presents for Emmy as well," Viv pipes up. The traitor. "As it is, she has a few things for her too."

"I wanted to do something for her because she was so disappointed today she couldn't come," I say defensively. "As for the gifts for Dex, I'm just happy I get to be part of his birthday. That's all. Been so long I've been able to shop for a birthday. It felt good." I shrug my shoulders.

When I look up, Gunnar wears a soft smile and Viv has tears in her eyes. Immediately she excuses herself, stating she has to get a good night's sleep in if she's going to pick up our slack at The Skipper tomorrow. I walk her to the car when she swings around and grabs me in a tight hug.

"I'm so fucking grateful for the day you came into all of our lives. I never was one for an active social life or had any girlfriends, but I'm grateful to have found one in you."

With a kiss on my cheek, she disappears into her car and takes off, leaving me gazing after her. *Me too,* I wanted to say, but she's already gone.

Gunnar is waiting for me on the front step. "You okay?" he wants to know. "I ... she ... yes, I'm okay. She just took off so fast I never had a chance to properly thank her for today." I stammer. Guiding me inside, Gunnar just grunts in response.

It takes a bit of coaxing, but eventually we jointly manage to get the kids upstairs, seeing as tomorrow is a regular school day, despite the fact it's Dex's tenth birthday. The only thing that finally convinces them to go is my promise there will be cake for the party. That's the only thing I'm willing to commit to since I'm not quite sure whether the plans I have for it will pan out. If I don't make any promises, there can't be any disappointments if I end up having to go to the store to grab a simple slab.

The plan is to bake a cake and then turn it into the shape of Batman's signal. I contemplated doing the Batmobile, but after looking at a complicated diagram online, I quickly changed my mind and opted for a simple logo. I decided on Batman because of one of the first conversations he and I had. Gunnar had picked up all the ingredients for baking and Viv and I stopped in at a Michaels craft store close to the mall for decorating supplies. I'm not even sure I can do this. I mean, I've done baking before, but remembering back, I never really did a birthday cake. I used to simply order one. The prospect of doing it myself is something I look forward to. But it's been hell not to spill the beans.

"Can you come tuck me in?" Dex calls from his room and I make my way over, finding him already in bed with his sheets pulled up to his chin.

"Excited?" I ask him and he furiously nods his head in response, making me chuckle before his little face turns serious.

"Syd? Do you think mom will come?"

"Honey, I'm sure she's gonna do her best to be here or at least call you. Dad left her a message reminding her over the weekend, but even if for whatever reason she isn't able to, we'll still have a great time and I'm positive your mom will make it up to you on some other day."

God, I hope I'm not lying to the kid. I'm keeping my fingers crossed that Cindy's going to pull her head out of her ass and give the kids the attention they are due.

Dexter pulls his arms from under the covers and holds them out to me, waiting for a hug, which I gladly give him.

"Are we good, Dex?" I ask him carefully and with his arms still wrapped around my neck, he mumbles, "We're good," before allowing me to pull back from his embrace.

I lean over to give him a kiss on his forehead. "Night, honey."

"Night, Syd," he says as he rolls over onto his side, pulling the covers up to his ear.

Once out back again, this time with a beer for Gunnar and a bottle of water for me, he clears his throat. "What you said earlier? I think it really brought home what you've been through. For me, and I'm guessing for Viv as well. Things we take for granted because we've never had to be without, like the ability to spoil a child—those things are precious to you. The little ways you have to make people around you feel cared for. I love that about you, and I hate it at the same time, because, Syd? If there was any way I could turn back time and take back the loss you suffered, even if it meant losing all that you are now? I'd do it in a heartbeat."

I can't speak. I'm so full of emotion right now, I'm overwhelmed. There is no way to describe the healing this man provides for my soul. He makes me think about the unthinkable, only to come up with the realization that you can't win the *what-if* game. Life is a trade off at times. Fate is cruel that way. Sometimes you have to accept the flow; letting go of one thing to be able to embrace the next. I'll never get over the loss of Daniel, or the part I played in it, but it's what brought me to this point in my life and that's something I could never regret. Gunnar, the kids, and even Viv and the pub; they are my future.

"Bird?" Gunnar's voice breaks through my revelation, a concerned frown marring his forehead. Putting my hand on his face, I try to smile through my tears.

"Love you." My voice cracks as I give him the only words I seem to be able to manage right now.

"Fuck, baby. I fucking hate it when you cry. Even more when I'm the one causing the hurt." He grabs me by the waist and hauls me on his lap, tucking my head against his shoulder.

"You're not hurting me, honey. You're healing me."

CHAPTER TWENTY-FIVE

Gunnar

"I want cake too!"

The horde of boys come running in from the deck where they've just finished four boxes of pizza like a pack of hungry wolves, each trying to out-yell the other after Syd calls them in from the back door.

Emmy went home with Tasha after school, not wanting to be around five boys all afternoon. Syd insisted we wait for her to get back before serving the cake and she was just dropped off by Tasha's dad. The cake is stunning; Syd worked on it for hours, cutting templates from sugar paste, replicating the printout she made on the computer. What was a thick, round double chocolate cake is now an oval, smothered in icing and covered with black and yellow fondant to make a perfect Batman logo image. Pleased as punch with herself, she grins at me from the kitchen, hiding the cake in the fridge until the boys are all situated in the living room with the blinds drawn and lights out for optimum effect. She pulls the cake out and setting it on the counter, sticks ten birthday candles around the perimeter, lighting them with the BBQ lighter.

"Happy birthday to you. Happy birthday to you," she starts singing as she carries the cake into the room, being joined by five other voices. I don't sing. Not going to start now, not when I'm enjoying the excited look on my son's face who's lapping up all the attention. Emmy comes to stand next to me and slides her arm around my back. I bend down to kiss her hair.

"You good, sweetie?"

She turns her smiling face toward me. "Good, Daddy. She makes everything better, doesn't she?" I follow her eyes that come to rest on Syd, who's encouraging Dex to blow out his candles and make a wish.

"She sure does," I tell my daughter softly.

With everyone supplied with a generous slice of cake, Syd is walking back to the kitchen when the doorbell rings. Motioning for her to continue, and that I'll get the door, I walk over and open it, fully expecting one of the parents to have arrived a little early. It isn't.

"Cindy ..."

"I'm not here to make trouble," she says, wiping the hair out of her eyes that look clear today. "I just want to say happy birthday to Dex. I've brought a gift." She holds up a gift bag with blue tissue paper sticking out.

I feel Syd's presence before I hear her voice from beside me.

"Of course. Why don't you come in and have some cake?"

Cindy gapes with her mouth open, her eyes flicking from one to the other. I'm not sure if Syd knows what she's doing, but trusting her, I follow her lead.

"Yeah. Sure, why don't you come in? Dex will be happy you made it."

I step to the side, leaving Syd to lead the way to the kitchen with a rather shell-shocked Cindy following wordlessly behind her.

"Sit." Syd directs Cindy to one of the stools at the counter and proceeds to cut her a slice of cake, setting it before her and putting a fork on her plate. "Some coffee?"

she asks and without waiting for an answer, she proceeds to make a fresh pot.

Cindy is staring at Syd's back, more demure and beaten down than I've ever seen her and I'm surprised to feel pity replacing the anger I've carried for so long. Never thought I'd see the day she'd be sitting in my kitchen, drinking coffee and eating cake. Well, technically, she's not doing either of those yet, but she will be. I'm starting to believe Syd can make anything happen. The kids haven't surfaced from their cake yet, but they will soon.

"Better dig into that cake. The kids are scarfing down theirs and may go after your piece next." Syd smiles as she slides a cup on the counter in front of Cindy. "What do you take in it?"

I see Cindy swallow hard before answering. "Cream and sugar, please." With a voice softer than I've heard from her in recent years, she asks about the kids while staring down into her coffee. "How are they? I ... I miss them."

I can see her struggling for composure. With a mind for the kids who could barge in at any time, I rest my hand on her shoulder.

"Kids are good, Cindy. They've been hurt and may take some time to get over the anger, but they're doing okay. I'm sure they miss you too." It takes everything to be nice to her—I've been treated to her brand of vicious too long—but I manage. Syd moved up to lean on the counter across from Cindy. Whether to show her support or to keep me from strangling my ex after all, I don't know. Guess is, probably the latter. Her eyes radiate warmth when she looks at me over Cindy's head. With a slight nod in the direction of the living room, she seems to dismiss me.

"Could you make sure the kids are okay? Maybe give us a minute and then let Dex know his mom is here?"

Yup. Definitely being dismissed. But I don't go without rounding the counter, putting my hand on the nape of her neck and tugging her close for a quick kiss. "Sure you'll be all right?" I ask her softly.

"Positive. Now get." With a little shove against my chest she sends me packing.

The living room is a bit of a disaster area. Lanky kids flopped all over the place, all watching Dex play his newest game on the big TV. Emmy sidles up to me as I plop down on the couch beside her.

"She gone?" she whispers.

I look at my daughter, surprised. "Your mom? She's still here, talking with Syd in the kitchen."

"Talking. Right," Emmy snorts, obviously expecting some new drama to develop.

"She is, Emmy. I don't know for sure what happened to make for this change, although I have a pretty good idea, but she seems to really be here just to see you guys. She even brought a gift for Dex." I try, but I don't think Emmy's sold. A stubborn set to her mouth I've become all too familiar with, and a demonstrative crossing of her arms over her chest would be a rather clear indicator she's not ready to buy into her mother's change of attitude. Frankly, I'm not sure I am either. If not for Syd setting the tone on this one, I'm pretty confident I'd have left her standing on the front step. She sure as hell wouldn't be eating cake and drinking coffee in my kitchen. Our kitchen. Shit, I keep having to remind myself.

"Mom's here?" Some of my whispered conversation with Emmy must've filtered through because suddenly Dex is up on his feet, throwing his controller at one of his buddies. But before I let him barrel past me, I pull him down on the couch with me.

"Easy, buddy. She's just talking to Syd, so give her a minute, okay?"

But Dex is up within seconds, having sat still for his version of a minute and I don't have the heart to make him wait any longer. More slowly, I follow him into the kitchen where he's already folded into his mother's arms. Now there's something I haven't seen in ... well, in forever. Not since he was a toddler has Cindy shown much affection. For either of the kids, actually, as is witnessed by the sharp inhale from Emmy who's come in behind me.

My eyes find Syd's and although they are a bit too shiny to my liking, the smile on her face is unmistakable. I wrap my arm around Emmy who seems frozen by my side.

"So what. You show up here with a gift and think that makes everything okay?"

Shit. Should've seen this one coming. Emmy pulls out from under my arm and stands in front of her mom with her hands on her hips. "Emmy ..." I try, but she shakes her head sharply, warning me off. I don't know if I can, but I appreciate she wants her say.

This situation could go to hell in a handbasket in seconds, especially seeing the look of confusion on Dex's face. But what surprises me is the calm look on Cindy's face as she turns to face her daughter.

"No Emmy, I don't. But I couldn't let your brother's birthday go by without doing something. I realize full well that making things *okay* is gonna take a hell of a lot more than that, and—" Cindy is cut off with a deriding snort from Emmy.

"Since when do you care? He's having a great birthday, with friends he was never allowed to have over at your house. He even has a cake Syd actually baked for him. She gives him a birthday, more than he's ever had from you!"

Every word is hitting Cindy hard and she's fighting to keep her composure when Syd's had enough.

"Emmy!" Syd draws my daughter's attention. "I get you're mad, and you have reason to be, but make sure *you* don't spoil things for your brother now." With a tilt of her head, Syd points to the birthday boy who's made his way to her side and is leaning against her. Close to crying, by the looks.

"Emmy," Cindy tries. "I'm gonna fix this. I may be gone for a while trying to get myself sorted, but I *will* fix this."

"Right. Well, I hope you don't mind if I don't hold my breath, *Mother*."

With that, Emmy slips past me and stomps up the stairs, slamming her bedroom door shut. Not going to run after her. Give her some time to process before we go up there.

The slump to Cindy's shoulders disappears when she turns to Dex, who's secure against Syd, her arm protectively around him.

"I've gotta go, birthday boy," Cindy says softly. "I might be gone for a while, but I'll be back when I'm better."

"You gonna call?"

"As soon as I can. I'll make sure your Dad has my number, okay? It's gonna be all right." With a straight spine she gets up and walks over to Dex. I notice he is getting tall; almost as tall as Syd and coming up to his mother's nose. Cindy bends down and gives him a kiss on his hair before facing Syd. "Take care of them?"

"You know it," Syd promises with a wobbly smile. A mouthed "thank you," in response before she turns to me. "Walk me to the door?"

I nod and follow her until we are outside on the step, Cindy looking away from me toward her car.

"I just wanted you to know that I've had my lawyer sign off on the full custody application. No contest."

She takes a deep breath before turning to face me. "I fucked up so bad, Gunnar. Made you hate me—made my kids hate me. I don't know if I can, but I'll try. For the kids, I'll give it all I have. I'll text you the address and phone number where I'll be." The pain is plain on her face and I can't help but want to reach out, but she wards me off with both her hands raised. "Don't, just ..." A shake as if to clear her head and she's down the steps walking toward her car.

"Cindy?" I call after her, making her stop and turn. "Good luck."

She's motionless for a moment before she nods once, turns, and slips into her car and drives away.

Syd

The moment Gunnar leaves the kitchen behind Cindy, Dex turns his face up to me.

"Do you think she'll really come back?" His voice is small and not hiding the fear in his words very well. My heart crumbles a little.

"I think so. I think your mom knows exactly what she needs to do to get well, but it isn't going to be easy for her. That's why she's going away—to get some help. But she has the best reasons in the world to make it happen." I cup his face in my hands. "I don't think there is anything more important to her than you and your sister, Dex. Have a little faith."

Poor kid is battling hard to keep the tears at bay.

"Why aren't you mad at her? She was really mean to you."

"Not today she wasn't. Besides, you've gotta know I'll always be grateful to your mom. If not for her, I wouldn't have two beautiful children to give all the love to that was locked inside me. You two are a gift to be treasured and for that, I will always be thankful. But she'll always be your mom and I know she'll be back so she can prove it to you."

I unwrap his arms from around my waist and plant a quick kiss on his head. "Now, I believe you have some friends who are waiting to kick your ass in that new game of yours."

Easily distracted, as is to be expected from a ten-year-old in the middle of a birthday party, Dex throws me a smile before running into the other room. His buddies, still focused on the TV screen, totally oblivious to the drama that just played out in the kitchen.

I'm just sitting down with a fresh cup of coffee when Gunnar walks back in.

"Well," he mutters, a little flustered. "I can't say I understand what just happened, but I dare say it's good, right?"

I smile at him, eliciting a small smile in return. "I'd say it was very good, although Emmy concerns me a little," I admit.

"Give her a little time to sort herself out," Gunnar offers. "I'm thinking this is a time a girl might need her mom most and hers has been missing in action for a long time, at least emotionally. It'll take her some time to get over that and I hope Cindy doesn't let her down. Good thing she's got you."

He walks over and insinuates himself between my legs, leaning down to kiss me—wet and deep—before lifting his mouth away.

"You know," I can't help but point out, "we're not so different, she and I." I push on, noticing Gunnar's raised eyebrows, questioning my statement. "We've had similar destructive ways in coping with our issues. I'd like to think that what I said to her had something to do with it, but honestly? I feel that she was probably already close to her breaking point."

"Hmmm," he hums, stroking his large hands over my back. "What did she say to you? I'm guessing she's heading for some kind of rehab?"

"She mentioned she hasn't had a drink since we saw her last Friday and she was sorry for going off the deep end on me. Apparently, she left Denise in the parking lot and drove straight to her doctor. She's been a mess, but rather than deal with her own issues, she focused all her negative energy on the kids, on you, and I guess on me. Her doc called her this morning to say he'd found a placement for her. That's why she came—she's scheduled to leave at nine tonight from Boston."

I dig my face into his chest, feeling sorry for Cindy who'd messed up such a good thing with this man and their kids. She knew it too, telling me I was lucky—that she'd been way too late in recognizing what she'd let slip through her fingers. Oddly, I don't feel threatened by her. Not anymore. Seeing someone's underbelly exposed has a tendency to at least balance the scales.

Both lost in our thoughts, the sudden ring of the doorbell and subsequent buzz of Gunnar's phone startles us. I chuckle, "Okay, I'll get the door, you get the call."

Disentangling myself from him, I head to the door and open it to the first parent picking up their child.

Within the next ten minutes, one after the other of the boys are picked up and I've taken up residence at the door with my loot bags until the last of them are gone. That's when I notice I haven't seen Gunnar and go in search of him, leaving Dex alone with his beloved game.

"Gunnar?"

Walking into the bedroom, I see him sitting on the edge of the bed, his head in his hands. Walking over, I sit beside him, running my hand along his back.

"What's up? Who was on the phone?"

"The Chief of Police, James Duffy," he sounds defeated. "Called to tell me he just came from an interview with Winslow and the department of Internal Affairs. Turns out Winslow was in Graham Bull's pocket, along with the pockets of a few other movers and shakers. He confessed to setting the fire in the shed, in hopes to gain further favor from Bull in his quest to get me shut down. A full investigation will be launched and Winslow is done."

Not quite understanding his mood, given what I take to be good news, I prompt him. "That's positive though, right?" I suggest, but when he lifts his eyes to mine, they're filled with guilt.

"You'd think so, wouldn't you? If it wasn't for his little girl wasting away in the hospital from a rare form of cancer, for which only uninsured experimental treatments are available, or the fact that his wife was admitted last week for severe depression. Don't agree with his choices, and I'm not saying I'd have allowed him to take down what's mine even knowing all this, but the man's been trying desperately to hold his life together by whatever means at hand. And somehow, I can appreciate that."

With a deep sigh, he flops back on the bed, his arm covering his eyes. I'm a twisted ball of emotions at this news. With tears filling my eyes at the tragic circumstances of Sergeant Winslow's private life, I lower myself next to

Gunnar. My head on his chest and my arm across his stomach. Automatically, his arm comes down to tuck me closer to his side.

"I love you, Gunnar," I whisper into his shoulder.

"Love you too, Bird. So much." His voice rumbles from his chest as he uses his other arm to pull me up so I'm lying on top of him. Stroking my hair from my face, he traces my features with his eyes. I can almost feel the touch on my skin. "It hits me how little we really know about the people that surround us. Viv was the first one to open my eyes to that. So much happened to her while she was under my nose, stuff still comes up from time to time and every time it hurts me to think I could've done something had I known. Then you came along and proved that point once again. I'd fallen for you long before I knew you—I mean, really knew you. And now this ... granted, I didn't care for the man, but in my hurry to control the impact he was having on my life, I failed to consider I might be having an impact on his." Another deep sigh expels from his lips. "Guess we really don't live in a vacuum, do we? Everything we do has a ripple effect, just like nothing that happens to us exists in isolation." He smiles softly at me. "But you know all this already, don't you? You live with that knowledge day in and day out. God, Syd. How you haven't been scared out of your wits every day of your life, knowing that any control you think you have is an illusion, I don't know. All I know is right now. Having kids to raise with the full realization I have no real control is more than a little daunting."

I hurt for my man. He's bruised and so I share his pain.

Leaning forward, I gently kiss his lips, brushing my own hand through his hair.

"We do our best, my love. You do your best every day. In the way you care for and protect your kids, and me.

Everyone around you, actually. You just have to come to terms with the fact you can't tuck us away, wrapped in tissue paper to ensure nothing bad happens to us. It doesn't work that way. Took me a long time to figure out that to stop breathing for fear of choking kills you anyway. Breathing is the better option. Trust me on that one. Can't close the doors and shut the windows to stop bad things from happening. Locking yourself away will only turn you to dust. This I know for a fact because I came from dust."

In a sudden move, Gunnar rolls and takes me with him. Lying on my back with him on top of me is a weight I welcome.

"You're remarkable, you know that?" he tells me, peppering my face with small kisses until he leans his elbow in the mattress beside my shoulder, his hand supporting his head.

"Can't help but notice you called me pet names twice today," he points out, a smile tugging at the corner of his mouth.

"Is that so?" I feign innocence, knowing full well I slipped up. Twice, just like he says.

"U-huh. I believe it was *honey* earlier, and just now you called me *love*. Can't quite believe it myself, but I've gotta say I kinda like it." The smile is now at full wattage and the sight of it directed at me gives me a little shiver all over my body.

"Well that's a relief. Since I'll probably let something slip here or there again at some point. Besides, you call me babe and Bird." I nudge his arm with my shoulder.

"I do at that. You'll always be my Bird."

CHAPTER TWENTY-SIX

Syd

"Syd! Call for you!" Viv yells from the kitchen just as I am walking in.

"Hello?" I offer when Viv pushes the phone in my hand.

"Ms. Donner. It's Matthew Simpson. Pam Hawkes contacted me this morning. She says you are looking for advice regarding some type of trust fund?"

"Wow, that's fast. I just spoke to her this morning."

Last night after Gunnar fell asleep from a slow, languid love-making session, I lay awake for hours thinking about that poor little girl—Winslow's daughter. Must've been closing in on two in the morning by the time I had formulated an idea I was eager to bounce off Pam this morning, given that she has not-for profit experience. She jumped right on board and said she would contact her lawyer who might be interested in working with us pro bono. His firm offers free work occasionally on select charity projects. According to Pam, my idea might fit their guidelines. I'm excited about the prospect of doing something constructive that would not only help this family, but would also give Gunnar a certain peace of mind. Ah, who am I kidding? It would go a long way to dealing with my own inability to change the past. We'd be doing something productive for a little girl's future.

A chuckle comes from the other end of the line. "Well, it just so happens that a complex case I was working on was just settled, so I actually have time on my hands and I'm due for my allotted hours of pro bono work. Your plan fits right up my alley, so in all honesty, we'd be doing each other a favor."

"Works for me."

I slip into the hall and look to make sure no one is within hearing range before outlining my idea for the foundation and my thoughts on raising funds. Until I have all my ducks in a row, I don't want to share. Don't want to look like an idiot if this isn't going to work. I talk for a good ten minutes, sitting on the stairs to the apartment, explaining what I'm hoping to accomplish before Matthew interrupts.

"Is this the officer whose name is all over the newspaper this morning? Winslow?"

"Newspaper? Erm ... I haven't seen it, but the father's name is Winslow, yes." I had only mentioned a family fallen on hard times and unable to afford the medical care their daughter needed. I never mentioned a last name or the father's profession, hoping to keep them anonymous. "How did you figure that one out?"

"The article mentions a sick child and your name comes up, as well as Mr. Lucas'. I learned to read between the lines, Ms. Donner. It wasn't that difficult," he chuckles.

"Oh."

I struggle to concentrate on what else he says. I'm too busy wondering what is in that article.

"Ms. Donner?"

"Sorry, my mind was wandering," I offer, trying to focus. "Oh, and please call me Syd."

"Very well, Syd. I was just saying that between what you've told me and what the article revealed, I can probably start laying the groundwork on the statutes for your foundation. I should have something for you early next week."

Just as I'm walking into the kitchen, having thanked Matthew and ending the call, I hear the back door followed by the chatter of the kids. Gunnar is back, and how perfectly timed. As the kids settle in at the kitchen table for their after-school snack, my mind starts working on how to tell Gunnar now that my idea seems a valid one.

Walking in behind the children, I can still see a shadow over his face. Despite the good talk we had last night— among other things—I can tell this whole situation is wearing him down. It's when I snake my arms around his neck for a sweet kiss that I notice the newspaper tucked under his arm.

"Is that today's? Can I have a look?"

I indicate the paper and almost reluctantly, Gunnar hands it over.

"Not much good in there today," he grumbles with a surreptitious glance at the children.

"Can I talk to you in the office for a minute?"

Grabbing his hand, I ignore the question on his face and pull him down the hall behind me. I hadn't planned on telling him before I had some more ideas on paper, but I can't stand seeing him dejected like this. Besides, I want to have a look at that article.

"Babe, all you had to do was ask," Gunnar jokes, some of his dark mood lifted with what he thinks is the promise of a quickie on his desk.

"I did ask, smartass," I shoot back with a grin, liking this mood much more, but once in the office, when I close the door behind us, the atmosphere turns dark again.

"Sit, please. I have an idea I want to talk to you about, but first let me quickly scan this article."

Sitting on the opposite side of the desk, I fold open the newspaper, cringing at the title: 'Skipper Central In Corruption Scandal.'

"Well that's inflammatory, if anything," I point out. "Clever play of words though. Could easily be interpreted a number of ways. You'd have to read the article to find out which one is correct."

"Don't bother. I already did. Aside from some minor innuendo, he basically sticks to facts. Problem is you're named several times in the article. I'm just listed as owner of The Skipper, but your name comes up as the victim of two crimes committed in relation to the pub," he admits gloomily.

"But only the fire was technically related, right? The other really had nothing to do with all of this."

"Yeah, but sick as it is, violence sells and I'm sure they'll justify its mention by saying it was used to provide context. My concern is that this is the kind of story that won't be limited to local events. This'll likely go state-wide at some point, if it hasn't already."

He looks at me, appearing to wait for something.

And then it hits me. My name could bring my past barreling back if seen by the right people. *Fucking hell.*

"Come over here," he says softly, turning his chair and gesturing with his hand. I don't hesitate, I'm around the desk and on his lap in an instant. "Whatever happens, we'll deal with it head on, okay? I'm not going anywhere and I'm not about to let you go either."

I only nod with my head tucked under his chin. For a few minutes we just sit, each lost in our own thoughts.

And then I've had enough.

"You know what? I'm not gonna worry about what might be. I've spent years living in the past I no longer had control over, I'm not about to start living in the worry of a future that may or may not evolve."

In the heat of my diatribe, I've got up and find myself flailing my arms about, standing in front of Gunnar. A slow smile morphs on his face and leaning forward, he grabs me by the hips and pulls me back onto his lap.

"You know it's hot as fuck when you get yourself riled up?" he growls against my skin, burying his face in my neck.

"Well, I was making a point," is my feeble defense for my perhaps slightly erratic behavior.

"And a good one it is." His laughter rumbles in his chest and I nestle in deeper against the vibrations.

"Exactly."

Pushing me back a little, he regards me, a smile lingering on his face. "How is it you manage to make everything better?"

"Ditto, big guy,"

"Big guy?" he mimics soundlessly, at which I lightly punch his shoulder.

"Oh!" Suddenly reminded of my reason to drag him into the office in the first place, I jump right in. "I still have something to tell you." I try to convey my ideas for financing Abby Winslow's medical care, watching Gunnar's face close down further and further. *Fuck.* I may have miscalculated here. Nervous about his apparent displeasure, I ramble on about checking things out through Pam and having just spoken to a lawyer. His silence when I run out of steam is unnerving to say the least. When he finally takes a deep breath and opens his mouth to speak, he takes me by surprise.

"I know I've said it before, and I'll probably say it again, but fuck me, Bird. You. Are. Remarkable."

A warm feeling blooms in my chest and spreads to the tips of my fingers and toes. A big smile cracks my face wide open. "Yeah?"

I get a twitch of his lips and a headshake before he cups my face and rubs his nose along mine.

"Fuck yeah."

Gunnar

This day sure turned around. I'm smiling into my beer when I catch Tim's elbow, causing me to spill beer all over myself.

"What are you grinning like an ape for?" He chuckles at my attempts to dry the front of my shirt with a stack of napkins from the table. "Do I even have to ask?" He looks pointedly in Syd's direction, who is serving a booth at the other end of the pub.

After a memorable make out session in my office chair, one I'd be happy to repeat, but naked when the kids aren't around, I walked around the pub with my own ideas forming. She totally floored me with her ideas. Hearing her explain how she wants to run a foundation in the name of The Skipper, raising funds through donations and events here in the pub—all to benefit families with children suffering from life-threatening diseases like Abby Winslow, who would be the first, had me stunned. If I didn't love her so damn much already, I'd have fallen in love with her right there and then. With her large heart and endless compassion, she's managed not only to offer those families some solace, but me as well. She's offering me a way to make some restitution of sorts to the Winslow family, and I'm just now realizing that there is some peace to be found in this venture for her as well. Her plans are solid, which I wouldn't have doubted with her financial background, and her ideas for fundraising manageable. The part she wasn't sure about was how to handle the requests for assistance and how to determine which family qualifies.

That's where I have some ideas.

I look around the table at the faces of my baseball team, representing just about every walk of life. Tim, who works for the city of Portland. Paul, who has an excellent grasp on social services available due to his stint on the street and now has a successful construction company. Douglas, who is a busy family doctor and Murray, who despite his non-stop foul mouth in his down time, is an acknowledged family therapist. Add Pam to the mix and you have the makings of a working board with connections to local government, local businesses, healthcare, and social services.

"Syd's got a plan, and it's a good one," I tell him in response before turning around just in time to catch Syd, who is just passing by.

"Babe, come sit and talk to us."

With a little blush staining her cheeks and a shy smile for all the guys, she perches on the edge of the chair I pull up.

"Guys," I quiet down the welcoming *hellos* around the table. "Syd is working on a project and I'd like to have her explain it to you. Better listen up, 'cause I have plans for some of you. I let my eyes run over the guys I have in mind, giving them a silent heads up.

Syd's almost jumping off the chair, looking at me with panic in her eyes. "But ..." she starts in protest, but I silence her with a hard kiss to her mouth, instigating various catcalls and whistles from the guys.

"Just tell them, like you told me earlier. And trust me?" I smile what I hope is an encouraging smile before I sit back, letting her take the lead.

For the next hour and a half, supplied with pitcher after pitcher of beer and a couple of orders of wings, we have jointly hammered out a tentative board for the foundation and plan of action for at least three fundraiser ideas that popped up around the table. Syd's face is beaming at the response she's getting, having lost her nervousness about two minutes into giving her impromptu presentation.

"Purpose looks beautiful on you," I lean over and whisper for her ears only, and when she turns that beaming smile on me, I fucking feel on top of the world.

I mean it too. Seeing her eager and interactive, listening to every word of feedback and forgetting all about her initial awkwardness, opens my eyes to the full scope of Sydney Donner.

Fuck, I'm a lucky man.

"Come for me, baby. Let me see your face."

My fingers deep inside her and my mouth hovering over her hard little clit, I wait for her to turn her head and face me.

I'm eager to finish what we started on the couch the moment the babysitter left. If Syd hadn't reminded me of the kids upstairs in their beds, I'd have had her stripped down and riding my cock in seconds. The alternative was upstairs in the sanctuary of our bedroom with a lock on the door. With Syd wrapped around me like an octopus, I took the stairs two at a time, while she was giggling all the way.

Now I have her at my mercy and seeing those big luminous eyes glaze over as she comes apart under my hands and mouth leaves me breathless. I slowly lower her down from the wall, where I had her perched on my shoulders, her legs wrapped around my head. Sliding her down, her hands firm on my shoulders and her eyes on mine, I pause with her pussy aligned with my cock.

"Ready, Bird?"

Biting her plump bottom lip with her teeth, she nods her head, eyes burning hot for me. Slowly I drop her more, easily slipping the head of my cock between her lips before dropping her the rest of the way on my throbbing erection.

"*Fuck!* Jesus holy motherfucking Christ," spouts from Syd's pouty little mouth, followed by a deep groan, freezing me with a stunned look on my face. Never have I heard that shit come out of her mouth.

"Don't stop—don't you fucking dare stop!"

Her head thrown back against the wall beside the door, mouth open in abandon, she's as beautiful as she's ever looked. With her hands clawing at me, doing certain damage to my back and shoulders, I let go. Her words have broken any control I had. Gripping hard onto her hips, lifting her up and dropping her on my cock again and again, I thrust up to fuck her as deep as I can reach.

It doesn't take long for her pussy to start pulsating around my cock and I know it won't be long before she comes again. This time, I want to come with her.

"Mouth ..." I need the taste of her on my lips, but she's lost in the preamble of what promises to be an explosive orgasm. "Bird! I need your mouth on me."

Her eyes clear and dart between my mouth and my eyes before her lips and tongue attack mine in a furious duel. My hips pump in rhythm with my tongue and I swallow her whimpers. With her taste in my mouth, her orgasm clasping my cock and her name on my lips, I thrust up one last time before spilling myself to completion inside her.

Lungs sucking in air like bellows and knees rubbery with my lingering release, I sink down on the floor, Syd's body languid and heavy on top of me. I try to get up, but she stops me.

"Don't move."

"Babe, gotta get rid of the condom and in bed," I try, but I feel her head shaking floppily on my chest.

"Sleeping right here ..." she mumbles before I lose her to sleep.

It takes a bit to get her off the floor and in one of my shirts and into bed, but I finally manage and with a quick trip to the bathroom to take care of business, I slide in behind her, pulling her tight against my chest.

Nothing better than waking up to the smell of coffee and bacon. I have both this morning. Taking a deep whiff of the smells coming from the kitchen downstairs, I roll over to check the alarm clock on the nightstand and shoot out of bed when I discover it's already ten thirty in the morning.

Fuck! The kids. Grabbing some sweats and a shirt from the drawer, I have them on in no time and quickly head to the kids' rooms to get them going. When I find both rooms empty, my next logical move is the kitchen. Two favorite things in my kids' lives right now is sleep and food. One day—hopefully thirty years down the road—they'll add sex to that list.

In the kitchen, there is no sign of my kids, only Syd who is humming something while cracking eggs in a pan.

"Where are the kids?" I jump right in. Syd turns around with one eyebrow raised.

"Good morning to you too. The kids are in school, where you'd expect them to be." There's a little bite I detect in her voice.

"How—?" I try, but Syd beats me to it.

"I drove them," she states matter-of-factly before turning around, trying to pretend something momentous didn't just occur.

In all honesty, it takes me a moment to appreciate its impact before I clue in that Syd doesn't drive. She never gets behind the wheel, not since ...

"You didn't ..." I state incredulously, making Syd turn with a little smirk on her lips. Fuck me. She *did.*

"How?"

"Turning the key in the ignition, backing out of the dri—"

My hand slapping her butt stops her mid-sentence, when it's her turn to look at me disbelieving as I drag her into my arms.

"That's not what I mean and you know it, smartass." I growl at her.

She shrugs her shoulders. "You were sleeping. The keys were right there and the kids were ready to go. I couldn't find any good reason why I shouldn't let you sleep some more and just drive the kids where they needed to go." Again with the shoulder shrug, implying it wasn't a big deal, when we both know it is.

"I'm so proud of you. Were you okay?" I ask cautiously.

Syd looks at me with a big smile on her face before responding.

"I was fucking terrified ..."

CHAPTER TWENTY-SEVEN

Syd

"Hey Syd? Where's Dad? I'm ready to go to Tasha's."

"Mowing the lawn, honey. Go tell him to get cleaned up."

Today is the first day of the kid's summer break and just like that, the weather has changed from wet and miserable to scorching hot within a week. First thing this morning, Gunnar went out to mow the lawn, which was about ankle high. Shirtless and with just a pair of old cargo shorts and sneakers, he's been outside, trying to get an early start.

The summer has been planned out for the kids. Emmy was invited to go on a two-week camping trip to Martha's Vineyard with Tasha and her family, and Dex is leaving for a wilderness camp in Vermont for the same amount of time. After that, we get them back for a week before Gunnar's mom comes out of the summer heat of Arizona to stay with us. Gunnar has planned it so that we spend time as a family—his words, not mine—during the days and then around four o'clock, the two of us will go into work while his mom stays home with the kids.

The kids will have one week at a sailing camp near Acadia Park, up the coast toward the end of their break and will spend the last week at home with us, getting ready for school.

I have mixed feelings about it. About all of it. First of all, the idea of not having the kids around for a two week stretch is gonna be so hard. I love them. They keep me securely invested in the here and now with their easy acceptance of me in their lives. I'll miss the morning snuggles with Dex, when he climbs into bed with us, even though he makes us swear not to tell anyone, him being ten and all. And his incessant chatter, which after the more quiet version of him I met first, is amusing ... most of the time. He loves me back without reserve, showing it as easily as his father does.

Emmy's opened up lately. Ever since she got her period last week and I found her trying to scrub her stained underwear in the laundry tub. Embarrassed at first, I simply showed her how I handle bloodstains when she insisted on washing them herself. Then there've been little things at school she started talking to me about. A boy she likes at school, a teacher being too strict, and a fight she had with Tasha. Little things to show me she's starting to trust me.

Yesterday afternoon at the pub, before Mrs. Danzel came to pick them up, she hugged me hard in the kitchen, telling me she'd miss me the next two weeks. Girl almost had me in tears because the truth is, I'm gonna miss them too. So much.

Then not in the least is the looming arrival of Emily, Gunnar's mom, who Emmy was named for. By all accounts she's a wonderful lady and I have to say the few times that Gunnar's shoved the phone in my hand when she was on the other end, she's been nothing but friendly toward me. But still, I've shacked up with her only son and her grandchildren and she knows little about me. I'm just not sure if she'll be as friendly when she finds out everything there is to know about me.

Finally there's being alone with Gunnar for two whole weeks. I'm just scared that without the kids here, without the constant distraction they provide, he'll see me clearly for once and it won't be enough. I know I'm being an idiot. Pam's told me this on more than one occasion, but it's difficult to imagine anyone feeling about me the way I feel about him.

Hands slide around my stomach from behind, and Gunnar's deep voice rumbles in my ear.

"I can see your mind spinning, Bird. You think too much." Turning to see his face, I catch my breath at the broad expanse of his chest, lightly coated with greying hair, and right now, glistening sweat. I curb my instinct to want to lick him, but not with the kids. It seems that once that line is crossed, we inadvertently end up tugging each other's clothes off. We've seen more of the inside of the laundry room than a few loads once a week requires.

"Better stop looking at me like I'm your next meal, Syd, or you'll have to come have a shower with me," he growls in warning. Tearing my eyes from his chest, I slide them up the strong column of his throat, his strong full lips, and finally come to rest on his own. The teasing sparkle there barely covers the heated passion lurking right behind and a small, but visible shudder runs down my back. "*Stop*," he whispers and I swallow deeply at the almost palpable need I hear in that one word.

Right.

Turning back to the sink, I try to bring my galloping heart back under control. "So, what's the plan?"

"Gonna have a shower, then we've gotta hit the road and drop off Emmy, pick up some water-shoes for Dex since he just found out he can't fit last year's, and then at noon we have to be at the school where the buses will be collecting the kids."

"Okay, I'll just—" I start, but Gunnar cuts me off.

"You'll just come along. It'll be fine, babe." And with a hard possessive kiss on my mouth that begs no discussion, he is off to have his shower.

He knows I don't like the idea of the kids leaving, probably not all the reasons for it, but I've told him I'm afraid of embarrassing them. I mean, what if I cry? An irritating side effect of opening up your heart again is the amount of *feeling* you do, and that comes paired with rather unfamiliar tears. Now? I'm a fucking fountain. Everything and anything can get me going and I appear to have little control. According to Pam, it's a normal adjustment to having come from a very solitary existence where I'd kept external stimulation of any kind to an absolute minimum to a very socially active one, where people seem to tear on my heartstrings on an ongoing basis. She says my emotions will find balance with time. I hope to God that's so.

Well I managed to hold myself together, saying goodbye to Emmy, who isn't one for demonstrative displays of affection and gave me a quick, barely there hug and a smile. Although I have to admit, she almost made me lose it when in the truck she leaned over the seat and whispered to me, "Take care of my dad for me?"

Dexter is a different story altogether. With the inborn male Lucas protective gene, he looks up in my face earnestly, his small arms wrapped around my waist and a little frown of concern shadowing his eyes.

"You sure you'll be okay, Syd? I'll be back soon. Two weeks will go by in flash, you'll see."

Gunnar is chuckling behind me while I'm turning into a puddle in the parking lot of his school, the bus loaded and ready to leave. I won't mention the throng of parents here to see off their respective children, most of them probably eager to see them go and have a breather. Not me. I stand out like an oddity, tears streaming down my face as Dex finally disappears up the bus steps, only to reappear in a window toward the back of the bus, waving frantically at us as it pulls out of the parking lot.

"You're a mess," Gunnar points out the obvious, amusement clear in his voice.

"Well, thanks," I bite off, adding, "I can't believe you're finding this funny!" My resistance is futile as he pulls me in the shelter of his arms, hiding my embarrassment from the curious eyes of a few parents walking past us to their cars.

"You're forgetting I've had time to get used to sending the kids off for weeks at a time, knowing that every time they go, they'll come back. I promise you'll get used to it." The rumble of his voice soothes me, as it usually does.

"I don't know that I want to get used to saying goodbye to them," I mumble into his shirt.

"And that, right there, is what I love about you. Come on, sad girl. Let's get some work done today."

With a kiss to my forehead, he grabs my hand, walking us to the truck.

Gunnar

"You bawled?"

"Shut up. Gunnar has a big mouth."

Viv chuckles and gives me a wink over Syd's head. Not hard, since she's about a head taller than her.

"You were eager enough for that mouth this morning," I can't help but tease, and then have to duck out of the way of a half-peeled potato Syd whips at me.

"I cannot believe you just said that," she says, her mouth open in indignant surprise at my words, or her own reaction. Maybe it's both, cracking Viv up in the process.

Picking up the potato, I dump it in the green bin before saying with a wink, "Well, I know when I'm not wanted."

Back in my office, I boot up the computer to look at sales from the last few weeks, which Syd put into a graph chart for me. By the looks of it, we haven't lost any substantial business as a result of the attempts at negative press on The Skipper. In fact, as of last week, and the press release prepared by Matthew, Syd's new lawyer for the foundation, business has been picking up and is currently over and above last year's for the same time. Given that last year was a record year, that makes me feel pretty damn good.

With Cindy admitted into a drug and alcohol treatment facility in Florida, as per her phone call last week, and the kids officially in my custody, I feel a huge pressure taken off my shoulders.

Having Syd to myself for the next two weeks in a house where there are no little ears to consider, I'd say I'm pretty fantastic. Of course, I feel the trepidation coming off her in waves. I know she'll miss the kids and is anxious about meeting mom face to face, but I plan to make her forget all about that. Other than that, she's settled in better than I could've imagined when I virtually forced her to move in on a permanent basis. She's confident in managing my kids and their daily lives, as well as the way she gives in to the easy banter and teasing with Viv and Dino here at the pub. She's still a little shy around Matt and the guys from the team, but it usually only takes a few minutes for her to relax in their presence. Still, there are things that remain unresolved for her. Most of them I can't do anything about. All I can do is wait for her to take the lead, but there is one thing I've looked into that I'm hoping to do with her sometime these next couple of weeks.

Yeah, nothing wrong with my life the way it is now, but having learned a thing or two, I realize things can change on a dime, and they often do.

A knock reveals Tim standing in the door opening, a big smile on his face and holding a bottle of Dalwhinnie, my favorite aged single malt Scotch, and two tumblers in his hand. "My guess is you're either here to butter me up over your unpaid bar tab, or you have some lurid confessions to make," I offer at the sight of him.

"You'd be off on both counts, my friend," he counters. "I come bearing news."

"And gifts? Must be good news then."

I make room on my desk for the glasses as Tim unseals the bottle—the fragrant scent of the twenty-five year old Scotch filling my nostrils. With two fingers carefully poured into the tumblers, he hands me one and raises the other.

"May those who live, truly always be believed, and those who deceive us, be always deceived."

Tim's attempt at a Scottish brogue is nothing short of funny with his 'Boston' showing through. "I'll say amen to that, but what's the occasion?"

"Thought it was appropriate, given the libation I brought and the cause I'm here to celebrate," he says with a shrug of his shoulders and a sip of his Scotch.

"Come on, man, don't leave me hanging. I'd like to know what I'm toasting to," I try to urge him to get to the point.

"Permit's been revoked. It would appear that someone put a bug in Portland's City Councils ears about a certain shark circling the waters of Casco Bay. Last Council meeting yesterday, a vote was passed to revoke the building permit granted for a certain nefarious former chef turned restaurateur." Tim has a big-ass smug smile on his face as he offers me the dressed up bit of news.

"You're fucking kidding me?"

"Not fucking anything much right now, but no, I'm not kidding. Bull and his wimpy sidekick have lifted their heels and have left Portland in their rear-view mirror. Not that the cops won't be keeping close tabs on them, but for all intents and purposes, the cook has flown the coop."

"Holy shit. That's good damn news," I smile back and raise my glass before tilting it to my lips, the rich flavor a great accompaniment to the release of tension I didn't realize I was still holding.

Slowly sipping our drinks, we bounce back and forth some ideas around Syd's foundation plans. I guess our foundation, since Syd's insisted only wanting to go ahead if I am involved. Fuck. There's no way I wouldn't be. The thought of being able to do something for the Winslow family and families like theirs, falling apart around a desperately ill child, has lifted me right out of my funk. Be good to give something back to a community that has supported The Skipper for decades.

In talking to mom this past week, she made it clear she wanted to be involved as well, and immediately offered her time and connections. She suggested she'd start making phone calls to people she'd stayed in touch with in Portland over the years to round up some support before we were even off the ground. Made me chuckle. For years after my folks handed over the pub to me, she'd been going through the motions of retirement, but it never quite seemed suited to her. The renewed sense of purpose seemed to energize her and I was seeing more of the active mother I grew up with, even at almost seventy years old. With a smile on my face, I'm thinking she's gonna be a dynamo when she gets here.

"Boss," Viv pokes her head in the door. "You may wanna come out here." The concern lacing her voice has me out of my chair in a heartbeat. I follow her to the doorway to the pub, where she halts me with a hand on my chest.

"Keep your cool, but the guy at the end of the bar says he needs to speak to his wife."

At my confused headshake she clarifies, "Syd. He's talking about our Syd, Gunnar."

One look at the perfectly groomed and distinguished looking asshole who's eyeing the pub with obvious distaste, has me fighting every instinct to go over there, pull him off the barstool and wipe the derision off his face. This is not going to be pretty.

Taking Viv's hand off my chest, I give it a little squeeze to assure her I'm in control, or at least pretending to be. Although, in all reality, I know it won't take much for me to snap.

"Keep Syd busy in the kitchen," I tell Viv softly. She eyes me with some trepidation, but finally nods and walks back into the hallway. Tim comes out of the office and walks up to me.

"Everything okay?" he asks with a hand on my shoulder.

"I knew this day would fucking come after those articles in the newspaper, dammit. Syd's ex is here."

"Oh shit," Tim so acutely points out.

"Shit is right. Up to Syd to share her story sometime, but I'll tell you now, that man sitting there has put my woman through a certain kind of hell."

"Right. Well, all I can say is don't kill him outright. Too many witnesses." With a supportive clap on my shoulder, he slips past me into the bar and takes a seat at the opposite end. A slight nod confirms he has my back, no words needed.

I take a deep breath in and make my way over to where the douche is sitting, wondering how what should've been a great day could tank so fast.

"Can I help you?" I ask the man who's been watching my approach with a look of distaste on his face. *Fucker.*

"Like I mentioned to the barmaid," he waves his manicured hand for emphasis. "I'm looking for my wife, Sydney Webster, although I believe she's using her maiden name, Donner, now. I believe she works here." He actually winces when he clarifies, as if the fact of her employment here causes him discomfort. I'll fucking show him and his sissy-assed name discomfort. Already the sound of his cultured voice grates on my last nerve.

"First of all, that—what did you call her? A barmaid?—is my manager and secondly, I can't help you."

I'm about to walk away when he reaches over the bar and grabs onto my arm. I throw a pointed look at his hand on my forearm and then up at him, not afraid to let my anger show through. Immediately he pulls back and raises the offending hand defensively.

"My apologies. Could I speak to your boss please?"

I turn fully to face him, folding my arms over my chest.

"No other boss here but me. Still can't help you."

Yeah, you idiot. He looks at me in disbelief, that someone dressed in faded jeans and a Henley shirt, could ever be mistaken for an owner. This is a pub, not a fucking country club.

"Look, you don't understand. She's been missing for years and we've all been worried sick. She has some problems ... mental problems. She left a psychiatric ward on her own years ago, and we've not been able to trace her, until now." Every word the man says makes me lose the edge I have on my temper, but his next words finally snap that precarious hold. "I feel I have to warn you. Sydney is capable of grave harm both to herself, and to others." Leaning forward, he continues in a conspirator's voice. "She killed our child during one of her fits."

That does it. I reach over the bar and grab the bastard by his necktie, as close to his throat as I can wrap my hand, and haul back with the other ready to plow my fist through his face.

"Don't!" Tim's shout barely manages to reach my ears, which are buzzing with rage. With some kind of sick pleasure, I watch the prick's eyes start bulging out of his head and if anything, squeeze my hand on his tie a little tighter.

Tim walks up behind me and I see Matt approaching Syd's ex from behind. "Let him go, Guns. Not worth it, ya know?" Tim says quietly.

Right. Not worth it. Slowly, I release pressure and immediately his hands come up to his neck in a protective gesture. "You ... you're as crazy as she is," he manages as he gasps for air.

"Hey, buddy," Matt grabs the man firmly by the shoulder. "You better quit while you're still breathing. In case you haven't noticed, you are seriously outnumbered here."

After throwing a sneaky look over his shoulder at Matt, douche bag turns back to me with a smirk on his face. "At least now I know she's—" he stops mid-sentence and looks over my shoulder at the doorway. I know without needing to look, just by the electricity in the air, that Syd just walked in.

CHAPTER TWENTY-EIGHT

Syd

I don't know why I know he's here. I just do. When Viv walks into the kitchen, I can tell something's going on. Her face is tight and although her chattering is not uncommon, the furtive looks she keep throwing in the direction of the door are. So when I hear a loud man's voice yelling, "*Don't*," I brush past her and barrel toward the pub.

He's just like I remember, only older and if possible, more arrogant in his appearance. I thought I'd be intimidated—freak out even—but instead I find myself eager to deal with him head-on. After the story about The Skipper's involvement in the corruption scandal came out, I knew it was just a matter of time.

With a cool resolve I can actually feel, I look my ex-husband in the eye and place a quieting hand on Gunnar's back, feeling the tension radiating off him.

"Jacob. I should probably say something inane, like, "It's good to see you," but you'll forgive me if I'd rather cut off my own arm than choke on those words."

I can tell from the widening of his eyes that he did not expect the challenge of my words. He's too used to intimidating and browbeating everyone around him into simmering submission, but not me. Not anymore. Where before I'd cower under his hateful glare, now I find myself entirely unimpressed.

Gunnar moves aside and allows me full view of Jacob. His tie is hanging limp from his neck and I don't need anyone to tell me that Gunnar was responsible for that. I'm surprised to find that it actually disappoints me not to find any marks on the bastard's face.

Watching me through now narrowed eyes, Jacob quickly makes adjustments, straightening himself; always keeping up the outward appearances. His eyes scan me head to toe and with his mouth set in a distasteful sneer, he pounces, just like I'd expected.

"Time hasn't been kind to you," is his opening volley, causing Gunnar to growl, but I grab the hand he reassuringly loops over my shoulder and show him I'm not affected in the least. This is what I lived with for years before I broke. "Honestly, Sydney. Standing behind a bar in dirty old jeans, your hair wild, and not wearing a stitch of make-up is not a good look for a woman of standing. And it hardly seems an appropriate place for a raging alcoholic. Judging by the company you keep, I shouldn't be surprised. You're lucky I found you."

I can't help the loud snort that escapes, to Jacob's horror, which only makes me laugh harder.

"I'm sorry, Jacob, but what exactly did you come here for? Amusing as it is, the way you are trying to assert yourself over me, it's also becoming a bit tedious."

"Your parents would be mortified," he tries to rattle me once more and this time, I have to grab onto Gunnar's hand and brace my arm in front of him to stop him from leaping over the bar at him.

"My parents have been mortified from the time I took my first breath, Jacob, so please, tell me something new. Now, why is it that you've chosen to seek me out now, after four years?"

"You're my wife, I have every right—" he sputters when I interrupt him.

"Was, Jacob. I was. I distinctly remember signing those papers. Now unless you tell me what it is you think I can do for you, I'd really like for you to leave. It's our busiest night of the week and you're causing a scene."

Immediately Jacob's eyes scan his surroundings, flinching slightly at the eyes he finds directed our way. A public scene would be too 'common' for his tastes.

"The house..." he bites out from between pinched lips.

"The house? What about it?"

"I need to sell it."

"So sell it. What does that have to do with me?"

"I've tried to for four years. I've tried, but it's not in my name. It's in yours."

I'm totally blindsided by that piece of news. I can distinctly recall him reminding me time and time again, that but for the grace of Jacob Webster, I wouldn't have a roof over my head or food in my stomach.

"Ran into some financial hick-ups shortly after... after Daniel, and didn't want to lose the house as well, so I had it put in your name." One thing I could never fault Jacob for, and trust me, there were plenty faults there, was his love for our son. He may have been a mostly absentee dad, but he loved that boy to distraction. To hear his voice crack with the use of his name, softens me, but only a tiny smidgeon. This man has done too much damage for me to have much sympathy for him and his feelings.

"You're saying the house is mine?"

"Only technically. We both know I put the lion's share into it, and all of it in past years. It's just a formality that was left in the aftermath of our divorce. Something we never settled."

That statement was debatable since it's not exactly how I remember things, but I care too little to argue with him.

"So what's the big deal now? Why do you need to sell it?" I'll admit, it feels good to have some power as I prod him to answer.

When he finally admits he needs the money to pay off his second ex-wife, who apparently got sick of his philandering, I can feel Gunnar's stomach shaking with what I'm sure is contained laughter. Karma is a bitch, but in this case, she's a sweet bitch. Apparently, he's come here hoping to intimidate me back under his control; at least long enough to have me sign the house over. Only thing not so clear is how he was hoping to get me to do that.

"Wait a minute. What were you planning to do with me?"

The way he avoids looking at me gives me a sick feeling in the pit of my stomach.

"You were a mess before. I expected ... I mean, it seemed—"

"Answer the woman, you dickhead," Gunner leans forward over the bar, his sheer size an intimidating factor that doesn't go unnoticed by Jacob who's fiddling with his tie again, his eyes darting about nervously.

"I thought I'd get her help."

Pompous, self-righteous son-of-a-bitch. I'm the furious one now, and it's Gunnar who's holding me back from climbing over that bar.

"You were gonna have me committed, weren't you, you miserable piece of shit?" My latent 'street-dweller' language makes its appearance, obliterating the measured speech pattern of New England's 'upper crust' I grew up with.

Something in my face must've impressed him, because he slides quickly off his stool and backs away from the bar.

Gunnar pulls me down and wraps his arms around me to stop my body from shaking.

"Tim, would you show this piece of trash out, please? Make it clear to him he is not to set foot on this property, nor is he to come anywhere near Syd, would you?" I hear him instruct Tim as I'm being ushered out the door, into the hall and into Gunnar's office.

"Fuck, honey. Even with all that lady-like composure and proper English you were spouting, you intimidate the crap out of even me. That was hot as hell."

Gunnar's eyes burn into mine as he pulls his desk chair around and sits down, pulling me onto his lap.

"You okay, babe?"

I let out the deep breath I've been holding, letting go of my anger and relaxing into Gunnar's body.

"I'm good now."

"You're more than good; you're exceptional. You decimated him, Bird." He chuckles, shaking his head at the memory. "He was so not expecting to find the fight in you. Figured he could come in here and squash you like a bug. Instead, you took him by the balls, crushed them in your tiny hands and handed them back to him. Such. A. Fucking turn on."

With his hand grabbing my hair, he pulls my head back and licks me from my cleavage and up my neck before taking my mouth in a hungry, claiming kiss. Mewling at the forceful invasion, I wiggle my ass on the hard ridge of his cock, eliciting a deep growl from his throat. The need to do some claiming of my own has me clenching my fist in his hair, countering every exploration of his tongue in my mouth.

"Jesus. You're killing me," he moans as he reluctantly pulls his mouth away from mine.

Both of us are breathing hard and the crotch of my jeans are damp with arousal. My body is primed and turned on, and I feel the loss of his lips when he sets me on my feet as he gets off the chair himself. The sudden chill sends a shiver down my limbs.

"Nothing I want more than to fuck you over that desk right now, but the crowd was already getting thick out there. Besides, the anticipation will be it's own reward once I slide my cock inside you."

"No fair," I manage to croak, clenching my thighs in response to his promise. A wolfish grin slides over his face as he tags me by the nape of my neck and pulls me flush against him.

"I promise to make it up to you, all fucking night."

With one last hard kiss, and with a hand in my back, he guides me out of the office and gives me a little shove in the direction of the kitchen. I stop, turn and grab his arm just as he's about walk toward the pub. Throwing my arms around his neck, I pull him down for another kiss. This one on *my* terms.

"Okay, take that shit back into the office. Dry squeaky vagina walking by here, in serious need of some TLC, and you're not helping." Viv scowls as she moves past us in the kitchen and I burst out laughing. Gunnar smiles down at me.

"I'll never get used to that sound. I never want to. Every time I hear you laugh it's the most unexpected, exhilarating experience."

Lifting up his arm, he pulls back his shirtsleeve. "Look. Gives me fucking goosebumps."

I stroke my finger over the bumpy skin, my smile lingering. "I like it. I like that I give you goosebumps. Only fair since you give me shivers with only a look."

Gunnar

God dammit. It's about the fiftieth time I've had to hide behind the bar to quickly adjust myself. My little game of anticipation is backfiring on me, big-time.

All evening I've been throwing Syd looks and stealthily touch her every time she comes within reach, but the last few times she's quickly turned the tables on me. First the licking and biting of her bottom lip, then stroking her hand from her neck, down to her cleavage. Now she's ramped it up by slipping behind the bar with an excuse and sliding in front of me, her ass rubbing against my cock. Intentional as hell, judging from the smirk on the little cretin's face. Damn woman knows she has me by the balls, no matter how much I try to convince myself otherwise. She's not fooled.

"Why don't you guys head out? It's ten. Kitchen's shutting down anyway."

Frankie, who is back on weekends for the summer, moves behind the bar to usher me out.

During the summer months, we stay open later Thursday through Sunday, with Frankie picking up the late shifts with Matt. Aside from Leanne and Matt serving, we brought in summer staff to help; most of them students. It was definitely needed with the patio up and busy already. For this early in the season, I have two outdoor heating units to ward off the chill that blows in from the water, but if there is any truth to the predictions for this summer, we won't need those for long.

"You'll be okay?" I check one last time with Frankie.

"Fuck yeah. Go home and take care of that woman. You've been eye-fucking her all night already." Frankie's loud, boisterous laugh rolls through the bar. Syd, who is wiping down tables, turns to look in our direction and when her eyes stop on mine, a lift of my chin is all that's needed to have her moving in my direction.

"We're leaving." And to Frankie, "Later, man. Thanks."

"Bye, Frankie," Syd barely manages when I take her hand and pull her toward the back where Viv's still cleaning in the kitchen.

"Shut it down, Viv. Time to go. Frankie and Matt've got this." I stop at the bottom of the stairs, thinking about the bed upstairs and how much faster I could get Syd naked if we stayed here. We have the next two days to ourselves, Sunday is our regular day off, and Monday the pub is closed, so going home now would mean we wouldn't have to surface for forty-eight hours.

Syd chuckles as I start pulling on her hand again, having come to a decision.

"Made up your mind?"

"What?" I pretend not to know what she's talking about.

"I could see the wheels turning, Gunnar. The bed upstairs must've seemed very tempting for a minute there."

"Hush woman. Need to get you home and out of those clothes."

Outside, the chill hits and I let go of Syd's hand to wrap my arm around her, rushing her down the alley to the truck. Just as we walk out of the alley into the dark parking lot, a dark shape moves away from the wall and steps into our path.

CHAPTER TWENTY-NINE

Syd

"Sydney."

I flinch at the familiar voice and curl myself tighter into Gunnar's side, whose grip on my shoulder becomes almost painful.

"Who the fuck are you?" Gunnar growls, making little impression on the looming figure before us.

"I see Jacob was right. You've obviously lost all of your senses working in the kitchen of a questionable establishment and consorting with the local riffraff."

"What are you doing here, Dad?" My voice sounds small and I hate that the man in front of me still has the ability to make me feel insignificant.

"Dad?" Gunnar tilts his head down to look at me with an eyebrow raised when another voice filters from the shadows of the parking lot.

"James? Did you find her?"

"I told you to stay in the car, Marilyn!" My father yells over his shoulder. Wonderful.

"And apparently my mother," I tell Gunnar, his questioning eyes still on me. Understanding floods his gaze and he gives me a quick wink before turning back to my father.

"A little unorthodox, to say the least, but nice to meet you, Mr. Donner," Gunnar tries for polite and letting go of my shoulder, he reaches his hand out to my father.

With a disdainful look, Dad ignores the proffered hand and turns his attention back on me.

"Sydney Rose Donner, you're coming with me."

His arm shoots out and grabs at me, but Gunnar seems prepared and grabs my father's wrist before he can pull me away. As it is, I'll probably have bruises from where his fingers pressed into my flesh.

"You don't want to do that," Gunnar warns, his voice low and threatening, but he doesn't know my father or his utter conviction in his superiority. Sensing a battle erupting between the two men towering over me, I pipe up.

"Stop it. Dad, let me go," I hiss, wrenching my arm from his hold and leaning into Gunnar who in turn, lets go of my father's wrist and wraps the arm around my waist instead, tucking my back to his front. "I don't know what you're hoping to accomplish here, but I'm not going anywhere with you. For your information, I'm not twelve."

My father is less than impressed, his lips pressing into a tight line. "You need help, Sydney. You're obviously not in the right frame of mind. God only knows what you've been up to these past years. Your mother and I have had a hell of a time trying to excuse your sudden absence, but we'll simply tell everyone you've been overseas." He drones on as if talking to himself.

"Is he for real?" Gunnar whispers by my ear.

"Afraid so," I mumble back. I shouldn't be surprised that my parents had been more concerned about the impression my disappearance would cast on them in their social circles than they had been about my well-being. Still, it stings. It also firms my resolve.

"James! Is she coming?" My mother deigns to stick her head out the window of a large sedan at the far side of the parking lot and yell, rather than coming to see me for herself. I can see her tidily quaffed hair glimmering in the sparse lamplight.

"Jesus," Gunnar mutters behind me and I can't help but giggle.

"I'll not have you soil our name any further than you already have, young lady," my father warns, ignoring my mom. "You've done enough damage to our reputation as it is. The newspaper articles and the horrid rumors they've spurned, as if killing your son wasn't damaging enough."

The moment the words leave his mouth—words I've heard many times before—I can feel the tension ratchet up. Gunnar has frozen behind me and anger radiates off him. My attempt to hold him back with my hand on his chest is futile as he lunges at my father, grabbing him by the neck and slamming him against the brick wall he was leaning against earlier.

"Gunnar," I try to get his attention. "It's not worth it."

"Not gonna let some pimped up, waste of space drag you through the mud," he grinds out as my father claws at the hands constricting his throat, gasping for air. "You listen carefully, you son-of-a-bitch. You may hold influence in your little Boston clique, but here in Portland, I hold all the fucking cards. Your daughter is loved here and she's not going anywhere with the likes of you. Your precious name will be gone from hers as soon as I can get a fucking ring on her finger, and you can stop worrying about your 'reputation'. As of this moment, you are done with her. Completely. She's mine to worry about and to care for, and that may not be much in your eyes, but it's a fuck of a lot more than she ever got from your miserable ass!"

With one last shove into the wall, he releases my father, who stands bent over with his hands on his knees, fighting to catch a breath.

"We'll sue you for assault." The cold voice of my mother, who is walking toward us, causes a small pang of hurt, but I straighten my shoulders and turn to face her.

"You try that, and I will go public, all over Boston's media with my sordid story, Mother. What you've accused me of for most of my life—being a blight on your name—will finally come true. Ironic, isn't it? I guess it's true what they say about those self-fulfilling prophecies."

She scoffs and looks at me with that little superior smile I know so well, but haven't missed even once in the past few years. "Still not the smartest knife in the block, I see, Sydney. You proved it when you backed up over Daniel and then proceeded to drink yourself into a stupor, and you're proving it now. Just like I always said. You go public on your 'sordid' story, your name would be ruined right along with ours," she says mockingly.

Unbelievable.

"You really are a lost cause, aren't you, Mother? Not only do you wave Daniel in my face as some well-honed weapon, but you are really too blind to see that I don't give a fuck about reputation." It gives me a rebellious hint of satisfaction when I see her flinch at my use of profanity. "This man, and these people I've come to love, they don't care about my reputation. All they care about are my actions; what I do as opposed to who I am or where I come from. It's beautiful, Mother. And something you will never have the satisfaction of knowing in your narrow-minded, cold existence."

Gunnar's arm comes around my shoulders and I realize I'm shaking. Whether from cold or emotion, I can't be sure, but his comforting hold feels good ... safe.

"Let's go, Bird. And don't look back," he says, walking me to the truck.

Once seated and buckled in, I can't resist a last look at the people who raised me. My father standing behind my mother, his hand proprietary on her shoulder. A picture of proper breeding and etiquette, and nothing I want any part of. I put my hand on Gunnar's leg and he places his hand on top to anchor me.

"Let's go home," I whisper.

Gunnar

"So was that some kind of half-assed marriage proposal back there?" Confused, I turn to a smirking Syd. The teasing twinkle in her eye unmistakable.

"You did tell my father you were planning to put a ring on my finger. I must say, I'm not sure that is the way to go about asking a man for his daughter's hand in marriage, but I could see he was persuaded." I throw my head back and laugh. Damn it feels good to let go of the tension and anger. Syd chuckles quietly beside me. Fuck, I'm a lucky man.

"You won't need to wonder when I'm asking—you'll know. And the question will be directed at you and no one else."

I squeeze her hand under mine and watch the sweet smile on her lips from the corner of my eye, but when her tongue slips out and licks her plump bottom lip before disappearing inside that delectable mouth, my foot gets heaving on the pedals and I beeline it home.

"Omigod, Gunnar. Please..."

"Tell me what you want, babe. What do you need?" I hum against her straining little clit. My fingers are poised at her entrance, keeping her strung like a bow.

The moment we walked in the door, I had her up against the wall in the hallway. With mouths and tongues clashing and taking, our hands make short work of the clothes and have us naked and rubbing up on each other. "Shower first," Syd mumbles into my mouth. I grab her behind the thighs and lift her up, her legs instinctively wrapping around me. With my cock sliding against her wet pussy with every step, I carry her up the stairs and into the shower, having the presence of mind to toss a condom from the drawer in the soapdish

"Fuck me. Please..."

Water cascading down our bodies, I shove two fingers deep while sucking her clit into my mouth. Her back is leaning against the tile and one leg is draped over my shoulder, spreading her wide for my onslaught. The tightening of her fingers in my hair and the shaking of her legs tell me she is right there. With the slight curve and the increasing pressure of my fingers, I bite down on her clit, sending her careening over the edge.

"Ohhh yessss. Fuck!"

My hands on her hips, I turn her to face the wall and push on her back to bend her forward. Without hesitation, I slam my cock inside her heat until I bottom out, balls slapping against the wet flesh of her rounding ass. The sight of that round perfection jiggling slightly every time I thrust inside her has me teetering on the brink of coming, but not without taking her with me once more. Curving over her back, I tweak her nipple with one hand while the other slides between her legs to press down on her clit. This time I feel, rather than hear, her orgasm with the clenching of her cunt around me. With a surge I swear puckers my asshole, I jerk my explosive release inside her.

"I can't believe something precious like you came from those soulless creatures claiming to be your parents," I mumble with my face buried in her still wet hair.

Exhausted from our explorations in the shower, and later once more on the bed, I've got her naked ass pressed against my groin and my hand cupping her breast.

"I used to think I was dropped off by aliens when I was little and a bit over-imaginative. I can see why now. They are like something from a different planet, aren't they?"

"Uranus, more than likely."

Syd chuckles softly at my lame joke and a sense of well-being settles over me.

"You know I love you, Bird. Right?"

"Hmmm, yes I do. Best feeling in the world when the one person you need to breathe, loves you back as hard. You make me strong," she says, turning her head to kiss my shoulder.

"I sometimes wish I'd met you when we still young. I wonder if I could've prevented—" Syd suddenly turns around in my arms and slams her mouth on mine in a punishing kiss.

"Don't." The word vibrates against my lips as she slowly pulls her mouth away and holds my face steady in her hands, all the love in the world shining in her eyes. "Everything that we've been through—all the pain and the anguish—has brought us right here, to this point in time." With one last kiss to my lips, she turns back and snuggles her backside tightly against me. "The only thing missing from perfection is knowing the kids are safe in their beds down the hall."

I squeeze my eyes shut to keep this perfect moment from leaking out.

"Where are we going?"

It's taken me forever to convince Syd to let me blindfold her.

"Won't be much longer," I tell her as I pull through the ornate gates and drive down the tree-lined path.

I made these plans a few weeks ago, but had been sitting on them for the right moment to put them into action. I'd even checked with Pam, to make sure I wasn't doing anything to move Syd back in time. Feeling guilty enough over going behind her back and calling in some help to get all the information I needed, Pam was able to assure me that the result would justify the means.

Still, I'm nervous for Syd's reaction when she finds out where I've taken her.

Pulling the truck to the side on the grass, I turn off the engine and turn only to find her fiddling with the blindfold. "Not yet, babe. We need to walk a bit first," I warn her, my hands pulling hers away from her head. "Sit right here."

I step out to make my way around to the passenger side to help Syd out. The moment she stands beside the truck, I grab her face in my hands and slide my mouth over hers.

"Hmmm," she hums when I release her lips, smacking them loudly. "Now I have a better understanding of the appeal of blindfolds in the bedroom; you tasted even more delicious than normal, and the sounds are so much clearer. Is that water I hear running?" She tilts her head to the side, trying to listen. All I can do is think about Syd naked and blindfolded on our bed, and my hand goes to my crotch immediately to adjust myself.

A warm chuckle has me lift my eyes to find Syd's face turned my way, a smile on her lips. "You were just groping yourself, weren't you; thinking about me wearing this thing in bed? I'm starting to read your mind, honey."

"Would appear so," is all I say, the nerves starting to squeeze my throat. With my arm around her waist to guide her, we move between the rows of markers. Some simple and plain and others quite ornate, bordering on ostentatious. Following the map I'd memorized, we finally come to a stop.

Syd's gone quite still beside me, all earlier light-hearted humor gone from what I could see of her face. Fuck.

"We here?" she whispers and I lean down to kiss her lips.

"We are," I say as I reach behind her head to release the knot in her blindfold. Syd lifts her hands to her eyes, but instead of pulling the cover away, she presses it back against her eyes.

"Tell me it'll be okay," she pleads, one tear and then another sliding down her face. Wrapping her in my arms, her hands still pressed to her face, I rest my cheek on the top of her head.

"I'm here. We'll be okay."

"I can feel him, you know? I've never been here before but I know where I am because he surrounds me. I feel him in my heart, against my skin—I can even smell the scent of his hair."

I don't question how she knows where we are. Whether she heard something to clue her in or could sense it from me, it doesn't matter. But I don't doubt for a minute her son is with her in this moment; invading all her senses. Hell, I know only too well how impossible she is to resist. How could anyone resist the quiet loving force she radiates, drawing everyone in? Why not from beyond the grave?

"I believe you, Bird."

With a little push against my chest, she steps away from me and lets the blindfold drop in her hands as she turns around to see her son for the first time in five years.

"Hi baby," she whispers as she leans over and presses her lips against the cold marble of his headstone.

I don't make any attempt to wipe the tears that are rolling down my face. I just stand here in awe of the love I can feel radiating from her.

"Mommy misses you so bad..." A soft sob escapes her and she sinks to her knees before going on. "I was lost for a while; wanted to turn to dust like you, but I wasn't ready. Someone special found me and he brought me to see you. But I want you to know I always carried you in my heart, even when I was trying to forget you."

The harsh sound of pain keens from her mouth as she rocks herself, sitting in the grass beside her son's grave and ripping a hole in my chest at the sight of her. I want to make it better, but I can't, so I stand here, crying at the pain I feel from her until finally I can't take it anymore and drop down beside her, pulling her in my lap.

The keening quiets and with a little time, the sobbing slows as well. "This is Daniel. He was the best of me," she says, now with a little smile on her lips before she turns and looks at me. "You're crying?" Her hand comes up to my face.

"Babe..." My voice croaks, sounding like the morning after a rough night, but I don't have it in me to continue. And I don't get a chance to before a soft voice breaks through the bubble of grief surrounding us.

"Rosie?"

I feel Syd's body stiffen under my hands as a woman who looks very familiar, tentatively comes closer, her hand pressed against her mouth.

"Rosie, is that really you? Oh my God, it *is* you."

I get up slowly, bringing Syd up with me who stands frozen in front of me, looking at the woman who stops about six feet away, her hands wringing together, and it hits me. The familiar look, the voice with the same timbre, *Rosie* must be a nickname for Syd from when they were kids. This must be her sister. Moments later, Syd confirms with a shaky voice.

"Sofie? What are you doing here?"

"I come every Sunday morning to read him Harry Potter." She indicates the fat book sticking out of the purse

346

hanging off her shoulder. "His favorite, Harry Potter and the Go—"

"The Goblet of Fire. Yes I know."

That's all it takes. The sisters are instantly in each other's arms.

Once again aware of my surroundings, I spot a bench not too far away and after tearful introductions are made, I lead both of them to sit there to talk while I walk around a bit to try and regain my man-status.

Fuck me.

CHAPTER THIRTY

Syd

"What time are they supposed to get here?" I ask Gunnar impatiently, who just eyes me with mild amusement.

"Anytime now, Bird. Anytime."

The past two weeks have flown by with the kids gone. Mostly because of the hours I've spent reconnecting with my sister after our dramatic encounter at Daniel's grave. I smile at the memory, bittersweet as it is. Gunnar's initiative had done so much more than he even anticipated. The first hurdle had been to hide his plan long enough for me not to bolt at the thought of having to face my child's grave. I hadn't even felt the urge to run once I got out of the truck, still oblivious, and felt Daniel's presence in every pore of my body. A cathartic experience of loss, grief and finally a sense of peace I hadn't thought possible to achieve. Surrounded by Daniel's sweet memory and Gunnar's love, I was able to find the missing piece of me that day. The final closure I needed to fully embrace my future, not by leaving Daniel behind, but by allowing him to live on in the part of my heart that was always reserved for him—and he filled it completely.

The cherry on top had been Sofia's appearance at his gravesite. This had not been part of Gunnar's plan, but the timing so perfect, the feelings at that moment so pure, I don't think any planning could have facilitated.

Three times I met with her after that day, finding out she had surprisingly settled somewhere between Boston and Portland, in Ogunquit, with her family. Apparently, her husband had had enough of my parents' daily negative influence in their lives, with their constant criticism of Sofie and the way they were raising their children. The first opportunity for him to move to a new location outside of Boston with the bank he's worked for for years, he took off, moving house, wife, and children into a beautiful townhouse in the center of the quaint little town. Last time I saw her was Monday, when Gunnar suggested we take up the invitation for dinner and make the forty minute drive down. Seeing Brad and the girls again was emotional, but in a very good way. It did hurt my heart to see my nieces, suddenly young women. Amazing teenagers with active social lives and a comfortable friendly manner about them. They'd get along famously with Emmy, I'm sure. The moment of sadness at having missed so much of their formative years passed quickly as Gunnar and Brad almost immediately wandered out the back door with beers in hand, to discuss the merits of the latest trades made by the Red Sox. Male bonding, So simple.

Gunnar insisted I see Pam right after we returned from the cemetery in Boston. He's been so worried he 'fucked me up,' worse than I already was. That made me chuckle and give in immediately, but still he apologized profusely after realizing what had come out of his mouth. Spent an exhausting hour with Pam, insisting Gunnar stick around so he could hear for himself the impact this experience had on me. Needless to say, some more tears were shed in that session, both on my part and Gunnar's. I swear I even saw Pam blink away a tear or two, although she'd vehemently deny that.

Seeing Gunnar cry was an almost surreal experience. From his first 'Who the fuck are you?', to the soft-hearted giant wiping the wetness from his eyes was a huge jump, and yet it so aptly paints Gunnar for the kind of man he is. It also feels like the best of compliments, to have a big burly man like that—one who will protect you at all cost—allow himself to show you how the sight of your pain can bring him to his knees.

He gives me everything I had forced myself to stop dreaming of, including two wonderful kids, both of whom are expected home today, although Emmy wouldn't come in until tonight.

"There's the bus," the main subject in my thoughts points out as the big lumbering tour bus hobbles over the speed bumps of the school parking lot.

Little faces are pressed against the windows, smiling big and waving wildly as some spot their parents.

"Where is he? I can't see him."

I can't wait to feel Dexter's arms squeeze me. Fun as it has been, being able to wake up in the morning and having Gunnar all to myself, I miss Dex's early morning snuggles.

The bus has come to a stop and I'm craning my neck to see if I can spot him.

"Here he comes," Gunnar rumbles in my ear, pointing slightly to the left of the bus where Dex is held up, backpack in hand and chatting up a little girl, or at least she's little compared to Dex, while waiting for their luggage.

"DEX!" I wave wildly when I see him scan the crowd at the sound of his name. Finally spotting me, a big smile breaks out on his face and with a big sigh, I settle back against Gunnar's chest, which is shaking with laughter. Bending over my shoulder, he says for my ears only, "You are *such* a mom." I elbow him in the side, but the smile on my face is beaming.

And it's still there moments later when Dex's lanky body slams into me from the front, trapping me effectively in a Lucas-men sandwich.

Dex's laundry already swirling in the washer, it's almost five when there's a knock on the door. Gunnar is out back, cleaning the grill in preparation of dinner tonight and Dex is down the street at his friend's place, regaling him with the camp stories he's already treated us to.

All I see is part of an arm in the narrow mottled window beside the front door. Pulling it open, I'm faced with an older, greying lady, a suitcase standing by her feet and a smile on her face. *Holy fuck, I'm not ready for this—I am nowhere near ready.* If I didn't already know from the evidence she's planning to stay a while, the voice would've given Gunnar's mom away.

"Oh, honey. So nice to meet you face to face. I see why my boy took a shining to you."

Before I have a chance to respond, I find myself wrapped up in arms that I bet could challenge Gunnar's in an arm-wrestling competition.

"Mom," I hear from behind me as Gunnar walks up and plucks me from his mother's breath stealing grip. "You're early."

"Missing my babies," her only explanation for showing up a week early, accompanied by a shoulder shrug before she holds out her arms to envelop her son. Despite easily towering over me, she's still dwarfed against Gunnar's big frame. He winks at me over his mom's shoulder when he sees the panic on my face. I'm still trying to figure out how to get Dex's laundry sorted and put away, as well as prepping the office/spare bedroom for his mom before dinner when she releases Gunnar, bends to pick up her bag, and moves easily past us and into the house.

"Close your mouth, baby. Flies are gonna get in."

With a snap, I close my mouth and glare at Gunnar, which only seems to add to his amusement.

"Where are my babies?" comes from inside the house as he walks in to join his mother who seems to be inspecting every corner of the downstairs. I follow closely behind after closing the front door.

"Dex is down the street at a buddy's house, and Emmy won't be back until tonight," Gunnar offers.

"Good, gives me time to bake some of my chocolate chip cookies for dessert."

Gunnar just chuckles while I frantically search my mind to the last time I cleaned the oven, which was well before the kids went away on their respective trips. *Shit.*

"Uhh, Gunnar?" I look for help from the man who a couple of months ago, couldn't crack a smile, and now seems to have one permanently glued to his face. Even under the invasion of his mother a week before she was due.

He walks over, tags me around the neck and plants a hard and wet one on my lips, making me momentarily lose my train of thought, before a chuckle, not unlike the man's whose lips are making a feast out of my mouth, pulls me firmly back to earth. Now if only it would open up and swallow me whole. Embarrassed at having been caught by his mom, I push off his chest and stare at the floor. Almost forty-years old, and reduced to this. Mercy.

"Yes, I can see why he's gone over you. Damn boy is virtually giddy; don't think I can't remember him like this since he fed his dog kibble soaked in rum, wanting to see what he'd look like drunk. He got his wish and a spanking from his dad that had his ten-year-old butt blue for a week."

I couldn't help it, I cracked up laughing at the story and the way she deadpanned it. And then, she melted me.

"Ahhh, yes. There it is. The sound of happiness. You'll do fine, girl. Just fine," she says with a smile before turning on her heels and taking possession of the kitchen. Stunned into silence with her words, I again turn to Gunnar for help, but he's just looking at me with hunger in his eyes.

"Told you about that laugh of yours. Fuck me, even my mother can hear it."

Gunnar

With mom in the kitchen, turning it into a sure disaster, and Syd upstairs, scrambling to create a 'comfortable space' for mom, I turn back to the cleaning of my grill. The panic on Syd's face was priceless, finding my mother, who on her best days is overbearing, standing on the doorstep a week early. She'd had plans to rip the spare room apart and clean it top to bottom for when mom came, something she had planned on taking a week for, but now only had half an hour, tops.

I know what has her so worried; the fact that I haven't formally announced Syd's living here to mom, but she doesn't realize it'll likely only make my mother happier.

353

Suddenly guilty for leaving her to deal with mom's early arrival by herself, I abandon the grill and go to find her. Instead of the spare room where I expected her to be, I find her face down on our bed, crying by the sound of it. Dammit. Sitting down beside her on the mattress, I rub a tentative hand over her back, trying to ignore the sight of her plump ass sticking up in the air. I thought she was irresistible before, but with the curves that have been gaining on her recently, I'll be damned if I can keep my hands off her at all.

"What's wrong, Bird?"

When she doesn't respond, I flip her over and lean down in her tear streaked face.

"Talk to me, Syd."

"I ha—had plans," she hiccups, not giving me anything more.

"I know you had plans, babe, but why the tears?"

"Because she's being so sweet to me and I don't want her to be disappointed when she finds out I'm shacking up with her son and his very impressionable young children. AND, on top of that, I haven't even got a spot ready for her yet."

Before I can set her straight, my mother comes walking into the room, unannounced. "Really mom?"

"Oh hush," she says, pursing her lips and her hands on her hips. Syd is doing her best to hide under the covers by now. "I could hear her crying downstairs. Now you toddle off to your grill and let me set this straight. After all, it's my fault for coming early she's upset anyway."

The groan Syd emits from behind my back has me chuckle, but I still ignore the fierce little hands digging into my sides, trying to keep me from getting up and exposing her to my mother.

"I'm sorry, I—you didn't upset me. I mean, I love that your early, it's just ... Argh!" With a frustrated groan, she throws her hands in the air dramatically, setting mom laughing. Turning to me, my mother reiterates her directive.

"Go on, get out of here. I've got your girl."

With a kiss on Syd's forehead, I leave, turning back at the door, only to see my mom sitting on the bed in the spot I just left, stroking her hair. Yeah, she's got her.

A few hours later, with Syd smiling and yapping with mom in the kitchen over a cup of tea, Dex and I are shooting the shit on the deck.

"Dad?"

"Yeah, kiddo?"

"Did you love mom? I mean, I was trying to remember when we all still lived in one house if you smiled that much then too."

Christ. My kid too? I turn to face him. "I did. I never loved her more than when she gave me you and your sister. Those days I swear I couldn't get the smile off my face if I tried. So yes, there were times when I would smile, but Dex, your mom and I? We were hoping for different kinds of things from life and were not smart enough to discuss those before we got married and had you guys. So in the end, it just wasn't helping you guys to live under one roof with parents who were constantly at each other's throats. I won't say there weren't happy moments, because there were, but those had mostly to do with you or your sister."

He nods his head in a show of understanding, although I'm not sure how much of what I'm saying really hits home. I wonder what brought this on, and specifically now, but with his next words, it becomes crystal clear.

"Is it bad that I like Syd living with us better than mom?"

"I don't think so. If that were the case, then it would be bad of me to feel that way too and I don't think it is. You don't get a lot of chances to do this 'love' thing right, so I consider myself a lucky man. I had one woman give me the best kids in the world, and another woman whom I couldn't love any more than I do. That's why I smile so much; I finally have everything I want, right here."

Emmy's squeals from the front of the house are a clear indication she is happy with her Grammy's early arrival, just like Dex was. Although in his case, I don't know whether it is his grandma, or the tray of hot chocolate chip cookies she had waiting when he walked in. Regardless, the arrival of the prodigal daughter has effectively put an end to Dex and my little man-to-man, but Dex gets the last word when he gets up and runs for the back door while shouting over his shoulder, "I love her too, you know," before slipping inside.

"Yeah, I know, buddy. I know," I whisper to myself as I trudge along behind him at a much slower pace.

The rest of the evening is spent munching on the saltwater toffee Emmy brought bags full home of—everyone but me, drinking beer, and this would be me exclusively, and listening to the kids regale stories of their two weeks away.

"And what did you do while we were gone?" Emmy asks. Luckily the question is directed at Syd, because first thing that pops in my mind is Syd bent over every surface in the house, naked as the day she was born. Undoubtedly knowing where my mind went, she pinches my leg in silent warning before smiling at Emmy.

"Actually, your dad took me to see Daniel," she says brightly.

"But isn't he dead?" my smart son from earlier tonight has morphed back into the tactless, ten-year-old clodhopper he really is.

"Dex!" his sister hisses, making him realize what just popped out of his mouth.

"Oh shit! I mean shoot. Sorry Syd, I didn't—"

"It's okay, bud. Yes he's dead, but I had never been to visit his grave. I didn't even really know where it was until your dad took me there." She says, swallowing hard.

"Was it sad?" Again, my filterless boy in action, and I wonder if he has that from me. *Ouch.*

"Yes, it was, but it was also really good to have a place to visit him and to really say goodbye."

My beautiful and much too sensitive Emmy is blinking away tears. "Do you think we could come with you one time? To visit him, I mean?"

Instantly Syd's eyes well up, and to be honest, I feel a little soft myself. Clearing my throat to hide the raw emotions of that day welling up, I address my girl. "I think that's a great idea, sweet girl. And I'm thinking—" looking over at Syd, I see she's valiantly fighting tears, "—I'm thinking Syd would love that idea too. It's actually a beautiful cemetery with lots of mature trees and a shallow, but fast moving creek running not too far from his grave."

"Cool," Dex says, but his eyes are on Syd who's lost the battle with the tears and smiles apologetically.

"I'll come too, if that's okay."

Every eye turns to my mom, whose chin is wobbling with the effort to maintain composure.

"I'd really love that," Syd says, smiling through her tears. "And I really love you all for making room for him ... or his memory, anyway."

"Shhhh..."

I have my hand loosely over Syd's mouth as she whimpers through her release on my fingers.

It took me a while to get her mind off my mother sleeping at the other end of the hallway, but at least she's forgotten about her 'new rule' of no sex in the house while Grammy is here. Yeah, right.

Shifting slightly, I settle myself between her legs and as I replace my hand over her mouth with my lips, I slide my cock inside her tight, warm, and extremely wet pussy, groaning when my balls hit her ass. *Jesus.* Every fucking time it's this good.

With slow, deliberate strokes, I bring her back to the edge of orgasm, never losing eye-contact. Never wanting to leave the world that plays behind her eyes, or the body that welcomes me freely. And with everything that I am, I pour myself into her as she gives herself completely, clenching down on my cock until the last drop is spent.

Freya Barker   FROM DUST

CHAPTER THIRTY-ONE

Syd

"*Syd,*" the voice I had missed every morning of the past few weeks is whispering in my ear. "Wanna come have Grammy's pancakes? She makes them with chocolate chips."

I turn my head to look at Gunnar, but he looks to be still asleep. After the day we had yesterday, and night, he deserves to sleep a little longer.

"Go on down, buddy. I'll be right there," I tell him softly, watching him sneak out the door.

The minute I turn back the covers and slide my legs over the side, Gunnar's arm tightens around my waist.

"Don't go." His voice croaking from lack of use overnight, he peels up one eyelid before closing it again with a smile. "Okay, now you can go. I just couldn't face waking up without seeing your face first thing. Go and eat mom's pancakes, they're the bomb." Slowly he pulls back his arm, releasing me. But instead of getting up, I lean back down in bed and kiss his smiling lips.

"I love you, Gunnar Lucas."

Then I get up and make for the bathroom for a quick shower, leaving Gunnar to fall back asleep, smile still on his face.

359

"Morning," Gunnar's mom Emily is stacking pancakes on a plate. The stack's high enough to feed all the neighborhood kids.

After my little meltdown last night, any discomfort I might have had was long gone.

She had come into our bedroom, basically kicked Gunnar out, and sat on the edge of my bed. I was absolutely mortified and swore I'd make Gunnar hurt for leaving me alone with her, but she grabbed my hand and told me that over the past years, she'd come to visit Portland at least twice a year and loved staying with her son and his kids because they didn't care she was a notoriously bad housekeeper. Great cook, but lousy in the cleaning department.

"It just never was my strength, and to be honest, for most of my married life, we lived and breathed the pub. A cleaning lady once a month to clear the cobwebs and the dust, and that was about it."

She smiled at me and stroked the hair that was plastered against my tear-streaked cheeks out of my face.

"You see, Gunnar's house is the one place where I don't have to be anything other than who I am. Don't have to do anything other than what I want to do. But if I'd known you had moved in..."

At my flinch, she continues stronger. "If I'd known, I would have called first, given you a chance to do what you feel you needed to do. Even though that spare room is plenty good the way it is and I don't care—heck, I don't even see dust or cobwebs, or less than pristine surfaces. If everyone in this house is happy, then so am I. Now, we have some talking to do, you and I, but now is not the time. Someday though, I'd like for you to trust me enough to share some of your painful history with me."

The warm smile on her face had me with a fresh batch of tears running down my face and a decision to take a leap in my heart. The moment she got up to grab tissues from the bathroom, I stopped her. "Can I just tell you one thing? Actually, two things. They're the worst things I've done and if you can still look at me after that, the rest will be easy."

Sitting back down, she grabbed my hand and simply said, "I'm listening."

-

"Morning. That's quite an impressive stack you have there," I point out with a smile.

"I know. I always go overboard when I do get to cook again. In Arizona, I only have a hotplate and a microwave, and my little kitchen is more set up for heating than it is cooking. Every time I visit Gunnar and the kids, I make sure to get my fix of cooking and baking. Hope you don't mind?" She stands with the spatula raised, as if the thought just occurred to her. Not having the heart to take away her few weeks of cooking, I shake my head.

"I don't mind. I mean, I love cooking, but with the time I spend in the kitchen at The Skipper preparing the daily and weekly specials, I get my fill anyway."

"Get out! Dino let's you at his stove? Already? It took Viv three years before he trusted her with the simple lunch requirements. And then, only on strict instructions, and he has you create and make the specials? You must be a miracle behind the stove."

I shrug my shoulders. "Just caught him on a good day, I guess."

"Well that makes me even happier," Emily grins widely while flipping the next batch. "Cindy was absolutely useless in the kitchen and besides, I never liked her enough to pass the traditional family recipes over to. Dino begged for years, but I just couldn't hand them over, no matter how much I like him. These are recipes, some of which date back three generations or more, but you—I can give them to you."

"But I'm not—" A flick of the spatula has me snap my mouth shut.

"Don't you dare say you're not part of this family. You should know better and I don't want to hear it." Her mouth is drawn tight in a straight line, making it obvious there is no argument to be had. The kids each have big smiles on their faces, apparently used to their Grammy's willfulness.

"Well, all right then. I'd be honored."

"Good. Now with that settled, sit down, grab a plate and load up. I have twenty-two pancakes ready to go and at least another ten or twelve to make." With that, she turns back to the stove, leaving me sitting with my mouth open. A stifled giggle beside me reveals Emmy slapping a hand to her mouth and beside her is Dex, who is grinning broadly. I bulge my eyes and mouth '*Twenty-two*' at them, causing both of them to burst into fits of giggles.

"I saw that," Emily says, having never turned her head. I takes me two minutes to figure out she's checking us in the reflection of the kitchen window; smiling at least as wide as Dex is.

"You know she does that all the time," Gunnar says, walking into the kitchen, giving his mom a kiss on the cheek before walking over to me. With his arm slung over my shoulder, he pinches a piece of my pancake off my plate. "Yeah, she used to drive me nuts. Could never get away with anything. She used to say she had eyes in the back of her head, terrified the crap out of me."

The kids are chuckling, obviously well-acquainted with the story.

"Did it to my kids too, but Emmy ... Emmy had her pegged pretty quickly. Didn't you, girl?" He smiles at his daughter before continuing, "I swear she couldn't have been more than five or so when mom pulled one of her stunts and Emmy just observed her, until suddenly her eyes slid to the kitchen window. And with a big smile on her face, she started waving at Grammy's reflection. Mom knew she was busted."

After eating five pancakes and feeling like a stuffed turkey at Thanksgiving, I offered to clean the kitchen, which Emily gratefully accepted, taking the kids with her for a trip to the mall where I'm sure she'd do her grandmotherly duty and spoil them rotten.

"I love you too, Rosie," Gunnar's voice rumbles close to my ear and I almost jump out of my skin making him chuckle. "Now you see, if you'd been keeping an eye on the kitchen window, you'd have been able to see me sneak up on you."

I turn my head back to let him kiss my smile.

"Why suddenly Rosie?"

"Just trying it on for size, but I think I'm sticking with Bird. What's with the Rosie anyway?"

"Sofia used to have trouble with my name and instead of Sydney, would call me Cindy." The wince on Gunnar's face makes me laugh, Cindy obviously not being one of his favorite names. "She would call me Syd for short and my parents hated it, so they suggested Rose, but Sofia changed it to Rosie. I changed hers to Sofie, another thing my parents hated and that was our little pre-adolescent rebellion. One that lasted into adulthood, I'm afraid." I chuckle at the memory. "I'm glad I got my sister back. She's the only one who ever cared."

Crowding in behind me, Gunnar blocks any possible escape by bracing his arms on either side of me on the counter.

"Not anymore. You have an entire family here. Here with me and the kids, and my mother." He rolls his eyes when he mentions his mom, putting a smile on my face, 'cause I know he loves her to distraction. "And in addition to that, you have the crew at The Skipper. They're as much your family as you are theirs."

I turn in his arms and wind mine around his neck.

"Thank you," I whisper against his lips.

"What for?"

"For the orgasm you're going to give me on that counter I just wiped," I smile at his pained groan.

"I like the way you think," he growls in my neck, his hands sliding down the front of my yoga pants.

"Thought you might..." I manage right before he finds me wet.

~Two weeks later~

"So are we gonna come back every week, just like your sister?"

We've just piled the kids and the leftovers of an impromptu picnic at the side of the creek in the truck. Emmy had insisted on bringing flowers and Dex brought his favorite ball cap, each putting their gifts reverently on Daniel's grave.

"I was thinking more like once a month," I say carefully, twisting in my seat so I can look Dexter in the eyes. "As much as I love feeling close to him, we have our lives to live and I think wherever he is, he knows we carry him with us in our hearts, even when we're not there."

"Okay." Dex nods his head as he gives his easy consent, but when I look at Emmy, she's studying me thoughtfully.

"Do you wish you could turn back time?" she asks, and Gunnar's hand holding mine clenches at the question, but I keep my eyes on her when I answer.

"That's a tough one, and I'm glad I don't have that choice to make because as much as I miss Daniel, I don't think I could ever give you and your brother up. Or your father. I love you all too much to let go."

The small smile that slips on Emmy's face is evidence enough that she likes my answer.

"Good enough?" I check, holding on to her gaze.

"Yes," she says firmly. "Good enough."

When I turn back to face the front, I notice the matching small smile on Gunnar's face, but other than a little squeeze of my hand, he says nothing.

He doesn't need to.

The rest of the ride is mostly silent and it isn't until we turn into the alley behind the bar that the kid's start talking in excitement. I let Gunnar field the questions about the big fundraiser his mom spearheaded in two short weeks. A ticket only function, with Emily preparing all the favorite family menu items that had ever graced The Skipper's menu over decades, with Dino's help. A veritable feast that would hopefully raise enough money to start Abby Winslow's treatments. It would also be the official launch of the foundation. At least fifty tickets had been sold already, thanks to the many community contacts Gunnar, his mom, and their friends have in Portland, and more would be sold at the door.

I watch the alley go by and contemplate how far I've come.

The remains of the shed where I'd started my rise from dust are still visible, although most of the loose rubble has long since been removed. Not so for the other side, where the building I was forced to defend myself is a stark reminder of how deep I've had to dig and how fierce I could be when it comes to standing up for myself.

The dumpster, where Viv first found me, half-starved and fearful, before she coaxed me inside with the promise of a hot meal. The first of many.

And finally we pull up to The Skipper, where I found a purpose, my self-worth and the man pulling open the door, reaching in to help me out. My love.

"Why are you crying?" he asks me gently as the kids skip up the steps and through the back door, none the wiser.

"Grateful, that's all. Been quite the journey," I suggest, looking back down the alley before lifting my eyes to his deep green ones. "But I don't regret where I landed. Not for a minute."

The soft but all-consuming kiss he shares with me holds no words, yet tells me everything I ever need to know.

"Oh for crying out loud!" Viv's voice bounces off the brick and concrete. "Would you get your horny asses in here already?"

Gunnar's mouth smiles against mine before pulling away.

"Ready to make some money?"

"Hell, yes." I smile as I grab his hand and pull him with me into the pub where a crowd is already gathering.

A banner on the far wall, opposite the bar, stops me dead in my tracks. And if I thought I couldn't love him anymore, I just fell a little deeper.

'**Daniel's Hope Foundation**' is printed in big bold letters.

Turning around I throw myself into Gunnar's arms to the clapping and whistles of the crowd. "Good enough?" he asks cautiously echoing the question I asked in the truck earlier and my face cracks open in a huge smile.

"More than good enough. It's perfect."

~~~~~*THE END*~~~~~

NOTE FROM THE AUTHOR:

The seed for 'FROM DUST' was planted a few years ago, when a local newscast reported on a tragic accident where a small child had been hit and killed in the family's own driveway. For some reason the story hit me hard. I didn't know the family, but I remember thinking the house they showed in the clip was so very similar to my house. It could've been my street—it could've been my family. And how does one survive an unimaginable tragedy like that?

That question plagued me for the longest time, because whichever relative was at the wheel that day, they would carry the weight of the entire family's loss and immeasurable grief for a lifetime.

How does one survive?

I didn't want to minimize the tragedy of such an event with 'FROM DUST', but being the eternal optimist that I'm sometimes accused of being, I did want to create a story of how such a person might find a way to 'live with it'. And hopefully find some closure along the way, because frankly, what other choice is there?

I hope I gave enough weight to the gravity of such a scenario, and that by the end of my story, albeit emotional, all of you are able to come away a little more hopeful.

Thank you so much for reading 'FROM DUST', it truly was a labor of love.

ACKNOWLEDGEMENTS:

To my beta-readers who know that I am not served by getting smoke blown up my arse. You need people who aren't afraid to provide constructive criticism, pick apart your manuscript and point out any weak spots, to built a good book. These people you KNOW have nothing but love and respect for what you do, despite the fact they find fault with your writing. And like you are invested in making you a better author.

I have been blessed with a group of betas that are all of the above and collectively they make my story so much better.

Kerry-Ann Bell, Debbie Bishop, Deb Blake, Pam Buchanan, Leanne Hawkes, Sam Price, Catherine Scott, Nancy Huddleston—I love you guys HARD!

I need to thank a few amazing women who have picked over the book to make sure every last wrinkle was ironed out. Daniela Prima and Karen Hrdlicka who combined pulled out more mistakes than I thought there were left! Oops. Love you girls!

The amazing Dana Hook, my editor and a woman I love with all my heart, who makes everything flow better, run smoother and look polished and spit-shined!

The reviewers who took the time to read the early and unedited version, giving me fantastic feedback and writing absolutely wonderful reviews that more often than not had me in tears.

My mom, who has read every one of my books, even at ninety years-old. She doesn't flinch at any sexual situation or description and is my most vocal and staunch supporter. Love you, Mom!

My family who once again have had to play second fiddle to my obsessive writing schedule. They do so with the occasional shrug of a shoulder or a shake of the head, but they love me through it beginning to end. And I adore them.

But most of all you, my readers, who have been growing steadily in numbers, supporting and encouraging me. Those of you who have come to visit me at one of the author signings, I so appreciate that! It's wonderful to have an opportunity to interact directly with readers. There is one reader in particular who made my signing in York in the United Kingdom the most magical experience. Vickie Watson fell into my arms crying, making me tear up as well. Her husband had warned me when he spotted me that tears would likely be shed, and he was right! Love you, Vickie! You're the best. xox

ABOUT THE AUTHOR

Freya Barker inspires with her stories about 'real' people, perhaps less than perfect, each struggling to find their own slice of happy, but just as deserving of romance, thrills and chills, and some hot, sizzling sex in their lives.

Recipient of the RomCon "Reader's Choice" Award for best first book, "Slim To None," Freya has hit the ground running. She loves nothing more than to meet and mingle with her readers, whether it be online or in person at one of the signings she attends.

Freya spins story after story with an endless supply of bruised and dented characters, vying for attention!

Freya

https://www.freyabarker.com

http://bit.ly/FreyaAmazon

https://www.goodreads.com/FreyaBarker

https://www.facebook.com/FreyaBarkerWrites

https://tsu.co/FreyaB

https://twitter.com/freya_barker

or mailto:freyabarker.writes@gmail.com

ALSO BY FREYA BARKER

CEDAR TREE SERIES:

SLIM TO NONE
HUNDRED TO ONE
AGAINST ME
CLEAN LINES
UPPER HAND
LIKE ARROWS
HEAD START

PORTLAND, ME, NOVELS:

FROM DUST
CRUEL WATER
THROUGH FIRE
STILL AIR

NORTHERN LIGHTS COLLECTION:

A CHANGE OF TIDE

A CHANGE OF VIEW
A CHANGE OF PACE
(Coming soon!)

ROCK POINT SERIES:

KEEPING 6
CABIN 12
(Coming soon!)

SNAPSHOT SERIES:

SHUTTER SPEED
FREEZE FRAME
IDEAL IMAGE
PICTURE PERFECT
(coming soon!)

CPSIA information can be obtained
at www.ICGtesting.com
Printed in the USA
BVHW050815180623
666010BV00023B/1427